RITA BRADSHAW

One Snowy Night

PAN BOOKS

First published 2019 by Macmillan

This edition published in paperback 2019 by Pan Books
an imprint of Pan Macmillan
The Smithson, 6 Briset Street, London EC1M 5NR
Associated companies throughout the world
www.panmacmillan.com

ISBN 978-1-5098-9808-4

1 3 5 7 9 8 6 4 2

A CIP catalogue record for this book is available from the British Library.

Typeset in Sabon by Palimpsest Book Production Ltd, Falkirk, Stirlingshire
Printed and bound by CPI Group (UK) Ltd, Croydon, CR0 4YY

Visit www.panmacmillan.com to read more about all our books
and to buy them. You will also find features, author interviews and
news of any author events, and you can sign up for e-newsletters
so that you're always first to hear about our new releases.

For Muffin, my precious little furry baby,
who helps keep his mum sane in this mad world.

Acknowledgements

The following books helped enormously with research for this story:

The Langhorne Sisters by James Fox
My Own Story by Emmeline Pankhurst
Tommy Turnbull, A Miner's Life by Joe Robinson
Durham Miners' Millennium Book by David Temple

Contents

PART ONE

Betrayal

1922

Chapter One

It was the first week of March. The bitter north-east wind was such that it sliced into flesh like a knife, and the young woman gingerly picking her way on the compressed snow was muffled up to the eyeballs, her felt hat pulled well down over her forehead and her woolly scarf covering the bottom half of her face. The deepening twilight was offset by the brilliance of the mantle of white covering the trees and hedgerow in the lane she was walking down, but Ruby Morgan was blind to the winter wonderland around her and the glow of the setting sun.

It was the eve of her wedding. She should be home dealing with the last bits and pieces that still needed to be done, she told herself, not tramping about in the freezing cold and getting chilled to the bone. Her mam had said much the same thing as she'd pulled on her outdoor things:

'What on earth is your Adam thinking of, Ruby, asking you to meet him in Snowdrop Lane tonight of all nights? It's a good fifteen minutes' walk and the pavements are lethal. You'll go a cropper and end up hobbling down the aisle with a stick tomorrow – that'd be a fine state of affairs, wouldn't it! If he wants to see you, what's wrong with him coming here? Barmy, this is, lass.'

Ruby hadn't argued. She agreed with her mother. But it had seemed disloyal to Adam to admit it, and so she had merely shrugged and continued buttoning her coat.

'Aren't you going to say anything?' Her mother had appealed to the other two people sitting at the kitchen table, her tone sharp. Ruby's father had disappeared behind his newspaper by way of reply, which hadn't surprised her. Since he'd come home from the war he was a shell of his former self, having watched both his sons die in the carnage of the Somme campaign and sustaining serious injuries himself in the last months of the war in the heavy fighting on the Western Front. But – Ruby's brow wrinkled – Olive had been unusually quiet. Normally her sister had an opinion about everything. Although Olive was only three years her senior she was as sour as an old maid and they had never got on. It was rare her sister missed an opportunity to add her two penn'orth to things, especially if Olive could side with their mam against her.

Catching sight of Adam waiting for her in a curve in the lane, all thoughts of her sister were gone. Raising her hand she walked faster, only to land up on her bottom in the snow as her feet slipped on a patch of ice. He reached her in moments, lifting her up, but then as she giggled and tried to talk she found herself pressed against his chest so tightly she could hardly breathe. When at last he released her she gazed in concern at his dear face, his handsome face. She knew every expression, every little nuance because hadn't they loved each other since they were bairns larking about in the playground? But she had never seen him looking as he was now.

'What's the matter? What's wrong?'

And when he didn't answer, merely staring at her with haunted eyes, she said again, 'What's the matter? Why did you want to meet here? I couldn't believe it when your Ronnie turned up at the shop with the note. Why didn't you come yourself?'

She didn't add that Mrs Walton, the owner of the costumier establishment where she had worked since leaving school some years ago at the age of thirteen, had been less than pleased to see Adam's grubby little brother, Ronnie, marching into her immaculate shop with his snotty nose and holey trousers demanding to see 'Adam's Ruby' as he'd smeared the contents of his nose across his face with the sleeve of his coat.

'I couldn't come myself,' said Adam, even his voice sounding different.

'But why not? You're on the early shift, aren't you?' Adam was a miner at the Wearmouth Colliery like his father and older brothers, and since they'd become engaged on Ruby's sixteenth birthday she had been collecting her bottom drawer. Adam had saved hard too after paying his board to his mam. They had both been determined to rent a two-up two-down terraced house when they got wed and to have enough money to partly furnish it too. A few weeks ago a house had come up in Wood Street, a stone's throw from the colliery, and Adam had snapped it up. They'd had a lovely time buying furniture, even if it was all second-hand, but she didn't mind that, nor it being a bit of a walk to her place of work in Southwick. She knew she'd landed on her feet when she'd taken up the position of trainee dressmaker with Mrs Walton. The elderly widow had no family and treated her more as the daughter she'd never had than an employee. Mrs Walton had helped her sew her wedding dress along with the two bridesmaid's frocks for Olive and Ellie, Ruby's best friend, and she'd insisted on paying for the material and the hundreds of tiny seed pearls on the bodice of Ruby's dress. It was her wedding present, she'd said, in a tone that brooked no argument.

Adam had been staring at her and now he said quietly, 'It's nothing to do with what shift I'm on. I – I had to talk to you without anyone else around.' He took a deep breath, his voice cracking as he muttered, 'Oh, Ruby, Ruby. I can't believe it's happening.'

'You're frightening me.' She took a step backwards.

'Promise me you won't hate me. Say it, say you won't.'

Ruby had always loved Snowdrop Lane. It was a favourite spot for courting couples, especially in the summer. She and Adam had often met here in the past when wild flowers dotted the grassy banks either side of the path and dappled sunlight slanted through the trees. Although only a short distance from the gridwork pattern of terraced streets stretching to the north and east of

Wearmouth Colliery in Monkwearmouth where a pall of smoke hung day and night, the air smelled different in Snowdrop Lane. You could almost imagine you were in the country. But tonight their special meeting place wasn't working its magic.

Again she said, 'Tell me what's wrong.'

'It – it's down to New Year's Eve.'

'New Year's Eve?' Ruby echoed in bewilderment. That was weeks ago.

'You know, when you and the others came to ours to see the New Year in.'

She stared at him. She remembered that night only too well – she'd hated every minute of it. She loved Adam and he was, thankfully, as different as chalk to cheese from his father and three older brothers who looked upon any and every occasion as an excuse for a drinking bout, as did most of Adam's relatives, it appeared. She hadn't wanted to accept the invitation from his parents, which had extended to her own parents and Olive, but her mother had insisted it would look rude if they refused and that with the wedding coming up it was better to keep everything nice and friendly. By ten o'clock most of the family and friends who were squeezed into the Gilberts' kitchen and front room had been the worse for the whisky and beer they'd poured down their throats, and even her own da had sat in an armchair smiling blearily at everyone and quite unable to form his words. She'd later found out that Adam's older brothers had made it their mission to get him drunk, partly, Ruby suspected, because Adam made no secret of the fact that he didn't want or need to drink the way they did, which had always riled them.

Carefully now, because she didn't want to make him feel worse than he already did about that night, she said, 'Isn't that all forgotten now?' By the time the New Year had been welcomed in Adam had been three sheets to the wind and wobbly on his legs, and his brothers had carried him upstairs to his bed and dumped him on it, rejoining the party and telling all and sundry they wouldn't let their little brother live it down. She had endured another hour at the Gilberts' before she had been able to persuade her parents and Olive to leave, and then she and her mother and Olive had had to practically carry her father home. The next day Adam had had a terrible row with his brothers and refused to accept their apologies, which he'd maintained – rightly as it happened – had been prompted by his mother. It was only the fact that his oldest brother was best man and Fred and Peter ushers that had brought them speaking again in the last few days. Whilst Ruby could see Adam's point of view, his tangible bitterness about the affair was a little extreme in her private opinion but she hadn't dared voice this, so angry was he.

'Forgotten?'

To Ruby's amazement he hit his forehead several times with the flat of his palm, and at this point she thought, he's ill, he must have banged his head down the pit or something. Accidents happened all the time but if they weren't serious the miners carried on working. Adam's father was living proof of this. Some years ago he'd fractured a bone in his ankle but had still dragged himself to the colliery each day, the threat of no work, no pay, getting him through. To the present day he walked with a limp.

'It's all right,' she said quietly. 'Whatever's the matter it will be all right.'

'You know how drunk I was that night, don't you? You know I wasn't in my right mind?' His voice almost a whimper now, he whispered, 'I love you, Ruby. You're everything to me.'

'Adam—'

'I hate her. She knew what she was doing, she wasn't as drunk as all that whatever she says now. She came upstairs to find me, didn't she? Is that someone who's pie-eyed?'

The chill that flickered down Ruby's spine had nothing to do with the weather. Through the feeling of dread she heard her voice saying quite calmly, 'Who is "she"?'

His face stricken, he opened his mouth but nothing came out for a moment. He swallowed hard, his eyes roaming over her face before he muttered, 'Her, Olive.'

'Olive?' She couldn't have heard right, not if what she thought Adam was saying was true . . . 'Olive, my sister?'

'She came up to the bedroom when the rest of you were downstairs and I thought at first it was you. I couldn't see clearly – it was dark – and she lay down. She was all over me, doing things, and I . . . Oh, hell, Ruby, don't look like that. She helped herself, that's the truth of it, because I was in no state to stop her. The drink, it made me—'

'You did it with Olive?' Shock kept her voice flat. From when they had first understood about the birds and bees, they'd agreed their wedding night would be special. Through all their fumblings, all the times when the temptation had been almost overpowering, they'd managed to stop. 'You took my sister down?'

'No, I've told you, *she* took *me*. I tried to throw her off but it was too late, and afterwards . . . I hoped it wasn't true, that I'd dreamed it or something, but she came to the colliery gates as bold as brass a couple of days later. She said I'd wanted it as much as her, that I'd been giving her the eye all evening, that I'd . . . Oh, all sorts of rubbish. She told me she was going to tell you if I didn't.' His jaw clenched. 'And I said I'd kill her if she breathed a word. I meant it an' all. And she knew I did because she didn't come back, not then, not till yesterday. She was waiting for me and she told me. I could have strangled her with my bare hands.' His face worked and his breath caught in a sob.

The sky above them was running rivers of gold. It was one of the most beautiful sunsets she had ever witnessed, and with the birds mostly having settled for the night and just the occasional faint noise from the industry lining the River Wear in the distance, Snowdrop Lane was magical. It added to the unrealness of what was happening.

Numbly, Ruby whispered, 'What did Olive tell you?'

'There's going to be a bairn.' He scrubbed at his wet eyes with the back of his hand. 'I didn't believe her, not last night when she told me. No one falls for a bairn the first time. I met her at Dr Upton's this morning because I said I wanted to hear it from him and he said it's true right enough. An' she's told Father McHaffie an' all. Apparently she went straight there to the church yesterday when she left Dr Upton. According to her, Father McHaffie's going round me mam's tonight to tell them I've got to marry her for the sake of the bairn.'

Feeling was surging in, hot and fierce, cutting through the initial shock. She wanted to hit him, to pound her fists into his chest; but instead she said, 'Why didn't you stop her when you realized it wasn't me? You could have done something, you must have known.'

'It was too late by then. She'd got me fired up and – and I hardly knew what I was doing.'

'You knew enough to give her a bairn.'

'Ruby—'

'No, don't say you couldn't stop because you could have if you'd really wanted to.'

He moved his mouth as though he was going to answer but no words came out, and as she stared at him she knew she had hit the nail on the head. In those minutes, when he had been with Olive, all that had mattered was the needs of his body. Hate spiralled up in her for both of them and it equalled her love for him, enabling her to say, 'If she's expecting a baby then you'll have to marry her. Father McHaffie will see to that.'

'I can't, I won't.' His voice throaty, he pleaded, 'You love me, Ruby. You've always loved me. I know we couldn't stay round here but we can go somewhere else, down south maybe, and get married there. She's brought this on herself – she'll have to weather the storm.'

Weather the storm? He knew as well as she did what Olive's life would be like if she was left to face this alone. They would crucify her, all the neighbours and folk hereabouts, the self-constituted avengers who would hide their pleasure at Olive's persecution under a banner of righteousness. And although at the moment she would like nothing more than to leave Olive to her fate, there was her mam and da to consider. The shame of his daughter giving birth to a bastard would kill her da, and that's what Olive's child would be if Adam didn't marry her. There would still be avid gossip and speculation because of the circumstances and some mud would stick, but the cloak of respectability that Adam's ring on Olive's finger would bring would stop the worst of the hounding and give the child protection.

This last thought caused Ruby to say, 'And what of the baby, *your* baby?'

He waved his hand as though that was of no consequence, and his next words confirmed it. 'It's hers, not mine. She did this on purpose to trap me, don't you see? She'll manage, she'll have to. There's your mam an' da, or if they throw her out there's the workhouse.'

Of all that had passed between them, this shocked Ruby the most. The workhouse, that huge bogeyman of bricks and mortar that hovered over the poor from birth to death and was the thing of nightmares – he would see his child brought up in those terrible confines?

'You don't mean that.'

'I do, I do. Please, Ruby, listen to me. We're young, we can make a good life for ourselves down south and we needn't ever come back here. Everything's better down there anyway – we'd be in clover, I know we would. I'll make this up to you, I swear it. We'll forget all this in time as long as we're together.'

She felt sick to her stomach and through the agony of mind he appeared almost a stranger. Not because he had slept with her sister but because of how he was talking now. A growing realization that she didn't know him the way she thought she did was frightening. He looked like he'd always done, like her Adam, but the person in front of her was not the lad she'd committed her life to. And if she didn't know Adam, if she'd got that wrong, then she didn't know anything or anyone. A horrifying panic made her feel as if she was shrinking, becoming smaller and smaller, and it was only when he reached out to her again, taking her arm, that she came back to herself.

The push she gave him took him completely by surprise and sent him sprawling backwards as his feet slipped on the ice and compressed snow. As he struggled up, her voice was like the crack of a whip.

'Don't touch me. Here –' she flung her engagement ring at him, which he caught instinctively – 'I don't want this.'

'Please, Ruby, no. Listen to me—'

'I don't want to hear any more, and as for us being together, that's over. You've gone with my sister, my *sister*. I hate you both and I always will. You disgust me.' There was a moment's stark silence. 'Whatever happens now, however things turn out, I never want to see you again so if you're going to run away from this and take the easy way out, don't use me as an excuse. I wouldn't have anything to do with you if you were the last man on earth, Adam Gilbert. I mean it.'

He could see she meant it. Adam looked into her great chocolate-brown eyes, the ring they'd chosen together pressed into his palm, and knew he'd lost her. It was inconceivable, unthinkable, but those drunken, exhilarating, shameful minutes on New Year's Eve had cost him his Ruby, his love. Never again would he run his fingers through her silky blonde hair that was such a striking contrast to her dark eyes, or hold her close to him. All the lads had been after Ruby from when he could remember, but he had always known she was his. She'd never played the coquette or flirted. Straight as a die, Ruby was.

Desperately, even while knowing it was hopeless, he whispered, 'Please, lass, please. I'll crawl on my knees if that's what you want. I'll do anything, anything, Ruby.'

Her face was bleached of colour, as white as the snow. He had expected her to shout and scream at him when he told her because she could be fiery at times, but all she said was, 'Go home, Adam. It's finished, we're finished.'

'I'll walk you home.'

'Why? In case something bad happens to me?' Now her words were coated in a bitterness that was tangible. 'I want you to go, all right?'

Adam stared at her. 'We can't leave it like this, not after all we've meant to each other. Please, Ruby, you must see that? We can sort it out. I promise you, we can sort it.'

She said nothing but her small chin rose a fraction and her mouth tightened. He wouldn't see her cry, she told herself.

'I love you, Ruby.' He wet his lips, one over the other. 'I've been a fool, but you know I love you, don't you?'

After a few more seconds when she neither moved nor spoke, his head twitched in a little jerk. 'I'll go now if that's what you want, but we have to talk some more. I won't take no for an answer.'

She remained straight and still as she watched him walk away, his shoulders hunched. It was only when he had disappeared from view that her body gave a visible shudder. In just a few short minutes her life had changed for ever – how was that possible? She had lost Adam and she had lost her sister too; however this turned out she wanted nothing to do with either of them again.

She wasn't crying. The pain was too fierce for the relief of tears, burning and consuming every emotion except that of furious rage. Now that Adam had gone, now he wasn't standing in front of her, her anger was directed at Olive. She shut her eyes for a moment, picturing her sister creeping upstairs like a spider, knowing all the time what she intended to do. How could any lass lower herself to trick a lad like that, but especially when it was her own sister's fiancé?

She shivered, although not from the cold; her coat was thick and warm and kept her like toast. It was beautiful, a deep rich gold. Mrs Walton had presented it to her as her Christmas present and she had been beside herself with delight at the time and overcome by the elderly lady's generosity. Her old coat had been worn and the sleeves too short, but she had been saving every penny for her forthcoming marriage and had been quite content to make do. She had floated home that night on cloud nine; now it seemed in another lifetime, a time in which she had actually been happy. How could she have taken her happiness for granted? But she had. Everything in the garden had been rosy and her future mapped out before her – she and Adam were both in work, unlike some, and he had been quite agreeable to her continuing with Mrs Walton, knowing how much she loved it there and how kind her employer was. Lots of men would have insisted their wives give up any outside work the minute they got wed, but Adam had said she could stay at her job until the first bairn came along.

This thought caused a shaft of pain so intense she gasped. She would never have Adam's babies now. How many times had she imagined how their bairns would look? In her mind's eye they'd been so real – gurgling, rosy-cheeked infants with Adam's brown curls and blue eyes, and maybe just one little lass with her brown eyes.

But it was Olive who would bear his first child. Her sister had set out to hurt her on New Year's Eve and her plan had worked better than perhaps even Olive had imagined.

She wrapped her arms round her waist, swaying slightly as though it could ease the agony.

Why had Olive done what she had? True, they had never been close. From a toddler, she'd learned to avoid being alone with her big sister unless she wanted a sly pinch or a slap, but this? This was something so huge, so fundamental, that she was forced to face the knowledge that she had always tried to bury. Olive didn't like her, in fact she must hate her. In the past she'd tried to convince herself that lots of siblings didn't get on, but it didn't mean the love wasn't there, deep down. Sisters and brothers argued and fought but when push came to shove, they were there for each other. Blood was thicker than water. She had believed that and she would certainly have been there for Olive.

Had she loved her? Ruby searched herself. Yes, she had. Olive was her only sibling now, the lads having being killed in the war, and family was everything. How stupid, how utterly stupid and credulous did that make her? The sound she made was dragged up from the depths of her, something between a moan and a wail, and somewhere in the hedgerow a blackbird protested at it, sending out a warning call. Well, she would never make the mistake of trusting anyone again; she had learned her lesson. The rose-coloured glasses were well and truly off now.

She stood for long minutes, gazing with burning-hot

eyes down the lane. Tomorrow was supposed to be her wedding day. Her bridal dress and those of Olive and Ellie were hanging in the bedroom at home she shared with her sister. Her mam had been baking for days for the wedding feast after the ceremony. Adam's family, and her mam's two sisters and their families, were coming, along with Ellie and Mrs Walton. Her mam had borrowed extra chairs from the neighbours, and her aunties were bringing more plates and cups and saucers and cutlery. Her mam had even gone out and bought a fancy new lace tablecloth for the occasion, although she could ill afford it, and the beautiful iced wedding cake was already sitting on the table that normally held an aspidistra in the front room.

Ruby shook her head at herself. Why on earth was she thinking of a cake, a *cake*, when her whole world was lying in fragments around her? And there was Olive, who had orchestrated the whole thing, sitting happily at home as though butter wouldn't melt in her mouth.

That was it, she had to go back. Through the raging pain a section of her mind told her what to do. Home was where her mam was and she needed her mam like she'd never done before.

For a moment tears threatened but then the anger rose up again, hot and fierce as she thought of her sister. She made herself begin to walk, putting one foot in front of another hesitantly in the way a blind person might move, but with each step her desire to leap on Olive and rend her limb from limb grew.

Chapter Two

Olive had watched from the kitchen window as Ruby left the backyard earlier. After a minute or two when she was sure her sister had gone, she went quietly into the hall and took her hat and coat from the row of pegs on the wall that held the family's outdoor things. Putting them on, she changed her indoor shoes for her stout ankle boots and walked back into the kitchen, there to be greeted by her mother who said in some surprise, 'Where on earth do you think you're going?'

'I'm just popping out for a breath of fresh air. I won't be long.'

'A breath of fresh air?' If Olive had said she was going to take off her clothes and dance naked in the snow, her mother's voice couldn't have expressed more amazement. 'It's bitter out there and I need you to help me get ready for the morrer. I thought I was going to have the pair of you here tonight, and there's Ruby gone off to meet Adam—' Her mother stopped abruptly. 'They haven't had a tiff, have they?'

'Not that I know of.'

Cissy Morgan breathed a sigh of relief. That would have been all she needed. She was up to her eyes in it as it was. Coming back to the matter in hand, she said, 'And now here's you skedaddling off an' all. It's not good enough.'

'I said I won't be long. It's hot in here and I'm feeling a bit off colour.' This had the advantage of being true. In the last days since the morning sickness had kicked in she'd had a job to hide it from her mother, but now the sickness seemed to be all day and the smell from the remains of their evening meal added to the heat coming from the range was making her nauseous.

'You do look a bit peaky.' Now Cissy's voice was anxious. She knew it was daft, but since the winter after the armistice when the Spanish flu had swept through the country killing tens of thousands of people, many of them young folk who, for some reason, had been especially susceptible to the terrible disease, she'd lived in fear of one of her girls being taken from her. Her lads were among the three-quarters of a million British soldiers who had given their lives for King and country, and George would never be well again, she knew that, but after the weeping and wailing she had come to terms with that. Thousands of women were in the same boat as her, and some of them without the blessing of one surviving child. She had told God she would shoulder her cross as best she could, at the same time pleading with Him to spare Olive and Ruby as the flu had picked off folk as near as in their own street. When the epidemic was over she had lit goodness knows how many candles of thanks in church and she never missed Mass – it had been part of her bargain with the Almighty. Now she said, 'You sickening for something, lass?'

'I'm all right, Mam.' Olive forced a smile. The roof was going to go off this house tonight one way or another, and much as she disliked Father McHaffie she needed the priest present when Ruby returned. Father McHaffie saw things in black and white and he ruled his flock with a rod of iron. Non-Catholics were in league with the Devil and on course for the fiery pit; his flock, one and all, were sinners and only confession each week and attending Mass regularly gave them any chance of avoiding the worse sufferings of purgatory, and lastly, and most importantly, his word was law. He had told her yesterday that Adam must marry her as soon as it could be arranged, just as she had known he would, and he had agreed he would be present when she confessed her sin and its consequences to her family, after which he would pay a visit to the Gilberts.

Pulling her hat well down over her forehead she walked to the back door, opening it and turning for a moment to say, 'I'll be just a few minutes, Mam,' and then stepping out into the icy-cold night.

She hurried the short distance to the little church of St Mary but then hesitated before opening the arched wooden door. Once she walked over the threshold the die was cast and Father McHaffie would take over. But no, she corrected in the next moment. The die had been cast before this night, right from when she had suspected she might be pregnant, in fact, or even before that, on New Year's Eve when she had crept upstairs to Adam's bedroom. She had known what she was doing, she couldn't pretend otherwise, but Adam hadn't exactly fought her off either. True, he had been as pickled as an onion, but he hadn't been so drunk that he was incapable, as the child growing in her belly proved. And he had known she wasn't his precious Ruby when he had taken her, cursing her even as he had repeatedly thrust and groaned until it was over. It had been painful and brutal and not at all what she had expected from her first time, and afterwards he had flung her off him with a ferocity that had frightened her, shoving her out of the room and turning the key in the lock for good measure. She had stood on the landing feeling sick with shame and humiliation, but even then the jealousy and loathing she felt for her sister had been enough to carry her down the stairs and act as if nothing had happened. She had watched Ruby in the time before they had departed from the Gilberts', and the knowledge that with the power of a few well-chosen words she could take the silly smug smile off her sister's face for good had been enough to sustain her.

Olive drew in a long shuddering breath. For years Ruby had flaunted Adam in front of her. All the lads had liked Ruby, but from when she and Adam were bairns they'd been as thick as thieves. Even so, why their mam had agreed for the two to begin courting at fourteen she'd never know. She'd told her mother that it was indecent and that Ruby would get herself talked about, but the only response she'd had was a pat on the arm and her mam saying quietly and kindly that her turn would come in time.

Olive's jaw moved as she ground her teeth. Her mam had known that was rubbish as well as she had. She remembered Ruby's engagement do when Adam's family had come round for a bit of a knees-up. His brothers had acted the goat as usual and everyone had been merry, going on about what a perfect couple they were. She'd suffered agonies that day, painfully aware of what the assembled throng had been thinking behind all the smiles and guffaws.

'Shame about the older sister and her as plain as a pikestaff. How can two sisters be so different?'

Oh, aye, she'd known, she told herself bitterly. No lad, not even the ugly ones or Wilbur Hardy with his club foot, had ever looked her way. Her nickname at school had been Scarecrow after one bright spark had said her face would frighten even the crows. She'd been eight or nine at the time and had pretended she didn't care when the lads had bandied it about in the playground and the girls, even those who were supposed to be her friends, had sniggered.

A sudden gust of wind prompted her to open the door of the church and as she stepped into the dimly lit interior the sweet, heavy scent of stale incense brought her stomach churning again. As a child she'd liked coming here, finding the services with their rituals and ceremony strangely comforting. Even the statue of Jesus lying in His mother's arms with blood coming out of His side and His hands and feet torn hadn't bothered her, although Ruby had had nightmares about it when she was a bairn. Olive's lip curled. That was typical of the spoiled brat she'd been and still was. Everything had been handed on a plate to Ruby from the moment she was born, with her big brown eyes and blonde hair and simpering smiles. Well, no more. Now her sister was going to have to face the real world. Her perfect Adam wasn't so perfect after all.

Olive stood at the top of the centre aisle looking down the church towards the altar where the black-clad figure of Father McHaffie was kneeling before the statue of Jesus in the Blessed Sacrament. For the life of her she couldn't walk or even move to sit in a pew, merely bowing her head and making a deep genuflection. She knew what the priest made of her conduct; he had made it abundantly clear at their last meeting.

After a few moments had passed, the lean, tall figure rose to his feet and then turned to face her. His eyes were small and hard, his mouth was thin and he had a sharp beak of a nose that dominated his face, and with his black robes he resembled nothing so much as a giant crow. As he walked towards her Olive thought he was terrifying. He stopped within an arm's length of her, his stare cold. 'Does your situation remain the same?'

'Yes, Father.'

'And you have made no mention of this to anyone other than Dr Upton and the father of the child?'

'No, Father.'

He nodded slowly. 'And the father, Adam Gilbert, still refuses to marry you?'

Olive gulped; her throat was dry with fear of the priest along with dread of what the next hour would bring. Her mam was going to be so disappointed in her, she knew that. She swallowed again before she could say, 'He – Adam's arranged to meet my sister tonight so I think he's going to tell her, but this morning, at the doctor's, he was still saying he wouldn't get wed to me. I told him you were going to speak to his mam an' da today.'

Father McHaffie surveyed this girl who had sinned and his thin voice dripped condemnation when he said, 'You have been wicked and foolish and as a result of your action the fruit of your womb will be tainted in the eyes of God unless Adam does his duty. The sooner he acknowledges his transgression before men and the Almighty, the sooner he can receive absolution. He will marry you as quickly as it can be arranged.'

There was no doubt in his voice that he would be obeyed, and much as Olive feared the priest she knew a moment of deep thankfulness for the power he wielded. Adam's family, like hers, were staunch Catholics, and although his da and brothers might drink themselves paralytic on a Saturday night, come Sunday they'd be at Mass and suitably penitent. Lowering her gaze, she murmured, 'Yes, Father.'

'Your father will accompany me to the Gilberts'. He is at home?'

'Yes, Father.'

'Then come along.'

He walked past and opened the door of the church, standing aside for her to exit first and then shutting the door before striding ahead of her, his head high and his black robes flapping. Olive had a job to keep up with him but he didn't turn to see if she was behind him at any point before they reached Devonshire Street. By the time she arrived at the house Father McHaffie had already knocked on the front door. Olive could imagine the consternation her mother would be feeling as she hurried into the hall; no one ever used the front door except the doctor and the priest, and apart from her mam scrubbing the front step and whitening it each week the door remained closed.

Sure enough, her mother's face expressed a mixture of anxiety and surprise when the door swung open and she said, 'Father McHaffie, we weren't expecting you tonight, were we? Come in, come in, the weather's dreadful, isn't it, and with the wedding tomorrow an' all. I was just saying to George—' And then her mother stopped abruptly as she caught sight of Olive behind the priest.

'Good evening, Mrs Morgan.' Father McHaffie swept into the house and straight down the hall into the kitchen, which further flustered Cissy. The priest, like the doctor, was of such standing in the community that he was only ever shown into Cissy's mausoleum of a front room. She cast a desperate glance at Olive before scurrying after

Father McHaffie. In the kitchen she found that George had stood to his feet and was rolling down his shirtsleeves as he said, 'Good evening, Father,' and now she twisted the corner of her pinny, saying, 'Won't you come into the front room, Father, and I'll make some tea? You must be frozen.'

'Here will do perfectly well.' The priest seated himself on one of the hard-backed chairs at the kitchen table, and Cissy breathed a sigh of relief that she had just cleared the remains of the evening meal and wiped the oilcloth over it before putting the pot of hyacinths which had been a present from Ruby into the middle of the newly cleaned expanse.

George had seated himself again once the priest had sat down. Cissy looked helplessly at her husband before she said, 'I'll make that pot of tea then, Father.'

'That would be most welcome.'

Olive had sidled just inside the kitchen doorway and she remained glued to the spot as her mother busied herself at the range. It was only when Cissy turned and said sharply, 'Bring four cups to the table, girl,' that she forced herself to move. From the tea set displayed on the kitchen dresser she took four cups and saucers of fine bone china. The set had been a wedding present from her mother's grandparents and as such was only used on special occasions. She placed them on the table before filling the little milk jug and sugar bowl. Her legs were wobbly and her hands were trembling and the cups had rattled in their saucers as she'd put them down, causing her father to glance up at her. She didn't meet his gaze, neither did anyone speak until her mother had filled the cups and everyone was seated.

Father McHaffie took a sip of his tea before he spoke, his voice cold. 'Olive has something to tell you and she asked me to be present. I must warn you it will be a shock, Mrs Morgan.'

As her mother's eyes shot to her face Olive licked her lips. She had gone over what she was going to say umpteen times but now the moment was here she found she couldn't speak.

Cissy, her eyes wide and questioning now, looked from her daughter's white face to that of the priest's, and then back to Olive again, but it was George who said quietly, 'What is it, lass? What's wrong?'

Olive took a deep breath as her stomach turned over. 'It – it was on New Year's Eve . . .'

When Ruby flung open the back door and walked into the kitchen, she was aware of several things simultaneously. Her father was sitting with his head in his hands, her mother was crying and Father McHaffie had a cup to his lips, but it was to Olive, whose head had jerked up as she'd entered, that she said, 'I hate you. How could you, how *could* you do that? You're dirty, disgusting.'

'That is quite enough.' Father McHaffie had put down his cup and stood up. 'Control yourself.'

'Control *myself*?' There was no respectful 'Father' and neither was there any deference in Ruby's attitude when she cried, 'You know what she's done and you tell me to control *myself*? She's done it to spite me, she planned it, and with *Adam*. She doesn't even like him, she never has, and yet she forced herself on him when he was drunk. She's worse than any dockside dolly.'

Ruby heard her mother gasp but she and the priest were glaring at each other and she didn't look her mother's way as Father McHaffie growled, 'What is done is done and this is helping no one. Furthermore, your speech and conduct leave a lot to be desired. Olive has confessed her sin and is repentant before God—'

'Repentant before God? And that makes it all right?'

'First and foremost it is against the Almighty that your sister has sinned.'

'Well, forgive me, Father, but I don't see it that way.' Ruby had always been afraid of the priest like everyone else but her sense of injustice had done away with the fear. For the first time in her life she was seeing Father McHaffie as merely a man, and a man who had been sitting at the table with her parents and Olive sipping tea as cosy as you like. It was this that caused her to say, 'If you think Olive is repentant then that's because she's pulled the wool over your eyes, and even if she is, which she isn't, a few Hail Marys and attending Mass till kingdom come won't take away the wickedness of what she's done to me.'

Father McHaffie had gone red in the face, and it was Cissy who said quickly and apologetically, 'Ruby is upset, Father. This has been a terrible shock for us all. She doesn't mean anything.'

'I know what Ruby means, Mrs Morgan, and of your two daughters I think it is the younger one you need to pray for the most.' The priest glanced at George who was still sitting at the table and his voice was a bark when he said, 'If you are ready to accompany me to the Gilberts' I suggest we leave now before your daughter further puts her soul in peril.'

'I haven't put my soul in peril by speaking the truth and God knows what's in Olive's heart even if you don't.'

'That's enough!'

The look that Father McHaffie gave Ruby as he spoke caused her to step back a pace, and even in her rage and pain she wondered how a man of God, a priest, could appear so devilish. It was the shock of what she had seen in his face that kept her silent as the priest strode out of the kitchen into the hall, her father following a moment later but stopping long enough to squeeze her shoulder as he passed her, his eyes full of pity and sorrow.

They heard the front door shut behind the two men and Ruby turned to look steadily at her sister.

'I don't know why you did what you did on New Year's Eve but I tell you this, you'll live to regret it. It wasn't a mistake on your part – you knew exactly what you were doing and the consequences. Oh, not the bairn, even you couldn't have planned that, but you wanted to spoil what me and Adam had, that's the truth of it. And all this talk of repentance that Father McHaffie was on about, I don't believe a word of it.'

'You shouldn't have spoken to him like that, hinny.'

Cissy's voice caused Ruby's gaze to swing from her sister to her mother.

'How can you say that after what she's done?'

'He's a priest, lass.'

'I don't care. He's still just a man.'

'Ruby!'

'Well, he is.' Ruby stared defiantly at her mother. For some time now she had been having thoughts about the way Father McHaffie scared the wits out of everyone and acted like God Himself, especially when he gave his fire-and-brimstone sermons about the damnation of non-Catholics. Mrs Walton wasn't a Catholic, but a kinder and better person you couldn't wish to meet. And there were other things too, such as the way he threatened his flock with purgatory every Sunday and demanded unquestioning obedience and acceptance of everything he said. She had tried to talk about it with Adam but he always changed the subject or said, much as her mother had done, that Father McHaffie was a priest as though that ended any discussion.

Before Ruby's eyes there rose a picture of Adam as he had looked walking away down the lane, and now she turned to Olive again, her eyes narrowed and her hands clenched. 'You're evil, that's what you are. You were determined to ruin my life, weren't you? And to trick Adam like that – you're beyond contempt.'

Olive stood up and now there was no trace of the penitent about her when she hissed, 'It takes two to make a bairn. I don't know why you're putting all the blame on me.'

'Because Adam told me how it happened and I believe him.'

'Of course you do. You'd hate to believe he could like someone besides you, wouldn't you?'

'He doesn't like you, not in any way. He loathes you, you sicken him. He wants me to go down south with him and get married there, and he said you could go into the workhouse for all he cares.' Ruby's words were dipped in the poison of her hate but nevertheless carried the unmistakable ring of truth. She saw Olive blanch and felt a moment of bitter satisfaction. 'But don't worry, I wouldn't let him touch me now if he was the last man on earth, not when he's been contaminated by you. You can have him but just remember he'll never forgive you for this any more than I will.'

'Ruby, lass, don't say such things.' Cissy tried to take her daughter's arm but as Ruby jerked herself free, she added, 'Olive is your sister, your own flesh and blood, and with the lads gone—'

'You're right, Mam. She's my sister but she's never liked me and you know that as well as I do. Nothing I've done has been right as far as she's concerned, not from when we were bairns. She's spiteful and cruel—'

'Lass, I know you're hurting and the good Lord Himself wouldn't blame you for feeling the way you do, but Adam's more to blame than Olive, you must see that? To give a lass a bairn . . . Well, it speaks for itself. And

Olive hadn't been with another lad – it was her first time.'
Cissy was desperate to pour oil on troubled waters. 'She
didn't know what she was doing, that's the truth of it,
and Adam was drunk and took advantage.'

'You're saying he *raped* her?' Ruby could hardly believe
her ears, or that her mother was so gullible. 'Is that what
she told you? Well, let *me* tell you, Mam, that there was
a raping all right, but not on Adam's side.'

'Ruby!'

The shock in Cissy's voice conveyed itself to Ruby,
and she said tightly, 'Don't look at me like that, Mam.
It's the truth.'

'No, lass, no. I don't believe that.' The reproach in
Cissy's face cut Ruby to the quick. Somehow she was the
one who had been put in the wrong. And when Cissy
further compounded her blundering by saying, 'This is a
terrible thing to have happened and my heart goes out to
you, hinny, you must know that, but Olive is as much a
victim as you are in all this,' she knew she had to get out
of the house before she said something unforgivable to her
mother. Her life was in ruins; it was supposed to be her
wedding day tomorrow and instead Olive had taken Adam
away from her, apparently with their mother's blessing.

She turned to Olive, her voice low and deadly as she
said, 'You've made your bed and you'll have to lie on it
but it'll be a bed of thorns, Olive Morgan. You think
you've won now but you haven't.'

The two sisters regarded each other for a moment
more; Ruby as white as a sheet but with her eyes blazing,

and Olive, the taller of the two, appearing even taller with her chin lifted and her thin mouth set in a grim line.

When Cissy said helplessly, 'Please . . .' it could have been directed at either of them, but it was enough to cause Ruby to swing round sharply and make for the hall. She ran up the stairs, not knowing what she was going to do or where she was going but only that she had to leave. Her suitcase was already partly packed with the clothes and things she had planned to take to her new home after the wedding celebrations here the next day, and now she added more to it, along with the money she had been saving for a little while to stock up the cupboards and buy bits and pieces for their new home. Adam had picked up the keys from the landlord two days ago and the second-hand furniture they had bought had been delivered that same afternoon, when Adam and his brothers had finished their shift at the colliery and could be present to put it in place. All her bottom-drawer linen and towels were there; they had even made the bed up that night two days ago amid much laughter and kissing. And then the next day Olive must have come to the colliery gates to wait for Adam . . .

She glanced at her wedding dress and the two bridesmaids' dresses hanging on the back of the wardrobe door. If she'd had a knife in her hand she would have slashed the frocks to ribbons. They had been a labour of love, and she and Mrs Walton had spent long hours on the finer details of her bridal dress, every stitch, every little aspect perfect and beautifully fitted to her figure. Olive had said more than once that she thought Mrs Walton would have been better spending her money on something useful like curtains or bedspreads, rather than on finery that would be worn for a few hours and then packed away in mothballs. Stupid, Olive had called her, when very soon Adam could well be on half-time at the colliery or even laid off the way the country was going.

Well, she had been stupid all right, Ruby thought bitterly, but not about her dress.

Taking the frocks off their hangers she rolled them up and tied them into a bundle with the cord of her dressing gown. They were Mrs Walton's by rights and she'd take them to her. It would be up to Mrs Walton what she did with them; she didn't care one way or the other.

Fastening the suitcase she picked it up, and with the bundle tucked under one arm she walked downstairs and into the kitchen. Olive was again sitting at the table and her mother was mashing a pot of tea; she looked up as Ruby entered and said quickly, 'I was just going to bring you a cup up, hinny,' before her gaze went to the suitcase. 'You're not going somewhere, not tonight?'

Did her mother seriously think she could bear to stay under the same roof as Olive for a minute more?

Ruby's face must have expressed how she felt because in the next moment, tears in her voice, Cissy said, 'No, lass, no, don't leave like this. Please, hinny, wait till your da gets back and we'll talk about things.'

Quietly, and without glancing Olive's way, Ruby said, 'I'm going, Mam.'

'But where, and at this time of night?'

She had known where to seek refuge from the moment she had looked at the dresses on the wardrobe door. 'I'll be at Mrs Walton's.'

'Lass, no, this is all wrong.'

No one knew that better than her. Again Ruby's face spoke for her and Cissy murmured, 'When will you be back?'

'I won't be coming back, Mam.' Somehow her mother's championing of Olive hurt more at this moment than her sister's treachery and Adam's betrayal.

'Of course you will, this is your home.'

Not any more. As Ruby looked at her mother she knew with a quiet certainty that she would never return to live under this roof with its memories of a life that might have been. Whether Olive remained here or whether Father McHaffie had his way and Adam married her sister, she was saying goodbye, and she made this clear when she said, 'I'll write and let you know where I am when I'm settled.'

'Where you are? What do you mean? You just said you were going to Mrs Walton's. She'll let you stay there for a bit, won't she?'

When Ruby made no reply Cissy walked across and hugged her, but her daughter's body was stiff and unresponsive and after a moment Cissy stepped back a pace, saying helplessly, 'Be careful, lass, the pavements are like glass. Do you want me to walk along of you?'

Ruby shook her head. She just wanted to get away.

She had reached the back door and opened it when Olive's voice behind her said, 'Whether you believe me or not I didn't want it to be like this.' Ruby paused for one second but she didn't turn round or speak before stepping into the bitter cold, leaving the door ajar behind her. She walked across their small yard and opened the gate into the back lane and again she left this open, and as she trudged down the track that was practically knee high with snow she expected any moment that her mam would come running after her calling her name, but the snowy night was silent and she was the only person alive in the whole wide world.

And now the tears streamed down her face.

Chapter Three

Vera Walton stared aghast at the young lass she thought of as a daughter. When Ruby had knocked on her door the evening before and had almost collapsed into her arms it had been some time before she could get the full story of what had happened out of the distraught girl amid her storm of weeping. Once she had become aware of the whole sorry mess she had made Ruby a hot drink, adding a good measure of the brandy she kept for medicinal purposes and which had been in the back of the cupboard for goodness knew how long. She'd then made up a makeshift bed on the sofa with thick blankets and a spare eiderdown. It was only after another mug of tea, again with a large dollop of brandy, that she had persuaded Ruby to lie down, a stone hot-water bottle at her feet. Ruby had dropped off within minutes, worn out by crying and no doubt aided by the amount of alcohol in her bloodstream.

Now it was seven o'clock in the morning and they'd just had toast and a pot of tea, but it wasn't Ruby's chalk-white face or the change in her persona that worried Vera – it was the fact that the lass had just told her of her intention to leave Sunderland that very day.

'Listen, m'dear, I know you are dreadfully upset and with good cause, but don't do anything hasty. You can stay here as long as you please, you know that. We can clear out the spare room where I store the material and whatnot and that can be yours. You'll be quite at liberty to come and go as you see fit, and I would be delighted to have you here indefinitely.'

Ruby forced a smile as she said quietly, 'Thank you, Mrs Walton, and I appreciate your kindness more than you will ever know, but I need to get away. Right away.'

'I can quite understand you thinking like that but all I'm saying is give it a few days until you are feeling a little better. Now is not the time to make such decisions.'

Ruby inclined her head. 'You are probably right but I can't stay. I have to go now. I – I don't want to see anyone I know.'

'You don't have to. I will make sure of that.'

She wouldn't be able to. Ruby looked at the old lady whom she thought of as more of a grandmother than an employer. She had never known her own grandparents – both her mother's parents and her father's had died before she was born – but they couldn't have been nicer than Mrs Walton. And she knew Mrs Walton was talking sense and that she meant well, but she had to leave the town now, today, before Adam tried to see her or her parents came round, especially her da. She might weaken if she saw her da and she couldn't afford to do that because she knew she would go mad if she remained in Sunderland. Adam would marry Olive; the combined weight of both sets of parents and not least Father McHaffie would see to that. Olive's stomach would swell and some time in the early autumn Adam's child would be born, and she couldn't, she just *couldn't* play the auntie when that happened.

'I'm sorry, Mrs Walton, but my mind's made up.'

Vera sighed and made one last effort. 'Ruby, you know how much I think of you, don't you? Having your company here for the last four years has made them the happiest of my life since my poor Maurice died.' She had told Ruby more than once how her husband had perished in the last few weeks of the Boer War, one of over a thousand British casualties lying dead in the hills at Spion Kop, seven miles from the garrison town of Ladysmith. She had mourned him ever since and still wore black from head to foot. 'I wasn't going to mention this until it became necessary but I made a new will a little while ago and you are my sole beneficiary, dear. This house is bought and paid for and the business provides a steady income. Moreover, you enjoy the work, don't you, and you have a gift for it, remarkable in one so young. Your life would be very comfortable and it would certainly mean a great deal to me if you stayed. We get on well, don't we?'

'Oh, Mrs Walton, I never imagined – I mean, I can't believe –' Ruby took a deep breath as she tried to pull herself together. She reached out and took the old lady's hands, and there were fresh tears in her eyes when she said, 'Thank you from the bottom of my heart. And I would have loved to continue here with you. I've always felt that you're like family, and you've been so good to me, but . . .'

She left the sentence unfinished and it was Vera who softly said, 'But you can't stay. I understand, I understand. But wherever you go, you will keep in touch, won't you? And we could perhaps see each other occasionally? You are very dear to me. Write to me as soon as you are settled so I know you're safe, won't you? Where will you go?'

'Newcastle way, I think.' She could lose herself in a big city and get work of some kind. 'But first I have to go and tell Ellie what's happened.' Ellie had been due to arrive at the house mid-morning to help her get ready for the wedding at one o'clock. 'Can I leave everything here while I go?'

'Of course, dear.'

It was Ellie's mother who opened the door to her knock. The big, blowsy woman with her enormous breasts and greasy grey hair screwed into a knot at the back of her head stared at her for a moment, her eyes bleary from last night's drinking, before recognition dawned. 'Ruby?'

'Hello, Mrs Wood. Could I have a word with Ellie?' For a moment Ruby's misery was secondary to her fight not to reveal what the smell emanating from inside the house was doing to her stomach. Although she and Ellie had been friends from their first day at school, she'd only visited the Woods' place a couple of times and that had been more than enough. It had been filthy and flea-ridden with mice droppings everywhere.

Ellie's father was a trimmer at the docks, a burly brute of a man who used his fists on his wife and children whenever he was in the house, and Mrs Wood had a bairn every year as regular as clockwork. Ellie was the seventh of the thirteen who had survived the violence and neglect, and since leaving school and getting a job in a bakery shop she made sure she was at home as little as possible, doing extra shifts and often working fifteen-hour days. Anything was better than being around her mam and da, as she'd said on more than one occasion to Ruby, and by getting home after eleven o'clock each night she could be sure they were blind drunk and dead to the world in their bed in the front room.

Ruby was saved from entering the house by Ellie appearing behind her mother in the next instant. She took one look at Ruby's face before saying, 'What's the matter? What's happened?'

Unable to reply at that moment for the swell of emotion in her throat, Ruby shook her head, at which point Ellie said, 'Wait there, I'll get me coat.'

Two minutes later they were walking away from the street at the back of Palmer's Hill Engine Works, and once round the corner, Ellie stopped, saying again, 'What's the matter? You look bad.'

Ruby faced her friend as she said simply, 'I'm not getting married, Ellie.'

Ellie blinked in surprise. 'Has there been a fall at the pit? Has Adam been hurt?'

She wished it was as simple as that. Forgive me, God, she thought, but I could have coped with that, however devastating, and been there for him. She shook her head. 'No, there's been no accident or anything, not in that way at least.' For a moment the irony brought the urge to laugh to the surface but she knew if she started she would never stop, like poor Mrs Longhurst two doors down who had lost her mind after her only son had been killed on his way home from the pit when the milkman's horse had bolted and the cart had crushed him against a wall. Mrs Longhurst had been calm at first, her mam had told her, and then she'd said, 'I prayed each day the pit wouldn't have him and it didn't, did it, but I never thought about a horse,' and she had started laughing, terrible laughter that had gone on for days until she had been taken away to the asylum.

'Ellie –' She paused. How could she word it? And then, swallowing hard, she shook her head almost in disbelief at what she was going to say. 'Adam's taken Olive down and she's expecting a bairn.'

Ellie gasped, her thin face with its great sad eyes stretching as her mouth fell open and her eyes popped wide. 'No, no, not Adam. She's lying, Olive's lying.'

'He told me himself. It was like this . . .' She told the story with painful flatness, willing herself not to break down.

Ellie continued staring at her for a moment after she

finished speaking, before saying in a low, aggressive tone, 'Her, your Olive, she wants stringing up. It's not your fault that you're so pretty and she's got a face like a hen's plucked backside.'

She knew Ellie hadn't meant to be funny – her friend's voice vibrated with fury, and in truth she wouldn't have imagined she could smile at anything today with her world in fragments – but from somewhere she found a laugh bubbling up, a real laugh, not like the way she'd felt a minute or two before. The feeling passed in an instant but it enabled her to say weakly, 'So the wedding's off and I'm going to leave here today, Ellie. I can't stay. Mrs Walton said I could live there but I need to get right away where there's no danger I could run into Adam or Olive.'

Ellie nodded. 'Where are you going?'

'Newcastle. I've got enough put by to rent a room in a house somewhere while I look for work, any work.'

'Right.' Ellie squared her narrow shoulders. 'I'll come with you.'

'Come with me?'

'You don't think I'd let you go by yourself? Safety in numbers and all that.'

'You can't just leave here, Ellie. What about your job at the baker's? You've done so well there and they think the world of you. You've had a rise each year since you've worked there.'

'That's because I work longer and harder than anyone else and old Fairley knows which side his bread's buttered,' said Ellie matter-of-factly. She knew no one else would start work at seven o'clock in the morning and work through till ten or eleven at night like she did, and she was agreeable to turning her hand to anything, from humping stones of flour into the bath tins first thing to start the bread-making process off, right through to helping Fairley's wife do all the fancy cooking like the teacakes and sugared buns and iced biscuits. Aye, Fairley knew it paid him to keep her feeling valued, but the bakery was a sanctuary away from her father's fists so it worked both ways.

'But what about your mam?' Ruby didn't mention Ellie's da. Everyone knew what Mr Wood was like although no one had ever confronted him, not even when he'd thrown one of Ellie's sisters down the stairs and she'd been in the infirmary for weeks. You can't interfere in the way a man is in his own home. That's what her own mam had said when she had told her about Ellie's sister. Ruby hadn't agreed with the sentiment and she'd said so, but her mother had just shaken her head and said it was the way things were.

Ellie shrugged. 'The only thing Mam will miss if I go is me wage packet each week. All she cares about is the booze. No, I'm coming. Look, I'll nip back in and get some things now, while me da's at the docks. It's his half-day an' he'll be back later.' She had turned as she'd spoken, but now swung back as she added, 'You don't mind me coming, do you?'

'Mind? It'll make all the difference.'

'All right then. Wait here.'

Ruby watched the too-thin figure of her friend dart

away, and for the first time since Adam had dropped his bombshell a ray of comfort briefly warmed her. She stood quite still, her mind in a strange vacuum until Ellie returned, and she couldn't have said how long she had taken. Ellie was carrying a bulging cloth bag and had her handbag over her shoulder and she looked excited, her tone reflecting this when she announced, 'I've said me goodbyes.'

'What did your mam say?'

'Not much. Just that me da'd take it out of me hide if I showed me face again, as if I didn't know that.'

'And you're sure you want to leave?'

'Never bin so sure about anythin' in me life.'

Ruby nodded. She could tell. Ellie's face was alight.

'And I hadn't given me mam me wage packet either. Old Fairley always pays me on a Saturday, but 'cause I was having the day off for the wedding he let me have it last night. They were in bed when I got home and blind drunk as usual. So, at least that's a bit towards things.' They'd begun walking, treading gingerly on the icy pavements, and as Ellie slipped her arm through Ruby's, she added, 'I shan't be sorry to get away from here, lass, I tell you straight.'

Neither would she. Oh, neither would she.

Ruby found she had to retract this thought for a few brief minutes as she said goodbye to Mrs Walton, because she realized at the moment of farewell that she was going to miss the little woman very much. But not enough to stay.

Nevertheless, as she and Ellie walked away towards the train station leaving Mrs Walton with a handkerchief pressed against her streaming eyes, the heartache of goodbye was pressing hard on her chest. Her employer had shown her nothing but kindness since the day she'd applied for the position of seamstress, and it was only now that she understood her affection for the refined little woman had long since matured into love. But she couldn't dwell on that or the way Mrs Walton had clung to her in the last few moments.

She had to be strong over the next little while, she told herself painfully. She mustn't think of Mrs Walton, or of Adam and Olive, and especially not of her mam. Her mam had made it plain that Olive could do no wrong in her eyes and that her sympathies were all with her elder daughter. The hurt this had caused had grown steadily over the last few hours, making her want to curl up into a little ball and die. But perhaps she should have expected it? Their mother had always favoured Olive. Strangely, though, it had never bothered her unduly before because she had known her mam loved her too. But now . . .

'—what to do.'

Ruby came out of her brooding to the realization that Ellie had been speaking. 'Sorry, what did you say?'

'I just said I'm a bit scared 'cause I've never been on a train before but at least you know what to do.'

Ruby nodded but didn't speak. The memory was too painful to dwell on. Adam had taken her out for the day as a surprise on her seventeenth birthday the year before.

It had been the beginning of February and bitterly cold, the snow lying thick in the fields they'd passed on the way down the coast to Hartlepool, but the train had chugged along impervious to the weather, billowing steam and snorting now and again. She and Adam had wandered round the shops in the town before having fish and chips followed by sticky buns in a little cafe, and then in the afternoon they had gone to a picture house to see Rudolf Valentino in *The Sheik*. It had been a magical interlude.

Ellie, realizing she had been less than tactful, trudged along silently now, telling herself she would have to watch her tongue in the days ahead because in this overwhelming happiness at her change of circumstances, she had to remember that Ruby was suffering. The joy and sheer jubilation she was feeling at escaping her mam and da and starting a new life with Ruby, whom she loved best in the world, had only come about through her friend's tragedy, and she wouldn't have wished it to be like this for anything. And as though someone had challenged this thought, she reiterated fiercely, I wouldn't, I wouldn't. Ruby had always been more of a sister than a friend, a big sister, even though they were the same age, and she'd always known she could count on Ruby no matter what.

Ruby had looked after her, protected her and never once made her feel a burden; she didn't know what she would have done without her. All the girls in their class had wanted Ruby to be their best friend but from the outset Ruby had chosen her, and woe betide anyone who had poked fun about her smelly clothes or holey shoes in those early days. Ruby had been on them like a ton of bricks, and through her friend's championing of her the other girls had accepted her.

Ellie hitched the cloth bag containing the sum total of her clothes and the indoor shoes she wore at the bakery further up her shoulder as she said in a subdued tone, 'We'll be all right, lass. You know that, don't you? We'll stick together like we've always done and things will work out. Olive will rue the day she started all this, but you'll come out on top. Your conscience is clear.'

That didn't feel as though it counted for much right now. Ruby forced herself to say, 'Thank you, Ellie,' because she knew her friend meant well, but this wasn't about winning or losing. She was leaving everything behind – Adam, her old home and the new one she and Adam had been going to move into this very day after the wedding celebrations, her mam and da, Mrs Walton, her whole way of life, the essence of what made her *her*. She supposed she ought to be feeling terrified, but ever since she had woken up this morning on Mrs Walton's sofa and realized the horrific nightmare she'd been having wasn't in fact a dream but the hard cold truth, she'd known there was nothing more to be terrified of. The worst had happened. Now it was a matter of getting through the rest of her life without Adam the best she could and she didn't know how she was going to do it.

Chapter Four

'What do you mean, she's gone?'

Vera Walton stared at the young man standing on her doorstep. She had been expecting Adam, knowing Ruby's mother would have to tell him where she had gone, and she had been all set to let fly once he was in front of her. He had hurt the girl she thought of as a daughter beyond belief, betrayed her in the worse possible way, and she was angry and bitterly disappointed in him. Moreover he was the means of causing the dear child to flee Sunderland, to leave *her*, and although she knew it was selfish to think of herself at this time, Ruby's loss was almost more than she could bear. Now though, as she looked at Adam, she couldn't bring herself to upbraid him. She had always thought him handsome with an air of virility she could imagine was very attractive to young women, but the man standing in front of her seemed to have aged ten, twenty years since the last time she had seen him. He looked ill; not just ill, she told herself, but broken.

In spite of herself and her love for Ruby, she found herself saying, 'Come in, Adam. We can't talk on the doorstep and you look as though you need a hot drink. Have you slept at all?'

'What?' He looked at her so vacantly she could see he was having trouble processing her words, and then he muttered, 'No, no, I haven't been to bed. I've been out walking since first light, trying to get myself together before I went to see Ruby but her mam said she left there last night to come here.'

Vera stood to one side and indicated for him to come into the house, and once inside she turned the sign in the shop window to 'Closed' and bolted the door. Leading him through the shop and into her small sitting room-cum-kitchen, she sat him down on the sofa Ruby had occupied the night before and then put the kettle on the hob. The blackleaded range took up almost one wall of the room and Vera kept the open fire in the middle of it going day and night, winter and summer. Consequently the room was as warm as toast and the contrast to outside caused Adam to shiver convulsively.

When Vera said softly, 'You're frozen, lad. Your lips are blue,' he didn't speak, but lowered his head swiftly as a rush of tears came into his stricken eyes.

It wasn't until Vera pressed a mug of hot tea laced with the brandy from the cupboard into his cold hands, that he raised his head.

'What am I going to do?' he whispered. 'I can't live without Ruby, Mrs Walton.'

'Drink your tea.' In a silence that was painful he did just that, much as a bairn would obey its mother, and as Vera watched him she thought, He's in a bad way sure enough. Oh dear, oh dear, what a tangle, and the pity she had felt when she had first seen him on the doorstep increased.

At length, when he'd drained the mug, he said quietly, 'Where has she gone, Mrs Walton? I have to see her.'

'It won't do any good, lad. Her mind's made up. Believe me, I tried to persuade her to stay.'

Aye, he could believe that. Mrs Walton thought the world of Ruby.

'Listen, Adam.' Vera sat down beside him. 'What's done is done and there's no going back. Perhaps if there hadn't been a bairn on the way it might have been different, I don't know, but if you love Ruby, and I think you do, you have to accept her decision.'

'I can't.' It was a helpless little whisper.

'You can. In fact, you must. It would be too cruel not to allow her to try and find some peace of mind.'

'All this is Olive's fault.'

'Olive played her part. A large part, I grant you that, but you must take some responsibility too.'

He shook his head, whether in repudiation of her words or in despair, Vera didn't know. There was quiet in the room for a few moments, and then Adam wetted his lips. 'Father McHaffie came to the house last night. He told my da I had to marry Olive and as far as my parents are concerned, that's that.'

Gently, Vera said, 'I don't know Father McHaffie. I'm not a Catholic, as you are probably aware, but forgetting him for a moment, I can't see you have any other choice. There is the bairn to consider, lad. The innocent one in all of this. From what Ruby intimated to me, she made it plain she couldn't see the child born out of wedlock, as much for her parents' sake as the baby's.' She paused for a moment. 'Adam, Ruby's gone and she isn't coming back, and to be brutally honest, even if she did, it's over between the two of you.'

'I know,' he whispered. 'In my head I know, but my heart . . .'

'I'm sorry, lad.' And she found she was as concerned for him as much as Ruby, which she hadn't expected. 'Can I get you another cup of tea?' The panacea for all ills, Vera thought ruefully, but not this one. There was no remedy for this.

'Thanks all the same but I'd better get going.' He stood up and Vera rose too, whereupon they looked at each other for a moment in silence.

'This was going to be the happiest day of my life,' Adam said, in a dead voice. 'We'd got the future all mapped out, Ruby and me.'

'I know, lad, I know.'

'And her, Olive, I could kill her for what she's done.'

'Don't talk like that, lad. That'll help no one.'

She followed him into the shop, unbolting the door and letting him pass her. In spite of the bitter cold the sky was high and blue and a white winter sun illuminated the snowy rooftops and pavements, promising that spring was round the corner. It was a perfect day for a wedding.

Adam stepped down onto the icy pavement and then turned to look at her as he said, 'Can it be right to stand before God and promise to love someone you hate with every fibre of your being, Mrs Walton? Because that's what I'll be doing, sure enough. But like you pointed out, I have no choice, do I.'

'Oh, lad.' His face now wore a closed, hard look and she realized that somewhere in the last hour or so while he had been with her he had become resigned to his fate. For a moment she almost retracted her words, almost told him to go and find his Ruby and try one last time, but what good would that do? Ruby's mind was made up and besides, there was the bairn. A bairn born out of wedlock would suffer for the sins of the mother round these parts; it would be made to feel shame and humiliation from the time it was out of nappies. The most vicious and determined predators in the animal kingdom didn't have a patch on human beings when they got going, especially some of the housewives hereabouts. And so she remained silent, and after a moment he walked away, towards a marriage made in hell, Vera told herself wretchedly, but then what could she do? What would be, would be.

Adam stood in Cissy's kitchen facing his future father-in-law. Earlier that morning when he had called asking to see Ruby, George hadn't been up and it had just been Cissy stirring a pan of porridge at the range. Now it was

George who said, 'What do you mean, Ruby's gone? Gone where? Not left Sunderland?'

Adam nodded. 'First thing this morning.'

Cissy gave a little cry. 'No, she wouldn't just disappear without saying goodbye.' Yanking off her pinny she threw it on a chair as she said, 'Mrs Walton knows where she is sure enough. I'll stay there till I get it out of her.'

'She doesn't. I was there for some time and she told me herself she'd begged Ruby to have her spare room but Ruby wouldn't be persuaded. She's gone and Ellie with her.'

Cissy stared at him before sitting down suddenly. The house was in a mess; her two sisters had been round half the morning after George had let them know the wedding was off. She'd been carting the chairs she'd borrowed back to the neighbours for what seemed like hours and Olive was refusing to come out of her bedroom. Adam's mam and da had sent a message to say they'd be round later to discuss things, and now here was the instigator of it all telling her that Ruby had disappeared to who knew where.

Turning her gaze on her husband, she said weakly, 'We have to find her and make her come home.'

It was to Adam that George said, 'Have you any idea where she might be? Has she talked about anywhere particular in the past, anywhere she would like to see?'

Adam swallowed hard. He knew Ruby's father was furious with him. It was there in his stiff face and deep-set eyes. He shook his head. 'We only talked about us, getting married and having bairns and things like that.'

It was too much for Cissy. She rounded on him as she ground out between her teeth, 'For two pins I'd throttle you. She only ever looked at you and she could have had her pick round here as you know full well. James Mallard was after her from when he was in short pants and his da owning the rope works and a string of houses, and Rory Stamp an' all and his family in that great big house in Southwick and his da tipped for mayor one day. But no, she only had eyes for you. And for you to take our Olive down, her own sister. Aye, I could swing for you, Adam Gilbert.'

Stung into retaliation, Adam bit back. 'No doubt Olive's painted me as the villain of the piece but let's face facts here, Mrs Morgan. Your poor innocent daughter came up to my bedroom on New Year's Eve when I was too drunk to know it wasn't Ruby and forced herself on me. Aye, forced. So don't go putting all the blame on me and acting as if she's as pure as the driven snow, not unless you want me to shout it from the rooftops.'

'Why, you little—' Cissy sprang to her feet.

'*Cissy*!' George's voice wasn't raised, in fact it was low and deep, but it vibrated with something that caused his wife to lower her hand and collapse onto a chair before bursting into tears. Over the sound of her crying, George said grimly, 'You swear that's how it happened, Adam? Now think before you answer because I can forgive most things but not being lied to.'

'I swear it.' Adam's face was drained of colour but his voice was steady. 'Get Olive in here and I'll repeat it in front of her. She was intent on doing the dirty on Ruby and she used me to do it.'

George sighed a long, heavy sigh, the significance of which was not lost on his wife.

Cissy scrubbed at her eyes with a handkerchief as she said, 'You don't believe him, do you? Olive wouldn't do that.'

George loved his wife. He always had. From the first time he had set eyes on Cissy one balmy Sunday afternoon when he and a group of his pals from the steelworks had been taking a walk Southwick way, and had come across Cissy and a couple of her friends, he had known she was the one for him. But his love didn't blind him to the fact that she saw only what she wanted to see, particularly in those she loved. He had recognized long ago that his elder daughter was jealous of the younger, and also that Cissy compensated for the marked difference in their appearances by favouring Olive to a degree that had bordered on the absurd at times. He had tried to talk to her about it on a number of occasions but to no avail.

Now, because of his love for Cissy, his voice was soft but it also carried a remnant of the tone he had used to check her when she was about to slap Adam, as he said, 'You ask me if I believe that Olive is capable of what Adam's alleged? Absolutely. And do I think he has spoken the truth about what happened that night? Again, aye, I do. For years her resentment of Ruby has been like a poison in this house and if you can't accept that now, after this, then I am sorry for you, lass.' He lifted his hand as Cissy went to speak. 'Hear me out. I love the pair of them – they're my flesh and blood and all we've got left – but if we are to survive this, it's time you stopped burying your head in the sand.'

He turned to Adam, and bluntly now, said, 'Are you prepared to give Olive your name?'

'I've no other choice, have I.' It was bitter.

George nodded slowly. Looking at Cissy, he said, 'Get her down here.'

'You know she won't come out of her room.'

'Tell her if she's not down here within a minute I'll come up and drag her down.'

Cissy opened her mouth to protest, took in the expression that made George almost into a stranger, and shut it again.

As the two men waited for the women to enter the kitchen George was aware of feeling sick to his stomach in a way that even the interminable slaughter of the war hadn't caused. He had witnessed horrors beyond a man's imagination and he still couldn't think of their Terry and Robert without wanting to scream and shout at God for the way his lads had died, but through it all he had held the images of Cissy and the girls deep in his heart as justification of what he was fighting for. Family was everything; it was what they had fought for and what his brave lads had died for. It made the sacrifice worthwhile.

When Olive walked in ahead of her mother her face was set in stiff lines and around her thin lips ran a white border as if painted on the flesh. She didn't look at Adam, keeping her gaze on her father. 'You wanted me?'

George didn't rise to her tone, which had been confrontational. 'Sit down, lass. We've things to sort out.'

For a moment Olive contemplated turning round and defying him, defying them all. Her mother had told her what Adam had said and it had shown covertly in her manner that, however unwillingly, she believed him. Gone was her mam's indignation and anger for her; instead Cissy's face had expressed bewildered disappointment and sorrow. Olive upbraided herself for being so hurt by it, knowing it was nothing to what she would have to put up with in the coming weeks. Adam marrying her would stave off the worst of people's derision, at least to her face, but she knew full well that behind her back the rumours would be scandalous. She would have to get used to scorn and contempt from now on. What folk didn't know they would make up. Sliding down onto a chair, she waited.

'Adam here has explained how this thing has come about,' George said quietly. 'I'd like to think it was a moment of madness on your part that got out of hand, but be that as it may, your jealousy of your sister has resulted in a bairn. That being the case, the one I feel the most sorry for in this whole sordid mess is the child, closely followed by Ruby. She's taken herself off to other parts, by the way, I don't know if your mother told you?'

Olive remained silent, merely shaking her head.

'Well, she has, so I think we can say that your intention to separate Adam and Ruby has been successful.

Adam's parents are coming to the house shortly and you will be present in the discussions that will have to take place. No disappearing to your room. Is that understood?'

'Yes.'

'Adam, do you want to say anything more before your parents arrive?' George looked at him, well aware that the lad's steely blue eyes had been fixed on Olive from the moment she had entered the room, and that if looks could kill, Olive would be six foot under. Like Mrs Walton, it occurred to George that the young happy-faced youngster he had always known was gone for ever, and in his place was a bitter and hate-filled man who looked years older. With this in mind, he added quickly, 'Recriminations are no good now, lad, and to be fair it always takes two to make a bairn.'

Adam didn't glance at his future father-in-law, neither did he speak. Instead his top lip curled away from his teeth as though he was surveying something putrid as he continued to look at Olive, and as she raised her head and met his gaze, her face paled to a dead whiteness.

Cissy stared at the pair of them, shocked by Adam's expression and wondering what on earth they were all going to do. Everything was in ruins, everything, and from what George had said to her a few minutes ago he held her responsible for the animosity between Olive and Ruby. The thought brought a trembling sensation into her throat and for the first time since Ruby had been born she questioned herself, and as she did so, she was forced to acknowledge that there was an element of truth in what her husband had said. Even when Ruby had been a babe in arms, Olive hadn't taken to her, but she had excused this by telling herself that Olive was just a baby herself at three years old and once Ruby could walk and talk, a big-sister affection would kick in. But it never had. And Ruby had been so bonny, so bright and beautiful, and there was poor Olive as plain as a pikestaff and painfully aware of it. Her heart had gone out to her. It still did, in spite of all that had happened. So perhaps George was right; perhaps she had brought this catastrophe on them all.

She lowered her head, drawing in a deep breath. She wanted to go back in time to when her two girls were bit bairns and do things differently; she wanted to make Ruby understand that she loved her just as much as Olive, and convince Olive that her baby sister was no threat and that having a sister was a precious thing if she'd open her heart to her. Instead she had made fish of one child and fowl of the other, and in so doing had unwittingly allowed Olive to justify her jealousy of Ruby in her mind. And now Ruby had disappeared, and her so bonny and young and innocent – what would befall her? And Olive, she'd brought disaster upon herself because however this turned out, her life was ruined.

Panic gripped her and it was all the more terrifying because she knew that nothing she said or did could change things now. Her house had always been well ordered and she was quietly proud of this. No matter what occurred outside its four walls – births, deaths, short-time or strikes – inside all was spick and span and her routine never varied. Monday was wash day. Tuesday she ironed even if Monday had been a wet day which had necessitated all the washing hanging on the lines above their heads in the kitchen in order to get it dry in time. Wednesday she cleaned the house from top to bottom, and Thursday she did the windows inside and outside and scoured and bleached the privy in the yard. Friday she shopped and whitened the front doorstep and blackleaded the range, and on Saturday she did her big bake. The birth of her four children had not been allowed to impact on this practice; neither had the death of her two sons or George returning from the war an invalid. But now the front room was topsy-turvy and in disarray, and the kitchen was a mess; Adam's parents were coming round shortly and normally that would have been incentive enough for her to be putting things to rights, no matter what was going on. But she didn't care.

She raised her head, her heart beating so rapidly it made her head swim. No, she didn't care; all the things that were normally so important had ceased to be of significance and this frightened her most of all.

To fight the panic she forced herself to stand up, saying to no one in particular, 'I'll make a fresh pot of tea,' as she walked over to the range. Her life had fallen apart and her family was going to be the talk of the street in the weeks and months ahead, and nothing she could do would change any of it.

Chapter Five

'This is the room. It's two bob a week, being the larger bedroom, an' the rent's paid a week in advance. I don't hold with no gentlemen callers or "friends" –' this was said with a meaningful sniff – 'and I lock the front door prompt at eleven o'clock. I only take lady lodgers here, it's a respectable house, all right? I don't provide no meals but you've the fire there to do a bit of cookin' if you've a mind.'

Ruby looked at Ellie who stared back at her silently. Since arriving in Newcastle at midday and emerging from the train station, both girls had been overwhelmed by the sheer size of the town. With no clear idea of where they were headed, they had set off clutching their bags and feeling very small and lost in the teeming streets of humanity. Before and during the Great War Newcastle had enjoyed a steadily increasing prosperity as world demand for its products – ships, engineering, chemicals – had grown, and although the richer inhabitants of the town had long since moved away from the quayside leaving their once fine houses to decay into rat-infested slums, new suburbs well served by public transport had mushroomed demanding a wide range of leisure and recreation activities for the middle and upper classes.

Ruby had expected Newcastle to be much like Sunderland but within a short time it dawned on her that it was far bigger, though the smells were much the same. They had walked aimlessly after leaving the train station to find themselves in a seemingly endless grid of streets, terraces of small mean houses with pubs and corner shops and the odd school and bathhouse leading to more of the same. It was only much later in the day, when Ellie said in a small voice, 'I think we've been in this street before, lass,' that Ruby realized they'd probably been wandering about in circles some of the time. She'd been so eaten up with misery and immersed in painful thoughts of Adam and Olive and her mam that she'd walked blindly without talking or being aware of her surroundings for hours, Ellie valiantly trailing after her and not saying a word. Now Ruby became aware that she was tired and thirsty and that Ellie looked ready to drop.

The street they had been standing in was much the same as many others they'd walked down, and as she had stared at Ellie her friend had said, still in the same tentative voice, 'I recognize the name, Bath Lane Terrace, and that sawmill we passed a minute or two back.'

'Oh, Ellie, I'm sorry.' She'd been full of contrition.

Relieved Ruby was talking again, Ellie said, 'There's been one or two cards in windows saying they take lodgers

– how about we see if that one over there is still free?'
She pointed across the road. A large white card in the
window of the two-storeyed terraced house said, 'Room
available within' in big black letters, but unlike some of
its neighbours the house looked as if it had seen better
times. The front door had flaking paint and the stone
step was unwhitened and soiled; the windows clearly
hadn't been cleaned for a while. But what did such things
matter? Numbly, Ruby had said, 'Come on then,' and
that was how they came to be standing in one of the
three bedrooms the house afforded. According to Mrs
Duffy, the owner of the establishment, the other two
bedrooms were considerably smaller than this one, which,
if true, meant they were little more than rabbit hutches.

Ruby dragged her gaze away from Ellie's hopeful face
and glanced about her. She was aware her friend would
have settled for almost anything at this point – it was
eight o'clock at night and dark outside – but even so she
contemplated leaving. The room was dingy and cold and
smelled of damp. It held a basic three-quarter-size bed
that was wire sprung and fixed onto a wooden frame
complete with a blue-striped mattress; two hard-backed
chairs tucked under what appeared to be a stained plank
of wood that had been fastened to the wall, and a battered
chest of drawers. The fireplace that Mrs Duffy had
mentioned was a small blackleaded affair which had a
bracket fixed to the back of it enabling a pot or kettle
to hang from a chain over the coals. To the side of this,
and about three feet from the bare floorboards, were two

shelves holding an iron kettle, a couple of pots and some other utensils. There was no other storage space and barely room to swing a cat.

The landlady, a little plump woman with hard eyes, pointed to an old wooden coal scuttle next to the fireplace. 'I always leave that full ready to start a new lodger off,' she said, her tone making it clear she considered this a great concession, 'and I should point out the mattress on the bed is brand new. My last lady ruined the previous one.' She didn't elaborate on this and Ruby didn't like to enquire further. 'And my house is mice and bug free, which is more than can be said for some in this street.' Another sniff punctuated this remark, something Ruby was to learn was habitual when Mrs Duffy felt she had a point to emphasize.

The landlady hitched up her ample bosom with her forearms before saying, 'The privy in the backyard is kept as clean as a new pin, winter and summer, and I expect my ladies to leave it as they find it, all right? There's a door at the end of the hall straight outside – you don't need to come into my kitchen. I have the downstairs to myself but the other two rooms up here are taken by single ladies. You'll meet them in due course if you decide to take the room?'

This last was said with raised eyebrows to Ruby and was clearly in the form of a question. Ruby glanced about her again. The walls were distempered in a faded brown colour and the thin curtains at the window were a shade or two darker. Altogether it was the most depressing and cheerless room she had ever encountered. But she was bone-tired and at the end of herself after what had been the worst day of her life. Taking in a deep breath, she forced a tight smile as she said to Ellie, 'Shall we?' knowing what the answer would be even before Ellie nodded.

'Right you are.' Mrs Duffy didn't give them a chance to change their minds. 'I'll go and get the sheets and blankets for the bed while you sort out the rent, a week in advance, please, like I said. And all your laundry is down to you but you can use the line in the yard to dry anything if you've a mind.' So saying she bustled out of the room leaving the two girls staring at each other.

The room was lit by a single gas jet on one wall and its flickering light, far from making the interior cosier, actually made the stark surroundings duller. Ruby walked across to the window and moved the curtains to look out, but the glass was a frosted mass of snowflakes and she could see nothing.

Mrs Duffy was back within a minute or two with their bedding, which proved to be barely adequate but at least was clean, and after Ruby had paid her the rent and the landlady had disappeared downstairs, Ellie said timidly, 'Shall I light the fire? Things will seem better when it's warmer.'

Nothing would ever seem better for the rest of her life. The thought brought with it the hot sting of tears at the backs of her eyes but before they could fall she blinked furiously. Now was not the time to give way. They had things to do, to sort out, and she had to get on with it. She had Ellie – she wasn't completely alone, even though she was gripped by such a feeling of utter and absolute loneliness that she would like to go to sleep and never wake up. The thought of having to go on, to find her way through a future that seemed barren and empty and devoid of everything she had ever wanted, had drained her to the core. And this wasn't her fault; she hadn't done anything wrong. She had loved Adam; she'd even loved Olive, come to that.

For a moment the flood of self-pity swamped her, making her want to howl and scream like a hurt child and shout against the unfairness and the arid months and years ahead.

'Ruby?' Ellie's voice brought her out of the maelstrom of pain and despair, and turning she found her friend staring at her with anxious eyes. She breathed out slowly, fighting for composure. She had always been the strong one in their relationship, the comforter and fixer, the one who sorted things out, and Ellie was waiting for her to take control now, to tell her what to do.

'Don't light the fire yet,' she said in a voice that surprised her with its calmness. 'We'll go out and get something to eat first. There was a pie shop on the corner of the street, we'll go there. We'll see to the fire and make the bed up when we come back, and come Monday we'll get some groceries and more coal and perhaps a thick eiderdown for the bed and a rug for the floor, before we look for work. We'll be all right, Ellie. Don't worry.'

Ellie nodded in relief. This was the Ruby she knew. Her friend never let anything get her down for long; Ruby would bounce back. She was tough, always had been. She would be fine.

Ruby knew exactly what Ellie was thinking and it added to the weight on her shoulders. Turning away, she reached for her handbag. 'Come on,' she said dully. 'We'd better get what we need before the shops shut. We'll buy enough for tomorrow too, it being a Sunday. I can't see Mrs Duffy helping us out with any food.' Or anything else for that matter. But that was the way it was going to be from now on, and the sooner she got used to it the better. She had made the decision to leave Mrs Walton's and strike out on her own; no one had forced her to come to Newcastle.

It was a fortnight later. Between them, Ruby and Ellie had transformed the once dark and uninviting room into a bright and cheerful little dwelling place. With Mrs Duffy's permission, they had painted the walls and ceiling a pale sunshine yellow, which had immediately made it a different environment. It had taken three coats of paint and a lot of elbow grease to cover the horrible brown colour, but the finished result had been worth the effort.

Ruby had noticed a small Singer sewing machine for sale in the pawnshop next to the hardware store where they'd purchased the paint, and had bought it with a view to making new curtains and a matching cover for the thick eiderdown they'd seen in a second-hand shop. She'd assured Ellie it was a good bargain at a third of the price of a new machine, and an investment for the future because she could make their clothes on it too.

But that wasn't the whole reason she'd wanted it. Even at school she'd excelled at needlework and since working for Mrs Walton her skill and expertise had grown, but it was the satisfaction she felt at turning a piece of material into something beautiful that was the important thing. It was an essential part of her, a true gift Mrs Walton had called it, and even though her world had fractured and she was all at sea, she didn't want to lose that part of herself. She needed it. It was all she had left.

Since moving in they had kept the little fire going night and day; initially to air everything and dry the paint, but then because it made the room feel more like home. Now the musty smell of damp was a thing of the past, and with the flowered curtains and eiderdown and a small clippy mat covering the limited expanse of visible floorboards, the place was unrecognizable.

Admittedly there was barely room for one person to live in the space, let alone two, but gradually they had begun to master the art of simmering a stew or broth over the open fire, which they would supplement with baked potatoes cooked in the ashes under the burning coals or a loaf of bread bought from the bakery in the next street. Breakfast was usually toast, and although they had lost the odd slice of bread when it had slipped off the toasting fork into the fire, their proficiency was growing. Ruby had even cooked them porridge one morning, and although it had had a slightly burnt flavour where the bottom of the pan had caught, it had filled a hole in their tummies.

Finding work didn't seem so straightforward. For the

first week they had spent every waking hour sorting out their new home, but then, with their money fast evaporating, they had concentrated on looking for jobs. Initially they had thought to find employment in a similar vein to what they knew – Ellie making enquiries at various bakeries, and Ruby at a couple of dressmakers and then a clothing factory. She had been appalled at the second-rate garments the latter had produced, the shoddy workmanship and cramped dark surroundings housing lines of weary-looking women depressing enough, without the leery foreman who had shown her round the premises and who had seemed to imagine he was God's gift to womankind. She could have coped with everything but being forced to produce substandard clothes that looked as though they would barely hold together, and after her visit to the factory she and Ellie had recognized they had to rethink their options.

It had been that night that one of the other two lodgers they had talked to a couple of times knocked on their door. Bridget Finnigan was an Irish lass who had come over the water a few years before. She had told them she was employed at the Newcastle Workhouse, which was situated a little over a mile from Bath Lane Terrace as the crow flies, to the west of the city at the top of Westgate Hill. This particular workhouse was an extensive complex that had come into being over eighty years before, when the Newcastle-upon-Tyne Board of Guardians had decided to replace the then existing four smaller workhouses in different parts of the town for one purpose-built facility.

Included were an administration block, dining hall, laundry, bakehouse, workshops, school, sick wards, lying-in ward, imbeciles' ward and inmates' quarters – the males on the western side of the building and the females to the east. An infirmary had been added thirty years later, but at the beginning of the new century any children had been removed and taken to live in the Union's new cottage homes that had been built on a seventy-acre rural site at Ponteland. The children's quarters had then become wards for the workhouse's aged and infirm population, and their dining room converted into a chapel.

Bridget had told them there were a couple of vacancies in the workhouse laundry, and had offered to put in a good word for the pair of them with the head laundress if they were interested? They would then have to be interviewed by the matron.

Ruby and Ellie had stared at each other. Their small hoard of cash was nearly gone and they couldn't afford to be choosy, but the thought of the workhouse was daunting. Neither of them had imagined they would willingly enter one of those fearful places. Having said that, Bridget seemed to be quite happy working there on the whole, and the fact that any employment was becoming harder to find since the brief euphoria after the Great War was a consideration. Ruby had written to Mrs Walton asking for a reference a couple of days after arriving in Newcastle and received a glowing commendation back by return of post, but Ellie was still waiting for something from her previous employer whom she imagined had turned awkward because she had walked out and left him in the lurch. This was an added problem.

With this in mind, Bridget had said persuasively, 'If you went after this, Ruby, you could vouch for Ellie if you applied together. I'm sure that'd do the trick for her. Your reference was so good, wasn't it, and it won't matter it's not the same kind of work. They go a lot on character an' all that at the workhouse – it was my old priest in Ireland talking to Father McGuigan who got me the job when I first came here. An' the money's not bad, eight bob a week an' lunch included, and it's good grub too. You'd eat in the officers' mess like me as we come in from outside. The officers and outsiders have their own kitchen an' dining room so it's separate from the workhouse kitchen an' dining hall. Even the smell of them poor devils' food makes you want to gag, take it from me, an' there was cockroaches in their porridge the other morning 'cause it'd been left to soak overnight in the kitchen.'

Ruby's face expressed her horror, and realizing she wasn't selling the job very well, Bridget added hastily, 'But like I said, the mess is lovely and clean, spotless, and the food's like you'd get in a hotel or something. We had roast lamb yesterday and baked haddock today an' it was beautiful, an' the cook's apple dumplings and custard can't be bettered.' Bridget was as round as she was tall and set great store by her stomach. 'Anyway, shall I say something to the head laundress and see if they've advertised yet? It's always better to get in first, isn't it.'

The upshot of Bridget's word on their behalf was that

on a bitterly cold morning in mid-March with the snow thick on the ground and more forecast, Ruby and Ellie caught the tram into the Arthur's Hill ward of the town. On leaving the tram they stood for more than a minute staring at the imposing three-storey building with a central archway at the entrance to the grounds of the workhouse. They knew from Bridget that this building contained waiting rooms and receiving wards on the ground floor, with a three-roomed residence above and then storerooms on the top floor. Looking at the forbidding Victorian frontage where people would enter into the soulless complex that made up the workhouse, Ruby shivered. Everything inside was run with a view to discouraging the poor from wanting to live at the expense of the community and life was deliberately hard and uncomfortable. Her da had always maintained that the workhouse made it seem as if ill health and destitution were crimes that deserved punishment, and that charity was an offence to God and man.

Ellie's voice was small when she said, 'I don't think I can go in there, lass.'

Ruby was talking as much to herself as to Ellie when she said briskly, 'Of course you can. Whatever it's like we shall be together and that's the main thing, and frankly, there doesn't seem to be much else going, Ellie, and we need to earn some money. If we get the jobs, having a good lunch will be a bonus. We can stuff ourselves and then just have some toast or bread and jam at night, which will help things.' She was finding buying coal for the fire, small as it was, expensive, and if they bought pies or bread or cakes the money just seemed to melt away. Somewhere with an oven would have made all the difference but of course that was impossible.

Ellie nodded slowly. Living with Ruby was wonderful, that's what she had to remember, and anything was better than being in Sunderland with her mam an' da. But the workhouse . . .

They were interviewed one at a time by Matron Henderson, an iron-faced woman whose husband was the master of the workhouse. Ruby was shown into the matron's office by a thin wisp of a girl clad in the workhouse inmates' uniform. Bridget had told them that only the officers wore black dresses and white aprons with caps and cuffs, and that paid hands from outside wore blue dresses and white aprons with caps. The inmates were dressed in grey smocks and mob caps of inferior-quality cloth, but it was their sad faces, Bridget said, that distinguished them the most.

The matron's office was as warm as toast compared to the chilly corridor outside, a good coal fire burning brightly in the large fireplace and thick gold curtains at the window. Matron Henderson was sitting behind a highly polished mahogany desk and although there was a chair in front of it she didn't suggest Ruby sat down. Instead she stared at her in silence for a few moments, eyeing her up and down, before saying, 'Your previous employer speaks very highly of you,' in a tone that stated she found it surprising.

Ruby didn't know what she was expected to say and

so she said nothing, but her shoulders straightened and her chin lifted slightly. Bridget had described the matron as a real tartar and having met her, Ruby could understand why, but she wasn't about to let herself be bullied by the woman, job or no job.

The matron continued to examine her, her eyes narrowed behind her black-framed spectacles. 'If you were as good at your work as Mrs –' she consulted the letter on her desk – 'Mrs Walton states, what made you leave Sunderland and come to Newcastle, Miss Morgan?'

Ruby had been expecting the question and she had already discussed her answer with Ellie. She would tell the truth, or the bare bones of it anyway. Quietly, she said, 'I was engaged to be married but things didn't work out and I wanted a new start somewhere. My friend offered to accompany me, and now we are settled in our lodgings we need a job.'

'A broken engagement. Does that mean the young man in question is liable to turn up and persuade you to go back to Sunderland?'

'Absolutely not.'

Even Matron Henderson couldn't doubt that Ruby was telling the truth. She stared at her for a moment more before saying curtly, 'Absolutely not, Matron.'

'Absolutely not, Matron.'

'Hmm. And unlike you, your friend has no reference to give me, I understand.'

'We left quite suddenly and there wasn't time to obtain one. She has written to ask but unfortunately has heard nothing back.' The matron's eyes narrowed further and Ruby added hastily, 'Matron.'

'Unsatisfactory, but if you are prepared to vouch for her perhaps I can stretch a point.' Matron Henderson settled back in her chair. It was clear that the girl standing in front of her was a step up from a mere laundry worker who did the washing and ironing, many of whom were workhouse inmates with limited intelligence. Just that morning she had been informed the laundry checker had sent word that owing to family problems she had been forced to give her notice with immediate effect, which was most inconsiderate in the matron's opinion, considering that the post was at junior officer level and carried a high degree of responsibility. She made allowance for the common workers to be flibbertigibbets, but not her officers. Still, that was beside the point. The fact was, the post had become vacant.

'Are you proficient in maths?' she asked suddenly.

Ruby blinked. What did maths have to do with working in the laundry? 'I suppose so, yes, Matron. At – at my previous job I did the bookkeeping for Mrs Walton.' The old lady had started her doing this when she had been with her for a while and it was only since Mrs Walton had revealed the plans she'd had for Ruby's future that Ruby had realized why.

Most fortuitous. Again the matron murmured, 'Hmm.' She had always prided herself on recognizing potential when she saw it. Coming to a decision, she said briskly, 'There is another post that has become vacant, that of laundry checker, Miss Morgan. It is a junior officer's post and each week the checker balances the ledgers, among other duties. You would earn eleven shillings a week and have three assistants to supervise, and you would report directly to the head laundress who reports to me. Obviously this post carries more responsibility than a laundry worker and your duties would reflect this. You would be asked to stand in for other staff on occasion, and once a month you would be expected to do the afternoon visiting duty in the workhouse hall. For the main part of any day it would be your job to check the dirty linen into the laundry and then account for its departure, but as I've said, other duties would be expected of you as an officer when need dictates. You would start work at eight in the morning and finish at six o'clock, Monday to Saturday. After three months you would be subject to a review and, depending on your performance, an increase in salary.'

Ruby stared at the matron, completely taken aback.

'Well?' Matron Henderson was watching her closely. 'What do you say? Do you think you are up to the job?'

Ruby pulled herself together. 'Yes, I do, Matron, and if you are offering it to me I would like to accept.'

The grim lips twitched just the slightest. 'I am indeed offering it to you, Miss Morgan.'

'Thank you. Thank you very much, Matron.' Eleven shillings with the prospect of a rise after three months. For the first time since she had arrived in Newcastle, Ruby felt a spark of her old self ignite deep inside. Unbeknown to Ellie and once her friend was asleep, every night she had lain awake for hours, tears seeping from her eyes and tormented by thoughts of home and what might have been. She had written to her mother to let her know she and Ellie were safe and had found lodgings but had not given her address for a reply, and in her letter to Mrs Walton she had asked the old lady not to divulge her whereabouts to anyone. But from this day she would take hold of her emotions, she told herself firmly. A phase of her life had ended, and with it had gone everything she had ever known and all her dreams for the future as a married woman and mother. That was over.

'Perhaps you would send Miss Wood in to see me and wait outside until her interview is over, Miss Morgan. If she proves satisfactory, one of my staff will take you both along to the laundry and show you where you will work before fitting you with the necessary uniform. You under-stand that your position is superior to that of hers, of course? I trust that will not prove a problem?'

'No, of course not, Matron. We're friends—' Ruby stopped abruptly as the matron held up her hand.

'A friendship that will be left at the front door when you enter this building and taken up again when you leave. My officers do not liaise with those beneath them.'

This one would. Ruby nodded sweetly. 'Yes, Matron.'

Ellie was sitting waiting on a hard-backed chair in the corridor outside and looked up anxiously as Ruby left the matron's office, shutting the door behind her.

'She wants to see you,' Ruby whispered. 'Just say yes, Matron and no, Matron and three bags full, Matron, and it'll be all right.'

'Is she awful?'

'She's fine. Go on, don't keep her waiting. Knock and wait for her to say you can go in.'

Ruby seated herself on the chair Ellie had vacated and once the matron's door was shut behind her friend, glanced about her. Everything was painted a dull green and there was a peculiar smell in the air, a fusty, unpleasant odour even though there didn't look to be a speck of dirt anywhere. She supposed that came from the waiting rooms and receiving wards where inmates were first taken before being processed through into the workhouse proper. Poverty had its own smell, she had found.

She swallowed hard. She would get used to it, she'd have to, and however hard the job was she would get used to that too. Mind over matter. She nodded to the thought. And no more wallowing in self-pity either. The Lord helps those who help themselves. How often had she heard her mam say that in the past? And it was right. She sat up straighter. This was the start of the rest of her life, that's how she had to look at things now, and if she could survive that night two weeks ago when her world had fallen apart, she could survive anything. She wouldn't let Olive beat her – she was stronger than that. She would make a success of her life, she would, and one day she would rub Olive's nose in that success. Her mouth set, she nodded again. Her day would come . . .

PART TWO

Choices

1924

Chapter Six

'You all right, man?' Walter Gilbert's voice was quiet, which was unusual. Even when he considered he was whispering it was normally a bellow.

Adam's answer was a curt 'Aye,' as he wrenched at the prop he was trying to move.

'Only you've not said owt for hours.'

'Nowt *to* say.'

'You had another barney with Olive?'

'Leave it, Walt.'

'Aw, man, come on. Look, Da's asked me to talk to you. He's worried. We all are.'

Adam now swung round on his belly from where he was lying in the cramped confines of the coalface. His shift of forty men were busy moving the face further in, which meant withdrawing the props to let the roof drop, always a dangerous part in the proceedings.

'I said, leave it,' he muttered, looking at his brother whose face was as black as his own.

'I can't.' Walter was the oldest of Adam's brothers at

thirty, and a trace of the importance he attached to his place in the family came through as he added, 'Like I said, Da asked me to have a word.'

'You've had it.'

'You and Olive and the bairn haven't been round to Mam's on a Sunday since Christmas, and even then you were like a bear with a sore head and as miserable as sin. It put a damper on everyone's day, I can tell you.'

'Good job I've stayed away then, surely?'

Walter swore, before saying, 'You're an awkward beggar an' no mistake but I don't like to see you like this, man. I know you an' her didn't have the best of starts but you've got the bairn now and she's a little cracker. Surely that counts for something? And Olive keeps the house nice and she's a good cook an' all. Mam reckons you could have done a lot worse, all things considered.'

'Is that right? That's what Mam thinks, is it?'

There had been a quality to these last words that warned Walter he'd gone as far as he dare. He'd purposely chosen to talk to Adam whilst they were working. With thousands of tons of rock, coal and slate above them his brother couldn't brush him aside and walk off as he'd done on numerous occasions in the last months, not when they were hemmed in like sardines in a can. Nevertheless, by the same token, if Adam got so riled up with him he made a mistake in what he was doing it could jeopardize not only his brother's life but the rest of the men in the low narrow tunnels.

Walter swore again before muttering, 'Have it your own way, I was only trying to help.'

Only trying to help. Adam wriggled forward, the heat and overwhelming humidity causing the sweat to run off him in rivulets. Walt and the others still had no real idea what they'd done that night two years ago, not even now. It was all right for them; they went home at the end of a shift to their bonny wives and families nice as you like, meeting up now and again as they'd always done down the pub for a jar or two where their chief topic of conversation would invariably centre around the coal owners locking men out and reducing wages and the rest of it, as if it mattered. As if anything mattered in this damn awful life he was trapped in. He didn't give a monkey's jig that working conditions were getting harder or the working day longer for less pay at the end of it. He wasn't daft; he knew as well as the next man that coal owners like the Duke of Northumberland or the Bishop of Durham had gone straight back to their old ways after the Great War. They had no regard for the safety of the men they employed in their deathtraps and took no responsibility for the injuries and crippling disabilities suffered by miners every day of the week. But what good did it do to bleat on about it? Did Walt and Fred and Pete and the rest of them really think that strikes and the unions shouting the odds would get them anywhere?

Adam looked up, the light from his lamp shining on the roof of the tunnel he was inching down. All it would take was it caving in and his problems would be over.

Before he had lost Ruby he'd used to have the occasional moment of blind panic when he was down the pit, his stomach flipping over so he felt like throwing up and his bowels turning to water. He'd had something to want to live for then, whereas now . . .

He began to work at another prop with the iron lever he was holding, conscious of Walter some feet behind him as his brother coughed and spat before saying, 'Easy, man, easy. You're going at that like a bull in a china shop, if you don't mind me saying.'

'I do mind.' He heard Walter mutter something that finished with '. . . miserable blighter,' but didn't respond. He wanted no truck with Walt, or Fred or Pete either. The three of them had ruined his life and even looking at them made him want to strike out. The number of times he'd told the three of them to leave him alone in the last couple of years must run into the hundreds, but still they persisted in keeping up the brotherly facade, especially Walt. But then they probably hadn't got the sense to believe what he said. Gormless, the three of them. Gormless and as thick as two short planks.

He should have gone down south. Even without Ruby he should have cleared off when Olive told him she was pregnant. Instead he'd let himself be bullied into marrying her, thereby saddling himself for life with Ruby's sister and her child. He never thought of their daughter as part of him – she was wholly Olive's – and this was apparent in his day-to-day dealings with the infant. He had never taken to her from the moment she was born, and he made no effort to hide his resentment at her coming, totally blaming the child and her mother for his present circumstances.

Telling himself to work and not think, he continued with the job in hand. Moving the conveyor belt towards the new face was always precarious for the miners withdrawing the old props, but the whole shift were working flat out as always, some men cleaning the conveyor itself, some hauling sections of it inch by inch in the confined space and others spreading stone dust to dampen down the danger of the coal dust exploding. No one needed to be told what to do; they worked as a team and each miner prided himself on doing the task in hand to the best of his ability. Lives depended on it.

A few hours later the new face had been established and the deputy had made his inspection before signing the shift off. Adam and his brothers, along with the rest of the men, made their way towards the main roadway where at last they could straighten up and ease their aching backs. All of the men walked along joking and laughing and swearing at each other, but although one or two glanced Adam's way they knew better than to try and talk to him. When he had suddenly upped and married one sister after being engaged to the other for a couple of years, there had been plenty of speculation, especially because – as one miner put it – the sister he'd been landed with had a face as rough as a badger's backside.

When they reached the cage that would transport them above ground there was the usual pushing and shoving and banter, but again Adam stood aloof from it all, merely making sure he didn't ride up in the same group of men as Walt. Because he had hung back he was in the last few of the shift to go up, and as the cage rattled its way towards the light he experienced none of the relief he'd once felt at the thought of seeing the sun and the sky again after hours in the bowels of the earth.

He knew he had changed, he told himself grimly as they reached the surface and he exited the cage and gave his lamp and token in. He hadn't needed Walt to tell him that. It had begun on the day he knew Ruby had left Sunderland and had washed her hands of him for good, and it had gathered pace since. He didn't recognize himself any more, that was the truth of it. The lad Ruby had fallen in love with didn't exist. And he knew just how absolute the change now was by the fact that this didn't bother him as it had done at first.

It had been some months into his marriage before he had acknowledged how angry he was with Ruby. Before that he had imagined it was just Olive he was furious with, but his anger against Ruby had been different. Olive he would always loathe for the way she had set out to trick him, but Ruby should have seen that in a way he was as innocent as her in it all. If she had loved him like he loved her, she would have understood; she would have agreed to leave Sunderland with him and go down south where they could have got married and put the past behind them. Instead she had assumed the moral high ground and cleared off leaving him in hell, a hell of fierce anger and pain and longing, a hell in which his corroding hate had gradually eaten away the core of him.

He made a sound in his throat, a harsh sound. He didn't know why he was thinking of all this now. No, that wasn't true, it was because of Walt, damn him, stirring things up. All he wanted was to be left alone – that wasn't too much to ask, was it? He could get by if he was left alone. Work, eat, drink, sleep, work again, and on a Sunday, come rain, hail or shine, he'd tramp the countryside for miles around until he was even more tired than when he had finished a shift down the pit. Thinking only tied him up in knots and brought the ever present rage to the surface, a rage that genuinely made him fear he'd do murder one day when he looked at Olive.

So, don't think. He nodded to the command, and like a child obeying a parent, made his way towards the wash house, his face set and his eyes cold and hard.

Olive glanced at the clock on the kitchen mantelpiece. He'd be home soon. Her stomach turned over. It was ridiculous, after two years of marriage, but every time Adam's arrival was imminent the trembling would start inside. Once he walked through the door she could cope with the bitterness and dislike that were evident in his every glance and word, but it was the waiting that caused her insides to knot. She supposed she should be grateful he hadn't taken to the drink like some men did to drown their sorrows, but if it had made him more mellow she wouldn't have minded. Anything would be better than the present state of affairs. But it was the way he was with Alice that hurt her the most.

As though her daughter had heard her name Alice gurgled in her highchair where she was chewing on a crust of bread Olive had baked in the oven until it was as hard as iron. The infant was teething and her mouth was bothering her, day and night. But she was such a good baby, Olive thought fondly, walking across and ruffling the silky brown curls. Even with the teething Alice rarely cried, although sometimes her plump little cheeks would be bright red with pain, and at twenty-one months old she was as happy as the day was long. Considering the misery of Olive's pregnancy, she was constantly amazed none of her anguish had communicated itself to the child in her womb.

From the day she'd married Adam, exactly a month after Ruby had left Sunderland, Olive had known that this mistake superseded anything that had gone before. Tricking him into sleeping with her, falling for a baby, the breakdown of his engagement to Ruby and her sister leaving and breaking their mam's heart, all that was as nothing compared to becoming Adam's wife. He was going to continue to make her pay for what she'd done to her dying day and by marrying him she'd effectively put a noose round her own neck.

Turning back to the range, Olive checked the tin of baked herring in the oven. It was the second week of June and the country was in the grip of a heatwave. Cloudless skies, backyards swilled daily to lay the dust, and the roads to the beaches jammed tight at the weekends as folk sought the relief of a sea breeze. Consequently, the old fishwives who plied their trade along the seafront and round the back lanes had been selling their glut of herring that the good weather had brought in for knockdown prices. Hannah, the old woman whose round included Olive's back lane, was a character, but then most of the fishwives were cut from the same rough cloth. Dressed in a cotton blouse, heavy woollen skirt and thick linen apron, an old shawl round her shoulders and her feet shod in black hobnailed boots, Hannah wasn't to be trifled with. All the bairns were fascinated by the coil of thick material on her head on which her fish basket was balanced, and by the way Hannah kept it steady when she walked. She never came in winter or bad weather when the herring were difficult to fish, but come the summer months her cry in the back lanes would ring out and housewives would appear out of their yards.

Fetching the baking tin with its rows of black and silver fish out of the oven, Olive left it on the side while she sliced a crusty loaf of bread she'd baked that morning into thick wedges. She had cooked the herring in vinegar and dripping, the oil from the fish adding to the mixture, and before she dished the fish up on their plates she would drain the gravy and tip it into two bowls in which she and Adam would dip the bread. Hannah had been anxious to get rid of the last of the fish in the back lane, and Olive had bought the herring for eight a penny, a bargain. It provided a cheap meal and one that Adam always enjoyed. While she had still been living at her mother's, her mam had always cooked herring with potatoes and vegetables, but she'd learned Adam didn't care for them that way, preferring the fresh bread as his mother had served them. It had been one of the more innocuous things she had had to come to terms with in her marriage.

Glancing again at the clock, she spooned the last of Alice's meal of mashed vegetables and gravy into her daughter's little rosebud mouth, and once the bowl was empty gave her another piece of hard bread just as she heard Adam walk into the yard. He objected if Alice made a mess when she ate; he objected to a lot of things concerning the child if it came to that, and from the day she had been born had insisted she slept in her own room rather than allowing the crib to be at the side of their bed for the first few weeks.

He didn't speak as he came into the kitchen and neither did Olive greet him, but Alice gave a little squeak of agitation at the sight of her father, which Adam completely ignored. Taking off his cap and frayed working jacket he sat down at the table and opened the newspaper he always bought on his way home from the pit, disappearing behind it while Olive dished up their meal. Only when his plate was in front of him did he put the paper to one side and pick up his knife and fork. They ate in the silence that permeated the house when Adam was home, a silence that was in no way a quiet, hushed thing but which vibrated with a dark energy that was alive. Even Alice felt it. Olive knew she did. Young as she was, her daughter seemed to instinctively understand that she must bring no attention to herself when her father was around. It was becoming more and more noticeable that Alice was afraid of him. This concerned Olive so much she'd mentioned it to her mother several times, but Cissy's reply was always the same.

'He'll come round, lass. Just give him a bit of slack and he'll come round. The bairn'll win him over if nowt else, she's that bonny, so don't fret. Have patience.'

But Adam wasn't coming round. Olive cast a sidelong glance at the man she'd come to hate and fear. She knew now he would never come round. And while she accepted that Adam's loathing and resentment regarding her was justified to some extent, she couldn't forgive his treatment of their daughter. Alice was completely innocent of any wrongdoing, she'd said that to him once in one of their rows, and he'd answered her by saying that the child was here, wasn't she? And her presence was fault enough. It had been from that day she'd stopped trying to make their marriage work.

It wasn't until his plate was empty and Adam got up from the table that he spoke. He always left the house after the evening meal, winter or summer and even in the worst weather, returning at bedtime. It was one of the many unspoken ways he made it clear he'd rather be anywhere than with her and Alice. It was unusual for him to speak, however, and in her surprise Olive looked at him, something she avoided if she could help it.

'I hear you've been talking to my mam behind my back.'

'What?' She stared at him, utterly taken aback.

'You heard what I said. Been round there, have you, crying on her shoulder?'

'I haven't the faintest idea what you're on about and the last time I saw your mam was when she called in a couple of days ago. I haven't been to theirs since we went on Christmas Day.'

His eyes narrowed. 'Still doesn't change the fact you've been whining to her about me.'

The sense of injustice at what she was being accused of kept her voice from shaking even though she could see he was spoiling for a fight. 'I have never discussed you with your mam. She pops in now and again to see Alice and have a cup of tea, that's all. She's Alice's grandma, for goodness' sake.'

He glared at her, dark anger glinting from his eyes under their narrowed lids. 'Don't give me that, I know how you work. Cunning as the Devil himself, you are, putting on an act of the poor misunderstood wife and trying to get sympathy. Well, I tell you now, I don't want my mam round here while I'm at work. I don't want no one here, is that understood? So you tell her next time she "pops" in she's not welcome.'

Olive continued to stare at him but for once she didn't acquiesce to what he demanded. Since the day she had got married and especially since Alice had been born she had taken the line of least resistance, hoping against hope that somehow they would find a way to be able to live together in – if not happiness – then at least civility, for the sake of their daughter. But if he expected her to cut off their families then he was in for a shock. Her parents' and his mam's support, and even his brothers' kindness to her on the rare occasions they met, was what kept her going half the time. She'd go stark staring mad if she couldn't have normal conversations with normal folk sometimes. And she had never said a bad word about Adam to his mam; to her own, yes, but never his. Her stare became fixed as she said, 'If you don't want your mam calling round to see Alice, then *you* tell her so. As far as I'm concerned she's welcome any day, same as any of your family.'

'You're refusing to do what I tell you?'

The tone of his voice was all the more threatening because of its quiet grimness, but Olive knew she was fighting for her very sanity. 'I'm saying it's up to you to tell her if you don't want her here, that's all.' She couldn't hold his gaze any more, standing up and beginning to clear the table of the dirty dishes and hoping he didn't notice the way her hands were shaking. He had never hit her – manhandled her out of the way on occasion, pushed her roughly to one side, yes, but never hit her – but she wouldn't put it past him. He liked to hurt her, that was for sure. On the nights he took her in their bed he was uncaring and deliberately brutish, sating his physical need without a word or the slightest caress and then rolling away so no part of him was touching her. Twice since Alice had been born she had missed a couple of periods but then on the third month each time she had miscarried, and in truth she hadn't known whether she was glad or sorry. Much as she adored her daughter the thought of bringing another child into the existence she was enduring seemed wrong in every way.

She wasn't aware he had gone until she heard the back door bang, and then she turned and watched him through the kitchen window as he disappeared out of the yard into the lane. He wouldn't be back until it was late, and with this knowledge the tenseness seeped out of her body but in so doing left her limp and trembling.

She had paid for what she'd done that New Year's Eve, she told herself as the ever-present humiliation and pain washed over her in a great wave, bringing her hands to her face as she rocked herself back and forth. She paid every day for it. And some nights. Oh, yes, some nights.

'Mama, Mama.' Alice's voice brought her out of the maelstrom of despair and she saw her daughter was holding out her arms to her, struggling to climb out of the highchair now her father had left. Whisking the child into her arms, Olive held her close, drinking in the smell and feel of her as two chubby little arms wrapped themselves round her neck and Alice's cheek nuzzled against hers.

This was what it was all about; for this she would endure what needed to be endured. Her bairn loved her because she was her mam; it didn't matter to Alice that she was ugly. Alice didn't wish she was someone else or think she was wicked or judge her wanting.

She didn't deserve her bairn, she knew that, but please,

God, keep her healthy and safe, she prayed as hot tears streamed down her face. It was a constant fear, loving her as she did, that she would be punished by losing Alice to one of the childhood diseases that swept the towns and cities every so often. Just the other Sunday Father McHaffie had preached that God wouldn't be mocked and sin had to be paid for, and he had looked straight at her when he had said it.

How she loathed that man. Immediately the thought came into her mind she was begging God to forgive her for it. It was the most heinous of crimes to criticize a priest, even if the criticism wasn't voiced out loud; everyone knew that, and if they didn't you could be sure they soon would when Father McHaffie preached his Sunday sermons. Priests were only one step down from the Almighty Himself and on the same par in holiness, if the father was to be believed. Eh, she was doing it again, and she had enough sins on her conscience as it was.

Shaking her head at herself, Olive set Alice down and once the little girl was occupied in playing with the brightly coloured wooden bricks Adam's mother had bought for her granddaughter, she finished clearing away the dirty dishes and washed up.

Once the kitchen was spick and span and knowing Adam wouldn't be back for a good while, Olive decided to give Alice a treat and take the old tin bath out into the yard and fill it with warm water for the child to play in before bed. The day had been hot and sticky and it would be good for Alice to tire herself out and have a wash at the same time. After bringing out a chair from the kitchen and setting it to the side of the tin bath, Olive sat in the sunshine watching Alice tipping water from one bowl to another with the fierce concentration only very young children bring to bear. As ever when she had a minute to herself, she found her thoughts drifting to Ruby and the bitter regrets she had regarding her sister. Before Ruby had disappeared out of all their lives, Olive would have sworn on oath that the only feeling she had for her sister was one of dislike. It had taken Ruby walking out for her to understand that buried under all the layers of resentment and jealousy and ill will was a feeling akin to love. She would give the world to be able to turn back time to that New Year's Eve and change things, but of course that was impossible, and anyway, she wouldn't have Alice if that night had been different.

Alice stood up in the water, her wet skin gleaming in the sunlight like a seal's, and offered her mother one of the bowls saying, 'Dink, Mama, dink.'

Olive took the bowl and pretended to drink. 'What a lovely cup of tea, thank you.'

Alice giggled delightedly, plonking down in the bath again and continuing her game. For the hundredth time it struck Olive just how like Ruby her daughter was. Alice had the same sunny nature and zest for life, the same ability to captivate folk and make them love her – everyone except her own father, that was. She bit down hard on her bottom lip.

She hadn't been too worried at first when Adam had

refused to have anything to do with the child. Lots of men were nervous of newborn babies and didn't want to hold them, but then as the days and weeks had gone by she had realized it was much more than mere male apprehension at dealing with such a little person that was bothering Adam. He didn't look at Alice if he could help it; in fact, he ignored her presence altogether. It was as if the baby didn't exist.

Things had come to a head one day when Alice was about fourteen months old and learning to walk, staggering around the kitchen holding on to the chair legs and every so often plopping down on her bottom before determinedly dragging herself up again. The baby had inadvertently grasped one of Adam's legs as he had sat at the table reading his paper while Olive had been busy at the range, and she had turned round with their plates in her hands just in time to see him jerk Alice off him. The child had lost her balance and smacked down so suddenly her little head had made hard contact with the stone slabs as she'd fallen backwards.

She had slung the plates on the table with enough force for the food to go everywhere, whisking Alice up into her arms and cradling the baby against her. Alice had screamed at the top of her tiny lungs, a visible bump already forming.

The row that had followed had been vitriolic on both sides, but whereas Olive had been beside herself with rage and fright, Adam had been as cool as a cucumber, his words icy and venomous, and showing not the slightest remorse. It had been later that evening, when Alice was asleep in her cot upstairs, that Adam had come in from his nightly walk and paused at her side where she was sitting doing some mending at the kitchen table.

'Let me make one thing perfectly clear,' he had said coldly. 'I bring home a wage each week that enables you and your child to be fed and clothed while you live under my roof. In return for that I expect my meals to be in peace and for my physical needs, in the bedroom and out of it, to be met at all times. I will not tolerate the sort of scene you made tonight again. Keep the child out of my way in future. Do you understand?'

She had looked up at him, into blue eyes as icy as his voice. 'Her name is Alice, and she's your child as much as mine.'

He'd said nothing for a moment, then he had walked across the room and paused with his hand on the door into the hall. 'Don't try my patience.'

Just four words, but they had chilled her blood. Even now, sitting in the warm sunshine with Alice splashing about and the sounds of normal life all around her – birds singing, the neighbours next door talking in their backyard and bairns shouting in the lane – she shivered. What was she going to do? She pushed a strand of hair from her brow. What *could* she do? Her da was so poorly now there was no chance she and Alice could go there, besides which, what could she say as a reason for leaving him?

'He won't have anything to do with Alice and he never talks to me or wants to be in the house.'

Her thin mouth tightened. She could just imagine how that would go down. She could actually hear her mam saying that most men took little interest in their bairns when they were as young as Alice, and as for talking, he was likely too tired after a day at the pit for conversation. Regarding his treks, she ought to count herself lucky. Some men were forever down the pub with their pals drinking the rent money away or spending it on the dockside dollies; what was a passion for walking compared to that? And she ought to be thankful not to have him under her feet in the house when he wasn't working; there was many a wife round these parts who would be only too pleased to see the back of their man. Oh, aye, her mam would say all that and then change the subject if she tried to discuss the state of her marriage. Her mam wanted to bury her head in the sand and pretend all was well; she'd actually heard her say to one of her sisters that everything had turned out all right in the end for her and Adam. It had been Boxing Day when they'd gone to her mam's for tea and Adam had set off for a walk as soon as they'd eaten. Her aunties and their families had been there and she could tell they had thought it strange that Adam hadn't entered into any jollity and then disappeared as soon as he was able.

The sunshine was warm on her face and as Alice played Olive found herself relaxing, her mind beginning to wander. How much longer could they go on like this before something snapped? She had only been Adam's wife for a little while when there had been an accident at the pit and a miner had been killed, and since then she had realized it wasn't an uncommon occurrence. Gas explosions that brought the roof down were the cause of nearly all the big pit disasters, but accidents involving the machines down the mine were frequent and could cause horrible injuries. Adam's brother, Walt, had been terribly shook up when they were at his mam's on Christmas Day due to his best friend being killed that same week. He hadn't gone into details but it had been something to do with one of the steel ropes and a saw. She'd heard him talking to Adam's father and his words had stuck in her mind.

'One minute Nat was there, chatting away, a whole man, and the next he was like nothing on earth, Da. I wish he'd gone straight away rather than having to hear him scream for his mam for minutes. She's been dead for umpteen years but he called for her like a bairn. Damn pit.'

Adam's father had shaken his grizzled head. 'I know, lad, I know, but at least he didn't linger for weeks. Remember Doug Turner? Now that was a bad do—' He had stopped abruptly, becoming aware of her listening, and that had been the end of the conversation, but now Olive mused that men died often, didn't they, so why not—

She came to herself with a horrified jerk, clamping her hand across her mouth as though she had been speaking out loud. What was she thinking? She didn't wish Adam dead, did she?

The answer, when it came, caused her to jump to her feet and whisk Alice out of the water. 'Bedtime, hinny,' she murmured as Alice protested at the sudden end to her fun, 'and Mam'll read you a story while you have your milk and a biscuit. You'd like that, wouldn't you? Course you would.'

She'd read her two; in fact, three. And when Alice was asleep she'd clean the kitchen from top to bottom and scrub out the cupboards and line them with fresh paper. She had been meaning to do that for ages. She needed to keep busy, that was the thing, and she wouldn't let herself think. It did no good to man or beast, thinking.

Chapter Seven

Ruby stared at Ellie in horror, and her voice was a reflection of her face when she said, 'You can't, Ellie. You can't. Think, lass, think. If he loves you as much as he says he'd marry you, wouldn't he? Not ask you to go and live with him in that house. He'd ask you to get wed first.'

Ellie stood facing her but she looked at Ruby without answering, merely shrugging her shoulders and moving her head in a way that could have meant anything.

There had been a great change in Ellie over the last couple of years, one that left Ruby at a loss at times. Within a few months of them being settled in Newcastle, Ellie had taken to going out at night and at weekends with Bridget and some other girls. Ruby had accompanied them once or twice at first, but it hadn't taken her long to realize she found the incessant chatter about lads irritating at best and a little shocking at worst if Bridget's friends really did get up to all they said they did. Ellie, on the other hand, seemed to admire and envy them. She had her hair cut in a bob and became obsessed with the latest fashions, regularly returning late at night smelling of alcohol and cigarette smoke. Ruby knew Bridget's pals frequented some of the less salubrious dockside pubs and gin houses where they let men buy them drinks for – as one of them had put it – a bit of slap and tickle, but Ellie always insisted she didn't get up to anything untoward when Ruby questioned her and had become increasingly hostile to any probing.

Ruby had reluctantly accepted that to keep the peace she had to let Ellie follow her own devices but she worried about her friend constantly, and could never fall asleep at night until she knew Ellie was safely home. Things had got worse in the last little while since Ellie had got herself an admirer, a young man called Daniel Bell. Initially when her friend had begun to mention one lad in particular, Ruby had been pleased. She'd hoped that having a steady beau would calm Ellie down. In a way she could under-stand the desire to make hay while the sun shone after the awful life Ellie had had at home, but it was that very thing that made her friend susceptible to a glib tongue. At the bottom of her, Ellie wanted to be loved and cared for, that was all. And now she was saying that she was going to up and move into the house that Daniel and one of his pals lived in.

Ruby tried again. 'Ellie, take some time and think this through. Please, for me. We're friends, aren't we? We've always been there for each other.'

'I don't need to think it through.'

'But to move in with him before you're married—'

'Howard's lass lives with him.' This was the other man Daniel shared the house with.

'That doesn't make it right for you.'

'You're so old-fashioned, Ruby. No wonder you're Matron Henderson's pet. Smoking, drinking, wearing make-up and dancing – she's against all that, isn't she, and forever going on about loose behaviour and suchlike.'

'I'm not her pet and I think for myself as you well know. There's nothing wrong with wearing make-up and dancing and the rest, but you know your reputation will be ruined if you live as Daniel's wife without being married. Men can do it, have mistresses and all that, and they're just considered a bit of a rake and a Casanova, but it's different for lassies. And I'm not saying that's right because it isn't, but it's how things are. But the main thing, the important thing, is that Daniel knows all that and he shouldn't have asked you.'

'He said you'd be like this. He said you'd be jealous because it's me he loves and not you.'

Ruby stared at Ellie in amazement, hurt uppermost. 'Do you believe that?'

Ellie had the grace to look discomfited. 'No,' she muttered, and then more strongly, 'no, I don't, but it's your own fault he thinks like that. You've never let him get to know you. I've told you he's suggested several times we could go out in a foursome with one of his pals, but you wouldn't. You've only met him twice.'

Twice was enough. Ruby remembered the first time

she'd seen Daniel Bell. She had gone with Ellie to a cafe in the town to meet him as Mrs Duffy flatly refused to allow a young man over the threshold of her house. She had been all set to like the lad who Ellie seemed clear mad on, and at first sight he was well-dressed, dapper even, and certainly handsome enough, with his blue eyes and blonde hair. He had been sitting at a window table waiting for them and had stood up as they'd entered, smiling and raising his hand. Ruby had noticed then how his teeth marred his good looks. They were discoloured and one or two appeared broken.

He had bought them both a cup of tea and a sticky bun but within a minute or two of sitting down Ruby had thought, he's bumptious, cocky even, and he certainly has a big idea of himself. There was no doubt he was silver-tongued and he had set out to charm her, which had the opposite effect, especially when he had let his hand rest on hers a mite too long when he had passed her the sugar, but it was more the way he had looked at her that had unnerved her. The only way she could explain it to herself was that he made her feel as though she didn't have any clothes on, that he had stripped her naked in his mind.

By the time she had left them, refusing Daniel's pleas to accompany them to the Picture Theatre at the junction of Lynwood Terrace and Westgate Road and then later for a meal and drink at a public house, her head was aching and she was acutely disturbed. Bridget had been in when she had got back to Mrs Duffy's and after knocking on the Irish girl's door she had asked her what she knew about Daniel Bell. Bridget had told her Daniel wasn't one of the crowd she and her pals hung about with, and that since meeting him Ellie had had little to do with her and the others, preferring to be with Daniel, and Daniel's friend Howard and his girlfriend, a lass called Daisy.

Ruby had suspected Bridget knew more about Daniel than she was saying but no amount of coaxing could get anything more from her, and she'd had to admit defeat. Later that night, when Ellie arrived home the worse for drink, they'd had their first row about Daniel. Since then she had met him again once when he had been waiting outside the workhouse when Ellie had left one evening. He'd been as slick and smooth-talking as before but this time Ruby had detected an edge of hostility beneath the urbane front and had guessed, rightly, that he knew her opinion of him.

Now, recalling Daniel's chilling gaze as she had walked away from the pair of them that night to catch the tram, Ruby said quietly, 'Ellie, however many times Daniel and I met we wouldn't get on, but that wouldn't matter an iota if he had your best interests at heart.'

'He does.'

'Not if he's suggesting you live with him.'

Ellie's face tightened. 'I'm not like you, Ruby, and frankly I don't want to be. All your reading at the library and taking night courses to better yourself and designing and making your clothes and that would bore me stiff, and I can't see how you care so much about the suffrage movement either. All those meetings you go to and them talking on and on – I mean, who cares that there's a couple of women MPs in Parliament now? And they're both "Lady"s, not ordinary women like us. The upper class couldn't give a monkey's about the working class, be they men or women, that's the truth of it. Life's passing you by and I don't intend to let it pass me by.'

'Ellie—'

'No, I mean it. I love Daniel and he loves me, whatever you say. I know he does. And we will get married soon. He's said so. When – when he's got time.'

Time? For two pins Ruby could have shaken her. Daniel had nothing but time as far as she could make out. For ages Ellie had parried the question of what Daniel did for a living, before admitting diffidently one night that he did 'this and that' and had a finger in various pies 'here and there'. He always seemed to have money in his pocket and clearly wasn't short of a bob or two, but Ruby had realized Ellie really didn't know what her beau did or where the money came from and, moreover, didn't care.

'Ellie, don't do this. Please.'

'It's too late. I've said I would.'

'Well, unsay it.'

'I can't. He'd – he'd be mad.'

'If he loves you—'

'Don't keep saying that,' Ellie interrupted a trifle wildly. Undeterred, Ruby continued, 'If he loves you he'll understand what a big step this is and wait.' This wasn't the first time she had detected an element of fear when Ellie had talked about Daniel, and now she took the bull by the horns, saying softly, 'Are you frightened of him, Ellie? Is that it? You can't let him bully you.' As Ellie stared at her Ruby knew she'd hit the nail on the head. Her voice even softer, she said gently, 'You are, aren't you? You're scared. Ellie, this is all wrong.'

'You don't understand. I've let him—' Ellie shook her head helplessly. 'I can't lose him now. No one else would want me.'

'Of course they would. Did he say that? Well, it's a lie. You're young, you've got your whole life ahead of you, and we can move away from here if that's what you want, go somewhere else and start again. We've done it once, we can do it again.'

For a moment Ellie wavered. And then she bent down and picked up the big cloth bag at her feet holding all her belongings. 'He's waiting outside,' she said dully. 'I've got to go.'

'No, wait.'

As Ellie opened the door Ruby followed her onto the landing and then down the stairs into the hall. Daniel was standing on the pavement when Ellie opened the front door, and as Ruby caught at her friend's arm, saying again, 'Wait,' he straightened, squaring his shoulders and narrowing his eyes.

'Well, look who it is. Little Miss Holier-than-thou,' he drawled softly, moving towards Ellie who was still standing on the step, and taking the cloth bag from her but with his eyes on Ruby. 'Bin saying your two penn'orth then? Aye, course you have.'

Ruby stared at him and said stiffly, 'If by that you mean I'm not in favour of Ellie ruining her reputation by living with you then you're right.'

He laughed. 'You have airs and graces coming out of those pretty little ears, don't you, and what are you but a jumped-up laundry worker. You might look down your nose at the rest of us but them that aim highest fall furthest, remember that. As for me an' Ellie, I'll thank you to mind your own business.'

'Ellie's well-being *is* my business.'

'Not any more, sweetheart.'

'She needs someone to look after her.'

He didn't answer her for a moment, instead saying to Ellie, 'You satisfied I'm going to look after you, love?' and when Ellie nodded, he raised his eyebrows at Ruby. 'From the horse's mouth, or as near as dammit.' Then the mocking persona vanished and he took Ellie's arm, pulling her down off the step onto the pavement whereupon he moved into the doorway so that Ruby was forced backwards along the hall. Bending over her so close she could smell his tobacco breath, he murmured, 'You interfere in my affairs again and I'll make sure you regret it, got that? I don't want to see hide nor hair of you, m'lady, and I'm telling Ellie to have nowt to do with you from now on. She won't be coming back to work so your paths won't cross again.'

'You can't do that.' In spite of herself, her voice trembled. She had been right about him; he was unprincipled, bad. Oh, Ellie, Ellie, what have you done?

'Don't fool yourself.' He smiled a smile that wasn't a smile. 'You think you're so clever, don't you, with your fancy meetings with them other men haters. Oh, aye, Ellie's told me all about it. But what you don't realize is that you can't win, none of you. It'd only take one dark night and you on your own for you to be brought down a peg and know who's boss. That's what you women were made for, to serve men.'

For a moment she couldn't believe what she was hearing. He was threatening her. He was actually threatening her with rape? If he had thought to intimidate her, it had the opposite effect. Now it was Daniel who retreated in surprise and nearly fell down the step as she all but sprang at him, her eyes flashing as she pushed him as hard as she could. 'Get out of here, you filthy-minded swine,' she hissed.

As he joined Ellie on the pavement, it was Ellie who said, 'What's wrong, what's the matter?'

Knowing Daniel had spoken so softly that her friend had been unable to hear, Ruby tried to speak, dragging in a long gasp of air through the shock that had gripped her before she could say, 'He threatened me.'

'Don't be ridiculous.' Daniel took Ellie's arm, turning her to face him as he said, 'I merely told her it would be better if she stayed away from us, disliking me as she does. I don't want you upset. We've our own life now,

Ellie. Ruby's made it very plain that it's me or her, and I've told her you've chosen me. That's right, isn't it?'

Ellie looked from Daniel's face to Ruby's. For a moment she hesitated and Ruby said quietly, 'I never said it was me or him, Ellie. I would never make you choose.'

'Your whole attitude is making her choose.' Again Daniel brought Ellie's gaze to him as he turned her chin, looking into her eyes. 'Listen to me, Ellie, and get this into your head. I'm not prepared to have her coming between us, all right? And that's what will happen. It's already happening. At the bottom of her she doesn't like men – none of them feminists do. They're not normal women, everyone knows that.'

Was this the sort of poison he'd been feeding into Ellie about her? Ruby glared at him. 'That's rubbish but then you'd say anything to further your own ends.'

'We're going.' Daniel took hold of Ellie's arm. 'And just remember what I've said. I won't have anyone interfering in my life. You'll keep your distance if you know what's good for you.'

Ruby watched Ellie give her one despairing glance as Daniel manhandled her down the street. It wasn't until they had turned the corner and were lost to view that she became aware that Mrs Duffy was standing a few feet behind her. Wondering how long the landlady had been there, Ruby said weakly, 'Ellie's moved out, Mrs Duffy.'

'Aye, I heard.' The ominous sniff followed. 'And I have to say she's picked herself a rum 'un there. I've seen his type before. He'll lead her a hell of a life, you mark my words.'

It wasn't helpful. Ruby bit hard on her bottom lip to quell the tears Ellie's sudden and unexpected departure had caused, and then her eyes widened in surprise as Mrs Duffy added, 'You look like you need a cup of tea, lass. Come into the kitchen, I was just making a brew.'

To Ruby's knowledge it was the first time anyone in the house had been invited into Mrs Duffy's private domain, which Bridget had irreverently named 'The Holy of Holies', and she was so taken aback she found herself following the landlady without a word.

Once in the kitchen, Mrs Duffy pointed to one of the four chairs set under a scrubbed wooden table. 'Sit your-self down and take a breath,' she said briskly but not unkindly. 'Bit of a shock, was it, Ellie going off like that? She didn't give you any warning then?'

Ruby shook her head, gazing about her covertly. The kitchen wasn't what she had expected, not with Mrs Duffy being the way she appeared. Certainly when she and Ellie had moved into their room it had been in a poor state, and the hall was always grubby, the lino rarely scrubbed and the brown walls dismal. But the kitchen was clean enough and had an air of comfort to it, a big rocking chair with padded cushions set to one side of the blackleaded range and the thick nets at the window white and starched into stiff folds. A small potted plant stood in the middle of the table with shiny green leaves and little white flowers, and all one wall was covered in paintings, one or two of them framed but mostly fixed with drawing pins. Ruby stared at one picture of a young girl in a meadow full of daisies and buttercups; it was alive with colour and warmth and involuntarily she said, 'Oh, that's beautiful. The picture, Mrs Duffy, it's lovely. They all are.'

'Aye, grand, aren't they.'

'Who painted them, if you don't mind me asking?'

'I don't mind, lass. It was me son, Michael. He had a gift that way.' Mrs Duffy paused in making the tea and gazed at the pictures with her. 'He was a good boy, none better. If he had lived he would have been a fine painter.'

'He – he died?'

'On his sixteenth birthday, two days after me husband passed. It was the influenza that took them, nearly thirty years ago now. I'd had a job to fall for our Michael and there were no more after him but me and me husband were content with him, he was one in a million.'

'I'm so sorry, Mrs Duffy.' For the last two years she had thought her landlady cold and unfeeling, and all the time she'd had this great sorrow to bear.

Mrs Duffy looked at her. 'Nearly went barmy for a time,' she said quietly, 'but you bear what has to be borne, don't you. The good book says, "The Lord giveth and the Lord taketh away, blessed be the name of the Lord," but it was a long time before I could bless Him again, I don't mind saying. Still have me black days even now.'

'Oh, Mrs Duffy.' It just showed you never really knew anyone else.

'Aye, well, there you are. I'd appreciate you keeping it to yourself, lass. I don't like others knowing me business but, well, you're a different kettle of fish to Bridget and Anne. Known your own sadness I dare say. But as for Ellie, you can't do nowt there. I've seen it all before, I'm sorry to say. He's got his hooks into her and that type don't let go easily.'

'He's played on her weaknesses.'

Mrs Duffy went back to mashing the tea, saying over her shoulder, 'Be that as it may, you have to let her find out herself now. There's only so much you can do. She's made her bed and she'll have to lie on it. But if she comes back wanting to live with you again, that's all right by me.'

'Thank you.'

'Now come on and drink your tea.' Mrs Duffy placed a steaming mug in front of her. 'And I've got a slice of bilberry tart to go with it.'

Ruby sat drinking the tea and eating the tart in a kind of daze. If anyone had told her this morning when she had woken up that Ellie would walk out of her life and Mrs Duffy would walk in, she would have said they were mad. But grief-stricken as she was about Ellie, she felt Mrs Duffy was going to become a friend.

Life was strange.

Chapter Eight

Over the next few weeks when it became clear Ellie wasn't going to return, Ruby was forced to take stock and acknowledge that yet another new chapter of her life was unfolding. The loss of Ellie was hard to bear, especially considering the circumstances in which her friend had left. Although in latter months Ellie had been out with Daniel every night, she had still been around first thing in the morning when they had eaten breakfast together and then gone to work. There was no denying Ellie had changed since she had been seeing Daniel, becoming quiet and withdrawn as time had gone on, which in Ruby's opinion was the opposite to how love should make you feel, but there had still been occasions where the two of them had talked and laughed together. But Mrs Duffy – or Mabel, as her landlady now insisted Ruby called her – was right in that Ellie had made the decision to burn her boats and live with Daniel, and she had to accept it. There was nothing else she *could* do. But it didn't stop Ruby worrying or having moments when she was on the brink of trying to find the house where Daniel lived. Ellie had been somewhat secretive about its location in the past, but she had let slip it was in Lombard Street, which was situated close to the docks.

One result of Ruby's introspection and self-analysis over this period was that her aim for the future became crystal clear. During the last two years when Ellie had been spending every penny she earned on enjoying herself, she had done the opposite. She had opened a savings account at the post office and the only money she had withdrawn from this apart from necessities like paying the rent and buying food and so on, had been to enrol in several night courses, one being elocution lessons, another advanced bookkeeping, yet another business management and a fourth in high-fashion dressmaking where she first heard the term 'haute couture'. The teacher on this eighteen-month course, a small Frenchwoman called Madame Poiret, was a perfectionist with an acid tongue who suffered fools badly. She had begun the first evening by stating that the creation of exclusive custom-fitted clothing was in the same realm as painting a masterpiece; it could only be accomplished by an artist who was prepared to sacrifice themselves for their art. High-end fashion demands high-quality, expensive and often unusual fabric sewn with extreme attention to detail, she had informed them, her ebony eyes sweeping over the nervous faces in front of her, and only the most gifted and capable dressmakers had any chance of succeeding. It was time-consuming, difficult, frustrating and not for the faint-hearted. They were to forget everything they thought they knew about dressmaking, she had continued, because inevitably it would be wrong.

Ruby hadn't been the only one who had finished that first evening regretting enrolling on the course, but unlike several others, she had returned the next week. And the next. She had practised what she had learned making her own clothes and those of Ellie at home, for a fraction of the price they'd have cost to buy, and all the time at the back of her mind thoughts of her own dress shop selling exclusive clothes copied from the London and Paris fashion houses were simmering.

She realized now it had been Mrs Walton revealing the plans she'd made to pass over her dress shop that had first seeded the idea in her mind, and although that was impossible, as she would never countenance returning to Sunderland, it didn't mean she couldn't do something herself. She had been promoted to assistant laundress at the workhouse after twelve months when the current one had left her job in a huff after falling foul of Matron Henderson, and this had meant a substantial rise in her pay packet. She now had a healthy little nest egg in her savings account, and she added to this week by week with unfailing determination. Her hours were long but the work was not physically arduous and the workhouse inmates who helped in the laundry did any unpleasant jobs, like sorting and counting the linen for the wash, some of which came down from the infirm wards stinking with filth. The worst part of her duties, as far as Ruby was concerned, were the Saturdays when it was her turn to supervise the afternoon visiting in the workhouse hall. In much the same way as criminals in prison, the workhouse inmates were allowed no private visitors, and the officer on duty was forced to witness the misery and heartache that ensued. Elderly parents visiting a grown handicapped daughter they could no longer care for; married couples who lived in separate wards after a lifetime together now unable to kiss or touch each other; young unmarried pregnant girls begging to be taken home – the list was endless. Ruby felt that all the grief and sorrow in the world was contained each week within the workhouse hall and it affected her deeply.

She often had the desire after one of these sessions to pick up her skirts and run back to Sunderland to see her mam and da, but she never did. There was no point, after all. She had written to her mother several times but without giving her address, and she knew from Mrs Walton with whom she regularly corresponded that Olive and Adam had a daughter. No doubt they were now all playing happy families and her presence would not be welcome at best and an acute embarrassment at worst. It was better she stayed away, she would tell herself, the bitterness that always accompanied such thoughts hardening her heart. But try as she might, she couldn't shut memories of her old life away completely, which was why she filled every waking moment.

It was now the beginning of August and Ruby had a week's holiday, something that was a mixed blessing. When she was working and then in the evenings attending her classes or a suffrage meeting, it only left the void of Sunday to plan for. She would clean her room from top to bottom, do her week's washing, complete any outstanding homework from her courses, write her weekly letter to Mrs Walton and generally keep herself busy. Now she had seven days to try and find tasks to keep her occupied, which was impossible. The year before, Ellie had been around and when they weren't doing things together, she had made sure she spent hours reading at the library or sewing a new summer dress for each of them. But Ellie had gone.

Ruby woke up on the Monday morning and lay staring at the ceiling. Ellie had said she didn't want to be like her, that life was passing her by, and she was probably right. It hadn't felt like that when she had company, but now she felt all at odds with herself. She was only twenty, for goodness' sake, and she was living like an elderly spinster. Just last week Matron Henderson had commended her for having an old head on young shoulders, saying she had the attitude and viewpoint of someone three times her age. It had been meant as a compliment but thinking about it now it didn't feel like one. Just the opposite.

Oh, what was the matter with her? Irritated now, she jumped out of bed and padded over to the small fireplace where the coals she had banked down the night before with damp tea leaves and slack showed a faint glow. Even in the warmest weather she kept the fire going; it was her only means of making a cup of tea or toasting bread or having a supply of hot water.

Stirring the embers into flames she added more coal and then hung the kettle she'd filled from the tap in the yard the night before over the fire. She would feel better when she'd had a cup of tea, and in truth she had plenty to be thankful for. She was comfortable enough living here; she had money in the bank and a good job that paid very well, more than lots of men earned these days with the dole queues growing and more than two million unemployed. And it wasn't even as if those families that could draw the dole were provided with an adequate means of survival; every week they were seeing more folk coming to the workhouse doors, either that or they starved in their own homes. She had to count her blessings and stop being silly.

She continued the mental pep talk as she made tea and toast and then got dressed. At least she could go to the suffrage meeting being held near the bandstand in Castle Leazes that afternoon, which she would have been unable to do if she had been at work. It was a special occasion and a friend of Baroness Stocks, the educationalist and a leading feminist, was speaking, according to the local branch of the movement to which Ruby belonged.

Later that day as she walked the half-mile or so through hot dusty streets to Castle Leazes, Newcastle's first big public park, she was recalling the evening when she had persuaded Ellie to accompany her to one of the meetings. It hadn't been a success. Ellie had clearly been uncomfortable as the meeting had progressed, and later, when they had walked home together, her friend had admitted she didn't see what all the fuss was about. 'I mean,' Ellie had said, 'it's not as if women can't vote now, is it.'

'Only women over thirty,' Ruby had reminded her. 'And even then most men in the government regard women as somewhat scatty, hysterical creatures who could never be trusted with any real decisions about the country and important matters.'

Ellie had glanced at her out of the corner of her eye. 'But men *do* have a better understanding of politics and all that, don't they? I mean, women's brains work different to men's.'

'Ellie, we're just as intelligent as men, more so in some cases. Some men I've met are as thick as two short planks.'

Ellie had giggled, but then continued, 'Still, it can't be right to do what some of those women did in the past. Blowing things up and hurting people.'

'I think the militants thought that desperate times called for desperate measures. Do you know that before the war the then Home Secretary tried to get the militant suffragettes to be certified as lunatics and put in asylums? He only failed because the medical profession wouldn't agree to it. Women like Emmeline Pankhurst were bullied and threatened and put in prison where they went through awful trials, and don't forget that in the beginning they only resorted to violence because they were lied to and let down by the government on numerous occasions. They got to the point where they couldn't justify another generation of women wasting their lives begging for the vote. Deeds, not words, was their motto and you can understand why when you look back on how they were treated.'

Ellie had stared at her doubtfully. 'My da always said that the suffragettes were mainly a load of upper- and middle-class women with nothing better to do than to make trouble because they were bored, and they dragged working-class women into their daftness through telling them a load of old codswallop.'

'Ellie, I don't mean to be rude, but your da is one of the men I mentioned who's as thick as two short planks.'

'That's true.'

'Think for yourself, lass.'

Ellie had grinned. 'Aye, all right, I will, but I tell you now them sort of meetings aren't for me, Ruby. To be honest I don't care about the vote, and if I could vote now I wouldn't know who to vote *for*. I'm not like you, am I. If I'm going to read anything, I'd rather it be *The People's Friend* or *My Weekly*, something like that, and preferably with a nice box of chocolates at the side of me.'

Ruby had had to smile. This was Ellie thinking for herself and so she couldn't argue. If her friend wasn't interested in suffrage, so be it. Everyone was different; her mam had used to say it was what made the world go round. And there the conversation had ended.

Ruby sighed heavily as she remembered how she and Ellie had walked home arm in arm that day; it seemed a lifetime ago now. What she hadn't fully appreciated back then was just how vulnerable her friend was. It wasn't that she wanted or expected Ellie to think or behave in the way she did, she just wanted her to be happy and contented and adored by the man she had given her heart to. And there had been no sign of that with Daniel Bell.

Ellie had been right in one thing she had said that day, Ruby thought now. Women's brains did work differently to men's and so did their hearts. For momentary satisfaction Adam had taken Olive, even though he didn't even like her sister. That side of the male sex was beyond her understanding. And if Adam could do that, what was Daniel Bell capable of? Of a sudden she decided she would try and find out the number of the house where Ellie was living and go and see her to make sure she was all right, even if it meant facing Daniel and braving his hostility. Once she knew Ellie was happy, she wouldn't bother them again. But she couldn't leave things the way they were.

It was a beautiful day and as she reached the outskirts of the park, the sweet scent of trees and ornamental flower beds was a welcome contrast to the terraced streets. The deep-blue sky was flecked with fluffy white clouds and the August sun was hot on her face as she made her way towards the bandstand in the distance. A large crowd had already gathered, mostly women but with a few men dotted here and there, and children were playing on the grass. She saw some faces she recognized from the local meetings she attended, but there were lots of new ones too.

It was clear that the speaker, a Lady Russell, had an entourage who were very definitely out of the top drawer of society. It was well known that such people financed the ongoing fight for equality, and in the last six years, since women had been eligible to stand as candidates for Parliament, women's suffrage had become slightly more respectable in some quarters. Lady Russell and her companions were sitting on chairs on the bandstand talking amongst themselves, and Ruby recognized one of the group, a Mrs Clarissa Palmerston. Mrs Palmerston had a large country estate just outside Newcastle where she lived with her husband, a brigadier in the army. Mrs Palmerston, Ruby had been told, spent a certain amount of time at her town house in London, but she had caused a stir some months ago when she had arrived at a local meeting in her chauffeur-driven Rolls-Royce Silver Ghost. The chairwoman of the meeting had been beside herself with delight, causing one woman to mutter darkly to Ruby, 'Look at that one, she's all over m'lady like a rash. They talk about equality but it's still them an' us when push comes to shove.'

Ruby had known what the woman meant – the chairwoman had been embarrassing in her effusiveness – but to be fair, Mrs Palmerston herself had seemed quite down to earth and happy to chat with anyone. It had been the chauffeur Ruby had felt sorry for. He had stayed with the car outside the hall where the meeting was held, and several times he could be heard by the women inside chasing off the local bairns to whom the beautiful vehicle had proved irresistible. Once or twice his language had been as colourful as a sailor's but Mrs Palmerston had appeared oblivious and hadn't so much as blushed.

It was another half an hour before Lady Russell was introduced with a great deal of pomp and ceremony. She was wearing an elegantly cut black suit, long in the jacket and the skirt mid-calf, her pale-mauve shirt collar spread across her shoulders and a three-cornered hat in the same colour shading her face. Ruby found herself assessing the cost of what was clearly an extremely expensive outfit for the first few moments and had to remind herself to concentrate on what Lady Russell was actually saying. In contrast to her serious and demure appearance, her speech was fiery from the outset, immediately holding the attention of the crowd.

'Do not think that because we now have women in Parliament the fight for equality can be less robust,' she began. 'In fact it is now more urgent than it has ever been. I have it on good authority that the courageous Lady Astor finds it necessary to engage in open, savage warfare with the most corrupt element in the House of Commons daily as she fights against untrue and possibly actionable slurs against her and her family. Hostility – petty, persistent and often vicious – is constant from certain male colleagues in the House, and these brave women are being put under unbearable strain simply because of an unwritten consensus among these bigoted males that a female MP is by nature wrong. Of course, the aim is to freeze women out of the government by any means possible and cause them maximum embarrassment and humiliation in the process, so discouraging constituencies from adopting other women candidates. Should we call these creatures men?' She raised her eyebrows. 'I think not. I have a better name for such persons but one that I cannot voice in the presence of children.'

There were a few murmurs of 'Shame on them,' and suchlike, before Lady Russell went on.

'Such tactics *are* shameful and only prove all the more how essential it is for us to continue to stand up against such tyranny. Such males wish to prove that Lady Astor and other women will be unable to cope with the work required of them. Lady Astor was refused a seat at the corner of a bench, thus forcing her to climb over men's legs to be able to take her rightful place in the House. They pretended that they couldn't find a lavatory for her and made her walk to the far end of the building. Before a debate on venereal disease they put the most graphic photographs imaginable in the lobby in an attempt to embarrass her, and made speeches considered unsuitable for a woman's ears. All this has been done and is being done, make no mistake about that. There is a very real feeling of hatred in the chamber but if these men imagine that the expansion of women's liberty will be intimidated by such aggression, then they are wrong. I repeat, *they are wrong.*'

Now some cheers rang out along with shouts of, 'Hear, hear!' Ruby, along with many other women in the crowd, was quite oblivious to the hot sun beating down, capti- vated by Lady Russell's passion and eloquence as she continued to speak for nearly an hour.

It was just after four o'clock in the afternoon when

Lady Russell said in closing, 'A decade ago, when the armies of every great power in Europe were preparing for war, another war – that of women against the injustices meted out to them by the government of the time – was put on hold. Women in all ranks of life in Britain put aside their own interests for the good of the nation, so they could nurse the wounded, care for the destitute, comfort the sick, nurture the lonely and be the solid foundation on which armies went forth to defeat the enemy. The struggle for enfranchisement of women was not abandoned, but, as women always do, they considered others' needs before their own. Something, sadly, some men find so difficult even to this day.'

'She's right there,' a stout matron standing just in front of Ruby said in an aside to her friend. 'Selfish toerags, most of 'em, and my Ned's one of the worst an' no mistake. Wouldn't even make a cup of tea when I was flat on me back pushing out our last bairn, the miserable blighter.'

Her friend shushed her as Lady Russell continued, 'A friend of the suffragists, Mr Wedgwood, made a speech in the House of Commons at that time, and he finished by saying that he believed no future government would repeat the mistakes and brutality of the Asquith ministry, under which women like Emmeline and Christabel Pankhurst, Annie Kenney, Mary Leigh and others suffered such horrors. He believed that the Cabinet changes which would of necessity occur as a result of warfare would make future militancy on the part of women unnecessary.

I leave it to each one of you to determine whether his hopes have been realized.'

'Don't have to think long an' hard about that one, do you,' the woman piped up again. 'My Ned'd knock me into next weekend if he knew I was here listening to her and there's plenty like him all over, including among the toffs. Men like power, that's the thing.'

It seemed Lady Russell agreed with her, as she went on, 'Suffice to say that a decade later women are still treated as inferior beings who only have the intelligence to vote at the age of thirty. Quite what the government imagines happens in a woman's brain between the age of twenty-nine and thirty, I have yet to understand, but apparently below this magic number we are merely considered as simpletons. But one thing that Mr Wedgwood stated was absolutely spot on.'

Lady Russell paused. She was well aware that she held her audience in the palm of her dainty hand and a slight smile touched her lips. 'It is an impossible task to crush or delay the march of women towards their rightful heritage of political liberty and social and industrial freedom. One day, perhaps not for some decades it is true, but one day a woman Prime Minister will rule this great country of ours and a woman Home Secretary will sit in office. Women will take their rightful place in the medical profession, in law, in business and in scientific research.'

As resounding cheers broke forth, the wife of the maligned Ned turned and shook her head at her friend. 'Never in a month of Sundays,' she scoffed. 'I'd love to see it, mind, but a woman Prime Minister? As much chance of that as hell freezing over.'

It *did* seem a pipedream. Ruby's gaze swept over the group on the bandstand and then took in the bright hopeful faces all around her. But then if you didn't believe you could make your dreams come true, what was the point in anything? Why not a woman Prime Minister and Home Secretary? Why not women rising up in the professions Lady Russell had mentioned? The only thing that would prevent it was women themselves and if this gathering was anything to go by, there were plenty who believed it could happen in spite of the woman in front of her. Change was in the air; it was almost tangible, and it was exciting.

Once the noise had died down, Lady Russell's piercing eyes surveyed her audience. 'My great heroine, Emmeline Pankhurst, was fortunate enough to have been brought up by parents who took an active part in the great struggle for human freedom in many areas. From a young child she understood the meaning of words like slavery and emancipation. At a time when, to their shame, propertied classes in England were largely pro-slavery, her family and the circle of friends they associated with were opposed to such wickedness. Her father, Robert Goulden, was a most ardent abolitionist, and her mother took an active part in raising money for newly emancipated slaves in the United States.'

What a different childhood to her own. Ruby didn't know if she envied Emmeline Pankhurst or pitied her.

Her own home had been a place where her mam cooked and cleaned and looked after them all, including her da, and the only time any conversation had been faintly political was when her da was reading the paper and commented about something or other like ex-servicemen reduced to a life of street hawking by the lack of jobs after the war. Before he had come home from France, her mam had never even bought a paper. Her childhood had been carefree on the whole, happy.

'And yet even in Emmeline's undoubtedly liberated environment where both parents were advocates of equal suffrage, she was aware of a difference in how her brothers were treated compared to her and her sisters,' Lady Russell's ringing voice proclaimed. 'The boys' education, for example, was considered a much more serious matter by their parents. Emmeline realized that men considered themselves the superior sex and that the best of women, her own mother, apparently acquiesced to that belief. The young Emmeline found this very difficult to reconcile.'

As Lady Russell paused to take a sip of water from the glass at her elbow, Ruby was aware of a sudden flood of homesickness sweeping over her. Whether it was the memories of her own happy childhood she didn't know, but she had to make a conscious effort to close her mind to thoughts of her mam and da. Her mam had chosen Olive. That's what she had to remember, she told herself sternly. When push had come to shove, and in the face of a huge betrayal from her sister, their mam had sided with Olive.

She took a deep breath, willing the momentary weakness

to pass as quickly as it had come. It was Ellie's departure that had made her so up and down in the last little while, that was all. But she couldn't dwell on that either, or how Daniel Bell might be treating her friend. It was too weakening. She just had to hope that Ellie would seek her out if anything was wrong.

She felt relief when Lady Russell began to speak again and she could concentrate on what the other woman was saying.

'When Emmeline Goulden married Dr Pankhurst she knew she was marrying a man of like mind,' Lady Russell declared firmly. 'He was a man who had lent the weight of his honoured name to the suffrage movement before it became popular, and who believed that society, as well as the family, stands in need of women's services. Their children would be treated equally in every respect, regardless of their sex.'

The crowd were hushed; even the woman in front of Ruby was quiet now. It was clear Lady Russell wanted to emphasize her next words as she moved to the very edge of the bandstand, bending slightly forward as she said, 'To any unmarried girls here, I urge you to choose very carefully when you commit yourself to your life partner. Politicians and leaders will fight on for the suffrage movement, but I believe it is in the family home, from cradle until adulthood, where the greatest changes are required. The values that children learn from their parents are the ones that will change the world for good or ill. Make it for good, young women of Britain.'

Ruby felt as though the last words had pierced her through. She stared at the woman on the bandstand, a hundred and one emotions causing her head to whirl.

She knew she had been slowly changing in many ways since she had left Sunderland and come to Newcastle, but suddenly half-formed thoughts and feelings had crystallized into one solid, inescapable fact.

If she had married Adam, sooner or later she would have become unhappy and she would have made him unhappy too.

She stood quite still as Lady Russell concluded her talk, not moving through the storm of applause that followed, even to clap like everyone around her. Her mind was grappling with the knowledge that had been thrust upon her.

A large part of her didn't want to acknowledge it was true, she realized, because to do so would effectively let Olive off the hook to some extent. And why should her sister get off scot-free when she had done her uppermost to wreck her life, and without a word of contrition? It wasn't fair. But – and she couldn't escape the fact – it *was* true all the same.

She shut her eyes for a moment but she couldn't put the genie back in the bottle.

Her heart thudding violently, she opened her eyes again and stared blindly ahead. Because she had loved Adam she had wanted to be his wife from when she could remember, but she had always known they felt differently about lots of things. Adam was a product of his upbringing and set in his ways, even as a child. When she'd broached the matter of her continuing to work for Mrs Walton after they were wed and he had agreed, he'd also made it clear it was a concession on his part and she had been grateful for it. As far as Adam was concerned, men went out to work and brought home the money and their wives raised the bairns at home. Once she'd had their first child she would have been destined to remain as a housewife for the rest of her days. And she knew now that wouldn't have been enough. Of necessity she had been forced to stand on her own two feet over the last two years and in so doing certain aspects of her personality had come into prominence. If she'd married Adam, she would still have developed in the same way, she realized that now, but the growth of the fledgling ideas and principles would have been slower to gain maturity. And he wouldn't have agreed with her on some of the things that had become so vitally important.

The crowds were dispersing now but still Ruby stood where she was, feeling as though her world had been turned upside down yet again. What Olive had done was horrible and Adam's betrayal had been devastating, but putting that aside, did the woman she was now feel the same about marriage to Adam as the girl of eighteen had felt?

The answer was stark and unequivocal and it rocked her to her core. She shut her eyes for a moment, trying to come to terms with the truth, and when she opened them again it was to see a riderless horse and gig fast bearing down on a woman who had just left the steps of the bandstand and who had her head turned away from the danger as she conversed with someone behind her.

Ruby called out as she ran, and she just reached the woman whom she recognized was Clarissa Palmerston when the galloping horse was feet away. Without thinking she threw herself on the woman and sent the pair of them hurtling through the air, the lethal hooves of the frightened animal missing them by inches. It was all over in a moment and the whole incident had only taken a minute or two.

She must have banged her head because for a while she was in a kind of whirling vacuum where she could hear voices around her but was unable to respond. And then the darkness receded and she opened her eyes to find herself being cradled in the arms of Clarissa Palmerston who was kneeling at her side, saying, 'She saved my life, she saved my life,' over and over again.

'Oh, my dear.' As Clarissa became aware that Ruby was conscious, she looked on the verge of crying, but instead murmured, 'That was the bravest thing, the very bravest thing. Are you all right, have you broken anything?'

'I don't think so.' The words were shaky as they passed her lips. In truth she felt most odd.

'Here.' Someone pressed a glass of water to her lips and she took a sip, and then a few more. Her head was clearing and the feeling of dizzy nausea passing.

'I landed on top of you, I'm afraid.' Clarissa supported her into a sitting position, keeping her arms around her. 'I just had no idea what was happening.'

To her great embarrassment, Ruby realized that Lady Russell and other dignitaries were in the circle of people peering down at her. She took another moment before she said quietly, 'I'm feeling better, thank you. Could you help me up?' to Clarissa, who immediately obliged but kept her arm round her waist once she was standing.

Looking into the distance she saw the horse and gig had come to a halt and that a man was holding the reins as another man, presumably the owner, came running over to them, saying, 'I'm sorry, I'm so sorry. A couple of dogs nipped his heels and he took fright and the reins must have come untied. Is anyone hurt?'

It was Lady Russell who answered and she was very much the aristocrat as she said icily, 'But for this young lady here, my friend would almost certainly be badly injured or worse. What were you thinking of, man?'

'I can't apologize enough.'

'Just make sure that the animal is secure in the future.'

'I will, I will.' He looked contritely at Ruby. 'We'd only just left him a minute before near the fountain with the other horse and traps while my wife and I had coffee with some friends at the park cafe. I couldn't believe it when I saw him galloping off but it was those damn – sorry, those dogs that unnerved him.'

'Yes, yes.' Lady Russell waved the poor man away, turning to Ruby and Clarissa as she said, 'Ineffectual individual. Now, Clarissa, you came by car, I understand?'

Clarissa nodded. 'And I'll see to it that Miss . . . ?'

'Morgan. Ruby Morgan,' Ruby said quickly.

'Miss Morgan gets home safely.'

'Oh, there's no need. I'm perfectly well now.' All Ruby wanted was to get away from the little group who had gathered around her. She had never felt so embarrassed in her life.

'Nonsense.' Clarissa smiled at her, a warm open smile, and her voice was softer than the somewhat acerbic tone of Lady Russell. Ruby had heard it said that Lady Astor, the feminists' champion, had an abrasive manner but that this characteristic was an advantage when dealing with male MPs who were waiting for her to fall flat on her face, so perhaps all these warrior ladies who were at the forefront of the fight for progress were the same? She could appreciate it might be necessary but it was a little intimidating, nonetheless, whereas Clarissa Palmerston seemed more understanding and gentle. She returned Clarissa's smile as she said, 'I really don't want to put you to any inconvenience, Mrs Palmerston.'

Clarissa's smile widened. 'Believe me, Miss Morgan, it would have been far more inconvenient to find myself under the hooves of that poor animal.' Clarissa had kept her arm round Ruby's waist and she now turned to Lady Russell, saying, 'I'll see you at Lord Rochdale's dinner tonight, Lavinia,' as she bent forward and touched the other woman's cheek with her lips, before guiding Ruby away from the others. As they walked, she said, 'I'm sure I've seen you somewhere before, Miss Morgan, but I cannot recollect . . .'

'It was at a suffrage meeting in town some months ago.'

'Ah, was that it? Yes, I remember the meeting. I made the mistake of getting poor Pearson to drive me in the Rolls, didn't I. He did suffer at the hands of those children. I've promised him I'll drive myself in one of the less ostentatious estate cars next time. I really thought the poor chairlady – Mrs Todd, isn't it? – was going to have a fit of the vapours at his language.' She cast a bright-eyed glance at Ruby as she added, 'Being married to a brigadier I've heard it all and much worse, I'm afraid. I've even let the odd word slip myself, on occasion.'

Ruby felt herself relaxing. There was something about Clarissa Palmerston that was very engaging and despite her upper-class accent and top-drawer friends, she seemed, if not ordinary, then . . . Ruby couldn't find a word that fitted and she gave up trying.

As they reached the Rolls-Royce where the said Pearson was waiting at attention with the door open for them, Clarissa asked, 'Are you expected at home, Miss Morgan, or do you have time to come and have tea with me? The brigadier is away at the moment and I do so hate having tea by myself. Pearson will drop you home later.'

Ruby stared at the other woman, totally taken aback. She was well aware that ladies of Mrs Palmerston's standing did not invite an assistant laundress from the workhouse home to tea. Mrs Palmerston was being kind because she had pushed her out of the way of the horse but it wouldn't be fair to take advantage.

She stood by the magnificent car thinking how to word her refusal when Clarissa further disarmed her by saying,

'Oh, please, do not say no, Ruby. May I call you Ruby? And you must call me Clarissa. Please come to tea. Look at it from my point of view. How many times in one's lifetime does one have the opportunity to have tea with someone who's just saved one's life? It will just be us two and we can sit in the garden and talk properly. One cannot converse with all the activity going on here. I want to know all about you.'

'There's nothing to know.'

Clarissa drew her into the back seat of the car, which was enough to take Ruby's breath away. Never in her wildest dreams would she have imagined herself sitting in the back of a chauffeur-driven Rolls-Royce. Cars of any kind were still mainly the playthings of the upper and middle classes, although now there were more Baby Austins and Morris Minors in the town to rival the 'Tin Lizzie', the Ford Model T. The only people Ruby knew who owned a car were the senior doctor at the workhouse and Mr Henderson, the master, and they both had one of the Fords. She'd read in the newspaper that down south traffic jams in the city of London were becoming a problem with the roads clogged by taxis and the new motor buses, but as yet Newcastle had no such difficulties.

'Now,' Clarissa continued once Pearson had shut the door and taken his seat in the front of the car, 'what made you come to hear Lavinia today?'

That was easy. As the car started, Ruby tried to relax again. 'I have a week's holiday from my place of employment and thought it was a good opportunity to hear Lady

Russell speak.' The car was moving now and Ruby found it much more disconcerting than riding in a tram or on the train.

'Oh, you work?' This was said not in a patronizing way but with keen interest.

Ruby nodded. Her head was aching, no doubt from the bump she'd received when she fell, and the car seemed very low down and unprotected compared to a tram. 'I'm an assistant laundress at the workhouse,' she said quietly. No good dressing it up.

'And you live at home with your parents?'

'Not exactly.' Ruby stifled a sigh. She had a feeling that Clarissa Palmerston, as well bred and ladylike as she was, was a person who, as her mam would have put it, made it her business to know the ins and outs of old Maggie's backside. Resigned now to her fate, she said flatly, 'I came to Newcastle two years ago following a broken engagement. My family's in Sunderland.'

'I see.' Clarissa didn't see at all but she was determined she would by the end of the afternoon. This beautifully dressed girl with the lovely face intrigued her. There was lots about her that didn't add up somehow. Her clothes were exquisite and clearly expensive for one thing; until she spoke one would imagine she came from the top end of society, but there again, although she had the northern burr in her voice it was soft and muted and her enunciation was perfect. But overall there was a sadness about her, not that she appeared dejected or downcast but more as though she had known heartache or grief. Of course, a broken engagement wasn't a pleasant thing for anyone to go through.

Decision made that she would wheedle out all that there was to know about Ruby Morgan, Clarissa settled back in the seat and deliberately moved the conversation to the meeting and Lady Russell, speaking lightly and humorously. She had plenty of time for her questions and the girl was looking rather pale and wan; she'd feel better after some refreshments.

The car was fairly flying along now as far as Ruby was concerned but after the initial apprehension she found she was enjoying the experience. She had read in the newspapers how most country people hated the cars and motorcycles that dashed at twenty miles per hour through narrow lanes bringing noise, fumes and danger; previously isolated villagers dreading the invasion of picnickers on summer Sundays with the attendant horrors of empty bottles and waste paper. There had been stories about ordinary working folk encouraging their children to throw stones at the passing gentry in their vehicles or to scatter nails and broken glass on the roads, and she had had sympathy with them, but now she had to admit riding in a motor car was thrilling. Some ex-servicemen had bought motorcycles with sidecars with their demobilization grants, and there were often a number of these to be seen parked in terraced streets, but now she realized that the luxury of riding in a motor car was something else entirely. How the other half lived.

It hardly took any time at all to reach the outskirts

of the town, and then they were travelling along country roads. Clarissa kept up an easy chatter and Ruby found she only had to respond with the occasional answer, which was just as well. In truth she was feeling quite over-whelmed by all that had occurred in the last hour and by the situation in which she now found herself.

They passed one or two farms, pale shimmering fields of freshly mown hay making mosaics against grain fields mellowing to the bronze of harvest and fields where sheep and cattle grazed contentedly in the late-afternoon sun, and drove through several little hamlets dozing in the sunshine. Thatched cottages with gardens bursting with flowers, children playing on a village green, hens clucking as Pearson sounded his horn to send them scurrying off the road and dogs barking at the strange and noisy appar-ition invading their domain. It was a different world to the town. Ruby had thought she was adventurous moving from Sunderland to Newcastle, but now it dawned on her that within a few miles of the towns lay a different England, one with so much open space it was incredible.

How long it was before the Rolls drove between massive open iron gates Ruby wasn't sure; she was feeling so befuddled it could have been minutes or hours. The car scrunched onto a gravel drive that could easily accommo-date several cars abreast, and this was bordered on both sides by ornamental privet hedges that were low enough to display the beautifully kept gardens beyond. These were a panorama of green lawns, bright flower beds and sculp-tured trees, but it was the enormous grey stone house in the distance that drew the eye. It was three-storey, its two large wings curving round a huge forecourt. Ruby gaped – she couldn't help it – and then snapped her lips shut, hoping Clarissa hadn't noticed.

The Rolls stopped in front of semicircular steps leading to a stone terrace and the entrance to the house, and as Pearson came round and opened Clarissa's door, she turned to Ruby with a beaming smile.

'Here we are,' she said as casually as if they hadn't just arrived at a residence that in Ruby's fevered mind resembled the pictures she had seen of Buckingham Palace. 'Let's have tea.'

Chapter Nine

It was two hours later. Ruby had had tea with Clarissa, sitting on a decorative terrace at the rear of the house that overlooked the gardens and a lake in the distance, and then her new friend – as Clarissa herself insisted she was – had escorted her round most of the vast establishment arm in arm, pointing out this and that as though she was a curator at a museum. Ruby by this time felt so comfortable with Clarissa that she had said exactly that, to which Clarissa had answered, 'But most certainly. Godfrey, my husband, was born in one of the rooms upstairs, as was his father and his father before him, but even he feels he's merely a glorified caretaker here. I mean, the house demands our service and we're obliged to give it, but truthfully it's never felt like home to me. It's beautiful but I much prefer our London residence. My childhood home in Sevenoaks is half the size of Foreburn and much more cosy.'

Ruby had nodded but said nothing. Even a house half the size of Foreburn would be a mansion outside most people's comprehension and could hardly be called cosy.

Now, as an ornate marble clock chimed six o'clock in the drawing room in which they were sitting, Clarissa said regretfully, 'Oh, I so wish I didn't have to attend this wretched dinner Lord Rochdale is giving for Lady Russell tonight. I would have much preferred for us to dine together.'

Ruby smiled but rose to her feet. 'I'll leave you to get ready,' she began, just as a knock came at the drawing-room door and a maid opened it to say, 'Mr Forsythe is here, ma'am.' A moment later a tall, handsome and distinguished-looking man strode into the room, smiling widely.

Clarissa jumped up, saying to Ruby, 'Oh, it's my brother Edward, he's escorting me to the dinner,' and then to her brother, 'I want to introduce you to the lady who saved my life this afternoon,' with a dramatic flourish worthy of an actress. 'Edward, this is Miss Ruby Morgan and but for her I would be lying mangled under the wheels of a horse and trap.'

Ruby had blushed hotly – she could feel the colour burning her cheeks – but Edward smiled, holding out his hand as he said in a deep, slightly husky voice, 'Now as introductions go, this is certainly one to remember. I am most delighted to make your acquaintance, Miss Morgan. Edward Forsythe, at your service.'

Ruby placed her hand into his hard warm grip and managed to say fairly steadily, 'How do you do, Mr Forsythe.'

'Very well, very well.'

Ruby had assumed Clarissa to be no more than a few

years older than herself but the man in front of her looked to be in his thirties, and this was confirmed when Clarissa said, 'Edward's my big brother, Ruby, but there are two more older than him. I'm the only girl and the baby of the family.'

'And more trouble when she was younger than the rest of us put together,' Edward grinned, then rumpled Clarissa's carefully arranged hair causing his sister to squeal in protest. 'But tell me, what's all this about Miss Morgan saving you from certain death?'

He had spoken with a twinkle in his grey eyes, and Clarissa's voice was reproving when she said, 'She did, she really did, I'm not exaggerating. You can ask Lavinia later if you don't believe me. We were at the meeting at Castle Leazes and a frightened horse bolted straight for me. Ruby flung herself into its path to save me.'

'Well, on behalf of myself and the rest of the family, may I thank you, Miss Morgan. We all decided a long time ago that Clarissa has been put on this earth to keep us on our toes but nevertheless, she is exceedingly precious.' He smiled at his sister, a warm, loving smile, and Clarissa smiled back. Ruby could sense the closeness between the two siblings even after only moments in their company and she found herself envying Clarissa. She had been ten years old when her two brothers had marched off to war and her memories of them had dulled a little with the passing years, but she didn't think she would ever have had the relationship with them that Clarissa seemed to have with Edward.

Knowing that Clarissa had to prepare for the evening ahead, she said politely, 'It's been very nice to meet you, Mr Forsythe, but I really have to be going,' at the same time as she became aware that next to his height and breadth – he must be at least six foot two inches or so and his shoulders were broad under his evening clothes – she felt unusually small and feminine and it wasn't an unpleasant sensation. There was a fresh clean smell emanating from him and although he was clean-shaven the faint bluish hue about his chin went hand in hand with his wavy jet-black hair. He was somehow disturbing, a small section of her mind told her, and not just because he was handsome although he certainly was. No, it was more the presence he carried with him. Telling herself she was being ridiculous and hoping she didn't appear as flustered as she felt, she said to Clarissa, 'Thank you for a lovely tea.'

'Oh, I enjoyed it immensely and don't forget you promised to come for lunch on Thursday,' Clarissa said, leaning forward and kissing her on both cheeks. 'I'll get Pearson to take you home.'

Had she promised to come for lunch on Thursday? Clarissa had asked her earlier when she was escorting her round the house, but to Ruby's mind she'd parried the invitation, hoping Clarissa wouldn't pursue it. Clarissa was being gracious, and she was clearly a genuinely warm-hearted woman, but the social gulf between them was so huge no amount of gratitude on Clarissa's part could bridge it. She must see that?

Highly embarrassed now, and wondering what

Clarissa's brother was thinking, Ruby said awkwardly, 'That's really very nice of you but I don't think—'

'But you're on holiday this week, you told me so,' Clarissa interrupted before she could finish. 'Oh, Ruby, please spare the time.' Clarissa took her hands, shaking them slightly. 'We can lunch down by the lake – it's lovely and cool there in the shade of the trees. Edward, tell her she must come.'

Edward looked at Ruby, a wry twist to his lips. 'She's like a miniature steamroller, Miss Morgan, take it from me, and always gets her own way. Thoroughly spoiled by our parents, I'm afraid, and Godfrey took over from where they left off.'

'Oh, you!' Clarissa pushed her brother with sisterly disapproval. 'You make me out to be a brat.'

'Well . . .' Edward grinned at Ruby and she had to smile back; they were like a double act, they really were.

'You'll come?' Clarissa said again.

Ruby nodded. 'Thank you.' Edward was right, Clarissa was an unstoppable force, and anyway she would be back at work next week and normal life would have to resume. Why not take this brief step out of reality and enjoy it for what it was worth – a glimpse into how the other half lived.

'Oh, goody.' Clarissa actually clapped her hands and Edward sighed in mock despair.

'See what I mean, Miss Morgan? She's never grown up.'

'I'm perfectly grown up but I refuse to be dull and

boring like you.' Clarissa softened the rebuke with a smile and then said, 'I'll ring for Gladys to tell Pearson you're ready to leave, Ruby.'

'Don't bother Pearson,' Edward said easily. 'If I know you you're going to take at least an hour or more to pretty yourself and I'll just be kicking my heels waiting. Why don't I pop Miss Morgan home?'

This was getting worse by the minute. Ruby's eyelids blinked rapidly but for the life of her she could think of no firm reason why Clarissa's brother shouldn't take her home. Somehow she managed to say weakly, 'Oh, I really couldn't put you to that bother, Mr Forsythe.'

'The name's Edward, and it's no bother at all. In fact, you would be doing me a favour. Shall we?' He smiled at her and held out his arm for her to put her hand in the crook of his elbow. She could do nothing but comply, especially with Clarissa beaming at them as though she had engineered the whole thing.

Feeling as though she had forgotten how to put one foot in front of the other, she accompanied Edward out of the room and into the vast hall, and once outside, Clarissa hugged her before standing on the steps and watching them as they walked towards Edward's car. It was another beauty but she had prepared herself for that, and it stood in gleaming midnight-blue splendour on the gravelled drive. As Edward helped her into the passenger seat, Ruby prayed for an aplomb she was far from feeling, and once he had slid in beside her and they had waved goodbye to Clarissa she searched for something to say.

The best she could come up with being, 'This is a lovely car.'

'Thank you.' As the car scrunched down the drive he smiled at her. 'It is something of an indulgence, I'm afraid. I mostly live and work in the city. I only use the car when I visit my parents, and Clarissa of course, and the odd visit to other family and friends in the country. Driving oneself in town is no longer the pleasure it once was.'

'You work in London?' As a son of wealthy parents Ruby hadn't expected Clarissa's brother to earn his own living. It was clearly unfair of her, but she'd had him down as one of the Hooray Henrys the newspapers were always on about, rich and mostly ineffectual young upper-class men who were fashionable and wayward and intent on a good time.

Edward nodded, keeping his eyes on the road ahead now they'd left the confines of the estate. It was dappled with late-evening sunshine and as the folding roof of the Daimler was fixed open Ruby had taken the precaution of removing her straw bonnet and placing it on her lap where it couldn't fly off.

'As I'm not the heir or even the spare,' Edward went on, 'I came to the conclusion early on that I was in the fortunate position of being able to choose what I wanted to do with my life. My two brothers are heavily involved with my father's estate and the farm we have. Cuthbert is being groomed to take over at some point and Leonard will manage the farm for him and so on. Anyway, my maternal grandmother, bless her, left me a sizeable inheritance when she passed on. She was a grand old lady in every sense of the word. My brothers and Clarissa were frightened to death of her but I never was and I think she liked that. I decided that the business world was beckoning and I entered in with gusto. After a somewhat tricky start I discovered I was actually rather adept at what my father likes to call "wheeling and dealing".'

This last was said with a tinge of bitterness, and Ruby felt that Clarissa's brother didn't see eye to eye with his father regarding his work. She glanced at him out of the corner of her eye but the handsome profile revealed nothing.

'And you?' he went on. 'Clarissa said you are on holiday this week? With whom are you staying, Miss Morgan?'

She suddenly realized that Edward had no idea of who she was or her station in life, and why would he? He had only met her minutes ago, after all. The clothes she was wearing were not those of the average working-class girl, and Clarissa had been unable to hide her surprise when she'd confided that she had made them herself from pictures she had seen of the latest fashions. Neither was her northern brogue as pronounced as it once had been; the elocution lessons had seen to that. Not that she was ashamed of her roots in the least, but if she was going to open her own high-class dress shop in the future she knew she had to speak properly with the right enunciation and delivery.

She looked straight ahead as she said quietly, 'I'm not staying with anyone, Mr Forsythe. I rent a room in the town and at present I have a week's holiday from my job as an assistant laundress at the workhouse.'

The car swerved slightly but other than that he showed no reaction. 'You rent a room? You have no family?'

'I have family in Sunderland but I moved from there to Newcastle two years ago.'

'That was very brave of you.'

'Not really.' She hesitated. No doubt he would get the full story from Clarissa if he bothered to ask, but she really couldn't go into it right now. She was mentally and physically exhausted after the events of the day and she knew she'd have bruises all over from her tumble at the park, but it wasn't so much all that as Edward Forsythe himself that had her at sixes and sevens. Now she said, her voice deliberately cool, 'Circumstances dictated the move, that's all.' Changing the subject, she added, 'London must be very exciting, Mr Forsythe.'

'Edward, please.' He slowed down to avoid a wood pigeon pecking at something on the dusty road and then sounded his horn when it showed no intention of getting out of the way, causing it to fly off with a great flapping of wings. 'Yes, I suppose you could say London's exciting – certainly there are more forms of entertainment than one can shake a stick at. And when the hotels and restaurants close and the theatres empty and so on, dancers can go on to one of the new clubs that have sprung up since the war like the Top Hat or Mother Hubbard's or the Kit-Kat Club and dance till dawn. The flappers make the most of that,' he finished somewhat sardonically.

She had heard the term before for the bright young things in flimsy dresses of muslin, chiffon and crêpe de Chine who shimmied the nights away in a whirl of fringes, tassels and beads, and who had a growing reputation for being frivolous and undisciplined and carefree. Again she glanced at him from under her eyelashes. 'You don't approve of the freedom of the modern woman?'

'On the contrary. I'm all for women having equality in every realm, be it in medicine or law, academia, business or politics, and certainly they should have been given the same voting rights as men decades ago. The fact that it was only last year that equal terms in marriage were finally awarded to their sex is shameful. However, I can't help thinking that the fight by the suffragettes in the past and which is continued by women like my sister and yourself today was for more than equipping the social butterfly type to flaunt her freedom by showing a distinct lack of morality.'

Now Ruby twisted in her seat to stare at him. 'So in other words, a woman should only have as much freedom as you approve of?'

'That isn't what I said.'

'I think it is.'

'No,' he said a little testily. 'I just don't think a brazen image of womanhood and seeming lack of seriousness or interest regarding the important issues of life this world faces is attractive.'

Neither did she, but that wasn't the point. 'If a young woman wants to have some fun before she settles down and raises a family, then that is her right, surely? It doesn't necessarily mean she is promiscuous or heartless. And if she chooses never to marry or have children, or makes a career for herself, then that is her right too.'

'Couldn't agree more.' His voice was laconic in the extreme now, which Ruby found immensely irritating. 'But your average scantily clad flapper with a haircut like a man's drinking umpteen Manhattans and getting pie-eyed constitutes a danger to herself and others, especially if they then decide to drive home in a car or on a motorcycle. I lost a dear friend this year when two silly girls in a little sports car one of their fathers had bought for her twenty-first birthday the week before lost control of the vehicle and mounted the pavement. They were so intoxicated they couldn't stand up when the police arrived on the scene.'

'That's awful, I know, but women like that are the exception to the rule. Surely you see that?'

He shrugged. 'Perhaps I'm getting a little cynical in my old age, Miss Morgan.'

It was the mocking note in his voice that made her say, and more sharply than she had intended, 'Well, forgive me, Mr Forsythe, but that's nothing to be proud of.'

There was silence for a long moment. The breeze had teased tendrils of hair from the chignon at the nape of her neck and her cheeks were flushed, more from their exchange of words than the rush of air in the open-top car. He had been kind enough to offer to bring her home and she had just insulted him, Ruby thought in dismay, but really, he was the most impossible man.

After an uncomfortable pause when Ruby remained

absolutely still and staring ahead, gripping her hat so hard her knuckles showed white, Edward said quietly, 'You are quite right and I apologize. Of course such individuals are the exception. It's just that Anthony left a wife and young child and I grieve for what might have been.'

'No, *I* apologize.' Ruby felt awful. He was mourning his friend and she'd shown as much empathy as a fly on the wall. Why, oh, why, had she ever agreed to accompany Clarissa home in the first place? 'That was totally uncalled for.'

'At the risk of disagreeing with you once again and incurring your wrath, I think you were right to reproach me, Miss Morgan. I was being boorish. Clarissa has taken me to task on a number of occasions recently on the same subject. Now –' he grinned at her for a second and as she met the dark grey eyes a little shiver snaked down her spine – 'with your permission, we'll begin again? Edward Forsythe, at your service.'

Ruby smiled. 'Ruby Morgan, Mr Forsythe.'

'I shan't believe I'm forgiven until you call me Edward.'

Feeling that the afternoon had got more surreal with every passing minute, Ruby had no option but to say, 'Edward.'

'And may I call you Ruby?'

As they were unlikely to ever meet again, Ruby could see no harm in humouring him, besides which she had little other option. 'Of course.'

During the rest of the journey Ruby discovered that Edward was skilled in the art of light conversation, and also very humorous when he set out to be. Nevertheless, she was immensely relieved when the car drew into Bath Lane Terrace where it immediately drew a great deal of interest from a group of children swinging on a rope they'd secured to the lamp post. Before they had even stopped a crowd of little people had surrounded the Daimler, and as Edward exited the vehicle and walked round the bonnet to open Ruby's door for her, one cheeky urchin, with his backside hanging out of his ragged trousers, shouted, 'Hey, mister, got a penny to spare?'

Well, he could certainly have no illusions as to her position in society after this, Ruby thought drily, as she said to Edward, 'Ignore them.'

He helped her out of the car and once they were standing on the pavement with all the children now clamouring for money, she said stiffly, 'Thank you very much for bringing me home, Mr Fors— Edward, and I hope you enjoy the dinner tonight.'

'The dinner will be tedious in the extreme, I'm afraid. I'm sure it's only to avoid such events that the brigadier devotes so much time to the army, but—' He broke off abruptly to shout at the snotty-nosed little lad who had first spoken and who had taken it upon himself to try and climb on the bonnet of the car using the mascot to pull himself up.

'I think you had better leave while you still have a car,' Ruby suggested, hiding her embarrassment as best she could when the waifs and strays took up a concerted deafening chant of, 'Mean as muck, no good luck,' as they retreated a few feet.

'It was very nice to meet you.' He smiled, as though unaware that the commotion the children were making had brought out some of their mothers. The women were now adding to the hullabaloo by yelling at their offspring whilst taking a keen interest in the grand vehicle themselves, and not least its owner. That a toff, and a handsome one at that, was chatting to one of Mrs Duffy's lodgers who he'd clearly picked up one way or another, was a tasty titbit to chew over.

Aware that her name would be mud in certain quarters, Ruby just wished he would go. There was nothing these old wives liked better than to get their knife into someone, and the gossip this incident would generate would go on and on until some other poor mug came into the firing line.

She smiled back, a tight smile, and said, 'Goodbye, Mr Forsythe,' before turning and walking away. As she opened Mabel's front door she was praying he would have the good sense to drive off without delay, and she closed it without looking round or waving.

Leaning against the wood she strained her ears for the sound of the car's engine, and as Mabel appeared from her front room-cum-bedroom where she'd obviously been peering out behind her nets, Ruby said, 'Has he gone?'

'Aye, he's gone, but who the heck is that? I thought you were going to one of your suffrage meetings. I've been worried to death for the last hour or so with it getting so late.'

Mabel sounded like her mother, but the landlady's tone was anxious rather than disapproving and it softened

Ruby's voice as she said, 'I'm twenty years old, Mabel, not two, besides which it's only half-past six and broad day-light outside.'

'That's as may be, but you never know these days. Things aren't like they were before the war, sorry to say.' This was one of Mabel's favourite sayings, covering everything from the milkman arriving late and the disgraceful – in her opinion – rise in hemlines, to the state of the country under the new Labour Prime Minister, Ramsay MacDonald. On taking office in January he had stated that there could not be a social revolution overnight, thereby alienating Mabel for good who had expected imme-diate benefits for the working class. 'So?' She eyed Ruby with a look that said she meant business. 'Who's the gent?' Then she added, 'Come into the kitchen and have a cuppa.'

Resigning herself to the inevitable, Ruby followed her landlady without protest and over a cup of tea filled Mabel in on the afternoon's events. Mabel listened without inter-rupting, but as Ruby finished speaking, shook her head. 'Them lot out there will never believe he's not your fancy man. You know that, don't you? Why on earth didn't you let him drop you off a couple of streets away so no one was any the wiser?'

In truth, Ruby hadn't thought of it, but her voice indignant, she said, 'I haven't done anything wrong so why should I?'

'All right, all right, don't have a go at me. I'm only looking out for your best interests, lass. Mud sticks, that's all I'm saying, and you know what they're like round here.'

Same as they were everywhere. 'He only brought me home.'

'Exactly.' Mabel pursed her lips and hitched up her ample bosom with her forearms. 'In a car. A great big one an' all. And him dressed like a gent. All that'll add fuel to the fire. Flaunting it, that's what they'll say. Not content with being some rich man's floozy, she's shameless with it. He'll be married with a couple of bairns by morning, you mark my words, for why else would a gent take up with a working-class lass if not to have a bit on the side?'

'He's not married.'

'That won't matter to them. The truth has little to do with it, believe me.'

'Oh, Mabel.'

'Now, now, don't look like that. What's done is done, and if owt's said to me I'll set 'em straight, believe me. Gossiping old biddies, the lot of 'em.'

Considering that Mabel enjoyed nothing more than a tasty bit of tittle-tattle this was a bit ripe, but Ruby was too downcast to see the funny side of it. Standing up, she said, 'Thanks for the tea, Mabel.'

'That's all right, lass, and if this Clarissa person sends her car for you on Thursday I suggest you're ready and waiting. What time did she say?'

'Pearson's collecting me at eleven o'clock.'

Mabel sighed. 'I dare say the curtains'll be twitching however nimble you are, and the bairns will report back to their mams anyway. The little beggars don't miss a trick.'

Leaving the kitchen, Ruby climbed the stairs slowly,

the beginnings of a headache causing her temples to throb. She was just about to go into her room when a 'Psst' behind her made her turn. Bridget beckoned to her with a finger to her lips, and as Ruby followed the other girl into her room, Bridget closed the door behind them carefully before she whispered, 'I don't want Mrs Duffy to hear.'

'Hear what?' Ruby had had enough for one day.

'About Ellie.'

'Ellie?'

'Aye. Mrs Duffy'd never have her back if she knew, not that that's likely to happen anyway, but just in case.'

'Bridget, what's happened to Ellie?' Suddenly she was frightened; Bridget's face was unusually solemn.

'It's him, that bit of scum she took up with. My friends had their suspicions about that fella Daniel shares a house with and his lass, but they weren't sure, but now there's no doubt. Daniel and his pal are running that house as a brothel and they've got the two lassies on the game, Ellie and Daisy. Flo, that's one of my pals, said it's common knowledge now.'

'No.' Ruby's heart was banging so hard against her chest she put a hand on her breast. 'No, I don't believe it. Ellie wouldn't.'

'Well, she has, lass. I wouldn't have told you if I wasn't sure. And apparently that Daniel is older than he looks, getting on for forty, Flo reckons, and that's not all. He's got a wife and bairns in Middlesbrough he ran out on years ago and he's mixed up in all sorts of things besides the whoring. Flo knows a bloke who's pally with a mate of Daniel's and this mate said Daniel's a nasty piece of work.'

'Nice sort of friend to have.'

'Aye. Well, anyway, he – this bloke Flo knows – said by all accounts Daniel isn't someone to get on the wrong side of. I thought I'd put you in the picture 'cause I know you were thinking of calling on Ellie some time but I wouldn't, I really wouldn't, Ruby. He might be there.'

Ruby looked at Bridget in amazement. 'Bridget, if what you've heard is right then there's even more reason for me to go. I've got to get her out of there.'

'And what if he turns violent?'

'I've got to see her.'

'She's completely under his spell, you know she is. Look what she was like when she was living here. It was all Daniel this and Daniel that, the sun shone out of his backside as far as Ellie was concerned.'

'If he's forcing her to do *that*, she might be feeling different now.'

Bridget shook her head. 'You're barmy, right barmy.' She stared at Ruby. 'Look how he was the day Ellie left. He told you to keep away then, threatening you with goodness knows what. You'll put yourself in harm's way and for what, lass? 'Cause I tell you now, Ellie won't leave him and if she tried he'd give her what for.'

'I've got to see her,' Ruby said again.

Bridget shrugged her shoulders, and then as she looked into Ruby's dark, pain-filled eyes, she gave a great sigh.

'Oh, what the heck, I'll come with you. You can't go alone, lass, take it from me. I'll see if a couple of me pals'll come with us, safety in numbers an' all that. They liked Ellie when she used to hang around with us before Daniel got his claws in her.'

'I can't ask you to do that.'

'You're not askin'.' Bridget patted her on the arm, an unusual gesture for someone who was not in the least demonstrative. 'Like I said, I think you're barmy but I'd like to think someone'd do the same for me if I was in Ellie's shoes.' They continued to stare at each other for a moment longer before she added, 'I'll have a word with me pals and see if any of 'em'd come along, all right? But whatever, I'll come. If he knows folk have got your back it's something.'

'Oh, Bridget. Thank you.' Bridget was Irish through and through, warm-hearted and straightforward. Travelling to and from the workhouse together and living in the same house the two girls had got friendly to some extent, but this was beyond what Ruby would have expected.

'Mind, I still think no good'll come of it. He sees Ellie as a means of earning money for him and Flo's not sure if it's just her and Daisy in there or if there's more girls – he won't let her go. But if you're set on seeing her . . .'

Ruby's face gave Bridget her answer.

Chapter Ten

Olive gazed at her mother in frustration. Why had she even bothered to try and tell her how things were between herself and Adam? She hadn't meant to. She had decided weeks ago that it would be pointless and so it had proved. Her mam had come out with every platitude she'd feared she would and more besides.

For her part, Cissy was well aware of what Olive was thinking but she couldn't, she just couldn't commiserate with her daughter. It would open up a whole can of worms she wasn't ready to face and besides, what good would it do? Olive and Adam were married and they had a bairn, that was the end of it. As George had said more than once over the last months, Olive had brought her situation on herself.

Nevertheless, her voice was gentle when she said, 'Lass, marriage is never easy, take it from me, but you have the bairn and that's a blessing. Now, let's have another cup of tea before you go and there's a slice of sly cake to go with it.'

Olive recognized the finality of the tone beneath the softness. She stood up, her face stiff. 'No, thanks, I need to get back and put the dinner on.' She picked up Alice who had been playing with her grandma's saucepans and pans on the clippy mat, bashing them with a wooden spoon and delighting in the noise she was making.

'Aw, lass, don't go in a huff.'

'I'm not, Mam. Like I said, I need to get the dinner on.' If it was late there would be hell to pay but Olive didn't voice this. Her father was having one of his bad spells and was in bed but she didn't go to see him, merely calling out goodbye as she put her coat and hat on and then leaving the house quickly.

The air outside was muggy and thick with the smells of the streets as she walked home, housewives gossiping on their doorsteps as bairns played their games on the dusty pavements and in the gutters. One or two women she knew called out a greeting as she passed, which she returned smilingly, playing the part expected of her. She wondered how many other women hid behind a mask, pretending their life was normal when it was anything but, and feeling like they were going mad inside.

But Adam wouldn't send her mad; she wouldn't let him. Her features tightened. Alice needed her, and no matter what happened, no matter what she had to put up with from Adam, she would make sure she was here for her daughter. She glanced down at the little girl in the second-hand pram her mother-in-law had bought for them in the weeks leading up to Alice's birth, and a bright, happy face immediately smiled back at her, bringing a smile from Olive in return. How could she bemoan her lot when she had such a gift?

Wrapped up in the child as she was, she didn't notice the woman approaching her until a voice said, 'Olive, lass, it's been a while since I saw you last. How are things?'

Looking up, Olive's heart sank although her face did not betray what she was feeling. She had gone to school with Susan Hannigan as she'd been named then, and Susan had been the ringleader of a group of girls who had bullied her relentlessly about her looks. Susan had been a spiteful, nasty girl and Olive had no doubt she'd grown into a spiteful, nasty woman. Keeping her voice neutral, she said quietly, 'I'm fine, Susan. How are you?'

'I'll be better when this is out.' Susan patted her enormous stomach. 'I've told my Bill this is the last one. Mind, I said that with our Annie and look at me. Got tiddly at Christmas and this is the result.' She gave a cackle of a laugh. Olive remembered that sound. Susan had always been at her happiest when she was tormenting someone, usually her.

Olive smiled and made to walk on, but Susan stepped directly into the path of the pram and then moved round to look into it. 'Bonny, ain't she,' she muttered grudgingly, as though it was a personal insult for Olive to have produced a pretty baby. 'Mind, her da's a looker. We always used to say that Adam and Ruby looked like one of them film-star couples – him dark and tall and her blonde and beautiful.' Hard blue eyes met Olive's. 'Biggest shock of me life when we heard she'd skedaddled to pastures new. How's she doing, your Ruby?'

Avid curiosity coated every word. Olive looked at her old enemy and now she didn't attempt to hide her dislike of the woman when she said coldly, 'Very well.'

'See much of her, do you, or would that be a bit . . . awkward?'

'Not at all,' Olive lied, her voice clipped. She wasn't fooling Susan and she knew it. Susan was vocalizing the eagerness to know the ins and outs of what had happened that was in most people's faces even to this day. Adam's family and her own had closed ranks and discussed the matter with no one, but the fact that Ruby had left Sunderland on the very day she was going to marry Adam, followed by her own marriage to Ruby's fiancé weeks later with the accompanying swelling of her stomach, had been proof enough of a scandal that would keep folk talking for years.

Susan stared at her, and the old venom was in her voice when she said, 'What goes round, comes round, that's what my Bill always says.'

'Really?' said Olive icily. 'But then your Bill never was the brightest spark, was he,' and with that she pushed the pram forwards, the wheels narrowly missing running over Susan's feet.

She was shaking as she walked home, a weariness gripping her that had nothing to do with physical tiredness. She would never be free of the condemnation of what she had done and what people suspected she had done, not while she lived in these parts, she knew that, but there was no hope of ever leaving Sunderland. Adam would never countenance it for one thing, and she felt this was perhaps more because he wanted her to live under the censure of people like Susan than anything else. It was part of what he saw as her punishment. And how could she leave her mam and da anyway, or provide for herself and Alice? And part of the time, when it was just her and Alice at home and she could hide away from the rest of the world, she could cope.

She squared her shoulders as she trudged on. Ruby had said that Adam would never forgive her for tricking him and her words had felt like a curse ever since. They were always there at the back of her mind and she knew they were true, but she hadn't realized how living with hate, day in and day out, affected every single little thing. But it was no good belly-aching about it. None at all.

Much later that night, when Alice was asleep and she and Adam were in bed, his snores punctuating the silence, she felt the old familiar pain in her belly and knew what was happening. She hadn't mentioned it to a soul but she had missed two periods again and had known she was pregnant. She had told herself, stupidly she admitted now, that if she kept it to herself she might, she just might carry this baby to full term. But it wasn't to be.

Sliding out of bed carefully so as not to awaken Adam, she pulled on her dressing gown and pushed her feet into her slippers. This was the third miscarriage now, and she knew she had to get downstairs to the privy to deal with what would follow.

The night was warm as she stepped outside into the yard, the moon riding high in a velvet-black sky surrounded by a myriad twinkling stars, and she felt small and alone and utterly bereft as she entered the privy, sliding the bolt behind her. The pain was stronger now, grinding away at her and making her gasp and moan when it reached peaks, peaks she knew were expelling another tiny little baby from what should have been the protection of her body. Tears were pouring down her face, not because of the agony she was enduring or the immense and harrowing loneliness she felt sitting in the dark in the silent night, but because of the grief she was feeling for the little boy or girl who would never see the light of day, never feel the sun on its face on a summer's morning or snuggle into her arms when she carried it to bed at eventide.

A tinge of pink was stealing into the sky when she opened the door of the privy some time later, spent in body and mind and as pale as a ghost. Adam would be up soon and she must get his breakfast on the table for when he came downstairs. She wouldn't say what had happened. There was no point. He wasn't interested in her or having another child, and there would be no sympathy for her, she knew that, just denunciation at her failure to achieve what other women hereabouts seemed to do so easily.

She paused for a moment in the small square of yard, staring blindly upwards as she murmured, 'You've won,

Ruby. Hands down, you've won, lass, better than you could have ever imagined.'

Somewhere not a million miles away, her sister was enjoying life with Ellie and other friends she'd made, no doubt, probably without a care in the world and certainly no guilty conscience to eat her up. And why shouldn't she? Olive bent over a moment as her stomach contracted with an after-pain. Ruby was blameless, after all.

It was that same day but in the evening, and if Olive had but known it, Ruby's conscience had kept her awake all the previous night telling her she should never have let Ellie leave with Daniel Bell that day weeks ago, that she should have wrestled Ellie away from him by force if necessary. She had *known* he was bad news.

As she and Bridget alighted from the tram in Castle Square where Flo, who'd agreed to accompany them to Daniel's house, was waiting, she was still feeling wretched. She knew Flo slightly from her early days in Newcastle, when she and Ellie had gone out with Bridget's group of friends a few times before she'd decided such evenings weren't for her. Flo's greeting was on the cool side. More by what Bridget hadn't said than what she had, Ruby had gathered that Bridget's pals thought her something of an upstart because she hadn't thrown her lot in with them as Ellie had, and now she said quickly, 'Flo, I can't thank you enough for coming with us today. I know you're doing it for Ellie and not me, but I'm so, so grateful.'

She was trying to hide the fact that the area was much

worse than she'd prepared herself for as Flo lived in the vicinity. She had known it was close to the docks with the attendant industry and all that meant, which resulted in grime and dirt and deterioration, but the overall poverty was shocking. As the centre of Newcastle had moved away from the waterfront in past decades, so had whole districts been left to decay into grotesque squalor with overcrowded tenements housing families of fifteen or more in one room.

Sandhill, where Lombard Street was situated, was one of these. The proximity of the slaughterhouses and the equally strong smells from the fish markets and stinking outside privies made the area as different to Bath Lane Terrace as chalk to cheese.

Ruby smiled at Flo who smiled back, somewhat mollified. 'Aye,' Flo said, 'like I said to Brid, Ellie's a nice lass but too gullible. I dunno if Brid's told you, but we all tried to make the lass see what Daniel Bell's like but she saw him through rose-coloured glasses.' She couldn't resist adding, 'I know you don't think much of us lot but none of us would get mixed up with someone like him. We just like to have a bit of a giggle, that's all.'

'I know, Flo. I do. And it's not that I didn't want to be friends but going out drinking just isn't my cup of tea, that's all.'

Flo grinned. 'Not your cup of tea, that's a good 'un.' She still thought that Lady Muck – as she and her other pals had christened Ruby – considered herself a step above, but to be fair Ruby'd always been a good friend to Ellie. Look at what she was doing now. And Bridget had said Ruby had been prepared to confront Daniel Bell by herself. That took some guts. No, there was something to be said for the lass but Ruby still got up her nose, truth be told. All these evening classes doing this and that wasn't normal for a young lass in her opinion, it was unnatural. Mind, Ruby might be about catching herself a rich husband; now that she could understand.

They began walking towards Lombard Street, the stink from the fish market hanging heavy in the warm air. There seemed to be an inn every few yards and despite the early hour – it was still only seven o'clock – from the noise within quite a few of the customers were already on the way to being drunk. They were walking along the quay-side and then as they turned into Lombard Street past a bank situated on the corner, the three girls saw two sailors leaving a house further down the street, laughing and nudging each other as they went.

'That's where Bell lives,' Flo said quietly.

Ruby felt her stomach turn over. Those two men . . . She glanced at Bridget who said, 'Don't think about it, and anyway they might just be mates of Daniel.' But neither of them believed that.

The three of them had come to a halt. Bridget looked scared to death and even Flo, who was a big hefty girl with arms on her like a navvy from her job at the rope and wire-making works, was biting her lip. Ruby had to swallow hard before she could say, 'You two stay here. If I get into any bother I'll say you're waiting outside and will raise the alarm if I'm not out in ten minutes.'

Bridget nodded, but Flo said, 'No, we'll come to the door with you and wait inside if we can while you talk to Ellie. Any funny business and I'll threaten the blighters with this.' She brought a cut-throat razor out of the pocket of her skirt, and as Ruby and Bridget's eyes widened, she said, 'It's me da's. He don't know I've got it, but I thought a bit of protection wouldn't do us no harm.'

Ruby's heart was thumping so hard it hurt. The street was like all the ones by the riverside, dirty and filthy, and there was a dead rat lying in the gutter along with other debris. A few yards away a group of children were playing on the greasy pavement. Their clothes were ragged and dirty and their feet were bare, and one of the little girls was sitting with a snotty-nosed baby on her lap, jogging it up and down when it cried. She couldn't have been more than three or four years old herself, her small frame thin and wasted and her fair hair lank and matted, but she still smiled and talked to the baby and even as Ruby watched dropped a kiss on its tiny forehead.

This was poverty such as Ruby had never seen. For a moment she thought of her childhood home and her mother. They hadn't had two pennies to rub together when she was growing up, but her mam had always seen to it that their stomachs were full, their clothes were clean and their shoes were mended the minute they developed holes in the soles; and she'd fought a determined and successful war against the body lice and nits some of the bairns brought to school too.

A pang of sudden and acute homesickness assailed her

and she found herself longing for a lost time, a time when she was a carefree child and her mam was the centre of her secure and happy world and everything was in its right place. Fear was gripping her, fear of what she would find when she knocked on the door of the house in front of her and also fear of Daniel himself, and she hated it, hated being afraid. The awareness of how she felt brought her chin rising and straightened her shoulders as her fighting spirit sprang up. Daniel Bell was scum and she wouldn't let him intimidate her, not while she had breath in her body. As for Ellie, she would do everything within her means to get her friend away from here.

She moved forward, Bridget and Flo falling into step behind her, and when she reached the flaking, battered front door of the house she grasped the brass knocker and banged hard twice. The door was opened almost immediately by a small fat man whose smile died on seeing the three girls.

'Aye?' He eyed them up and down. 'Whad're you want?'

Unconsciously, Ruby brought all she'd learned at the elocution classes to bear as she said crisply, 'I am here to see Ellie Wood, Mr . . . ?'

Howard Riley blinked. Women didn't call at this house, especially not ones who spoke and dressed like this one. His gaze flickered from Ruby to Bridget and then Flo behind her, and it was to Flo he said, 'I know you, don't I? I've seen you around?'

'Aye, you might have done. I know you an' all – you're Howard, Daniel's pal. Well, like she says –' she flicked her head at Ruby – 'we've come to see Ellie.'

Flo was as rough and ready as they come, and this had the effect of reassuring Howard. He knew how to deal with lassies like her. His small piggy eyes narrowing into black slits, he said mockingly, 'Oh, aye, want to see Ellie, do you? An' who's she when she's at home and what makes you think she's here?'

'We know she is here so don't take that tack.' Ruby's tone wiped the smile from his face. 'Unless you want a great deal of trouble I suggest you call her immediately.'

Howard hesitated. He couldn't weigh this one up and that concerned him. She was a classy piece and perhaps it wouldn't do to get on the wrong side of her. Gathering himself, he said, 'An' who might you be?'

'That's none of your business.' She had recognized she had an advantage with this crony of Daniel in that he was unsure of her standing in the community and she wasn't about to give her name in case Daniel had spoken of her. Trying to imagine how Clarissa, or perhaps Lady Russell, would address such an individual, she kept her shoulders back and her head up, her chin not out but drawn slightly into her neck. Her voice cool and clear-sounding, she said, 'Now do as I say and fetch Ellie.'

Howard knew Daniel wouldn't like a piece like this one coming into the house asking for Ellie, but what could he do? Decision made, he stepped back from the door. 'Come in a minute and I'll see if she wants to talk to you.' Once they had filed past him into the brown-painted hall, he nodded to the front room to the left of them. 'Wait in there.'

The smell of stale tobacco and alcohol was strong as they walked into the room, which held three sofas clustered round a long low table holding a couple of ashtrays and several glasses. There was no other furniture and the heavy thick curtains at the window were closed, the only illumination coming from two gas lights on the wall, which gave the place a dim, claustrophobic feeling.

Daniel's pal had shut the door after them but Ruby opened it and stood in the aperture, and she heard him talking to someone in one of the rooms upstairs. Bridget and Flo were standing in the middle of the room; none of them wanted to sit down, and after whispering, 'Stay here,' Ruby retraced her steps into the hall and quietly climbed the uncarpeted stairs. The house was three-storeyed and a century ago had probably been the home of a rich merchant, but now it was crumbling and in a state of disrepair, and Ruby didn't doubt that the others in the street held umpteen families in each property.

A door was slightly ajar on the first landing and Ruby could hear Howard quite clearly as he growled, 'I tell you she asked for you. Now why would a lady come here, eh? What you bin up to? Dan won't like it, you know that, don't you?'

As she pushed the door open wide, Ruby's eyes registered several things at once. The room, unlike the rest of the house thus far, had a thick red carpet covering the floor and held a double bed with rumpled sheets. Either side of the bed stood two pedestals with an oil lamp on each, and the light from them showed Ellie cowering back against the profusion of satin pillows with Howard bending over her. Without pausing to think, Ruby shouted, 'Get away from her, leave her alone,' even as her eyes widened at Ellie's transparent negligee under which she was naked.

At the sight of Ruby, Ellie gathered up the top sheet, wrapping it round her, and Howard turned, glaring at her as he yelled, 'Hey, you, who said you could come up here?'

Ignoring him, Ruby cried, 'Ellie, you have to come with me right now,' and as Howard sprang and seized her arm she yanked it free, pushing him hard as she shouted, 'Don't you dare lay a finger on me.'

The commotion had brought another scantily clad young girl into the doorway, and as she said, 'What on earth's going on?' Ruby turned just in time to see a partially dressed man pulling on his shirt over his trousers as he hightailed it down the stairs.

'Get the hell out, Daisy.' Howard manhandled the girl onto the landing, and as he did so, Ruby quickly shut the bedroom door behind him and turned the key in the lock.

Ellie still hadn't said a word, but now, as Ruby repeated, 'You have to come with me,' she pulled the satin sheet tighter round her. Thinking Ellie didn't understand, Ruby approached the bed. Her voice was soft as she murmured, 'Ellie, it's me, Ruby. Don't be frightened. Look, Bridget and Flo are downstairs. We've come to take you home.'

Howard was banging on the door and shouting obscenities, and Ruby could hear Bridget and Flo's voices too, but trying to keep calm in the bedlam, she put out her hand to Ellie, only to see her shrink back into the pillows.

'Ruby, you have to go, quick, before he comes back,' Ellie muttered.

'Who? Daniel? I'm not scared of him, Ellie.'

'You should be.'

'Ellie, he's forced you into this, he's scum, rotten to the core. I'll go to the police if I have to.'

'No.' Ellie's face was white, her eyes wide and terrified. 'It'd do no good. Daniel's got them in his pocket, paying them backhanders to look the other way.'

'Not all of them, there'll be some who are decent men.'

'You don't know what he's like. You don't cross him.'

'Then we'll leave Newcastle, all right? Go somewhere else. We left Sunderland, didn't we?' Ruby was getting frantic but trying not to let it show in her voice.

'You don't get it, do you? I can't. He'd find me and kill me.'

'No, he won't. I promise you he won't. We'll disappear, Ellie. I've got money, we can start somewhere new.'

Just for a moment Ruby thought she saw a ray of hope in Ellie's eyes, but then her face went blank and she shook her head. 'I'm – I'm not the lass you once knew.'

'Yes, you are, you *are*,' said Ruby fiercely. 'I don't care what you've done, what he's made you do. Underneath you are still Ellie Wood.'

Again Ellie shook her head and now her voice was weary when she muttered, 'You've no idea, Ruby, no idea. You live in such a different world.'

'Listen to me.' Ruby sat on the edge of the bed and took Ellie's hands. For some reason it registered that they were soft and white, unlike when her friend had worked in the laundry. 'I know you're frightened of him and I'm not saying without cause – I can imagine what he's like – but if you want to leave here with me I'll make sure you are safe. I'll move heaven and earth, Ellie. I swear it.'

'It wouldn't be enough, and anyway . . .'

'What?'

Howard had stopped banging on the door and Ruby could hear voices downstairs.

'No decent man would want me now. And – and Daniel does look after me.'

Ruby couldn't believe her ears. She shook the limp hands in hers as she murmured, 'This isn't looking after you, lass. Letting men do that to you. Don't you see?' And when Ellie just stared at her, she said fiercely, 'He's nothing but a nasty little pimp. They both are, him and this Howard. Scum of the earth.'

Again Ellie gave her no answer but now she shut her eyes, shaking her head.

Ellie, Ellie. Ruby wanted to shake her until she saw sense but gather her up in her arms at the same time. The room reeked of cheap perfume and another mustier odour that was distinctly unpleasant. Swallowing hard, Ruby said, 'Get dressed and we'll leave here for good, lass.'

As though she hadn't heard Ruby, and still with her eyes shut, Ellie whispered, 'It started with him asking me to do a pal of his a favour. Daniel said this man had lost his wife and was knotted up inside and that if I was kind to him it would help him get back to normal. I said no.

Once I came here I knew Daisy had men in her room but I thought . . . Oh, I don't know what I thought. Anyway, Daniel got angry, he said if I loved him I would do it for him, it would prove how much I thought of him. He said we could start thinking about getting married. So –' Ellie opened her eyes – 'so I did it. The – the next day I think he must have put something in my drink because we'd been out, Daniel and me, and Daisy and Howard, and I came over a bit funny and that's all I remember till I woke up in bed with – with two men I didn't know. Daniel said I'd agreed to it, that me and Daisy had said we wanted some fun, but I wouldn't have. I know I wouldn't have.'

'Of course you wouldn't, I know that.'

'He got angry again when I argued with him and . . .' Her voice trailed away. She took a deep breath and whispered, 'He's all right if I do what he says, but he *would* kill me if I tried to leave, you must believe me, Ruby. And you, he'd kill you too. You don't know some of the things he's done. He'd find me wherever I went and—'

'Ellie, he's told you this to scare you but he's not omnipotent, he's not God.' The Devil, more like. 'If we go far enough—'

Now it was Ellie who interrupted Ruby, her voice gentle and almost pitying when she said quietly, 'It's no good, lass. It's too late. You have to accept that. And – and it's not too bad when you get used to it. Some of them just want a bit of comfort.'

Ruby stared at her aghast, but before she could say anything more they heard footsteps running up the stairs and then such a loud thumping on the bedroom door that they both physically jumped. Ruby stood up, but Ellie shot out of bed on the other side and pressed herself against the wall, shaking from head to foot.

'Open this damn door. You hear me, Ellie. You open it right now or I'll flay you alive.'

'It's him.' Ellie's face was chalk white and her eyes were wide with terror, like those of a trapped animal. 'You should never have come, he'll blame me.'

The thumping came again. He must be using both his fists, Ruby thought, as the door rattled and groaned on its hinges.

'I'll break it down, you hear me?'

There followed a spate of such vile obscenities that Ruby's face screwed up against them. When he paused to take breath, she swallowed deeply and willed her voice to be steady and strong. 'Mr Bell? This is Ruby Morgan, Ellie's friend.'

There was silence for a split second and then his voice came deep, like a growl. 'Aye, I know who you are, all right.'

'Then you will understand why I came to visit Ellie.' There was no point in beating about the bush. 'I came to beg her to come back home with me but she didn't know I was coming. This is all down to me, Mr Bell.'

'I don't doubt that for a second, *Miss Morgan*.' His voice was scathingly mocking now, with a dark edge of intimidation. 'And I suggest you get the hell out of my house and take them two trollops downstairs with you.'

As he finished speaking Ruby heard Flo call, 'We're here, lass, don't fret, and I've told him we're going nowhere without you.'

'Ellie, *please*.' She had to try once more, because one thing was for sure, she would never be able to come back here, not after this. 'Please come away with me now.'

Ellie bowed her head, drawing her bottom lip into her mouth. It was a habit of hers in moments of deep distress and one Ruby recognized from old. After beatings from her father or some other trauma it was as if Ellie was trying to make herself as small as possible, to shut the world out. 'I can't,' she said after a moment.

There was a finality in the two words Ruby couldn't fail to be aware of. 'Ellie, I'll go now but you know where I am and any time, any time at all you can come to me. Everything I've said holds true. We'll disappear, do anything, all right? I mean it.' Ellie didn't raise her head or look at her, and as Daniel banged on the door again, Ruby said, 'I love you, lass. You know that, don't you? You've always been like a sister to me, a proper sister, not like Olive. I'll do anything for you.'

Ellie took in a shuddering breath. 'Then go now. Go, Ruby.'

She had failed. She was going to have to leave Ellie with him, this monster. Her inward moan of protest was like a physical pain. Walking across to the door she turned the key in the lock and opened it.

Daniel had moved back a couple of paces as he had heard the key click and was now leaning against the wall, his arms folded across his chest and his eyes narrowed. She watched his mouth stretch into a sneer as he realized Ellie was staying put. 'You show your face here again, with or without the whore with the razor, and I'll do for you,' he said very softly. 'That's a promise.'

So Flo had shown him her razor, had she? Good for her. Ruby didn't look back as she walked to the stairs, but as she reached the top one, his hand came out and gripped her arm. 'One little push, that's all it'd take,' he murmured, still in the same quiet tone. 'And it'd give me great pleasure to do it.'

'Take your filthy hands off me.' She didn't shout or even raise her voice, but the steel-like quality was devoid of the fear she was feeling inside.

He let go of her but she could tell she'd got under his skin when he growled, 'Ellie's mine and she stays mine. Got it? She don't want you here no more than I do.'

She didn't reply to this but walked down the stairs to where Flo was standing with Bridget behind her. As she reached the hall, Flo said, 'The other one's in the kitchen with his lass nursing a cut lip. Daniel punched him in the gob when he found out Howard'd let us in.'

Ruby nodded. At this present moment words were beyond her. The thought of leaving Ellie here was almost more than she could bear.

'He was about to have a go at us but Flo waved the razor under his nose,' Bridget put in, her tone one of awe. She could never have squared up to him like Flo had.

'She's not coming?' Flo looked up the stairs as she spoke.

Daniel had gone into Ellie's room and shut the door and all was quiet.

Ruby shook her head. 'She's too frightened of what he'd do to her.'

Flo nodded. 'Aye, his type always pick a lass they know they can push around. I've seen it a hundred times. Meself, I'd wait till the swine was asleep and then use a knife on his wedding tackle. Still, we're all different.'

Bridget had turned and opened the front door and as they walked out of the house into the hot street Ruby paused and looked towards the stairs one last time. 'Bye, Ellie,' she said under her breath. 'I'm sorry.' Sorry for bringing her to Newcastle; sorry for not seeing what Daniel was earlier and doing something about it; sorry for leaving her here now in a life of fear and degradation . . . This was all down to her. Somehow she should have protected Ellie better.

As though Flo had read her mind, she said, 'You've done all you can, lass, and this isn't your fault.'

They began to walk, Flo and Bridget either side of her, and despite telling herself she couldn't break down, not here, in the street, Ruby's voice was choked when she said, 'I feel like it is.'

'Well, don't,' Flo said stolidly. 'She's not a bairn, she made her choices. You're not the only one who didn't like him, none of us did. We all tried to warn her not to get mixed up with Daniel Bell but she wouldn't have any of it. One of me sisters was the same. Our Kitty was a bonny lass and nice with it, you know? But she was determined to have this bloke who worked at the docks from the first time she laid eyes on him. Wouldn't hear a word said about him, even though we all felt there was something strange about him. He had a way of looking at you, I can't explain it. Anyway, they'd only bin wed some six months or so when she broke down to me mam one day and told her what'd bin going on in the bedroom. An animal, he was. Unnatural isn't the word for it. Me mam an' da said she could come home to them, and me da and brothers went round and knocked ten bells out of him that same night, but Kitty wouldn't leave him, don't ask me why. It was another month or two and then they found her with her head in the gas oven. Eighteen, she was. Me mam's never got over it.' And then, realizing the story was less than helpful in the circumstances, she added, 'Anyway, all I'm saying is that you couldn't have stopped Ellie going with him. The blighter played her like a violin from day one.'

The three of them parted company at the tram stop. Bridget and Flo had arranged to meet the rest of the crowd they hung about with and they invited Ruby along, 'to take you out of yourself' as Bridget put it. But all Ruby wanted to do was to get back to her lodgings. She felt as desolate as when she'd found out about Adam and Olive, but, as she told herself as the tram rattled along, she'd had Ellie then . . .

'I didn't know she was coming.' As Daniel closed the bedroom door and stood staring at her, Ellie was frozen with fear. 'I swear it, I had no idea. I couldn't believe my eyes. I haven't seen her since I came here, you know that. I wouldn't, Daniel.'

He continued to stare at her, enjoying the scent of her fear. Without speaking he crooked his finger, beckoning her forward, and when she was standing trembling in front of him he raised his eyebrows. 'That the truth, Ellie?'

'Yes, aye, I swear it.'

'Then you've nowt to worry about.'

'You – you believe me?'

'You might be stupid, Ellie –' he paused, then lifted her chin with one finger – 'you know you're stupid, right?' and at her nod he smiled. 'But stupid as you are, I don't think you're dim enough to go against what I've told you. Bad things happen to people who do that as I've told you before, but we won't go into that now.'

'No, Daniel.'

'And although you're none too bright and nowt to look at, I love you, don't I?'

She nodded.

'And I look after you, don't I?'

She nodded again.

'Aye, that's right. But for me you'd still be slaving away in that workhouse laundry but now you have this nice comfortable room and plenty to eat and drink, and we have fun, you an' me. I took you to the picture theatre in Westgate Road the other day, didn't I? You enjoyed that.'

Ellie stared at him. They'd left the theatre to go to a pub where Daniel had arranged to meet some 'pals', and these same pals had subjected her to two hours of rape and buggery in a room upstairs. She had found it difficult to walk or sit down for days afterwards, but when she'd cried and said she couldn't accommodate any customers for a while, he had drugged her and still let men come to the house. She said none of this, however, merely bowing her head and drawing her lip between her teeth.

'Look at me when I'm talking to you. Did you enjoy it?'

Her head shot up at his changed tone and she gabbled, 'Yes, aye, I did.'

'Aye.' He softened his voice again. 'That's a good girl.'

She was still unsure of what he was going to do, knowing from grim experience that he could be unpredictable, so when he said, 'I blame Howard for this, he should never have let them three into the house,' she sagged with relief. She had realized within twenty-four hours of moving in that Daniel called the shots and Howard did what he was told, same as most folk Daniel came into contact with. Howard was the one who let the customers in and out and remained in the house, but Daniel was always out and about somewhere. Daisy had told her that Daniel had a finger in plenty of pies and had some other girls working the streets for him. They were lucky, Daisy had said, that they had a room each here and weren't one of his lassies working the docks or the pubs. Some of them had come to a sticky end. Funny, but she didn't feel lucky, Ellie had said back, to which Daisy had just shrugged. The top two rooms of the house had been converted into one, and it was here that Daniel ran his gambling den most nights. After this finished in the early hours it was understood that she and Daisy 'entertained' any gamblers who felt so inclined.

Daniel turned, opening the door as he said, 'Put something on and come down to eat,' and for a moment she found it difficult to obey his command for amazement that she had got off so lightly. Gratitude that he wasn't going to beat her or worse brought her scrambling to comply, and once she had pulled on a dress and knotted her hair at the back of her head she found him waiting for her at the top of the stairs.

Just as he had caught hold of Ruby's arm, he now did the same with Ellie, his voice quiet as he murmured, 'I let your pal leave here in one piece this time but that don't mean I'm going soft. You know that, don't you?'

He had propelled her to the top of the steep narrow stairs as he'd spoken, and she looked down, the terror he always inspired making her stammer as she said, 'Ye– yes, I – I know.'

'Good.' He held her arm for a moment more and then said softly, 'Stop trembling. I'm not angry with you, not this time. Come and have a bite and something to drink. You've put on a bit of flesh the last few months but you're still too scrawny. Men like a lass with a bit of meat on her bones. I need to fatten you up.'

It was for all the world as though he was talking about a cow being fattened up for market, and as she followed him down the stairs, Ellie reflected that was exactly what she felt like. Cash on the hoof.

Chapter Eleven

Edward Forsythe was well aware that the young woman who had, by all accounts, saved his sister's life, would not take too kindly to him turning up on her doorstep when she was expecting Clarissa's chauffeur to call for her. There had been a finality to her goodbye on Monday evening that had stated quite clearly she wished him gone, and thinking back over their conversation when he had driven her home he had come to the conclusion that he hadn't acquitted himself particularly well. He had said as much to Clarissa when he had returned to the house and his sister, with her gift for cutting through all the flannel and getting right to the bone of something, had raised her eyebrows and said, 'And that matters to you?'

He had brooded on it all evening through the endless dinner at Lord Rochdale's before finally admitting to himself that yes, it mattered. It mattered a great deal. For some reason he wanted Miss Ruby Morgan to like him. It was as simple as that. And it was because of this that he had stated casually over breakfast the morning after the dinner that he thought he might stay in the country for a few days rather than returning straight to town, if Clarissa was happy to have him? Clarissa had been happy, as he'd known she would be. His had been a lonely childhood – his parents had had little to do with any of their offspring, preferring to leave them in the care of their nanny and the other servants, and his two older brothers had been more like twins with only fifteen months between them – but when he had returned home for the summer hols from his prep school one day when he was eight years old and found a small gurgling baby sister installed in the nursery, he'd been enchanted.

He smiled to himself as he drove, remembering how Clarissa had changed his times at home from that point. She had been a demanding baby and a stubborn toddler who had grown into a wilful and determined little girl and then an indefatigable young woman with a mind of her own, but she was also warm and generous and loving, and he had adored her, and she in her turn had adored him right back. Their parents had been nonplussed by this cuckoo in the nest who wouldn't be put in her place of being seen but not heard, and who defied them in a way he and his brothers wouldn't have dreamed of doing. They had attempted to marry her off to an earl when she was eighteen years old and had been upset at her adamant refusal of what they considered an excellent match, and when she had rebuffed the attentions of another gentleman with excellent connections the following year had been beside themselves, especially considering her interest in suffrage. And then she had met her brigadier.

Edward's smile widened. Twenty years older than Clarissa and a widower to boot, Godfrey was an army man from the top of his head to the bottom of his boots, but the two had fallen in love and nothing his parents could say had prevented the match. Godfrey was the last man in the world he would have expected his sister to marry if he was truthful but they were sublimely happy and living proof that opposites attract. Their union had, to some extent, restored his faith in the concept of true love, although he had never been assailed by the emotion himself and had no wish to be. His work was his life, and with his business interests growing in the United States of America the knowledge that he could just take off at a moment's notice without any ties to hold him down was important.

He nodded to himself, and then said out loud, 'Yes, damn important,' as though someone had challenged him on the subject. He enjoyed the company of women, both in bed and out of it, but had never felt the desire to make any of his relationships permanent, always choosing ladies of like mind. His present attachment was with a married woman in his social circle whose husband's mistress was also part of their set. Arabella and her spouse had what she called an 'open' marriage, neither one objecting to the other's dalliances elsewhere as long as there was a certain amount of discretion employed by all parties.

Thinking of his association with Arabella had wiped the smile from his face and he shifted in his seat uncomfortably as he remembered his conversation with Ruby. Arabella was typical of the social butterfly he had denounced so forcibly, he thought wryly, before justifying his hypocrisy by telling himself he had been talking about the young, unmarried flappers with their motto of 'anything goes', silly little girls who were a danger to themselves and everyone else. The excuse didn't sit well, however, and he gnawed at his lower lip for a moment, asking himself what the hell he was doing in trying to further his acquaintance with Ruby Morgan.

He brooded about it for a full minute before brushing his conscience to one side; he had had a lot of practice doing this over the last years and it came easy. Concentrating on the road, he put everything out of his mind except enjoying the feeling of being in command of the powerful car.

Ruby hadn't slept well for the last two nights, tossing and turning and worrying about Ellie, and then when she did fall into a restless slumber having disturbing nightmares she couldn't remember the moment she woke up. She had spent the previous day with Mabel, taking her landlady out to lunch before she had treated her to a Charlie Chaplin film at the local picture house. She'd long since realized Mabel was lonely and that her gruffness was a way of coping with the grief she felt about her husband and son, but in spite of their friendship which had grown over the last months, she also knew Mabel was narrow-minded and fixed in her views and if she had breathed a word about Ellie's circumstances to the land-lady, Mabel would never countenance Ellie stepping over her threshold again.

Not that there was much chance of that, Ruby reflected miserably as she got ready for her proposed lunch with Clarissa. Ellie was completely under Daniel's control and while she was useful to him he would make sure she went nowhere. Part of her wished Bridget had never told her the truth because the pain of knowing was raw. She had never liked Daniel, but before Bridget had confided in her she had been able to comfort herself that Ellie was happy. Or perhaps fool herself was the right word? Whatever, the reality of Ellie's life now was so much worse than anything her worrying had conjured up in the past.

She dressed carefully in a simple pale-grey skirt and jacket she had only finished making some weeks before, teaming it with a buttercup-yellow blouse and stylish hat in the same shade that framed her face and gave her brown eyes gold tints. It was the first time she'd had an occasion to wear the outfit, which she'd copied from a picture in *Vogue* magazine; it was too grand for everyday life and definitely upper-class, but it had been the last project before she had left her classes with Madame Poiret and she had wanted to impress her tutor. The little Frenchwoman had been fulsome in her praise of her star pupil, so much so that Ruby had been somewhat embar-rassed when she was held up as the goal the others should model their aspirations on.

'This, *this* is what makes my life worthwhile,' Madame

Poiret had said dramatically, clasping her hands together under her bosom and rolling her eyes. 'For this I endure what has to be endured.' Her black eyes had swept over the rest of the class sitting in meek silence, leaving each person in no doubt they were part of the endurance Madame was suffering. 'Miss Morgan, she listens to her mentor, yes? Not only listens but applies herself to what I say. And the result?' Her voice had risen to a rapturous quiver. 'Perfection. Yes, I say it again, perfection.' She had unclasped her plump hands and taken Ruby's and for a moment Ruby thought Madame was going to waltz her round the sewing room. Instead Madame had contented herself with a wide smile. 'Exquisite work, my dear.'

Ruby now surveyed herself in the mahogany cheval mirror she had bought shortly after beginning the classes with Madame Poiret, when she had realized the import-ance of seeing the whole of her reflection and how the clothes she was making hung on her frame. The suit was plain but screamed exclusivity and a hefty price tag; no one would dream she had made it herself. Madame had taught her the importance of cut and cloth and a hundred things beside, and she had absorbed every single detail like a sponge. Another year, maybe two, and she would have saved enough to start thinking about taking her dream to the next stage, because she didn't intend to work in a laundry for the rest of her life.

Her eyes narrowed as she adjusted her hat. Neither would she put her future happiness in the hands of any man. She intended to be in charge of her destiny. This was a new era for women but it didn't mean the fight against men's exploitation of them at every level of society was over. Far from it. Lady Russell had outlined some of the basic reforms Lady Astor was agitating for, reforms that had seen her come under savage attack by her male colleagues time and time again. Things like nursery schools, votes for women at twenty-one, equal guardianship for mothers and fathers, the abolition of the death penalty for expectant mothers, the protection of married women who lost their citizenship if they married a foreigner . . . To society's shame the list was endless.

She picked up her handbag, checking her reflection one last time, and as she stared at the woman in the looking glass who looked every inch a lady, it dawned on her how bizarre the last few days had been. One moment she'd been feted by a member of the upper class in surroundings so grand they'd taken her breath away, and the next it had been the other end of the pendulum when she'd visited Ellie down by the docks in filth and squalor. And she? Where did she fit in? she asked herself. Nowhere. She knew Flo and the others, and probably Bridget too although she wouldn't say so, thought she was an upstart, but surely you could aim to better yourself without having that tag applied? She would never deny her beginnings and she was proud of what she'd achieved thus far, but she wanted more. Much more. Not just her dress shop, although that would be a start, but she wanted to make a difference in the world somehow. But as to where she fitted in she just didn't know any more and it was a strange feeling. There were times since Ellie had gone when she felt she was alone in a little boat in the middle of the vast ocean with no one to really care if she lived or died.

Oh, for goodness' sake! Now the stare became a glare and she swung round, disgusted with herself for the brief pangs of self-pity. It was all this with Ellie that had depressed her, she told herself as she heard Mabel call her name, and no wonder, but she had to accept what she couldn't change and hope for the best for her friend. And yes, it meant she was on her own, but there were worse things than that.

Mabel called again as she opened the bedroom door, and she looked down the stairs to see the landlady standing in the hall, beckoning her furiously. She was only halfway down when Mabel hissed, 'It's him, the brother. He's just drawn up outside.'

'What?' Clarissa's chauffeur would have been bad enough but Edward Forsythe again? Oh, the neighbours would just *love* this.

'I thought she was sending *her* car?'

'So did I.'

'Well, it's him.' Mabel tucked her chin into her neck. 'What are you gonna do?'

There was nothing she could do but brave it out. Ruby's heart was racing but she took a deep intake of breath and said quietly, 'He must be staying with Clarissa for a few days and probably fancied a run out in his car, that's all.'

Mabel didn't answer but her look said everything.

'I can't stop him coming, Mabel. I didn't know, did I? Perhaps the chauffeur was busy.'

The knock came at the front door and now Mabel whispered, 'You be careful, lass. That's all I'm saying. Them nobs are a breed apart, everyone knows that. He'll be after turning your head with all his la-di-da ways and fancy talk, but them type only want one thing from a young lass and once he gets it he'll be off quicker than a dose of salts, back to his own kind.'

'Mabel, I'm going for lunch with his sister, that's all.'

'You might think that and the sister might an' all, but take it from me, lass, that beggar's got something else on his mind than lunch.'

'Oh, Mabel.' It wasn't funny, her name would be mud in the street, but Ruby couldn't help giggling at the older woman's outrage. On impulse she bent forward and placed a swift kiss on Mabel's cheek.

'What's that for?' Mabel asked in surprise.

'For caring,' Ruby said softly.

Taken aback by the show of affection and not a little embarrassed, Mabel shook her head. 'Go on with you, you soft ha'p'orth,' she muttered to hide the lump in her throat the caress had caused. It had been a long, long time since anyone had kissed her.

The knock came again and they looked at each other for a moment before Ruby whispered, 'If I'm not back by midnight send out a search party.'

'Many a true word has been spoken in jest,' Mabel

said darkly. She didn't go back into the front room but stood just behind Ruby and when the door was open stared silently at the man standing on the pavement.

Edward was smiling, his voice light as he said, 'We meet again, Miss Morgan.'

'Hello, Mr Forsythe.'

He was well aware her tone was cool and that the middle-aged woman standing behind her was staring at him with open hostility. Nevertheless, he allowed his eyes to rest on the little woman for a moment as he drawled, 'I'm sorry, we haven't been introduced. I'm Edward Forsythe, Clarissa Palmerston's brother.'

Flushing slightly, Ruby turned, saying, 'This is my friend and landlady, Mrs Duffy.'

'How do you do?' Edward extended his hand and unsmilingly Mabel took it but didn't say a word, her eyes narrowing.

Far from wanting to kiss Mabel, Ruby now had the desire to shake her. Stepping down into the street, she said, 'Shall we?' to Edward, and as he opened the car door for her and she settled herself down into the plush leather seat she stared straight ahead without so much as glancing towards the house.

As Edward walked round the car's bonnet she was aware of him looking at her but she didn't return his gaze, and not until he had slid in beside her and started the engine did she say, 'I'm sorry about Mrs Duffy, Mr Forsythe. She's something of a mother hen with her lodgers.'

'I'm just counting myself fortunate that hens don't have teeth.'

She kept her lips tightly together to suppress a smile; then she actually laughed aloud when he added, 'But I hear they can give a nasty peck on occasion.'

'She – we – were expecting Clarissa's chauffeur.'

'And that would have been more acceptable to Mrs Duffy?'

She didn't know how to put what she had to say. She didn't want to give the impression that she imagined he was interested in her in any way – she knew that was ridiculous for a man of his station in life and furthermore they hadn't exactly hit it off a couple of days ago – but at the same time she felt she owed it to Mabel to explain. Awkwardly, she said, 'I think she was considering how the neighbours might view someone like you arriving on her doorstep. Gossip is the lifeblood of most of them.'

'Someone like me?' he asked interestedly.

He must know what she meant. Her voice slightly reproving now, and determined not to feed his ego in any way, she said, 'Let's just say that most of the men hereabouts have a bicycle in the way of transport, and that's if they're lucky.'

'Ahh . . .' And then he sat up straighter, shooting her a swift glance as he said, 'I haven't compromised you in any way, have I? I never intended . . .'

'It's quite all right.' It wasn't, but she could hardly say, 'Yes, they'll all have me as your mistress by nightfall if they haven't already.'

A silence ensued between them for a moment; then Edward, his voice devoid of the thread of laughter it had held thus far, said quietly, 'Please accept my apology, Miss Morgan. I didn't think—' He stopped abruptly. 'But I should have, I see that now.'

Of course he didn't think; his world was so far removed from hers as here to the moon. She didn't doubt that it was perfectly acceptable among the fashionable upper class and Hooray Henrys for men and women to socialize and get up to who knew what without an eyebrow being raised. But no, that wasn't quite fair; whatever Edward Forsythe might be, he wasn't a Hooray Henry. She slanted her eyes towards him and saw that he seemed genuinely concerned.

'If narrow-minded gossips add one and one and make ten, that's their mistake,' she said softly.

'Yes, but—'

'Did you enjoy your dinner at Lord Rochdale's?'

Taking the hint, Edward bowed to the change in conversation. 'Let's just say that enjoyment and Lord Rochdale don't go hand in hand,' he said drily, 'although I have to admit Lady Russell's presence livened things up a bit. I should have known, being one of Clarissa's friends, that she wouldn't be shy about making her opinions known, but once or twice I don't think the poor old boy knew what had hit him. He's old school and set in his ways and used to having everyone agree with him, so when they locked horns neither would give way.'

'Good for Lady Russell.'

He grinned. 'I thought you might say that. She's certainly a born fighter.'

'Most women are – we have to be.'

'Because it's a man's world?' The mocking note was back.

'Because men have always been determined to make it so and still are, despite the fact that not one of you would be here if it wasn't for the privilege of being carried in a woman's body for nine months.'

'Believe me, I'm for you, not against you.'

'Really?' Ruby said coolly, resenting the slightly patronizing quality to his voice. 'Have you ever really thought about the judicial unfairness, lack of impartiality at every level of government and the exploitation by men of women and children both in the home and at work and society as a whole? Any show of aggression by women is condemned outright, and yet the male cult of hard drinking in all classes and the violence it causes, and the confrontational attitude to change by men, is considered "natural". You live and work in the city, Mr Forsythe. How many women are given the same chances of employment as men in your type of business? Don't tell me you are for my sex until you are prepared to stand up for equal rights and opportunities, even if the "best man winning" means the person concerned is a woman.'

This time the silence stretched on for a while. Ruby was conscious of the view outside the car; of streets flashing by, bairns playing, women standing and gossiping at open doors or walking with shopping baskets, of horse and carts, bicycles and the odd car or two, but it was all on the perimeter of her mind. She was vitally aware of the man at the side of her, of the bulk of him, the clean fresh smell she'd noticed previously, of his hands at the wheel, and most of all his quietness. Had she offended him? she asked herself, her heart beating faster than was comfortable. Well, that couldn't be helped. He had been laughing at her. Oh, not in a nasty way, she'd give him that, but nevertheless there had been an element of condescension, like the way some folk talked down to a bairn.

They had reached the outskirts of the town and had turned onto a country road with farmer's fields on either side when he spoke again. 'You're not an easy person to be around, Miss Morgan.'

For a moment she felt a sense of deep hurt, before telling herself not to be so pathetic. She hardly knew this man and she didn't care what he thought of her. She had spoken the truth and if he couldn't handle it, that was his problem.

'But an extremely interesting one, nevertheless,' he continued before she could summon a suitable reply. 'Tell me, are you always so forthright?'

'I think so, yes.'

'Then it's not just your disapproval of me?'

She had to wet her lips before she said, 'I don't disapprove of you. How could I? I barely know you,' speaking out her earlier thought.

'No, that is true, you don't.'

'Look, Mr Forsythe—'

'And never will if you persist in being so formal.' The black eyebrows came together in a frown. 'Edward really isn't such a difficult name to say, is it? Now if it was Ethelbert like one poor devil I know, or perhaps Egidius, I could understand it. Egidius was a pal at university and his parents had apparently thought it clever to give him the Latin form of Giles. Needless to say he didn't agree.'

Ruby stared at him. 'You're making that up, about Egidius.' She couldn't imagine parents calling their son Ethelbert either, come to that.

'Not at all.'

'Poor thing.'

'Quite.' A few moments passed before he said quietly, 'I wanted to call and take you to Foreburn today, I won't pretend otherwise. I felt our previous meeting didn't go too well, Miss Morgan.'

Oh, dear. Perhaps he *was* one of the womanizers Mabel had spoken of, after all. Keeping her voice light, Ruby said, 'And you think today is going better?'

Now he actually laughed out loud. 'Oh, no,' he said ruefully, 'I'm afraid not. We seem to meet head on if we say more than two words to each other, don't we, and I don't quite understand why. I was being completely genuine when I said I support all the aims that you and my sister campaign for. I totally accept that the expansion of women's liberty needs women like Lady Astor who aren't afraid to call a spade a spade and stand up to bullies. I applauded the way she handled that swine Bottomley when she first came to the House, for example.

He'd cowed most of his colleagues into a state of submission through being the proprietor of that muck-raking journal, *John Bull*, and thought he could do the same to her by printing a pack of lies and innuendos about her marriage, but she responded with dignity and courage and showed him up for the paragon of unpleasantness he is. I do wonder if he'd have been sent to jail for financial impropriety a couple of years later but for her. But that is by the by. Suffice to say I am not your enemy as I have said before, Miss Morgan.'

'I never imagined you were.' Quite what Edward Forsythe was, however, she wasn't sure. Coming to a decision, she added, 'And the name is Ruby.'

It was highly unlikely their paths would cross again after today; his sister had been generous in her invitation to lunch, but their different stations in life meant that once this holiday week was over and she was back working at the laundry, normal life would resume. There was no need to be concerned about Edward taking liberties. She would never see him again.

Edward smiled to himself. The first battle had been won, but he fancied there would be many more in the future. Because one thing was for sure – meeting Ruby Morgan again confirmed what he now admitted he had known since the moment he laid eyes on her in Clarissa's drawing room: she was going to be part of his life. He would make sure of it.

PART THREE

Goodbyes, Reconciliations and New Beginnings

1926

Chapter Twelve

The start of another year. Olive gazed across the bedroom to the faint light coming in the window. Although it was only five o'clock in the morning and still dark outside, the thick snow that lay on the rooftops and made the roads and pavements treacherous brought illumination into the room. *How could she endure another year like the last one and those before it?*

Adam stirred at the side of her, his snores faltering for a few moments before he grunted and turned over, one arm falling across her waist. Olive lay absolutely still, scarcely breathing, and when she was sure he was fast off again she slid slowly out of the bed. Only when she stood up did she start to breathe normally.

The room was like an ice box. Dressing swiftly and silently, she told herself she'd have a good strip-down wash later when Adam was at work. She'd bring the tin bath through and fill it in front of the range when Alice had her midday nap. Until then she would have to put up with the smell of him on her.

He hadn't bothered her for some weeks before last night – she supposed she ought to be thankful for that – but he had been three sheets to the wind when they'd got back from the New Year's Eve jollities and carry-on at his mam's. Once she'd settled Alice down and come into their room, he'd been waiting for her.

She shut her eyes for a moment. It had only been in the last year that he had started drinking and then, to be fair, not often, but the indignities he inflicted on her when he was in his cups were ten times worse than his usual demands. Whilst most of the women hereabouts complained about their men's reduced pay packets and longer working hours, calling Churchill and his gang every name under the sun, she was grateful that it meant there just wasn't the money for Adam to spend on beer, not normally. But there were still the times when his da and brothers persuaded him to keep them company after a shift, or the infamous Gilbert family gatherings to celebrate something or other. The first time he'd got drunk again, after the fateful night Alice was conceived, was the New Year's Eve before this one, and when, the next morning, she had remarked that she thought he was against getting legless, he'd stared at her with red rimmed eyes and mumbled something about, 'If you can't beat 'em, join 'em.'

She turned, staring at the humped form under the mound of blankets and thick eiderdown.

She would never have believed that Ruby's Adam – the happy, funny boy who'd grown into a happy, funny youth

– could have turned into the man he was today. Even his own mam said he had changed beyond recognition and she knew everyone blamed her for the way he was. And it *was* her fault, she knew that. Losing Ruby had infected him like a malignant disease.

Before going downstairs she checked on Alice. Her daughter was just over three now and every day Olive marvelled how something so bonny and perfect could have come from her body. Alice was fast asleep, curled under the covers like a small animal in its nest, and as Olive gently turned back the clothes a few inches she could see the outline of her child's face in the dim light, her amazingly long lashes lying like a dark smudge on her sleep-flushed skin and her beautiful chestnut hair tumbled about her face and shoulders. Everyone adored Alice – everyone except her father that was, Olive thought as her thin mouth pulled tight – and her two grandmas were besotted with her. How much that was to do with the fact that Adam would have little to do with her, she didn't know. His mam had been the only one, besides herself, who had dared to take him to task on the matter and by her own account she'd received short shrift. But no amount of love and fondness by the rest of the family could make up for the lack of it in Alice's own da, and the child, small as she was, was affected by his coldness towards her.

Olive tiptoed out of the bedroom, the familiar weight of self-condemnation and remorse heavy on her heart. She would give her life for her child without a second thought, but through something she had done Alice was the one who had to pay for it every day of her life. The look in her bairn's eyes sometimes when her da pushed her away or spoke sharply was almost more than she could bear, but for some reason the older Alice had got the more she tried to please him, to get him to love her. It had been easier in one way when Alice was a baby and had been frightened of him, much as she'd hated that, but over the last year that fear had gone and she didn't understand why.

Once in the kitchen, the only warm room in the house, she stoked up the fire in the range, which she'd left banked up with slack and damp tea leaves the night before, and went out into the small yard, which she tried to keep clear of snow. There had been a light fall during the night and the tap in the yard had frozen again in the sub-zero temperatures that had persisted for weeks, but she had been expecting this and had brought a small roll of burning paper to push up the spout. It took a couple of trips back indoors and more burning paper before she was rewarded by a trickle, but once the water was flowing she filled up the big iron kettle and set it on the hob in the kitchen. She normally left the kettle full before she went to bed but Adam had decided to sluice his upper body and wash his hair before they had gone to his mother's the previous night. She hadn't refilled it before they'd left and it had been after two in the morning when they'd got home.

Fifteen minutes later when Adam came downstairs she

had a pot of tea on the table and within moments set his bowl of steaming porridge in front of him. He sat down and began eating as she poured him a cup of tea before seeing to his bait, which was four thick slices of bread and jam and a bottle of cold tea. Once she'd packed it into his knapsack and he'd finished the porridge, he reached for his jacket and cap, thrust his feet into the big steel-capped boots by the back door and left the house with the knapsack over one arm. Not a word had passed between them, but once the back door had closed behind him Olive let out a long deep breath, consciously relaxing tense muscles, and plumped down on a kitchen chair.

After a few moments of staring into space she glanced round her. The kitchen was as clean as a new pin and the blackleaded range was shining, the coal in the open fireplace glowing a deep red and this, combined with the flickering light from the oil lamp in the middle of the table which she had lit first thing, lent a cosy comfort to the surroundings. For the hundredth time since she had married Adam, she told herself she could be happy if only things were different between them. She didn't mind that they had to watch every penny and rob Peter to pay Paul every week, or that life was a daily struggle to make ends meet; wasn't it the same for everyone? Adam was earning less than when they'd first wed and working longer hours for it, and everyone knew that when the government stopped paying the coal owners the subsidy at the end of April, the unions and the coal owners would go head to head. Life was uncertain now but it would get ten times worse then. The owners and the Tories were determined to have a contest of strength with the miners and destroy the unions once and for all; the men had talked of nothing else at the get-together last night, and Adam's mam and his brothers' wives had confessed they were worried about what the year would bring.

Olive rose to her feet and made another pot of tea, and once it was mashed she poured herself a cup. She and Adam drank it black now; his wage didn't run to them having milk and sugar although she made sure Alice had her milk each day.

The sky was lightening outside the window but it was low and heavy, threatening more snow. For once, Olive let her mind wander, probably because she was tired after the late night and not least bruised and sore after Adam's rough handling of her.

It was nearly four years since she had last seen Ruby. There had been times, in the dead of night when the rest of the world was asleep, when she had imagined herself going to Newcastle and searching and searching until she found her sister. After begging Ruby to forgive her a reconciliation would follow, and then Ruby would accompany her home to see their parents. Their mam and da missed her, and since their da had become bedridden twelve months ago she knew he brooded more about things. But then, in the cold light of day, she accepted it was an impossible undertaking. Ruby wrote to their mam every two or three months to say she was well and doing all right but never gave any hint of where she was living or working; it would be like looking for a needle in a haystack. And how would Adam react if he saw Ruby again? Things were bad enough as it was.

She heard the patter of little feet on the wooden stairs and the next moment Alice came bounding into the kitchen clutching her teddy bear. The bear was threadbare and patched and missing an eye; it had once been hers, and probably because of that it was the child's favourite toy and she wouldn't settle down for sleep without him.

Olive held out her arms and Alice threw herself into them, snuggling into her mother's chest before she drew away and said, 'Milk, please, Mam.'

Olive hugged her daughter tight and then lifted her into her highchair. The day was beginning and she had no more time for introspection, which was a good thing. Alice slept well but when she was awake she was on the go a hundred per cent. 'A live wire,' her da called his granddaughter, and Olive could remember that Ruby had been the same. In fact, there was a great deal about her daughter that reminded her of Ruby.

Shutting the door on that particular avenue of thought Olive busied herself with Alice's beaker of warm milk, and as she fell into the routine of the morning, listening to the child's chatter and watching her sunny little face, she counted her blessings.

As long as she had Alice nothing else mattered.

Olive would have been amazed to know that Adam was thinking about Alice too as he stepped into the cage that would take him and the rest of the fore shift into the bowels of the earth. Neither the gate slamming shut nor the cage taking off with a clash impinged on his thoughts; this had been his daily experience for years and the speed and seeming lack of control with which they descended was second nature to him.

Unbeknown to Olive, he had looked in on Alice before he had gone downstairs to the kitchen. He often did this when he could be sure Olive was occupied downstairs, because he would rather have been hanged, drawn and quartered than admit to his growing affection for his daughter. He hadn't wanted to become fond of the child and he had fought the emotion since the day she was born. It had been easier when she was a baby. He had been able to say to himself that the infant was merely a biological product of an act of lust on his part and cunning manipulation on Olive's, and that, along with her mother, she repulsed him. Through her conception he had lost the woman he loved and become trapped in a living nightmare – why wouldn't he hate and resent her? He *wanted* to hate and resent her. And then one day just over twelve months ago Alice had been toddling about in the backyard when he'd come home from his shift and had fallen over in front of him, grazing her knees. And it was what the child had done next that had got to him. Through her tears she had lifted her arms to be picked up and said, 'Dada.'

The word had cut through all his carefully built defences like a knife through butter. He had stood there like a moron staring down at her, and but for Olive rushing out into the yard and whisking Alice up into her arms he would have betrayed himself then and there by picking her up and comforting her. Olive had glared at him and even accused him of pushing the child if he remembered correctly, and in the row that had followed the moment of weakness had passed. But it was from then that something had changed, as much with Alice as himself. He had still maintained the stiff, unapproachable facade and it fooled everyone but the child herself. It was as though his daughter had *seen* what he'd felt – that was the only way he could describe her sudden lack of fear regarding him – and it had melted his heart. He hadn't wanted it to happen but now it had he was powerless before the emotions it invoked. She was his daughter. This perfect little creature with her huge eyes and sweet nature was part of him, and although the new awareness was hard because it constantly tore him apart inside when he told himself Ruby should have been her mother, he couldn't fight the love. He had imagined the drink would help and when he got legless it did put a balm on the rawness for a few brief hours, but once he was sober again the knowledge of what a hell of a mess he'd made of his life would grip him even more strongly.

The cage clanged to a stop and he let the other miners go first, several of whom – including his brothers – looked as hungover as he felt. His father was the last one to leave in front of him and as they walked into the main road, which was well lit, unlike where they'd be working, his father turned and said, 'All right, lad?'

He nodded. He knew his mam and da worried about him but he didn't want their concern or their pity; he just wanted to be left alone.

'Your mam was wondering if you and Olive and the bairn'd be round on Sunday?'

He shook his head. 'Things to do,' he said briefly. He knew if he went it would turn into another drinking session with his father and brothers once Sunday tea was over and the women and bairns took over the front room while the menfolk stayed in the kitchen, and he wanted neither the drink nor the conversation which would centre exclusively on the coal owners and what the unions should do. He had to get a handle on the drink, he knew that; he couldn't carry on as he was.

His father shrugged. 'Please yourself,' he said as he turned and walked on ahead. 'But you know you're always welcome, and your mam likes to see Olive and the bairn.'

Adam gritted his teeth but didn't reply. He had no real beef with his parents except that they seemed determined to forget how Olive had tricked him into getting wed and to act as though their marriage was a normal one. They'd even grown to like Olive; his mam in particular showed her approval in a hundred little ways that grated on him every time they were round there. 'No one makes a fruit cake like Olive.' 'There's not a bairn as well turned out as our little Alice.' 'Never seen a speck of dirt in your kitchen, lass.' Oh, aye, he'd heard it all.

He walked behind his da and the others as the road got narrower and the roof got lower until they were all doubled up and only the light from their lamps pierced the darkness. No one hung about. They only got paid from the time they reached the place where they would begin work and that could take half an hour or more. It was now pitch black, blacker than the darkest night. When he was a little lad he had shut his eyes in bed sometimes and imagined that was how it was down the pit, but on his first day down he'd realized that the pit's blackness was something beyond that. It was the kind of primeval malignant darkness where you can see nothing at all no matter how long your eyes take to get used to it, something that could turn you into a gibbering idiot if you let it. That blackness could accomplish what the mice and rats and blacklocks – huge, ugly, shiny black-backed beetles with feelers as long as bootlaces and a nasty habit of dropping down your neck – couldn't do, and that was why he and the other miners took care of their lamps as though they were made of solid gold.

Once he reached the face where he was working, Adam brought his mind to bear on the job in hand and put all thoughts of his tortured private life out of his head. It was a relief to think of nothing. In fact, he often told himself his hours down the pit each day had kept him sane the last few years, and he dare bet there wasn't another miner in the county of Durham who would know what he meant if he was foolish enough to voice such a sentiment out loud.

Chapter Thirteen

It was the middle of March and for the first time in weeks the pavements were free of ice and snow due to a sudden thaw. Although still cold, the day had been bright and sunny with a clear blue sky and a smell in the air that heralded spring was definitely around the corner. A thick twilight had fallen by the time Ruby and Bridget left the workhouse, but nevertheless it felt good not to be walking along Bath Lane Terrace in complete darkness when they got off the tram. The winter had been long and hard, unemployment was rising slowly and insidiously, and several choking pea-souper smogs which had blanketed the skies over Newcastle for days on end had affected the very young and very old adversely, increasing the intake into the workhouse for the latter when illness had proved the last straw to staying in their homes. Ruby had seen first-hand that the fine line between merely being poor, and living in a poverty that became unsustainable, could be as simple as the loss of a couple of wage packets.

Bridget was in the middle of telling her about a family

that had been admitted to the workhouse the day before who had been riddled with nits, lice, ringworm, impetigo and fleas, the father crippled with arthritis and the five children bow-legged with rickets and barely able to walk, when she stopped abruptly, peering through the gathering gloom. 'Is that Daisy?' she said, as a figure stepped out of the shadows and came hurrying towards them.

Ruby's stomach turned over and her heart began to race. It had been over eighteen months since the traumatic visit to the house near the docks, and in that time she had heard nothing from Ellie. Flo had told Bridget that she'd seen Ellie in the company of Daniel a couple of times and that she'd seemed all right, but aside from that, nothing. She had written several letters to Ellie, begging her to keep in touch, but after the fifth note had been ignored like the ones before it Ruby had conceded defeat. Ellie knew where she was. Hopefully, if things became too unbearable with Daniel, Ellie would seek refuge with her.

Ellie had to come to the point herself where she felt staying with Daniel Bell was worse than the possible repercussions if she left him. It had been Edward who had said that, and Ruby could see it made sense. It said a lot for both Clarissa and Edward's persistence that Ruby now counted them as friends, but Clarissa had been determined from day one not to let the social gulf that Ruby pointed out time and time again come between them. Edward had followed his sister's lead in using a steady drip-drip approach to overcome Ruby's misgivings about their acquaintance, and had put himself forward in the guise of simply a friend. As such, Ruby accepted his presence in her life. And when his frustration at the role he was playing became too much, he would tell himself that Rome wasn't built in a day.

'Daisy?' As the other girl reached them, Ruby stared at her. The girl she remembered seeing on Daniel's landing that day had been young and, if not exactly pretty, had had a certain attractive pertness to her. Now Daisy looked scared to death and the air of jauntiness was gone. 'What is it? Is Ellie all right?'

'No. It's about her I've come. I can't be long. Dan'd kill me if he knew I was here and I've got to be there when he gets back to the house, but Howard an' me are worried she'll—' She broke off, and with a little sob, said, 'She's bad, real bad.'

'Bad?' said Ruby and Bridget in unison.

'Daniel took her to old Aggie's last night. She didn't want to but he made her. An' she was awful when she come back, I could hear her moaning and crying all night, but he don't care.' Daisy's voice was bitter. 'Went off this afternoon as happy as you like to see to some business down at the docks, an' Ellie not knowing what to do with herself. When Howard said about gettin' someone, Dan went for him, but the bleeding won't stop.'

'Daisy, who's old Aggie?'

'One of the backstreet midwives who'll fix you up if you pay for it, but they use dirty crochet hooks an' all sorts. Ellie was terrified he'd make her see one of 'em when the castor oil and hot baths didn't do it – scalded herself, she did, she had the water so hot, but nothing worked.'

Ruby's blood had run cold.

'He's a maniac, that Daniel,' Daisy went on. 'Howard's had enough of him and this is the final straw. We're gonna clear off down south on the quiet, but don't tell him that,' she added, looking suddenly terrified.

'I've got to go to her.' Ruby looked at Bridget. 'Make some excuse to Mrs Duffy about where I am, say there was an emergency at the workhouse and I've agreed to stand in for someone, something like that.'

'You can't, lass. What if he comes back and finds you there?' Bridget was literally wringing her hands in distress.

'I don't care. She needs a doctor.' They'd had a young girl left at the workhouse doors just the other day who'd had a botched abortion. Terrified at the shame of un-married motherhood, the fifteen-year-old had attempted to terminate her pregnancy with the help of her mother using a home-made purgative containing soap and aloes and liquid paraffin, and when that hadn't worked, her mother's knitting needle. She wouldn't give her name or say where she lived and had died in agony of an incomplete abortion that had also punctured her bowels, and had been buried in a pauper's grave without even her name to mark the place. Ruby had spoken with Clarissa about it and her friend had said it was one of the things Lady Russell was campaigning about; up and down the country the gynaecological wards in hospitals were full of women suffering terribly for the same reason and many died, most of them from the working class.

'Widespread ignorance about sexual matters is a huge national hazard,' Clarissa had stated without a trace of embarrassment, 'and some married women don't know how a baby is born even when well into their first pregnancy. It's a disgrace. Most women have no idea they can take measures to prevent conception, and many men can't be shaken from the belief that any form of contraception leads to sterility. I mean, French letters were distributed to soldiers in the war to prevent the spread of sexually transmitted diseases – what's wrong with using them in peace time? Of course, the fact that a packet of ten costs ten shillings could have something to do with it for the poor. Lady Russell believes they should be free if necessary. How else are we going to stop unwanted pregnancies or tragedies like the poor girl you mentioned?'

When Ruby had confessed that she had no idea what French letters were or what was involved in the birth of a baby, it had led to a frank and revealing conversation that had opened her eyes good and proper about many things she'd hitherto only had a vague idea about.

Now, armed with that knowledge and the realization that Daniel clearly hadn't seen fit to protect Ellie in any way from getting pregnant by one of her customers, either with one of the Dutch caps that Clarissa had told her about or by providing French letters for the men to use, Ruby was angrier than she had ever been.

Leaving Bridget staring anxiously after them, Ruby

and Daisy hurried away to catch a tram, which thankfully arrived just as they reached the tram stop. They didn't talk much during the journey – there wasn't much to say after all – but Daisy sat biting at her nails and giving little worried glances every minute or so as though Daniel was going to appear out of thin air.

It was as they left the vehicle and sped off towards Lombard Street that Ruby said, 'Why didn't she leave him and come to me, Daisy, when she knew she was pregnant? I could have helped her, she must have known I'd do anything for her.'

'She was frightened for you, lass.' Daisy shook her head. 'You've got no idea what Dan's capable of – he's a devil, I tell you straight. Howard got mixed up with him before he knew what Dan was really like and then he was too scared to leave, and he's a bloke, not like Ellie. I said to Ellie to come to you but she said she couldn't let anything happen to you because of her. She – she thinks the world of you, lass.'

Through the lump in her throat, Ruby managed to say, 'I think the world of her too, Daisy.' And this time she was going to get Ellie out of there. She didn't care if Daniel Bell came back before she managed to spirit Ellie away – she'd fight him physically if she had to – but she wasn't going to leave Ellie in his clutches a moment longer.

When they reached Lombard Street Ruby saw three or four women with shawls over their heads standing huddled together close to Daniel's house. As she and Daisy approached them, one called out, 'Your man's bin sticking his head out of the door every two minutes since you've been gone, but the other one's not back yet. Reckon old Aggie's done for her – she oughta be locked up, the dirty old crone.'

Daisy didn't reply to this; instead she gestured at Ruby. 'This is Ellie's pal, the one I told you about earlier. She's goin' to get Ellie away from here, Moll. Away from him.'

The woman looked at Ruby, taking in her fashionable coat and hat and her feet shod in smart leather shoes. Her tone doubtful, she said, 'You ought to have brought a bloke an' all, Daisy. There'll be ructions if Bell turns up.'

Daisy shrugged her shoulders and opened the front door of the house. A groaning wail was coming from upstairs and it was spine-chilling. As they climbed the stairs it changed in pitch so it didn't sound human, more the sort of shriek an animal might make if it was caught in a trap.

Howard came out of Ellie's room to meet them and his face was as white as a sheet, his former bravado gone. 'She's not stopped since you've been gone,' he muttered to Daisy. 'I can't stand no more of this.'

He couldn't stand any more? Ruby brushed past him and the metallic smell of blood hit her as she walked into the room. The bed was soaked with it and there were pools on the floor; she wouldn't have believed a human body had so much. Ellie was lying with her knees up to her stomach on her side moaning softly now, and then the awful cry came again, shrill and stretched out, and Daisy began to sob.

It was as she reached the bed that Ruby saw the pitiful little creature between Ellie's legs. The miniature human being was perfect but so tiny the little girl had had no chance of surviving out of her mother's body. Telling herself she had to concentrate on Ellie and with tears streaming down her face, Ruby looked at Howard who was standing transfixed in the doorway, visibly shaking. Ellie was a hundred times worse than she could have imagined; they were going to need transport to get her to hospital.

'There was a horse-drawn cab outside the bank on the corner when we passed a minute ago,' she said huskily. 'See if it's still there, pay the driver anything he wants, and if it's gone, get something else. Here, take my purse.'

Howard shook his head, turning as he said, 'I've got money.'

Thanks to her conversation with Clarissa, Ruby knew what to do to separate mother and child, and after Daisy had fetched a pair of scissors and a clothes peg, they did the necessary and then stripped Ellie of her nightclothes and dragged the filthy sheet from under her, pulling a clean nightie over her blood-caked body and wrapping her cocoon fashion in a fresh sheet. Ellie seemed unaware of what was happening and although still moaning was a little quieter, but already blood was seeping through the sheet.

Sick with fear, Ruby kept up a steady stream of reassurance as they pulled a thick eiderdown round Ellie, but she doubted if her friend could hear her. She herself was now smeared with Ellie's blood as was Daisy, and as they heard Howard running up the stairs, they both sagged with relief.

Howard came panting into the room. 'I caught the cabby an' explained what was what. He wasn't too keen to have her in his cab at first but I gave him five bob on account and told him we'd pay whatever he asked if he gets us there.'

Ruby was glad of Howard as she and Daisy had tried to lift Ellie out of bed after they'd changed her clothes and they'd all nearly landed up on the floor. Howard simply bent down and lifted her, eiderdown and all, into his arms, carrying her out of the room behind Ruby. It was as Ruby reached the head of the stairs that Daniel walked in the front door.

He looked up at them, his face showing his surprise for a split second before he said, his eyes unblinking, 'And where do you think you're going?'

'I'm taking Ellie to hospital.' Funnily enough, now he was here the fear of him had fled and all she felt was a rage that had her wanting to tear him limb from limb. If she'd had a weapon in her hand she would have used it without compunction and relished doing so.

His gaze moved to Howard behind her. 'Take her back to her room,' he said softly. 'I'll deal with you later. And as for you, my fine lady, I told you what I'd do next time you poked your nose in my business.'

'She's going to hospital.' Far from being cowed, Ruby began to walk down the stairs, praying that Howard and

Daisy would follow. If they stood by her she could still get Ellie out.

His eyes narrowed. 'The hell she is. She'll be right as rain in a day or two and I'm not having no doctor asking questions about this and that.'

She had reached the hall and he was between her and the front door, which was slightly ajar. Howard was behind her and Daisy now moved up to stand at the side of her. Their combined attitude of defiance wasn't what Daniel had expected, Ruby could tell that, but neither was he giving way. Ellie was quieter than she had been – whether she was unconscious or not Ruby didn't know – but then she gave one of the animal-like moans and Ruby didn't hesitate. Walking up to Daniel, her voice almost a growl, she said, 'Get out of my way, you Devil in hell.'

His answer was to raise his hand and slap her so hard across the face that she catapulted into Daisy and then slammed hard against the wall. She didn't have to think about what to do next. She launched herself at him, swinging her handbag wildly so it hit him full in the face, and suddenly it was Daniel screaming. He clutched at his eye, blood spurting between his fingers. Ruby realized the metal clasp must have caught him. She'd cut her finger on it only the other day, but as he stumbled towards the kitchen it was their chance to escape. Once outside, she bundled Howard and Ellie into the cab, she and Daisy climbing in after them, and the cab driver needed no encouragement to be off. They were halfway down the street when Daniel emerged with a roar from the house, clutching a bloody towel to his face and shouting and swearing at the cab driver to stop.

Ruby instructed the cabby to drive straight to the work-house where the hospital was situated. Five years previously the administration for the infirmary was separated from the rest of the workhouse and the infirmary's name was changed to the Wingrove Hospital, and it was now an efficient and well-run building within the work-house. Once they'd arrived, the fact that Ruby held a position of authority at the workhouse enabled her to cut through the normal red tape involved with admissions, and when Matron Henderson was called by the officer in charge she aided Ruby in this, whilst making it clear she thoroughly disapproved of Ellie's circumstances.

The chief gynaecologist was called in, and he operated on Ellie within an hour of them arriving at the hospital. Once Ellie was back on the ward and heavily sedated, he didn't mince words with Ruby who had obtained special permission from Matron Henderson to remain sitting by Ellie's bed.

'She's been butchered,' he said grimly. 'I've done all I can but she's very ill indeed. You're her friend, I under-stand? Do you have any idea who's done this to her?'

Ruby stared at Ellie. She was drained of colour and completely still. She already looked like a corpse. Only the faintest of pulses told the nurse consigned to check her every few minutes that her patient was still alive.

'Oh, yes, I know.' She dragged her eyes from Ellie. 'A woman called Aggie did the abortion, but it was the man Ellie lives with who took her to this Aggie and made her go through with it. She didn't want to but he forced her.'

The gynaecologist nodded. He already had a pretty good idea of the relationship between his patient and this man, having seen it all a hundred times before. Prostitution was rife in the city and had got worse as the slump had continued. The men who controlled these girls were ruthless and only interested in the money they could earn.

He stared at the well-dressed young woman in front of him. He knew from the matron that Miss Morgan was a respectable and intelligent individual and he wondered how she had come to be mixed up with the poor girl in the bed. But that was by the by. It made his blood boil to see what he'd seen this night.

His voice grim, he said, 'It's rare that names are named in circumstances like this. Are you prepared to speak out, Miss Morgan? To tell the authorities what you know?'

She nodded. 'His name's Daniel Bell and I want him to pay for what he's done to Ellie.'

'Is there anyone who can support your accusation?'

'The couple I came with know what happened.'

'So you have no objection to the police being informed?'

'None at all.' She just hoped Daisy and Howard would be prepared to stand up to Daniel Bell. They had left the hospital shortly after Ellie had been taken to theatre, but Daisy had promised her she would come back to see Ellie in the morning, although it had been obvious the pair of them were terrified at the prospect of facing Daniel after what had happened at the house.

Ruby spent the rest of the night holding Ellie's limp hand in hers, crying and begging God to spare her. Ellie couldn't die, she told herself – and God – over and over again. Her friend had had such a horrible life with her mam and da, and then since meeting Daniel Bell it had got so much worse. She couldn't bear to think of what Ellie must have been subjected to. Once she was over this, she would take care of Ellie for the rest of her life or as long as Ellie needed her. She'd forget the dream of a dress shop; compared to Ellie's well-being it was nothing. She could use the money she had saved thus far for a deposit on a small house for the two of them and carry on working at the laundry. Matron Henderson had hinted more than once that the job of head laundress would be hers in due course. She would do anything, *anything* if Ellie could get well; her life couldn't end in this terrible way.

It was seven o'clock in the morning when Ellie gave a great shuddering sigh and opened her eyes. She didn't ask where she was or move so much as a finger – it was clear she didn't have the strength – but she looked straight at Ruby as though she had known she'd be there, giving her such a sweet smile that Ruby's eyes filled with tears despite the promise she'd made to herself that she wouldn't let Ellie see her cry. She had to be strong for her.

'Ruby . . .' It was the faintest of whispers.

'Hello, lass.' Ruby kissed her cheek, stroking a strand

of hair from her forehead. 'You frightened me,' she said softly, 'but you are all right now and I'm here and I'm staying.'

'I . . . I didn't want to do it.'

'I know, lass, I know. Don't talk. Save your strength to get well.'

'He – he made me drink something and then I couldn't stop him taking me there. My baby . . .'

'Don't think about that now, please, Ellie, don't.' Ruby wanted to make it all better but she couldn't. 'You're safe and I promise I'll look after you from now on. We'll get a little house together – you'd like that, wouldn't you? Just the two of us where we can be together again.'

Ellie whispered something but Ruby had to lean right over her before she could make out what her friend was trying to say. 'Daniel . . . Be careful.'

'Forget about him, he'll never hurt you again. No one will and I'm not frightened of him, Ellie.'

The great eyes in the chalk-white face were pleading for something, but again Ruby had to put her ear to Ellie's mouth, so faint was the whisper. 'Do you think I'll be with my baby?'

'Oh, Ellie, lass, don't talk like that, you're going to get well,' Ruby murmured softly as she straightened up. 'I promised I'd call the nurse if you woke up – I won't be a minute.' But then, as Ellie's fingers moved to grip hers, she whispered, 'All right, I won't go, but shut your eyes now and go back to sleep. I'm here and I won't leave you.' She bent over and kissed Ellie's cheek again, and when she drew back it was a few moments before she realized what had happened. Ellie had gone. Just like that.

She stared at the still figure, an emotion tearing through her that was too great to express and compounded of such grief and loss and disbelief that its very intensity was numbing. This wasn't real, it couldn't be. In a minute or two Ellie would take another breath and then another and another. Anything else was unthinkable. She sat willing it to happen, believing it, screaming it in her head because if she didn't accept that Ellie was gone, then it wasn't true.

Even though she knew it was.

Chapter Fourteen

Daisy and Howard arrived at the workhouse just as Ruby walked out through its gates. The weather had changed again and a few desultory snowflakes were beginning to drift from a low, leaden sky as she saw Daisy jump down from the horse and cart Howard was driving and come towards her. As Daisy reached her, she said softly, 'Oh, no, lass, no. She's not passed?'

Ruby nodded, she couldn't speak. She felt her heart had been cut out, the feeling a hundred times worse than when she'd found out about Adam and Olive. She had remained sitting by Ellie until the nurse had come to check her again, and when the girl had said quietly, 'I'm afraid it was too much for her,' and had leaned across to pull the sheet over Ellie's face, she had made the nurse jump when she'd said sharply, 'No, don't do that, she likes the light, she's always liked the light. Her da used to shut her in a cupboard when she was little and she's frightened if she can't see anything.'

The nurse hadn't said anything to that, but when ten

minutes later she still hadn't been able to persuade Ruby to let go of Ellie's hand, she had fetched her superior, who in turn had sent for Matron Henderson. She hadn't cried in front of them – the shock of Ellie's passing had been too great for tears – but she had been adamant they weren't taking Ellie down to the morgue. It would be Ellie's worse nightmare to be shut in there.

It had been Bridget coming on duty that had broken the impasse. Matron Henderson had brought Bridget to her and after a while Ruby had been persuaded to leave Ellie's side. Bridget had taken Ruby through to the laundry and everyone had been very gentle with her, helping her to wash and then sponging down her coat and dress, which had Ellie's blood on them, and cleaning her shoes. Ruby had submitted to their ministrations in a kind of vacuum. It had only been when they'd tried to persuade her to eat something that she had protested. Matron Henderson had come to see her shortly afterwards and had insisted she go home and rest and she hadn't argued. In truth, she felt nauseous and her head was thudding.

Now, as Daisy put her arm round her, she said, 'Come on, lass, me an' Howard'll take you home.'

Ruby looked across at Howard sitting holding the reins. 'No, it's all right. I can catch the tram.'

'We're taking you, lass. You're in no fit state. Besides, I need to fill you in on what's been happening while you've been at the hospital.'

It was only as Daisy helped her climb up onto the

thin plank seat of the cart that Ruby noticed the back held a number of boxes and bags. As Daisy followed her gaze, she said, 'We're going down south, lass, to make a new start. When we got back last night Dan was ranting and raving about the mess you've made of his face. I reckon he might have lost the eye, it looks real bad. Anyway, him an' Howard had a fight and Daniel said he was throwing us out an' Howard said that was fine by him. Me an' Howard went to get this horse an' cart from a pal of Howard's, paid through the nose but beggars can't be choosers, an' while we were out, Moll said the Old Bill turned up saying it was to do with Ellie. Did you give 'em his name?'

Ruby nodded.

'Oh, lass, you shouldn't have done that.'

Quite why she shouldn't, Ruby wasn't sure, but thinking about it she supposed in reporting Daniel it might have put Howard and Daisy in an awkward position.

'Anyway,' Daisy went on as the horse began to trot and the cart bumped along the road, 'these coppers weren't the usual ones Daniel deals with, if you know what I mean. They gave him short shrift when he tried to buy 'em off an' he lost his temper and went for 'em. I think he was all riled up about his face – put some store by his looks, Daniel did – but he cooked his own goose sure enough. Moll said he was like a looney throwing his weight about and after he'd floored one of 'em, they arrested him and then searched the house. Course, that was the last thing he wanted with what he stashes in that upper room but Howard always said Dan's temper would be the ruin of him one day.'

Ruby looked at Daisy, and in answer to her unspoken enquiry, Daisy said flatly, 'Drugs. He's got all sorts up there for when his gambling pals get going. Finger in lots of pies, has Daniel.'

'Not any more.' It was the first time Howard had spoken and now he glanced at Ruby. 'He'll go down the line for this for a time however many strings he pulls and I wouldn't want to be you when he gets out of gaol. I'd make meself scarce if I was you, disappear to pastures new and don't let anyone know where you are. He's a vicious so-an'-so when he gets going.'

Ruby stared back. 'I won't let him drive me away,' she said bitterly. 'He killed Ellie. Oh, he might not be the one who did the abortion, but he made her go there even knowing what this Aggie was like. He's filth, scum.'

Daisy shook her head. 'Be that as it may, you can't fight someone like him, lass. You're just a woman.'

Ruby didn't reply to this. She was exhausted and sickened and heartsore, but what she did say was, 'I want him to pay for his part in what he did to Ellie.'

'He won't do that.' Howard avoided looking at her now as he spoke. 'He'll deny he knew anything and no one can prove he was involved.'

'But *you* know, you and Daisy. If you tell the police—'

'We're telling the police nowt.' It was unequivocal. 'We're leaving today and that's that. The coppers have got enough on him to send him down for a stretch with what they found – you'll have to be content with that.'

'You're frightened of him,' Ruby said disgustedly.

'Aye, you're right, I am, and if you had half the sense you were born with, you would be too. Me an' Daisy are going to make a new life down south. We might even tie the knot, eh, lass?' he said to Daisy. 'We're done with Newcastle.'

It was no use, Ruby could see that. No matter what she said they were going to disappear, but she made one last appeal to Daisy. 'Ellie was your friend. Don't you want justice for her? Don't listen to Howard, Daisy. Do the right thing even if he won't.'

Daisy visibly bristled. 'Howard helped us get Ellie to the hospital, didn't he? He needn't have done that. An' I agree with him, if you want to know. Daniel Bell will go down the line now anyway an' that's all that matters. Old Aggie was the one who caused what happened to Ellie. I don't want Daniel to come after Howard because he rats on him.'

It was a different world with a different set of rules. Daisy had spoken about Howard as though he was some kind of hero, not the man who had put her on the game and who lived off her earnings. Unbelievable, but she actually seemed to have an affection for him. The feeling that had taken possession of her mind and body when she knew Ellie was gone was stronger, and Ruby knew she would say something terrible if she was with these two a minute longer.

'Stop here,' she said. 'I can catch the tram from here and you can get away.'

Howard reined in the horse immediately. He clearly couldn't wait to be rid of her, but Daisy said uncertainly, 'Are you sure? You look a bit peaky.'

'I'm sure.'

'Oh, all right then. Well, look after yourself, lass.'

She didn't reply, *couldn't* have replied, and once she'd scrambled down from the plank seat the horse and trap pulled away at once. Daisy turned round to wave but she didn't respond, and after a moment the other girl settled herself closer to Howard and put her arm through his.

The snow was falling thicker now and Ruby stood and watched the horse and cart until it was swallowed up in the distance. She didn't wait for the tram but began to walk and now her tears all but blinded her as her heart cried out, 'Ellie, Ellie,' with every step.

She was soaked through and her shoes were sodden by the time she reached Bath Lane Terrace. She had no sooner opened the front door and stepped into the hall than Mabel was there, cluck-clucking at the state of her before she noticed Ruby's red-rimmed eyes. 'What is it, lass?' she asked worriedly, taking Ruby's cold hands and drawing her along to the warmth of the kitchen. 'Bridget said there's a bad case at the workhouse but why did you have to stay? And all night an' all. Taking liberties they are, if you ask me.'

'It's Ellie, Mabel.'

'Ellie?' Mabel pushed her down on a chair and removed

her hat and coat as though she was a child, saying, 'Get them shoes off and I'll put some mustard in a bowl of hot water for you to soak your feet in. You'll end up with pneumonia at this rate,' before repeating, 'Ellie?'

'I should never have agreed to her coming to Newcastle with me. She didn't like the bakery much and her da was a horrible brute of a man, but she'd still be alive if she'd stayed in Sunderland.' That thought was tormenting her.

Mabel stopped her bustling. 'What are you saying, lass? She's not dead?'

Hearing it put so starkly caused Ruby to flinch. She nodded, she couldn't speak for a moment.

Mabel stared at her, her mouth falling open, before she shut it with a little snap. 'I'll get that bowl sorted and a cup of tea – you need warming inside and out. Now sit quiet, you'll feel better with something inside you.'

Ten minutes later, with her hat and coat gently steaming on the clothes line strung across the kitchen ceiling and her shoes drying in front of the range, Ruby had stopped shivering. Her feet immersed in hot, mustard-smelling water and a blanket round her shoulders, she struggled through the slice of toast Mabel insisted she ate, the cup of hot sweet tea going down easier. It was only when every crumb had gone and she was holding a second cup of tea, that Mabel said quietly, 'Tell me.'

And so Ruby did tell her, omitting nothing, and when she had finished the sorry tale there was silence for a short while before Mabel said, 'Hanging's too good for scum like that Bell.'

'He won't hang, Mabel. Hopefully the police will be able to put him away for a time on account of the drugs they found, but without Daisy and Howard it would be my word against his regarding Ellie, and I wasn't even there when he made her go to this woman.'

'And there's no chance her friend, Daisy, will change her mind?'

'Daisy does exactly what Howard tells her, and he's too worried about his own skin, both regarding Daniel and the police too. He clearly knew about the drugs and so on, and he's Daisy's pimp, after all.'

'Dear, dear.' Mabel clearly didn't know what to say, which was a first.

She stayed with Mabel for a little longer before going upstairs to her room, ostensibly to get some sleep, although strangely, in spite of having been on the go for over twenty-four hours and feeling exhausted in mind and body, she knew she wouldn't be able to drop off. Her mind was buzzing and going round and round in endless circles as she lay in bed staring up at the ceiling she and Ellie had painted together. She would give the world to be able to go back in time to the moment when she'd agreed that Ellie could come with her to Newcastle. No, even before that, to when she had stood in Snowdrop Lane and listened to Adam tearing her world apart. She should have gone home, packed a bag and left Sunderland that very night, and written to Ellie later. Different scenarios poured through her head, each one more extreme than the last, and at some point she must have fallen asleep because she awoke to a room filled with twilight and Mabel knocking on her door with a cup of tea.

And once she was alone again, she realized something had happened during the time she had been sleeping. She needed to go and see her mam and da, and yes, Olive too. She had been putting it off for a long time, but it needed to be done if she was ever really going to lay the ghosts of the past. Ellie's passing was at the back of this decision but as to the reasoning she couldn't search herself now; it was too painful, but it was all mixed up with Ellie being like family to her.

She sat on the bed sipping the tea as her thoughts began to clarify. She would take two days' unpaid leave from the laundry and explain she had certain urgent family matters to attend to in Sunderland, which was the truth, after all. She needn't be more specific than that. And once she had been home, she would see about looking for a property where she could make the dream of her dress shop come true. There were too many painful reminders of Ellie connected both here with this room and with her present job. She would go stark staring mad if she didn't have something to occupy her fully in the months ahead, and her position at the laundry no longer did that. She could have done the work in her sleep the last year or so.

She realized now she had never really believed that Ellie wouldn't be part of the future. She had always imagined Ellie with her in her fledgling business, maybe talking to clients and taking measurements and making tea, things like that, because Ellie had never been any good at needlework at school. She'd always pricked herself with the needle so many times her fingers had resembled a pin cushion, and working the little sewing machine the class had taken turns on had filled Ellie with dread.

She shut her eyes tightly but still hot tears spurted beneath her lids and squeezed down her cheeks. She couldn't believe that Ellie wasn't in the world any more, that she would never see her again. It seemed impossible. And the way she had died . . . But she couldn't think of that now. She had to carry on and if she thought of Ellie's last days she wouldn't be able to, it was as simple as that. And the baby, oh, the baby . . .

She got up swiftly and walked over to the window, opening it wide in spite of the flurry of snow that blew in her face and breathing in the cold air. Help me, God, she prayed silently. Help me to find a way through this. Help me to believe that Ellie and that tiny little girl are in a better place and that this life down here isn't just some monstrous terrible joke, where the evil win and the innocent lose, because that's what it feels like right now. Help me, God, because I feel like I'm losing my mind.

Chapter Fifteen

Edward Forsythe stared aghast at his sister. 'What on earth were you thinking of to let her go back by herself?'

'Edward, I'm Ruby's friend, not her keeper.'

'Why didn't you tell me what she intended to do?'

'Truthfully? Because I knew you would react exactly as you are doing now and Ruby didn't need that on top of the distressing death of this girl, Ellie. I made it clear that I would be glad to accompany her and be at hand if she needed someone, but she was adamant this was something she had to do alone. She's a grown woman, Edward, and one who has proved she is perfectly capable of looking after herself as you know full well.'

'Oh, believe me, Clarissa, I'm under no illusions in that regard.'

'And there's no need for that attitude. Ruby's independence and strength of character are to be applauded.' Clarissa stared in exasperation at the brother she adored. Edward had just arrived from London for the weekend; this had been happening a couple of times a month since she had introduced him to Ruby and whilst she was always glad to see him, it worried her that the feeling he had for Ruby seemed to border on obsession at times. Next to Godfrey she loved Edward best in all the world, but her affection didn't blind her to her brother's self-centredness or the fact that Edward was used to getting what he wanted. Like herself, he had a strong character – their brothers Cuthbert and Leonard were weak men in comparison – and also like herself Edward could be selfish and stubborn. But then wasn't everyone selfish to some degree or other? More gently now, she said, 'Ruby will be quite all right. Sunderland is hardly a den of iniquity, no more than anywhere else, anyway, and she will be back on Monday evening. She's only gone for a long weekend.'

Edward wouldn't be soothed. He was furious with Clarissa. By her own admission, Ruby was heartbroken at the death of her childhood friend and the circumstances as related by Clarissa would be enough to stop even the most hardened individual in their tracks. And Ruby wasn't hard. Oh, she might put on a tough front – he supposed that was necessary for a single woman making her own way in the world – and yes, she was determined to be autonomous and stand on her own two feet as he had learned to his cost, but the soft centre she tried to hide was there all right and it could be her undoing if she saw this fellow who had let her down so badly again. What if she still loved him? She had never spoken about the matter to him and he had no idea if this was the case, but Ruby's refusal to have anything to do romantically with the opposite sex pointed to some feeling still being there.

Glaring at Clarissa, he growled, 'You should have told me.'

'No, I shouldn't, Edward.' Clarissa was well aware of what he was thinking, and although she felt sorry for him and could understand that having to keep his true feelings about Ruby hidden was a continuous strain, she was irritated too. A part of her suspected that it was the fact that Ruby wasn't interested in him that had strengthened the fixation. Edward had been used to women throwing themselves at him all his adult life, after all. But she could be being unfair here. Certainly she had never seen him this way before. When she had perceived his interest in Ruby, they'd had a conversation in which she had warned him that even if, in the future, Ruby returned his feelings, a match between them would be impossible. They were from different backgrounds, different worlds, and like it or not, a different class. She had no doubt, she had said, that Ruby was equipped to fit into society at any and every level, but he knew as well as she did that people could be horribly cruel. Ruby's life could be made untenable. And if he was imagining that Ruby would be willing to become his mistress like so many before, he could think again. The young woman she had got to know so well would never agree to such a thing.

Edward had rounded on her at that point as though she had suggested something obscene, which in view of his previous chequered history she had thought a bit much, but his reaction had convinced her that he wasn't after a seedy, hole-in-the-wall affair. Which in some respects had worried her even more.

Remembering their conversation that day, Clarissa said, 'Edward, my dear, don't you think it might be time to accept that a relationship other than friendship between you and Ruby is not possible? If you were of the same class and inclination—'

'That's enough.' His glare deepened. 'I would have thought you, of all people, would appreciate how ridiculously outdated this absurd notion of class is. The war changed everything in that regard.'

'The war might have blurred the edges a little, and I do mean a little, but that's all. You know as well as I do that the class system is still alive and well.'

'And always is likely to be if thinking men and women who have got a bit about them don't challenge it.'

Clarissa nodded. 'Yes, I give you that, but are you really saying that if something did develop romantically between the two of you, you would be prepared to expose Ruby to women like Belinda Ferne-Rice or Rosaleen Marchbanks – or even our own mother, come to that? Ruby is beautiful and accomplished enough to win the men over, but the women would cut her to pieces with their tongues.'

'Belinda Ferne-Rice has slept with most of her husband's friends and half the men in London.'

Clarissa's fine eyebrows arched. 'You included, if I remember rightly, and that being the case it would make her even more spiteful and malicious. Human nature,

Edward. I seem to recall you tired of her rather than the other way round?' As was always the case with her brother.

He flushed, opened his mouth to say something, thought better of it and then flung himself down into a chair. 'Damn the lot of them,' he muttered angrily. 'There's not one worthy to lick her boots.'

'I give you that too, but unfortunately it makes not the slightest bit of difference.'

'What about Nancy Astor, the woman all your lot hold up as the shining light?'

She sat down opposite him, saying calmly, 'If by "my lot" you mean those determined to bring equality between the sexes about sooner rather than later, I don't think we hold Lady Astor up as anything but what she is.'

'That's just it, she's a *Lady* and as upper class as they come, but in all the elections she's fought she sets up like a street preacher, standing on a box, and in the roughest districts there are, and she wins them over. She shouts and struts and harangues her Labour opponents and the common people love her for it. She cuts through the divide of class like a knife through butter.'

Clarissa sighed. 'Edward, Nancy Astor is a tornado, one of a kind and no one respects her programme of social reform more than I, but she has no relevance to what we're discussing. She can talk the language of the working class and break down class barriers while she does it, but when she goes home it's to wealth and opulence and her own kind and she makes no apology for it. That's simply the way it is. Ruby would be like a fish out of water in your world, and you would be the same in hers.'

Edward said nothing for a few moments. Then, as he leaned forward, his elbows on his knees and his head in his hands, he whispered, 'I love her, Lissie. I've never felt like this before and I know I never will again.'

The use of his old childhood pet name for her melted Clarissa. She stood up and moved to sit on the arm of his chair, hugging him as she murmured, 'Oh, Edward. Maybe I'm wrong, maybe it can work out, I don't know, but unless Ruby feels as strongly as you do I *do* know it wouldn't be possible. And I'm sorry, my dear, I really am, but as yet I see no sign of that. But who knows what the future will bring? If you are prepared to wait, of course.'

'I have no other choice, do I? Not feeling as I do.'

'I suppose not.' For the first time since she had met Ruby, Clarissa found herself regretting the impulse that had made her persuade the other woman to become her friend. If she hadn't brought Ruby home that day after the incident in Castle Leazes, Edward would never have met her and would have continued on his merry way, heart intact. But he *had* met her and what had been done couldn't be undone. And she herself had a great affection for Ruby; in fact, one could say she loved her like the sister she had never had. It was a tangle. And the person at the centre of the tangle seemed unaware of it, which didn't help matters.

She hugged Edward again and then rose to her feet, pulling him up. 'Come on, let's go for a walk in the grounds and then we'll have cocktails before dinner. Godfrey will be home soon and I warn you now all he'll want to talk about is the ins and outs of Scotland beating England for the Calcutta Cup for the first time in the history of the competition. He's taken it as a personal insult, bless him.'

Edward smiled as he acquiesced, while all the time inside he was saying, Two opposites, that's what you and Godfrey are, with very little in common beyond the fact you love each other, but however diverse your opinions are on most things, that's all right, isn't it, because when it comes to class and the division between upper, middle and working class, you both sing from the same hymn sheet. That's what you think, Clarissa, and it makes me angry. It makes me very angry.

Clarissa was holding the drawing-room door open for him to pass through in front of her, and as he looked at her dear face he suddenly felt a pang of guilt. Before he had met Ruby he'd probably thought the same, he acknowledged ruefully. But he *had* met her and it had changed him in many ways, not least because it had caused him to question the rights and wrongs of men and women being bred to think of themselves as superior. The aristocrats, the landed gentry – who were they, after all? You only had to delve back into the history of the Royal Family to find a trail of murderers, poisoners and miscreants second to none.

He stepped into the splendid panelled hall, and as a maid appeared as if by magic, he wondered what his sister would say if she could read his mind. And if he added that he was lonely, that even in the midst of family and friends and no matter what he was doing he was heart lonely for Ruby, would Clarissa understand that his love was no passing fancy?

But he had said more than enough for one day. He nodded mentally to the thought as the maid fetched his hat and coat. And all the talking in the world couldn't make Ruby love him or alter the fact that in her own way she was just as rigid about the class issue as his sister.

Once Clarissa was ready they walked out into the snow-dusted grounds. Godfrey's gardeners had cleared a path that wound away from the house and into the ornamental garden past majestic old trees clad in their mantle of white, and although it was bitterly cold a pale winter sun shone in the dying afternoon. He glanced at Clarissa muffled up in her furs, and as he did so a picture flashed onto the screen of his mind of a scene he had passed on his way up from London. He had driven through a pit village in Durham just as a group of miners, the coal dust of the mine still on them, had left the pit gates after their shift. The snow hadn't been thick, just a light covering as in Newcastle, but the contrast between the men and the white purity of their surroundings had been stark. Their caps pulled low over their eyes and their shoulders hunched against the bitter wind, they'd walked as one, their shabby jackets and big hobnailed boots creating a powerful image in his mind. To them the snow was the enemy, yet another obstacle in their hard lives to overcome, but here in the grounds of Godfrey's estate it was merely enchanting, creating a pretty scene to be enjoyed before one went indoors to the warmth of a roaring fire in the drawing room, cocktails in the comfort of Clarissa's comfy sofas and a six-course dinner to follow.

Ruby's childhood sweetheart, the man she had been betrothed to, was a miner. She had grown up among such people. And the woman he had glimpsed standing at the open door of her house, a baby in her arms, looking towards the group of men, could have been Ruby if the circumstances had been different.

A weight settled on him compounded of fear of an enemy he didn't know and had no understanding of, an enemy who was in Ruby's blood and who had been fed into her along with her mother's milk. Something more powerful than a mere man. A community.

Ruby stood staring down Devonshire Street, an army of butterflies creating havoc in her stomach. She'd travelled by train from Newcastle, and on leaving Central Station she'd caught a tram to Ellie's parents' house and told her mother what had happened to Ellie, feeling it was her duty to acquaint them with the news. She hadn't expected an outpouring of grief and there hadn't been any; she hadn't even been asked over the threshold. She had walked away from the house shaking with rage but knowing she had fulfilled what had needed to be done. But now she was home, she told herself; in the street where her mam and da lived and where she'd spent the first eighteen years of her life, happy years on the whole, but although the surroundings were familiar, she felt as though she was a stranger. She hadn't expected the sense of detachment and it was a little unnerving.

Devonshire Street was devoid of bairns for once. The older children would be in school, and the bitterly cold weather would have kept the toddlers indoors, but the lack of noise and activity added to the unrealness that had gripped her.

She took a deep breath of the icy air, knowing she couldn't stand where she was all day. She had made the decision to come back and she had to follow through on all it entailed; it would be ridiculous not to now, but what if Olive was visiting her parents with the bairn when she turned up? She wasn't ready to face her sister, not yet, not until she had talked to her mam and da.

It was beginning to snow a little in the wind, and again she told herself to move, smoothing the lapels of her coat and adjusting her hat. She had packed an overnight case with a few bits and pieces but even now she wasn't sure if she was up to staying at her mam's, or whether to find a room in a hotel.

That was assuming her parents would want her to stay; she'd walked out of their lives, after all, and then had stayed away for four years. They might have washed their hands of her. The letters she had written to her mother during that time had been devoid of real emotion and very short, just notes to inform them she was still alive and well and doing all right. And she was a different person now to the girl they had known, she knew she was. Sometimes, when she thought back to the young, trusting eighteen-year-old Ruby, she felt a deep sense of pity for what that girl had gone through but it didn't hurt any more. She'd had to lose Ellie to know what real grief and sorrow were. Or perhaps it was just that time had healed and in the healing she had understood that a narrow confined life like the one she'd have been expected to live as Adam's wife would never have been enough?

She shook herself mentally, suddenly irritated with her introspection. Mabel always said that navel-gazing was good for neither man nor beast, and she was right. She only had to think about Edward to know the truth of that. She knew he was in love with her, but she also knew that anything beyond friendship was impossible. Even if Edward asked her to marry him – and he might not be thinking along those lines at all but rather to setting her up somewhere as his mistress, but if his intentions were honourable where she was concerned, marriage would be the death knell on any happiness they might share. He would be committing social and business suicide to take a wife from the working class and he must know that, and that eventually he would feel the price had been too high. And she would never put herself in a position where his family and friends and acquaintances could look down on her. Right or wrong, she had too much pride for that. She wouldn't be able to suffer slights and injustice in silence, which would make things even more intolerable. But neither was her nature such that she could bear to live a life in the shadows as a man's mistress, even Edward's.

Again she mentally checked herself, but now with an impatience that brought her walking along the street. She would be no man's wife or mistress; she had made that decision a long time ago when she had left this place and that, at least, had not changed. She wanted to be autonomous and in charge of her own destiny and she would never willingly put herself up to be hurt again. Men, even the best of them, weren't to be trusted. She had learned that the hard way, but having learned it, she would only have herself to blame if she ignored it.

She paused as she reached her mother's front door. She had briefly considered going through the back lane and into the yard and knocking on the kitchen door, but it had felt wrong. It would be suggesting an intimacy that was no longer hers by right.

Swallowing hard, she told herself to lift her hand and knock. If her mam and da weren't pleased to see her, if they had decided to cut her out of their lives as, in all honesty, she had done with them, then that was fair enough. She hoped they could exchange a few civil words and she could leave on a good note, but if not then she would have to deal with that. Steeling herself, she raised a trembling hand.

It seemed like minutes but in reality was only probably twenty or thirty seconds before the door was opened. Her mother stared at her for an unending moment before reaching out and grabbing her, as though she thought Ruby was going to disappear again, but without saying a word. Ruby found herself gathered into her mother's embrace and borne into the house, still clutched so tightly she could barely breathe.

'Lass, oh, lass, lass.' Cissy was half-laughing, half-crying. 'Oh, Ruby, thank God, thank God.'

They stood together in the hall and now Ruby was clinging on to her mam and they were murmuring incoherently, tears streaming down their faces, unable to let go of each other. It was only her father's voice calling from the front room that broke them apart and enabled Cissy to say through her sobs, 'Come an' see your da, lass. He's never given up hope of seeing you again. He's kept me going in my darkest moments. "She'll come back," he's said, an' he was right. Thank God, he was right.'

Now Ruby was thrust into the front room and she saw immediately that it had become her parents' bedroom and the reason for it. The figure in the bed was all skin and bones but at the sight of her the gaunt face lit up and it was her da again. She flew to his side, kneeling down beside the bed, and as he opened his arms she leaned into them. 'Aw, lass, lass.' His voice was thick. 'I've prayed for this day. Oh, aye, every night since you've bin gone. Me bonny lass.'

Flooded with guilt and sorrow, she sobbed, 'I'm sorry, Da. I'm so sorry.'

'Nowt to be sorry for, lass, not on your part leastways. You needed to find your own path after what happened, I understand that, but I'm glad you've come. By, lass, I am.'

Cissy had followed her into the room and now, as she

wiped her face with a handkerchief, she said huskily, 'You sit with your da, lass, an' I'll get a cuppa. When did you have something to eat last?'

'This morning. I had breakfast.'

'Why, it's past two now. You sit tight an' I'll bring you a tray. I did me baking yesterday an' you've always been partial to a bit of ham-an'-egg pie.' Having said that, she didn't move, staring at Ruby as though she couldn't get her fill of her, and adding, 'Oh, lass, can you ever forgive me?'

'Forgive you?' Ruby stood up and covered the space between them in a heartbeat, holding her mother tight. 'There's nothing to forgive.' And in that moment there wasn't. Seeing her mam again and the love that had poured out of her had wiped away the hurt and resentment that had been festering for a long time. She had been right to come home.

Ruby had sat with her father for more than an hour until he had dropped off to sleep, holding his frail hand and talking about Newcastle and her life there. She had told both him and her mam about Ellie after her mother had enquired after Ruby's friend shortly after she had brought her the tray with a large slice of ham-and-egg pie. They had been shocked and saddened but Ruby hadn't mentioned Daniel Bell, merely saying Ellie had got mixed up with a bad crowd. The last thing she wanted was for them to worry about her when she went back.

Now it was four o'clock in the afternoon and she had

quietly tiptoed out of the front room and joined her mother in the kitchen where Cissy was preparing a pot pie for dinner. It was snowing heavily and had been for a while, and as the light had vanished earlier than usual the kitchen was lit only by the glow of the fire. Her mother never lit the gas light until it was well and truly dark outside.

Her mother looked up and smiled, saying, 'Sit yourself down, lass, and I'll make a pot of tea once I've finished this.'

'I'll do it.' She made the tea and brought two cups to the table, sitting down and watching as Cissy tipped the chopped steak and kidney and onion into the pastry-lined pudding basin, half-filled it with water, dampened the edges of the pastry and then put on the remainder as a lid for the pie, sealing it by pressing her fingers round the bowl. Once it was covered with greaseproof paper and steaming on the hob, her mother sat down close to her and reached for her cup.

Ruby had found it immensely comforting watching her mother work; it was something she had done a thousand times throughout her childhood and it brought countless memories of happier times. Once Cissy had sipped at her tea, Ruby said softly, 'How bad is Da, Mam?'

Cissy put down her cup and placed her hand over Ruby's. 'It's his heart, lass. He had a funny turn two years ago and he's got worse bit by bit since then. The doctor says the injuries he got during the war have played their part and there's nowt to be done. Mind, he could go on for years, there's no knowing, and he's better in the summer. This cold doesn't suit him. You've caught him in a bad spell. Sometimes he can go for weeks on end without struggling for breath, but once that starts I make him stay in bed.' Cissy looked at her daughter. 'Adam's been good,' she said quietly. 'He'll do any jobs that need doing and I know I can always call on him.'

The mention of his name pierced Ruby through but she made no sign of this, saying evenly, 'How are they? I heard they had a daughter,' as she removed her hand from under her mother's.

'Aye, little Alice. By, she's a bonny piece.' Cissy paused. 'As to how they are, well . . .' She shrugged. 'It's not a happy home, lass.'

If Ruby had voiced her inward response to this it would have been that her sister and Adam had got what they deserved, but she didn't want to upset her mother. She had enough on her plate with the emotional strain of caring for her da. But neither could she be a hypocrite. Flatly, she said, 'Did they move into the house in Wood Street?' The house that should have been hers and Adam's.

'Oh, no, lass.'

Her mother sounded as shocked as if she'd suggested something indecent. Ruby thought this was a bit rich in the circumstances, considering Olive had stolen Adam and had a baby by him. Occupying the house that should have been her marital home was nothing in comparison, surely?

'No, they've got a place at the back of the sawmills.' Cissy paused again. 'Hinny, it was wicked what she did,

I know that, lass, an' it grieves the heart of me, but she's been made to suffer for it. I don't get involved – you can't come between man and wife, can you – but he can't stand the sight of her an' that's the truth.'

In spite of how she felt about Olive, it was now Ruby who put her hand over her mother's. Her mam looked so old and tired and to have all this at her age, it wasn't fair. 'It's probably not as bad as you think.'

'And he's never took to the bairn.' Her mother stared at her, pain in her eyes. 'Olive's told me on the quiet she'd never dare leave Alice alone with him for fear of what he might do. Your da don't know that and I'd never tell him, but it plays on my mind.'

Now it was Ruby who was shocked. 'Adam would never hurt a bairn, especially his own.'

'Not the Adam you knew perhaps, but he's changed, Ruby. I've never seen such a change in a man. Even his own mam said she don't know him any more.'

'I don't care, I know he would never hurt a child, Mam. Believe me on that if nothing else and stop worrying.'

'Oh, lass, I'm so glad you've come back.' Cissy was crying again but silently this time, great tears welling up and trickling down her lined cheeks.

'So am I, Mam. So am I.'

Chapter Sixteen

The confrontation with Olive came the next day.

Ruby hadn't slept well in her old bed. The room was as cold as the grave for one thing, especially compared to her little abode at Bath Lane Terrace, which she kept as warm as toast in the winter months. But it wasn't just the temperature that had her tossing and turning into the early hours. Coming home had invoked a hundred and one memories of her past life, and with her father so poorly every one had taken on a poignant significance. Even with Olive being the way she was, her childhood had been a happy one, but the way she had left the family home had coloured her thoughts about it since and that was wrong. She understood that now.

In spite of having had only a few hours' sleep, she was downstairs early. She spent some time with her father after breakfast, then left to see Mrs Walton. Although they corresponded regularly and Ruby had invited the old lady to lunch many times, Mrs Walton's health had deteriorated shortly after Ruby had left Sunderland, and

Vera had been disinclined to travel even a short distance. It was enough to potter about the shop, she'd explained in one of her letters, and still do a little dressmaking for one or two of her favourite customers.

It had stopped snowing when Ruby left the house and the day was bright but bitterly cold as well as being perilous underfoot. By the time she reached Vera's, Ruby had nearly gone full length a few times. They spent an emotive but happy hour or so together, although Ruby was secretly shocked at how frail the old lady had become in her absence. She left promising that she'd return in the near future when she paid another visit to her mam and da. With her father's health the way it was, and now Vera appearing old and enfeebled, she had already decided that she would try and make regular visits home. But she wouldn't return for good. On that she was crystal clear.

Her mam had told her she was making panackelty for their lunch, and as Ruby walked home, treading gingerly on the ice and snow, she could almost taste it. No one made panackelty like her mam so that the potatoes absorbed all the flavour of whatever meat and stock she used and the onions almost caramelized, the whole dish going deliciously crusty at the edges. Her mouth watering, Ruby remembered how she and Olive had used to fight for the privilege of scraping round her mam's roasting tin for the remainder of the crust.

The meal was ready almost as soon as she got home, and once she had taken her father's tray in to him, she and her mother sat down at the kitchen table, eating together in a companionable silence that Ruby would have thought impossible only the day before.

They had just cleared away the dirty dishes and her mam was at the range making a cup of tea when the back door opened and Olive walked in, Alice in her arms. Olive stopped dead in her tracks as she saw Ruby, her face lengthening with her surprise and her mouth falling slightly open.

Ruby stood up, but although she had gone over this scenario a hundred times in her mind over the last few days, now that it was happening she found herself tongue-tied. They were standing regarding each other now, both unsmiling, and Ruby could feel the same hot colour in her cheeks that was staining Olive's face red.

It was the child in Olive's arms, squirming and calling, 'Gamma, Gamma,' that broke the deafening silence, and then Cissy bustled forward, her voice over-loud to hide her own embarrassment as she said, 'Come to Grandma, my little angel, and let's get your hat and coat off, and then you can say hello to your Auntie Ruby.'

Auntie Ruby. The words hung in the air. Ruby dragged her eyes away from her sister's face and looked fully at Adam's daughter. Her mother had just taken the child's woollen pom-pom hat off and as brown silky curls sprang round small cheeks flushed by the cold, Ruby waited for the pain she'd prepared herself for. It came but it was bearable.

Alice wriggled out of her coat and then stood by her

grandmother's knee, one arm round Cissy's leg as she peered shyly at Ruby.

'Hello, Alice,' said Ruby softly. 'I'm your Auntie Ruby.' She bent down and smiled into the little face. Alice didn't look like Adam or Olive that she could see, or anyone in the family come to that, but she was a pretty little girl with the biggest green eyes Ruby had seen on a child.

'Hello,' Alice whispered back, before glancing up at her grandmother as though she wasn't sure what to do. Ruby knew just how she felt.

Cissy whisked the little girl into her arms, saying, 'Come and see Granda. He was hoping you would come today,' and without further ado left her two daughters to each other.

As the door closed behind them, Ruby turned to face Olive. 'She's beautiful,' she said quietly.

Olive stared at her. The red had drained from her face leaving its usual sallow colour, and it occurred to Ruby that her sister looked much older than her twenty-five years. Olive hadn't moved from her spot just inside the back door, and now Ruby said, 'Mam's just made a pot of tea. Do you want a cup?'

'When—' Olive's voice broke and she had to clear her throat before she could say, 'When did you get back?'

'Yesterday afternoon.'

'Are – are you back for good?'

'No, just till tomorrow.'

Olive nodded, and Ruby thought she saw a flash of relief in her sister's eyes. Rage spiralled up in her as suddenly as if someone had flicked a switch and she walked across to the range where, standing with her back to Olive, she said again, 'Do you want a cup of tea?' Her voice was cold and tight.

'It's only that I don't know how he'll be if he sees you again.' Olive had come up behind her and now touched Ruby's arm. 'Not that I don't want you to come home.'

Ruby cleared her throat, took in a long breath and turned round. 'But you don't, do you, Olive? Want me to come home again, I mean. Out of sight, out of mind. Is that it?'

Olive didn't answer this directly. What she did say was, 'We're sisters, aren't we?'

'It's a bit late to remember that.'

'I don't blame you if you don't believe this, but – but I've missed you.'

Ruby searched the thin plain face. She had long ago begun to discern that her sister was a complex human being, even before the bombshell that had torn their family apart. She herself was relatively straightforward, she felt. She was like her da in that way, and her mother wasn't exactly complicated either. But Olive – she was different. Whether it was her looks, or lack of them, that had made her sister so, she didn't know, but Olive was impossible to fathom. One thing she did know, though, was that Olive never lied. There were times in the past, especially where she herself was concerned, when Olive's honesty had a poisonous edge to it that could cut to the quick, but she always spoke the truth.

Now Ruby said quietly, 'If you say so, I believe you. I'm surprised –' her eyebrows lifted wryly – 'but I believe you.' A slight smile touched her lips as she added, 'I bet you were surprised too.'

Olive stared at her and then her tense face relaxed a little. 'I didn't plan that night at Adam's mam's, not – not exactly. I mean, not in the way of days beforehand or anything like that. When his brothers carried him upstairs and I went up after I was only thinking if he thought I was you and I got him to kiss me, it'd cause a row between you. I didn't think . . .' She shook her head. 'I was stupid. Stupid and spiteful and horrible, and I know saying sorry can never be enough.'

'Why did you hate me so much? What did I ever do to you to make you want to hurt me?'

'Nothing. You didn't *do* anything. You were just you. Pretty, popular, funny, clever; everything I'm not, I suppose. Right from when you were born people compared us. I used to see them and I knew what they were thinking even if they didn't say it out loud, although some did, of course. Great-Aunt Alma – you can't remember her, I shouldn't think, she died before you started school – well, every time she came round she used to pat me on the head and say to Mam, "Poor Olive, it's a crying shame." Every single time. When I knew she'd died I was so glad.'

'Oh, Olive.'

'And the bairns at school, they were so cruel, especially the lads. When Alice was born I was so thankful she didn't take after me. But it wasn't your fault, I know that now. Perhaps I always knew but I had to have someone to blame and so I told myself I hated you, that if you hadn't been born everything would have been all right. If you tell yourself something often enough, you can make yourself believe it.'

Ruby bit on her lip. It was some seconds before she was able to say, 'And now?'

'You're my sister,' Olive said again. 'I always thought the saying about blood being thicker than water was a load of old codswallop, but it's not. I – I care about you. I know you hate me and could never forgive what I did, but if it helps at all you were right about me making a bed of thorns for myself. If it wasn't for Alice, I'd have walked down to the river and thrown myself in long before now.'

Ruby had always imagined it would be impossible, unthinkable, to forgive Olive. It would mean that her sister had effectively got away with what she had done, that she was off the hook, and that the pain and devastation her actions had caused were of no account, actions that hadn't affected just her but her mam and da and others too. Mrs Walton had been left alone with her plans for the future spoiled, and Ellie would be alive now if she'd stayed in Sunderland. But she had to let go of all that. Forgiveness was only forgiveness if it was absolute.

She reached out and took Olive's hand. It was cold and thin, and it occurred to her that this was the first time she could remember them holding hands. 'I don't hate you. Like you said, we're sisters, and four years is too long to hold on to hate.' She felt Olive's fingers quiver in hers although her sister's face was strained. 'And I forgive you, Olive. The past is the past and I think we should leave it there from now on.'

When the tears spurted from Olive's eyes and her sister practically collapsed against her so that she was holding her up, Ruby was totally taken aback. The sobs that were shaking the sparse frame were harsh and painful, and as Ruby held Olive close, her body shook them both with the force of her agonized weeping.

Ruby was unaware of her mother putting her head round the hall door and then disappearing again; she continued to murmur words of comfort without really being conscious of what she was saying. After thirty seconds or so when the crying hadn't abated, she guided Olive to a kitchen chair and sat her down, sitting next to her, still with her arms round her. It was a good couple of minutes later when Olive pulled herself free and searched blindly for something on which to dry her eyes, and as Ruby pushed her handkerchief into her sister's hand, Olive wiped her streaming face. Between gasps, she kept saying, 'I'm sorry, I'm sorry,' but it was another full minute before she could cease crying.

'Here.' Ruby placed the cup of tea she'd poured while her sister gained control into Olive's hand, adding, 'Drink it, it'll help. I looked for some brandy or whisky to add to it but I couldn't find any.'

'Probably –' Olive gulped deep in her throat and then took in a long breath – 'probably just as well. The state I look, if my breath smelled of whisky the neighbours would say I was pie-eyed. They don't miss a thing in my street.'

'You all right, lass?'

Olive didn't give her an answer to this, but what she said was, 'I've made such a mess of things, Ruby. I'll never forgive myself, never as long as I live. I've ruined your life and Adam's and Alice's—'

'Hey, no, stop right there.' Ruby shook her head. 'You haven't ruined my life – far from it, I promise you. And from what I could see of Alice she looks a happy, bonny little girl. As for Adam, he's not exactly blameless in all of this.'

'He doesn't look at it like that.'

'Nevertheless, it's true.' Ruby took a sip of her own tea. 'And if he can't accept that after all this time, I feel sorry for him. Life has to be lived looking forwards, I've learned that. It's the only way.'

'You're different.' Olive searched her face. 'You even *sound* different.'

'That'd be the elocution lessons.'

'*Elocution lessons?*'

Ruby smiled. 'I've done a lot of things in the last four years I would never have dreamed of when I left here.'

'Tell me.' Olive leaned slightly forwards. 'Tell me it all. And how's Ellie? Is she with you?' Then, at the look on her sister's face, she murmured, 'Oh, no, lass. What's happened?'

Ruby began at the beginning and told her sister everything, from the best to the worst, and when she had finished, they sat in silence for a few moments before Olive said, 'And this Daniel Bell? He's in prison for how long?'

'I don't know, for a few years I would think.'

'And will you do what Howard said and move away before he's let out?'

'Perhaps.' Ruby shrugged. She had no intention of letting Daniel Bell frighten her away but she wasn't about to tell Olive that. 'And don't tell Mam and Da about him, all right? They'd only worry and there's no need.'

'I don't know about that.'

'We'll see.'

Olive could see that was the end of that particular subject. 'And Edward? Do you . . . like him?'

'I told you. He and Clarissa are friends, as far as they can be, anyway, with them being top drawer. We move in different worlds.' Ruby glanced at Olive's face and smiled. 'There's nothing like that going on, I promise you.'

Olive nodded, but from what Ruby had told her and bearing in mind how beautiful her sister was, she doubted it. Certainly on Edward's part, anyway. A man didn't travel all the way up from London every two minutes just to see his sister as Ruby had intimated. And Ruby hadn't really answered her question as to whether she liked Edward in that way, which spoke volumes. 'So you think you'll look for shop premises when you go back, even with the slump getting worse?'

'It's time,' said Ruby simply.

Their mother brought Alice through to the kitchen in the next moment so there the conversation ended, but as

Ruby got to know her niece a little better, her last words to Olive were at the forefront of her mind. Coming home, seeing her mam and da and especially Olive, had settled something inside her. The next stage of her life had to begin. The thought terrified her as much as it excited her, but sink or swim, it *was* time.

When Ruby left the house for the train station the next day it was snowing again, big fat flakes that settled on the previous ice and snow and made walking even more treacherous. It had been an emotional leave-taking and even her father had shed some tears, and it was him Ruby was thinking of as she waved once more to her mother, who was standing on the doorstep, before turning the corner of the street. Her head down and her thoughts with her father, she almost jumped out of her skin when her arm was taken and a deep voice said, 'Hello, Ruby.'

'Adam!' Putting her hand over her heart, which was trying to leap out of her chest, she said weakly, 'I didn't see you there.'

He didn't say he had been standing watching the house since six o'clock that morning when he should have started his shift, or that he had lain awake all night since Olive had told him Ruby was home on a flying visit. He knew, of course, that Olive wouldn't have said anything but for the fact that Alice had talked about her Auntie Ruby when they'd been having their evening meal. He stood looking at her, his gaze taking in her clothes, the way she held herself, but most of all the face that haunted his dreams. She was even more beautiful than he remembered, but of course four years had passed. The girl had turned into a woman.

'How are you?' he said huskily.

'I'm – I'm well.' She tried to pull herself together. Adam had always been tall but now he was much broader in the shoulders, and like Olive, he looked older than his years. He was still handsome in his rough-hewn way but now there was a brooding quality to his face that hadn't been there in his youth. 'And you?' she said more composedly. 'How are you? I met Alice yesterday and she's enchanting.'

Enchanting. It wasn't a word the old Ruby would have chosen but it fitted in with the way she now spoke, everything about her, in fact. The hat and coat she was wearing must have cost a fortune, even he could see that, and he knew nowt about women's fashions and the rest of it. It was painful to look at her face, the cheeks a soft, creamy pink, the heavily lashed eyes and her small but full mouth. He remembered how it had felt to kiss those lips . . .

'You were going to go without seeing me.' He voiced the thought that had sat like a lump of lead in his chest since Alice had spoken of her Auntie Ruby being home the evening before.

It was a statement, not a question, but Ruby answered it as though it was the latter. 'Well, yes, I only came to see my mam and da for a little while. I have to get back to work tomorrow.'

He would have walked to the ends of the earth for a

glimpse of *her*. His Adam's apple moved swiftly and he swallowed, but no words came through the anger and hurt.

'I have to catch my train.' It was a covert request for him to move out of her way but he ignored it. 'I need to go, Adam.'

'I think of you all the time.' He was painfully conscious of his dirty working clothes, his big hobnailed boots and his old cap in a way he had never been before. She looked so perfect, so – what was that word she'd used about Alice? Oh, aye – so enchanting. 'There's not a day, an hour, when I'm not thinking of you.'

'Stop it.' She was stepping back away from him, an expression of something akin to distaste on her face. 'You have a wife and a beautiful little daughter, it's them you should be thinking of.'

'Don't you ever think of me?' he ground out, hot colour flooding his skin.

She looked him full in the face. 'Not in that way, no. I remember the good times, the happy times, of course. You were part of my childhood and youth, after all. But everything's different now. I've moved on with my life, Adam, and so should you. You have a family and you could be happy if you put the past behind you.'

Rage was uppermost. He could, without the slightest compunction, have throttled her at this moment. How dared she have dismissed him from her life so easily? So completely? When he existed in a living hell because of her?

They stared at each other for some seconds and Ruby, recognizing what was in his face, kept perfectly still. She had decided the night before, as she had lain in bed going over everything she and Olive had said, exactly how she would deal with Adam if they met up in the future, which was highly likely now she had determined to pay regular visits home. She just hadn't expected the confrontation to be so soon.

'You've changed,' he said at last, his voice bitter. 'You've become hard.'

Her expression didn't alter although his words hurt. 'I'm sorry you feel that way but it doesn't alter the facts. If you gave Olive a chance—'

'Don't tell me what to do.' His glare was almost maniacal and she watched the effort it took for him to gain control before he said, 'Go on, go and catch your damn train.'

She forced herself not to scurry past him, frightened as she was. This man was not the easy-going, amiable lad she remembered – he had changed beyond all recognition. Her mam had been right. And yet the old Adam still had to be there, surely? The Adam who would carefully take a spider out of the house rather than killing it and who had traipsed round the streets for hours finding homes for the kittens his da had wanted to drown in the privy. His da and brothers had taken the mickey and called him soft, but she had loved that side of him.

Quietly, she said, 'I only meant that in letting go of the past you could make something good of the future, Adam. For you as much as anyone. Alice is a lovely little girl and bairns bring such joy.'

It was some seconds before he said gruffly, 'She should have been yours.'

What could she say to that? It was what she'd thought herself every minute she'd been with Alice the day before. Seeing her mam and da with their grandchild and the way Olive was with her had brought a physical ache into her chest, and she'd had to battle against something akin to grief the whole time.

She met his eyes and for a moment the look they exchanged took them back to when they were just a young lass and lad making plans for the future they'd share together, a future in which they had never pictured anything else but having their own little home and family, of growing old together and watching their grandchildren arrive in their golden years. Through her whirling emotions, she said softly, 'But she *is* yours, your daughter, part of you.'

'Oh, Ruby.' It was a groan and the echo of it was in her own heart. In the time since she had left Sunderland she'd told herself that she and Adam would never have been totally happy together, that in maturing as she had it would have caused problems between them sooner or later, that their marriage would have suffered the more she thought for herself and threw off the tight confines of life as a working-class wife and mother. And all that was probably true. But it didn't lessen the ache within her right now for what might have been.

Pulling herself together, she said quietly, 'Try and be happy, Adam.' Something warned her not to mention her sister's name, so she just said, 'For your sake and Alice's.'

He made no reply but his chin jerked slightly.

Holding out her hand, she said, 'Can we part as friends?'

'It should be me saying that after what I did.' He took her small gloved hand in his own rough one, holding it as he stared down at the fine leather. No women in their community would have worn gloves like this. It further emphasized just how different their lives had become.

The next moment she was walking away, and as he stood there in the whirling flakes of white and watched her go, the pain was as intense as on that snowy night four years ago. More so, perhaps, he acknowledged grimly, because ridiculously, deep, deep down in his subconscious, he'd always harboured the tiniest hope that one day they would get together again, that a miracle would happen. But that most fragile of dreams was over, gone, finished. Just by her lack of condemnation and bitterness towards him she had destroyed it. It was as she had said: she had moved on with her life and there was no place for him in it now.

He removed his cap, banging the snow off it against his trousers and putting it back on his head.

Maybe he had always known it was only an impossible dream but that didn't make it any the easier to let go of it.

She was lost to view now but still he didn't move; not until a couple of nattering old wives passed him, staring curiously before continuing their gossiping, did he force his feet to begin walking, and then it was slowly, like an old, old man.

Chapter Seventeen

Olive carefully placed Adam's evening meal in front of him and then fetched her plate from the side of the range and sat down at the table before she said, 'Well, we knew it was coming, didn't we?'

It was the last day of April and the coal owners had closed every pit in the country, the miners being locked out once again. As soon as the New Year had started it had been obvious that the coal owners and the big employers in every industry had been set to crack down on the working man, and miners in particular. Her da had explained it to her by saying that countries like Japan, America, Germany and others were now producing cheaper and better goods than Britain, but instead of British manufacturers making something better or different, they were carrying on in the same old way and dealing with the competition by lowering their prices; and the only way they could do this without touching the profits that financed their great big houses and extravagant way of living was to reduce the wages of their

workers and increase their hours whilst cutting expend-
iture on safety.

In the last weeks, the phrase, Not a penny off the pay,
not a minute on the day, had been adopted by the miners,
but her da, like many others, hadn't held out any hope
that a showdown could be averted. 'Churchill is itching
for a fight,' he'd said the last time she'd called round
with Alice a couple of days ago and told him Adam
thought a strike was inevitable, 'and Baldwin will leave
it all to him to deal with, you mark my words. Baldwin's
more concerned with keeping his job as Prime Minister
than anything else.'

'Aye, we knew it was coming.' Adam looked at her.
There wasn't a jack man who hadn't known what the
owners were about. 'But it will get nasty, you know that,
don't you? There's no negotiating with them up top,
whatever they might say to the contrary. The only hope
we've got is if the TUC follow through and back us and
the trade union leaders bring every working man out in
the country.'

'Do you think that'll happen?' Part of Olive couldn't
believe they were having a conversation like any normal
married couple. There had been a change in Adam, and
if she pinpointed to when it had begun, she could trace
it back to the time Ruby had visited. It had been around
then that he had started to talk to her civilly and show
an interest in their daughter. She'd spent days tormenting
herself by wondering if Adam and Ruby had met and
what had gone on between them, and whether the

mellowing in his manner had been a result of Ruby taking him to task. And then reason had asserted itself. It didn't matter how the change had come. It was enough that it had happened. She had decided at that point that she'd ask no questions, not of Adam nor of her sister when she saw her next, whenever that might be. She had no right to be jealous that Adam still loved Ruby. That was what she told herself a hundred times a day.

Adam swallowed the mouthful of meat roll in his mouth before he said, 'Do I think it'll happen? Maybe, but I have me doubts whether men like Jimmy Thomas or Walter Citrine will put their necks on the line for us miners if push comes to shove. They've not got the backbone to take on the government, in my opinion.'

'So all this will be for nothing?'

Adam shrugged his broad shoulders. 'Who knows?'

Alice had been busy tucking into her dinner – meat roll was her favourite meal – and now as she scraped the last morsel from her plate, she said, 'More please, Mam?'

Olive smiled. She loved to see the child eat well. 'That's all there is, Alice. Mam'll get you a bit of stottie cake.'

'Here.' Adam tipped a good half of the meat roll left on his plate onto the child's, and as Olive made a sound of protest in her throat, he said, 'She's a growing bairn, aren't you, hinny?' and Alice beamed at him.

Olive said nothing more but got up on the pretext of bringing the teapot to the table. There was a pain in her that had been growing over the last little while, and it wasn't just that Alice seemed to have transferred the main source of her affection to Adam – although if she was honest that did hurt – but seeing Adam's tenderness with the bairn caused a physical ache she couldn't define deep inside.

He hadn't touched her in bed for weeks, and at first she had been relieved and thankful. She was still relieved and thankful, she told herself fiercely. Of course she was. Who wouldn't be? Every time he had taken her it had been in the form of a punishment, she knew that, but in this relaxing of his attitude towards her she had thought that maybe . . .

What? she questioned herself bitterly as she poured a cup of tea for herself and Adam, black and without sugar – any milk was still for Alice. That he might grow to like her? Want her? Not for the release of his body but because . . .

She mentally shook her head at herself and her stupidity, but her train of thought had forced her to recognize something she had been fighting in the last days and with it came a bitter humiliation that exceeded anything she'd suffered thus far. She cared about him. It had only taken this change in him, after all he had put her through, for her to absolve him of the years of torment, which was as degrading as it was mortifying.

Adam was talking again, saying something about the number of Royal Commissions various governments in the past had set up to look into the wages and working conditions and safety in the coal industry, and how they weren't worth the paper they were written on, but although Olive made the appropriate responses, her mind was working on a different plain altogether.

He would never love her and there was nothing she could do to change that. It wasn't just that she was as plain as a pikestaff and with about as little shape as one, but she'd been the means of him losing the woman he loved. Not just loved – worshipped, adored.

She became aware of holding her cup so tightly that her knuckles shone white, and she made herself put it down carefully and then relax her fingers, one by one. She had thought she'd been glad when Ruby had returned and they had made their peace, and she was, in one way. But in another . . .

She drew in a long, silent breath. In another way, her sister's visit had opened a whole different can of worms, for her, at least.

'Here, look at this.' Adam passed her a piece of paper and she saw it was one of the local trade union bulletins. 'They're quoting something from a paper called the "Fifth Report" that was apparently written at the end of the war by a committee of churches looking into the working conditions of miners and factory workers and the like. Our leaders are saying it sums up what we're fighting for now, but another way of looking at it is, if the government and the upper classes didn't take any notice then, why are they going to now?'

Olive forced herself to concentrate as she read:

'By "a living wage" we mean not merely a wage which is sufficient for physical existence but a wage adequate to maintain the worker, his wife and family, in health and honour, and to enable him to dispense with the subsidiary earnings of his children up to the age of sixteen years. By "reasonable hours" we mean hours sufficiently short not merely to leave him unexhausted but to allow him sufficient leisure and energy for home life, for recreation, for the development through study of his mind and spirit, and for participation in the affairs of the community. We hold that the payment of such a wage in return for such hours of work ought to be the first charge upon every industry.'

When she'd finished reading the paper, Olive raised her head and looked at her husband as Adam said, 'That's what I want for us and for the bairn. It's a basic human right, surely? And yet if we voice such things the working class are held up as a lot of useless whingers who haven't got the sense to do anything more than to labour like animals.'

Olive stared at him. She hadn't heard anything past the 'us'. It was the first time in her marriage Adam had referred to them as such.

'I might be looking on the black side, Olive, but I can't see that a strike will persuade them at the top to regard working people as human beings. I hope I'm wrong, but when I see pictures of Churchill in his nice suit and with a cigar the size of a bazooka sticking out of his mouth, it's like he's from another planet, and the same goes for the rest of the government. They talk about us as the "New Red Threat" and being "Worse than the Hun", but I work with blokes who fought in the war and would fight again if their country needed them. No, this is going to be a long bitter fight and I've no idea whether it'll be worth it in the long run.'

It was the most he'd said to her at one time in the whole of their four years together. Quietly, she said, 'We'll get through, Adam. You're fighting for Alice's future and all the other bairns who weren't born with a silver spoon in their mouths.'

He raked back the curls that always fell over his forehead as he muttered, 'I don't know if you'll still see it that way when we can't pay the rent and there's nowt to put on the table.'

It struck her anew how handsome he was. 'Oh, aye, I will, have no doubt about that.'

He met her eyes and as she held his gaze, he said softly, 'I believe you will at that.'

It was a start, she thought, her heart thudding painfully. If nothing else, it was a start.

Three days later the General Strike was on. Workers in almost every industry laid down their tools and walked out. Buses, trams and trains stopped, factories and docks were deserted and even offices were empty. And in the same breath, the government went into action. A formal state of emergency was declared and a class war split

Britain as undergraduates, stockbrokers, barristers and other white-collar professionals realized boyhood fantasies and climbed on the footplates of strikebound trains and worked up steam. Others drove London's buses and lorries filled with essential food supplies, and still more lined up in the quadrangle of the Foreign Office to sign with the Organisation for the Maintenance of Supplies, or queued at London police stations to be sworn in as special constables. It was a lark, a break from routine, they said, and although they had a good income and many came from wealthy families, the government was paying them £1 15s a week to do the work, as well as a further £1 14s 6d for food and 5s for clothing. A total of £3 14s 6d a week for work that ordinary folk could do far better, and were fighting for the right to do for much less.

'They're laughing at us,' Adam said bitterly to Olive a few days into the strike. 'The TUC has given a guarantee that their members will supply food, hospital supplies and essentials, and carry on doing slum clearance and building hospitals, but Churchill will have none of it. He wants to paint us as black as the ace of spades. There's the navy mooring its submarines and destroyers along the docks of all the major rivers, marines marching with fixed bayonets to escort trams, the army driving through streets in armoured cars and tanks rolling up, and the police using their truncheons to knock hell out of us every chance they get. Churchill's declared war on us and now he's gone this far he can't be seen to lose. And them damn university students and the rest of the upper classes who'd never stoop to dirty their hands in the normal run of things think it's all great fun to drive buses and load lorries and play at driving trains.'

Olive stared at him. She wondered what his reaction would be if she told him about Edward Forsythe. Ruby had one foot in the working class and one foot in the upper, and that wouldn't go down well, not how things were. And Ruby's great friend, Clarissa, sounded even grander than her brother. Ruby was consorting with the enemy, that's how Adam would see it, she knew that.

It was on the tip of her tongue to speak. To say something casually, wryly perhaps, like, 'I wonder if Ruby's new friends are doing their bit then,' but as she looked at Adam's troubled face the words died before they were voiced. She knew he was worried to death about the outcome of the strike. It was clear now that the government, and in particular Churchill and his cronies, had been setting up the O.M.S., the Organisation for the Maintenance of Supplies, for a long time, probably since the 1921 lockout, in fact. The stockpiling that had gone on was evidence that they had anticipated a national strike and had been organized and waiting to spring into action. Adam and her da and others were sure that it had always been Churchill's intention to let the strike happen so he could show the working class who was boss once and for all, and keep them on their knees for ever. She didn't know about that, she was no politician, but if Adam said it, it was good enough for her.

And so she now said, 'I was round Mam's today and

Da said Churchill's brought out a new newspaper called *The British Gazette* and he's saying whatever he likes in it.'

Adam nodded. 'Aye, I heard about it from one of the lads. There'll be nothing bad about the government in it and nothing good about us, you can be sure of that.'

They were sitting in the kitchen and it was dark outside, Alice had long since been in bed. Olive was seated at the scrubbed table doing some darning by the light of an oil lamp, and Adam was reclining in a battered armchair in front of the range, his slippered feet on the fender. It was a scene that would have been unthinkable just weeks ago, and this was at the forefront of Olive's mind as Adam continued to talk about the ins and outs of the strike. He and his brothers had congregated at his mam's that afternoon to chew things over together with their father, and he had taken Alice with him, saying Fred was going to bring his three bairns and it would be nice for Alice to play with her cousins. Fred's wife was overdue with her fourth and as big as a house.

For practically the first time since she'd had Alice, apart from once or twice when she had left the child with her mother for an hour or so when the weather had been atrocious and she'd needed to do some shopping, she had been on her own and she had hated it. It had seemed an eternity until she had heard them in the yard, Alice giggling on Adam's shoulders, and she had felt ridiculously tearful when Adam had walked in.

Not for the first time, she wondered how she was

going to fill her days when Alice started school after her fifth birthday. She knew Adam wouldn't agree to any suggestion that she work outside these four walls; as far as he was concerned, once a woman had a bairn her place was in the home and that was that. Admittedly they were in a better position than many families who had several bairns and just one wage packet coming in, but things were still tight. She had to watch every penny and she was canny with her housekeeping, only buying scrag ends and brisket and other meat that needed long, slow cooking and could stretch to a second or even third meal when the leftovers were used for broths and stews or meat rolls and panackelties. She knew of families in her own street who existed on a staple diet of tea, bread, margarine, potatoes and cheap jam, the shadow of the workhouse forever hanging over them. Even the butcher's offal was beyond their reach, or the herring that was often plentiful at the height of summer.

Adam had lapsed into silence, staring into the glowing coals of the fire in the range as his mind turned over some of what had been said between the men that afternoon, things he wouldn't worry Olive with. Since the statement from Downing Street encouraging strikers to go back to work by saying the government would protect them from any loss of trade union benefits and that the courts would take action against any union that expelled a member for returning to work, and that anybody caught jeering or insulting such a person would be liable to a fine of forty shillings, things had taken a nasty turn. Men were being arrested, quickly convicted and sentenced to hard labour, and anyone found picketing on main roads could now be jailed for 'interfering with the King's Highway'. Trade union offices had been ransacked, private papers, printers and typewriters removed, funds frozen and anyone in the building at the time arrested. His da had heard on the grapevine that in some places the mounted police along with their bruisers on the ground had laid into folk with their truncheons, and that university students, members of sporting clubs and the Fascist Movement were looking on attacking the strikers as entertainment. They were being thrown to the wolves, his da had said, and when Lord Londonderry, the Durham coal owner, had said publicly that he wanted 'them smashed from top to bottom', he was only voicing what the government and the upper classes were thinking.

It didn't look good, his da had said quietly, and he just hoped the trade union leaders in every industry would hold firm. This was a once-in-a-lifetime opportunity to make the coal owners and other big manufacturers who controlled the docks and the railways and factories and the rest of it treat their employees fairly. But if one of the trade unions caved in it would rock the boat and they'd all sink. It'd been bad enough in 1921 when every colliery in the country was closed and padlocked by the coal owners for thirteen weeks to force miners to agree to their wages being reduced and the working day being longer. The miners had lost that fight. They couldn't afford to lose this one.

Adam stretched and reached for the cup of tea Olive

had placed by his elbow ten minutes ago. It was cold now but he didn't mind that; he took a bottle of cold tea to the pit each day along with his bait and he'd grown to like it. You could get used to anything if you had to.

The last thought brought his eyes to Olive for a moment. The old saying as he remembered it was that familiarity bred contempt; well, he'd started off his married life full of contempt for the woman who had tricked him into marrying her and ruined his life, but over the years that emotion had faded. Living with her, and in spite of himself, he had to admit, he'd slowly come to reluctantly admire her strength and grit. He'd put her through hell on a daily basis, and even now he felt she'd brought that on herself, but whatever the ins and outs of it she had never whinged or complained. Nor had she refused him his conjugal rights in spite of the way he'd handled her. His meal was always ready when he came home of an evening; his slippers would be warming on the hearth, and she kept the bairn and the house spotless.

The fire in the range spat and for a moment a deep cavern showed in the glowing coals like a mini hell. Before Ruby had left, he'd always imagined hell was like Father McHaffie described, a physical place of intense heat where you burned day and night with the smell of sulphur in your nostrils and nothing to soothe your scorching body, but he knew different now. Hell was worse than anything the priest could drum up to frighten his flock witless. It was knowing you had made a mistake there was no coming back from, a mistake that soured and coloured every single aspect of your life. That was the torturing part that had driven him mad, and although he'd excused himself at first by putting all the blame on Olive, he knew there had been a few moments on that New Year's Eve when he could have stopped it happening. And Ruby had known it too. He would forever remember her face when he had told her, the look in her eyes.

But – and here his thinking became so painful that he screwed up his eyes against it for a second – there had been no sign of that terrible desolation when he had met her in the street a few weeks ago. She had changed. He knew everyone said he had too – his mam certainly was one for calling a spade a spade – but Ruby had changed in a different way. Deep inside he knew he was still the same, even though because of self-survival he'd put on a tough front the last years, but as he'd stared into Ruby's face he had known she wasn't the same person he had loved so passionately. Even the way she had been with him – understanding, gentle even – had told him the feeling she'd had for him was dead, and the old Ruby, the girl who tormented his dreams, was no more. He would have welcomed bitterness, anger, accusations from her rather than the kindness. He'd stood there in his work clothes looking at this creature from another lifetime who had transformed into someone who could have been from the upper classes, and he'd felt sick to the soul of him.

Looking at his wife, he said quietly, 'I saw Ruby before she went back to Newcastle.' He hadn't meant to ever mention it and he had no idea why he had.

'I thought you might have done.'

The words sounded calmly indifferent and if he hadn't seen the way her face had tightened he would have thought she was unconcerned. Even more quietly, he muttered, 'She's different. Not just in the way she dresses and speaks, I mean, but *she's* different. Did you think that when you talked to her? That she's changed?'

'No one stays the same. She's a woman now – she was a girl when she left here.'

'I suppose so.' He swallowed the last of the tea and put the cup down before saying, 'I told her she'd become hard.'

Olive's hands became still and she looked straight at him. 'I don't think that's true. She had to find a way through what happened, that's all, and make a new life for herself. Did she tell you Ellie's dead?'

'Ellie? No.' He was shocked. 'We didn't talk as such, just exchanged a few words in the street as she had to catch a train. What happened to Ellie?'

Olive told him but made no mention of Daniel Bell or the fact that because Ruby had sent the police to his house he was now in the hands of the law. Ruby had asked her not to mention Daniel Bell to anyone, but it was less her promise to her sister and more the fact that she didn't want Adam charging off to Newcastle like a white knight on a charger that caused her to hold her tongue about it. She finished by saying, 'I think Ellie's passing was what prompted Ruby to come and see our mam an' da and make her peace with them.'

'And you.'

'Aye, and me.' She had no idea how he felt about that.

As if he was reading her thoughts, he said, 'Before she came back I would have imagined I'd feel angry if you two made up.'

'Because it would mean she'd forgiven me for what I did.'

He nodded.

'And do you? Feel angry?'

He didn't answer this but said, 'Do you hate me?'

Visibly shocked, she said, 'Hate you? Of course I don't hate you.'

'I could understand why if you did.'

'Well, I don't.' Terrified she would betray how she really felt about him, which would be the final humiliation, she added, 'You're Alice's da and she loves you.'

A smile touched his mouth, which had settled into stern lines over the last four years. 'Aye, she does. Funny that.'

'I don't think so. It's natural for a bairn to love her da.' She picked up her mending again to give her hands something to do and so she could look away from his face, which was paining her.

It came to Adam as he continued to stare at her bent head that Ruby wasn't the only one who had changed. This thought unsettled him more than the rest of their conversation but he didn't want to examine why. He stood up, stretching as he said, 'I'm for bed. I'm meeting the lads first thing to plan the week ahead although to my mind it's a bit like shutting the door after the horse has bolted. We should've been more organized from the start. None of our lot took into account that the government would use the newspapers and the wireless to turn the British people against us, but how can we come back and challenge their lies with no voice? They're saying the strike's against law and order and King and country and calling us enemies of the state, and there's that Cardinal Bourne telling the whole nation the strike's an offence against Almighty God an' all. That's even put the wind up Catholic workers, let alone the middle class. It's a mess, I tell you straight.'

'I'll be up in a minute when I've finished this.'

Once he had gone upstairs Olive put down her mending. She couldn't see what she was doing for the tears blinding her and streaming down her face. He hadn't forgiven her. He would never forgive her, and the fact that it was only what she deserved didn't make it any easier to bear.

Chapter Eighteen

Ruby's heart was pounding fit to burst. She stood in the middle of the establishment that until recently had been a sweet shop, looking about her. Shafts of sunlight slanted through the mullioned bay window and sounds from the street outside filtered through into the empty room. The walls were lined with shelves which had held large glass jars of every kind of confectionery, along with boxes of chocolates and bonbons, trays of coconut ice and different varieties of toffee, and other treats. The lingering smell made her mouth water, but all that was left now were the little scales and small brass scoop on the long wooden counter.

This was hers, she told herself, still hardly able to believe it. This shop, the one-bedroomed flat above and the small annexe that took up most of the tiny backyard, was *hers*.

She had first noticed the terraced shop near the library in the centre of Newcastle a couple of days after she'd returned from Sunderland. She had been in the area because Bridget had told her that Daniel Bell was being brought up before the magistrate, and she had gone along to the court to see what transpired. She had been more than a little apprehensive, but had needed to be sure he'd be put away, if not for his crimes against Ellie for which there was no proof, then for the possession of the drugs the police had found when they had searched the house after she had given them Daniel's address.

She had got something of a shock when she had seen him in the dock. He had a black patch over one eye from which a livid red scar ran down across his cheek, puckering the skin. Daisy had told her about the injury, of course, but even so it had given her a start. Not that she regretted her action, not in the least; he deserved that and more for what he had put Ellie through. He had been impeccably dressed in a dark grey suit and white shirt and striped tie, and his general demeanour as he'd stood there had been meek and mild. His counsel had insisted that the charges against his client were a terrible mistake, and that the person responsible for the drugs being in the house was a man called Howard Riley. His client, the defending counsel had said, had given this man a room in his house out of the kindness of his heart and had been quite unaware of what went on in it, and as it had been at the top of the house he had had no reason to go there himself. He had been as horrified as anyone at what this rogue, Riley – who incidentally had fled who knew where – had been about. Mr Bell strenuously denied any involvement in any wrongdoing and it was this same Mr

Riley, an aggressive, violent individual, who had given poor Mr Bell the recent injury to his face when he had told Mr Riley to find other lodgings the day before the police had come to the house.

Many eyes had turned towards poor Mr Bell who had suffered such abuse from nasty Mr Riley, and for the first time Daniel had raised his downcast gaze and glanced around the court sorrowfully. It was at this moment he realized Ruby was present and the transformation in him had been immediate and ferocious. Far from being the pitiful wretched victim of a cruel misunderstanding eliciting sympathy, he had revealed who he really was, screaming obscenities and threats, the main thrust of which was that he would get even with her if it was the last thing he did for what she had done to his face.

It had been a gift to the prosecuting counsel and one they had made the most of, the result being that Daniel Bell had been sent down for a minimum of three years' hard labour.

It had been that very day when, shaken and at the end of herself, she had passed the 'For Sale' sign on a quaint and charming old shop on her way home. It was the prettiness of the building that had first caught her attention, the white-painted bricks and big bay window with a window box full of flowers standing like a rose between two thorns from the austere-looking solicitors on one side and chemist on the other. If nothing else it had taken her mind off the disturbing scene in the courtroom when she had thought Daniel was going to leap out of the dock and fling himself on her. The two policemen either side of him had clearly been of the same opinion because they had pinned his arms and done their best to restrain him, with the three of them wrestling in a very undignified manner on the floor in the end. It had been bedlam, and by the time she had left the court she had been trembling uncontrollably.

She had told Edward and Clarissa about the sweet shop when she had gone to Foreburn for Sunday lunch, along with the visit to the courtroom. They had both been full of enthusiasm about the shop and horrified that she had gone to the court alone. In Edward's case, excessively so, and he had been angry as well, saying that anything could have happened. She had said she hardly thought so – it was a court, after all, and by its very purpose populated with officials and policemen – but he wouldn't be coaxed round and lunch that day had been a somewhat stiff affair.

The next evening, however, Edward and Clarissa had picked her up at seven o'clock and the three of them had met the estate agent who was selling the property outside the shop. He had been a small rotund man with a hearty manner and hadn't been able to hide his surprise at Ruby having such wealthy and influential friends, almost tripping over his own feet as he had shown the three of them round the premises. Apparently the old lady who had owned the shop had moved down south to live with her sister, so it was vacant possession. Always a bonus, he'd said ingratiatingly.

All the houses on that side of the road were shops or businesses, and the rest of them comprised the solicitors and chemist either side of the premises, along with a cabinetmaker, a hairdresser, a dentist, a grocer and, at the far end of the street, a butcher. None of the other properties had bay windows, and neither did the houses on the other side of the road. Besides the large room in which Ruby was standing, there was another smaller one which had apparently been used as a storeroom, and beyond that, a tiny back hall from which a steep staircase rose to the one-bedroomed flat. On inspecting this with Edward and Clarissa, Ruby had been amazed to discover that besides the tiny kitchen, small sitting room and bedroom, the flat boasted the modern innovation of an indoor closet, bath and washbasin. The estate agent had told them the bathroom had been installed in what had been the box room only the year before on the insistence of the owner's married son who had been worried about his mother's increasing frailness. She was well over eighty, he'd continued, but had been determined to stay in her home and run her little business, but unfortunately a bad fall resulting in a broken leg and other injuries had put paid to that. The annexe in the yard still housed an old privy and wash house, and at the end of this the coal bunker.

Despite the renovation and refurbishment that would be involved, Ruby had fallen in love with the old shop. She had learned from the estate agent that the old lady had been born in the bedroom of the flat, as had her mother before her, and the premises had been used as a sweet shop for well over a hundred years. She didn't think the house would mind its new role as an exclusive dress shop, though. She felt, even from that first time she had stepped across the threshold with Edward and Clarissa, that it had welcomed her.

She shook her head at her fanciful thoughts, smiling to herself. But it was true. Edward had helped her with the buying of the property by recommending a solicitor friend of his who had dealt with the legalities involved, guiding her through the process of putting down a credible deposit and taking out a mortgage with all the paperwork that had generated, but the house had been hers long before the sale was completed and she'd received the keys. At least that was how she felt.

But now began the real hard work. Ruby took a deep breath and then let it out in a satisfied sigh. She had finished at the laundry for good on Saturday lunchtime and today was Monday morning, the first week of her new life.

She knew exactly what she was going to do both in the shop and her little home above. This larger room would be the place any potential clients saw first and she intended to make it both sumptuous and elegant, the decor screaming luxury. Comfortable chairs and small tables, with one wall holding racks of clothes for the women to browse through, and perhaps one or two dressmaker's dummies modelling particularly beautiful creations. And she wasn't going to cram the window full of clothes like so many shops did; maybe just one costume and hat on display with a pair of shoes and a handbag.

The room beyond would be the fitting room and she intended to steal some of this space to have a small cloakroom built with a toilet and washbasin and mirrored walls. She could see it quite clearly in her mind's eye. The annexe she intended to convert into her workshop but that might have to wait until the business got going. She had kept a portion of her savings back for the work she needed to do and she intended to do as much as she could herself, but money would still be tight. She would make her creations upstairs until the work on the annexe could be done. The important thing was to get the shop and fitting room ready before she added to the frocks and costumes she had been working on for the last months. She had a number ready to sell but not enough to open the shop as a viable business.

The refurbishment of her living quarters would have to wait too. The small flat was dark and shabby and smelled strongly of cabbage, but a good scrub from top to bottom with plenty of disinfectant and bleach would sort that. The old lady's son had removed all his mother's furniture and belongings and the flat was empty, although he had left the curtains at the windows, so she wanted to get cleaning immediately. She'd arranged for a bed to be delivered at the end of the week, along with a table and chairs she'd seen in a second-hand shop and that would do for now. A kettle and a few pots and pans and items of crockery for the tiny kitchen would suffice; there was a small gas stove installed in there and the sink had a tap with the luxury of running water, another convenience which the son had had carried out at the same time as the bathroom had been installed. This had thrilled Ruby as much as the indoor toilet; no more mornings melting the ice on the tap in the yard in the depths of the northern winters.

She had broken the news to Mabel that she was moving out of the house at the weekend, and although Mabel had tried to persuade her to stay until all the work was completed, offering to waive the rent, Ruby wouldn't budge from her plans. She would be able to work as late as she liked and rise whenever she wanted and the thought of being in her own home was heady. Besides which – and now the glow that the joy of ownership had brought to her face faded – she needed to fill every moment, to be so exhausted she could fall into bed each night and sleep. Grief for Ellie, and to a lesser extent her father, although she kept telling herself he was still alive and could go on for years, kept her tossing and turning for a good while most nights. Now that she had left the workhouse laundry and was her own boss, so to speak, she intended to pay another visit home within the next few days. What she would encounter she didn't know because since the TUC had called off the strike a couple of weeks ago the embattled miners had voted to fight on alone. Her mother wrote to her every week now she had her Newcastle address, and in her last letter she'd said Adam had been round to see her da the night before and said he and the other miners were preparing for a long, hard and bitter fight. The government had deemed the strike unlawful, which meant the workers could claim no relief, not even from their own union funds, and the Ministry of Health had already told workhouse guardians throughout the country that it was now a matter of law that no able-bodied man was to be given any money or vouchers of any kind. The Co-op's headquarters had told all their branches to give no credit as they hadn't been paid back from the 1921 lockout yet, and little corner-end shops could only give tick for so long before they went out of business themselves. It was up to the lodges in every district of every coalfield to look after their own people, Adam had said, and to raise money the best they could. There was no doubt in any miner's mind that the strike had become a war against us and 'them', them being the government, the middle and upper classes and even the higher end of the working class.

Ruby walked across to the old wooden counter, trailing her finger in the dust that had accumulated. She had saved every penny she could over the last four years, going without and working extra hours at the laundry whenever possible in order to accrue more funds towards her dream of owning her own dress shop, but would her family see it like that? If she had rented a place it might have been different, but in becoming a property owner she had moved into another stratum, that would be their view. She was elevated into the 'them', but in her case she would be labelled an upstart too. Perhaps not by her mam and da, or if they thought it they wouldn't say it, but Adam . . .

She brought herself up sharply. What Adam did or didn't think was of no account. And she wouldn't apologize for being ambitious, not to anyone, but she could appreciate that the timing of buying the shop was perhaps not ideal, not where her own folk were concerned. Businesswise, it made sense, though. The estate agent had told her that because of the way the depression was beginning to take hold, she had got the premises for a good deal less than they would have been just a couple of years ago. And the signs were that things would get worse, for the working class at least. The upper classes and the gentry were a different matter, of course. Being born with a silver spoon in your mouth meant your whole view of life was rose-coloured. She'd said as much to Edward and when he had protested that he was a self-made man and his little business empire had come about by his own financial astuteness, she had reminded him, rather cuttingly she remembered now, that his maternal grandmother had had rather a lot to do with it too.

As though her thoughts had conjured him up there was a knock on the door of the shop and when she peered through the window there he was, grinning widely and looking as pleased as a dog with two tails.

What on earth? As she opened the door she stared at him in astonishment. He had been up for the weekend as usual but she had expected him to be on his way to London by now. By the look on his face she didn't think there could be anything wrong with Clarissa, but she said anyway, 'What are you doing here? Is Clarissa all right?'

'In the pink. I left her tucking into her eggs and bacon this morning.' When she continued to stare at him, he said, 'Can I come in?'

'What? Oh, yes, yes, come in.' When she'd shut the door she turned, saying again, 'What are you doing here?'

'Isn't it obvious?'

'Not to me, no.'

'I've come to help you get started.'

'Help me . . .' She shook her head. 'What about your work?'

'I've taken a week's holiday. Even entrepreneurs like me need the occasional break.'

She was completely taken aback. 'But you never said anything yesterday.' She had been at Foreburn for lunch and he'd had plenty of opportunity.

'I'm saying now.'

'But I'm going to be cleaning and painting and . . .' Her voice trailed away. 'Oh, this is ridiculous. I bet you've never held a paintbrush in your life.'

'Well, that is where you are wrong. I do a very fine watercolour, as it happens.'

'I didn't mean that sort of painting.'

'I know what you meant, Ruby.' He wasn't smiling now. 'And I can assure you I can get my hands dirty as well as the next man.' He turned, walking away from her and still talking. 'Clarissa will be along at lunchtime with refreshments for the workers so I suggest we get started? I know you need to get the flat clean and I do agree that rather pungent smell needs to go, so I presume we start upstairs? I also know you've got a builder coming by later to discuss the alterations down here.'

'But—'

He turned, the smile back as he said, 'For once, just once, don't argue, Ruby. Let me help you. It's what friends are for, after all. And I come bearing gifts, I might add – every kind of cleaning product on the market is in the boot of my car.'

'Oh, Edward.' She didn't know if she wanted to kiss him or hit him. In the event she did neither. 'Some holiday this will be.'

'My choice.' The mercurial grey eyes that could be a soft dove-grey or might darken to a stormy sky on occasion held an expression she couldn't quite fathom. Their gaze locked for a moment and then he said easily, 'I'll bring in those things from the car, shall I? And you'll need to boil some water on the stove. A couple of the packets said something about mixing with hot water to get the best effect.'

'Right.' She suppressed a grin. He sounded almost knowledgeable. And this *was* kind of him, but . . . She pushed the but aside. Friends. That's what he'd said. And that is what she would treat this as, one friend helping another. She wouldn't think beyond that.

They worked steadily all morning and Ruby had to admit that until they'd got started she hadn't fully appreciated just how dirty the flat was, especially the kitchen and bathroom. It had clearly all been too much for the old lady long before her fall. When she took the curtains down to wash them and clean the windows they fell into tatters, the moths clearly having had a good meal or two, and the floorboards were thick with grime where the couple of rugs that had been on the floor hadn't covered them. By the time Clarissa arrived with a champagne lunch – of all things – they were both covered in dirt and hot and tired, and had barely made inroads into all that needed to be done, but once they'd eaten and drunk and Clarissa had sailed off again, they got their second wind.

The builder arrived just after six o'clock that evening and Ruby was glad that Edward was around in the background while she dealt with Mr McArthur. He seemed a nice enough man but she rather suspected he might have added an extra few pounds here and there on his estimate if Edward hadn't asked the occasional pertinent question and made it clear she wasn't a soft touch. Which she certainly wasn't, she told herself silently, but perhaps a little naive at dealing with builders, it must be said.

Mr McArthur told her he and his two sons could start work the following day, which suggested they were among the many struggling in the present declining economic market, and once Edward had got him to write down his quotation – not an estimate, Edward had insisted pleasantly, which legally didn't tie him to the amount stated – and sign it, off he trotted.

'You've accomplished a lot in one day.' Edward smiled

at her as she closed the door on the builder. 'How about I pop you home so you can change and we'll go out for a meal somewhere?'

'Mabel said she'd keep something hot for me and to be honest all I want to do is to eat and fall into bed. Do you mind?'

'Of course not.' The skin round the grey eyes crinkled as he smiled. 'Your wish is my command. You know that.'

In spite of his words and the casual manner he'd adopted she knew he was disappointed. She didn't want to hurt his feelings but neither did she want any intimate tête-à-têtes, and dinner alone with Edward could be . . . The word that came to mind was dangerous but she substituted awkward. It could be awkward. She saw him mostly with Clarissa at Foreburn and although they'd gone out for the occasional excursion she'd always made it clear she expected Clarissa to be present, which Edward had accepted without comment. She and Clarissa and Edward had gone to the theatre just before Christmas to see a pantomime, and she had found herself in a beautiful little box overlooking the stage far below, sitting between Edward and Clarissa. It had been fun until a rather grand couple with two children had swept into the next box and turned out to be people that Clarissa knew. She had seen the woman talking in an aside to the man once the introductions had been made, and she had just known they were speculating as to who she was and why Clarissa's brother was with her. She had been on edge the whole time after that. Fortunately Edward had arranged for drinks to be brought to the box in the intermission so she hadn't had to converse with Clarissa's friends in the foyer, and once the show had ended she'd declared she had a headache – which was perfectly true, brought on by her tenseness – and they'd left immediately. She'd declined any further trips out.

As Edward drove her home he kept up an easy conversation that required little response from her, which was just as well; she really was feeling utterly exhausted. Once they'd arrived outside her lodgings he jumped out of the car and opened her door for her with his usual grace, and she turned and smiled at him on the doorstep as she said, 'You really don't have to come back tomorrow, Edward. I mean it. You've helped enormously today and—'

'I'll pick you up at nine o'clock sharp.' He waited until she had opened the door before sliding back into the car, and as he did so she noticed the curtains in a couple of the houses opposite twitch.

Blow the nosy old biddies, she thought as she stood and waved him off, making something of a show of it. She would be leaving here soon and they'd have to find someone else to gossip about. As Edward disappeared round the corner of the street, one of the curtains drew aside slightly and Ruby caught a glimpse of a face. Looking straight at the woman she raised her hand and smiled before turning on her heel and entering the house. Put that in your pipe and smoke it, she thought with immense satisfaction, even though it would undoubtedly put another nail in her coffin.

'Brazen, she is,' they would say, full of self-righteousness as they enjoyed their tittle-tattle. 'Right brass neck on that one.'

Mabel was waiting with a plateful of stuffed cod and pease pudding that she'd kept warm in the oven, followed by a generous helping of baked jam roll. Once she had eaten and had a cup of tea with Mabel, explaining all that had gone on in the day, Ruby went straight to bed, her legs leaden as she climbed the stairs.

She fell asleep as soon as her head touched the pillow and for the first time since Ellie's death, there were no bad dreams. Unfortunately, though, there were plenty about Edward. She was finding out more and more that where he was concerned, she couldn't control her subconscious desire and longings as easily as she could her conscious mind.

Chapter Nineteen

Adam stared at his father. He and his brothers were in their mam's kitchen, drinking tea that was so weak it was just hot water, after going on yet another march. Adam wasn't the only one in the room who thought the marches to get people's attention were a waste of time. No matter how well behaved the men were the police always arrested somebody, either for 'conduct likely to cause a riot' or 'thinking about causing a riot' or some such thing. The police were out to get certain men whom they considered troublemakers and they would hound them until they did; in Adam's opinion the marches just gave the law the perfect opportunity to trump up some excuse and cart the men off to jail. But his father didn't see it that way and Adam, along with his brothers, knew their da was one of the men the police were targeting and for that reason they always accompanied him on the marches. Their father had been a puffler for the last few years at the pit, which meant that if any of the men's wages had been docked unfairly or a miner had another grievance, it was he who went and argued their case with the deputy, and the overman too if necessary. It meant their father had got under the owner's skin, which meant in turn he was now labelled an 'agitator'. His card was marked.

'So.' Adam's father looked at his sons one by one. 'We meet back here tonight and come armed.'

'Armed?' Adam shook his head. 'That's asking for trouble.'

'Don't be daft. You'll not have to use it but we need to show 'em what's what.'

What's what. For as long as he could remember that had been one of his father's expressions and could cover everything under the sun.

It must have been the look on his face that revealed what he was thinking, because now his father's voice was aggressive. 'So what'd you do, eh? Let the beggars bring in the scabs and doff your cap at 'em while they're doing it?'

'Of course not.' He was as mad as anyone at the way some miners – those who had given in now the strike had been going on for months – were being drafted into some of the northern pits from elsewhere by the police and the army. But however much it riled him, he didn't see how a physical confrontation would help them. What good were pick handles or poss sticks against rows and rows of mounted police? And it wouldn't be just a few either. For some time the reinforcements had been arriving, well-drilled ranks of big tall men, and the horses were different animals to the gentle beasts used down the mine. The police horses were great muscled giants with massive hooves and huge teeth, and from their vantage point on the animals' backs the police used their batons like hammers. 'But they're expecting us to picket the gates at the colliery, you know that. Even if our lot go easy the police'll make sure there's a fight. They're aching for it. They'll provoke it and knock ten bells out of everyone and then stand back and say it was us who asked for it, same as they've done all over the country.'

'He's right,' Walt said quietly. 'You know Adam's right, Da.'

Angry colour reddened his father's sallow skin. 'Well, if you four are too lily-livered to come along that's all right by me, but I'm going.'

'Me too. Can I come, Da?' Ronnie might be the youngest and still at school but he considered himself as much a man as his older brothers. He had marched with them on various occasions, along with his mother and other bairns and womenfolk, but Adam had always been strongly opposed to this. It was one thing for the miners to put themselves at risk, quite another for wives and children. He had forbidden Olive to join them, as had his brothers with their wives and families, and his father had taken this as a personal criticism, which it undoubtedly was. Adam knew his father loved his mother dearly and why he would encourage her to expose herself to danger was beyond him.

'This isn't a march, Ronnie, and there'll be ructions.'

Adam was speaking to his brother but looking at his father as he added, 'You and Mam'll be best off here.'

'You can't tell me what to do.' Ronnie turned, appealing to his father. 'I can come, can't I, Da?'

'Aye, course you can,' said John Gilbert. 'It's good to know at least one of me sons hasn't got a yellow streak running through him.'

'That's not fair, Da. Me and the others'll come, you know that, but this'll end badly – any fool can see that.'

'Oh, I'm a fool now, am I?'

'For crying out loud.' Adam's exasperation was clear as he stood up so quickly that his kitchen chair tipped over, clattering on the stone slabs. 'I'll be here at seven-thirty, all right?'

It was dark and raining in the wind when the six of them joined the large crowd of miners gathered round the colliery gates later that evening. Adam was glad his mother wasn't feeling well and had stayed at home – it was one less thing to worry about – but there were quite a few women and older bairns with their menfolk in the big mass of people milling about.

Directly in front of the locked gates were more police than Adam had ever seen at one time, some on horseback and some on foot standing in regimented rows and patting the palms of their hands with their batons in a way that was obviously meant to intimidate. Walt, on Adam's left side, swore softly, and Fred standing behind them muttered, 'Look out for Da and Ronnie once the fun starts.'

The words hadn't left his mouth when the blacklegs who had been working down the pit came into the colliery yard, some forty or fifty men in all and each one looking terrified. At the sight of them the crowd started shouting and cursing and throwing stones, and one of the policemen on horseback began reading the Riot Act in spite of the fact that no one could hear a word he was saying. The moment he finished speaking the rest of them acted. As Adam said afterwards to his brothers, it was like the charge of the Light Brigade but there were no women and children in that battle, unlike this one. Although it could hardly be called a battle, more like a massacre.

The police on horseback galloped into the crowd, lashing out indiscriminately with their truncheons as the horses knocked men, women and children over and trampled them underfoot. Hemmed in as he was, Adam tried to reach his father and Ronnie who had been standing in front of him and Walt moments before but were now a few feet away having been swept up in the people trying to escape the horses. The police on horseback were twisting round in their saddles and smashing their thick heavy truncheons down on unprotected heads with enough force to crack skulls open, leaning out as far as they were able. They had no mercy on anyone, not even women or children. The yelling and screaming were deafening, people falling as though they were dead, blood spraying over the crowd and police and horses alike, and blood-curdling shrieks such as Adam had never heard before.

Of one mind, he and Fred fought to reach Ronnie and their father, aiming to stay on their feet amid the bodies on the ground and those folk struggling to get up to avoid being trampled by the horses' hooves. He was close enough to Ronnie to see his little brother's terrified face and his father slightly bent over the lad as he tried to protect him, when it happened. One of the policemen, who couldn't have been more than nineteen or twenty, saw what his father was doing, and purposely aimed for him. He brought his truncheon bang smack into the middle of John's forehead, and as he crumpled, the policeman stretched right up in his saddle to take another swing at Ronnie who had frozen with fright. For a split second it was like watching something in slow motion, something that you know is going to happen but which you are powerless to prevent.

Who threw the half-brick that hit the young policeman in the middle of his face Adam would never know, but there was no doubt that whoever it was saved his brother. One moment the raised baton had been aimed to smash down on Ronnie's head, the next it had fallen from the policeman's hand as he collapsed on the horse's neck. As Adam grabbed Ronnie, Fred reached them, and then the three of them were pulling the inert figure of their father up off the ground. Somehow they struggled to the edge of the crowd, expecting any moment to have their skulls caved in. People were trying to get away and scattering here and there, some being chased by running police who were still striking out with vicious intent, and others, like them, lugging the injured along as best they could.

'Pete and Walt?' Fred gasped as he and Adam lifted their father between them and stumbled away from the crowd, Ronnie not saying a word for once.

'They'll have to look after themselves. We need to get Da home.' And Ronnie too, by the look of it, although Adam didn't voice this. His brother was covered in their father's blood and where the red wasn't showing stark and vivid, his face was as white as a sheet and he was clearly in shock.

By the time they reached their parents' house John had been violently sick twice and had regained consciousness enough to keep up a steady animal-like moaning. This sound, together with the sight of her husband covered in blood, vomit and horse faeces, was enough to send Adam's normally unflappable mother into a panic. After stripping his clothes off him down to his vest and long johns, Adam and Fred cleaned their father up the best they could and put him to bed. He had a lump the size of an egg on his forehead and was mumbling a load of gibberish, both eyes were swollen shut and blood was still oozing from his nose although it wasn't streaming as it had done at first.

Ronnie had the skitters and had already been in and out to the privy umpteen times when Walt and Pete came in a while later, both bloodied and bruised but two of the walking wounded, unlike some of their comrades. According to Walt, a number of men had been arrested and taken away, and still more carted off to hospital and

– Walt had added grimly – to the morgue if the sight of them was anything to go by.

It had been a disaster from start to finish.

The streets were quiet and deserted when Adam walked home some time later, and as he walked he knew he had made up his mind about one thing. No more marches, no more picketing, not for him at least. He wouldn't be a scab, but neither would he put himself in the way of harm and leave Alice without a da. It was as simple as that. When this damn strike would end he didn't know but somehow he'd have to see that his family got through. He owed Olive and the bairn that.

Chapter Twenty

Adam looked down at his plate. He had been expecting a bowl of the dirty-looking water that went under the name of fish soup that he and Olive had eaten for the last three days since he had found some fish and vegetable scraps under a stall at the market. He had managed to snare a rabbit a few days before after walking four miles into the country and waiting for nearly twenty-four hours in the bitter cold before one took the bait, and that had been eked out with potatoes each day for Alice. But this wasn't rabbit.

He said nothing but raised his eyes to Olive who had just sat down herself. It was late and Alice was in bed; he had been walking for hours, going as far as Washington knocking on doors and asking if the householder wanted any odd jobs doing, all to no avail. It was October and the strike had been going on for six months; people had given all that they had in money, food, clothing or little bits and pieces they didn't want any more but which could be sold for a few pennies.

Olive met his gaze. She had always been thin but now she was skeletal, her skin pasty and her long, narrow face appearing almost fleshless. He knew that ever since the strike had started she had been going without so Alice could eat, the spectres of consumption or pernicious anaemia ever present. Although Alice was pale and washed-out-looking, up to now Olive had been able to prevent the ringworm and impetigo that practically all the bairns hereabouts were now suffering from, along with mouthfuls of ulcers, bleeding gums and eyes full of sties.

Her hands clasped together but her voice calm, Olive said, 'It's a couple of slices of the brawn my mam brought round and a few potatoes and peas.'

He noticed that the slice on her own plate was paper thin and this moderated his tone when he said, 'And how did your mam get the shin beef and cow heel and ham bone to make the brawn? They're slowly starving on your da's war pension as it is.'

'It was given them.'

'By her.'

'By Ruby, aye. She is their daughter, after all.'

Keeping hold of his temper with some effort, Adam said tightly, 'And she would have meant for them to eat what she gave, not give it away, surely?'

'She—'

'What?'

He knew the food was for them, Olive thought. In July when the strike had still dragged on Ruby had come on a visit and brought their mam various things and left a shopping bag full of food for Adam and Alice and herself too. She had made the mistake of telling Adam this rather than hiding the food and slowly doling it out, which in hindsight would have been the sensible thing to do, but she hadn't expected his reaction. He'd been furious that day, refusing to eat anything Ruby had given them and telling her that she and Alice must have it between them, but that she wasn't to accept another thing from her sister. She didn't tell him that there had been five shillings along with the food that day, and when Ruby had visited their mam twice since then and each time left shopping and a few shillings for them, somehow she had managed to conceal it from Adam. It had meant Alice was fed and for that she would have defied the Devil himself. But Adam was looking ill and his clothes were hanging off him and today she had made the decision that enough was enough.

Very quietly, she said, 'You need to eat and keep your strength up, Adam. How are you going to be able to work down the pit when the strike's over if you're ill? Ruby – Ruby wants to help us.'

'I don't want her help.' Now his voice was like the crack of a whip. 'Let her play the Lady Bountiful with your mam an' da – I'll look after us.'

It was on the tip of her tongue to say, 'But you can't,' but she bit it back just in time. When the strike had first begun it hadn't been so bad. Adam had joined his da and brothers and other men fishing the rivers and the sea, and she and Alice with the women and children picking winkles, crabs, seaweed and sea coal. Adam had fetched sand from the beach, washed it in buckets and sold it to builders and anybody else who could use it, and as a family they'd gone to the farms dotted around the countryside near Sunderland and picked potatoes and turnips and got paid a few pennies by the farmer or given swedes and kale and other vegetables by way of payment. She and Alice had gone to the lodge hall and joined the little army of women and bairns making clippy mats and tea cosies and scarves and socks with old woollens kind folk had donated, and the men had set to digging gardens, fixing roofs, cleaning chimneys and even doing tinker's work by repairing kettles and pans and doing soldering jobs. Everything and anything they'd done as a community, all pulling together and united by common purpose, and in spite of the worry of where their next mouthful of food was coming from and how the rent was going to be paid, she'd found she was actually happy. Adam had been different; they'd been standing shoulder to shoulder like a real married couple and he had talked to her and even laughed now and again. But he hadn't touched her in bed. It was as though in his softening attitude towards her that side of things had become unimportant to him, which she didn't understand. He was a man, wasn't he, and men had needs as he had demonstrated since their marriage night.

And not just men. Since she had admitted to herself that she loved him, she had longed for the very thing that she had feared for so many months and years; for his hands on her body, him inside her, needing her, wanting her, if only for the slaking of that primeval physical hunger on his part. When he took her he knew it was her and not Ruby beneath him. But he still cared about Ruby; even the way he was over her sister trying to help them out proved that. He didn't want to appear any the less than he had always been where Ruby was concerned. It shouldn't hurt, but it did.

Bone weary and suddenly bereft, she spoke what was in her heart for once. 'She's not looking down on us, Adam. Ruby isn't like that, you know she isn't. And you need something in your belly.'

He moved his head from side to side but he didn't snap at her as she had expected. Instead of demanding she be quiet, he said softly, 'I didn't expect you of all people to be championing your sister.'

'Why? I did her a great wrong, not the other way round. And – and I ruined your life too.'

He was silent for a moment. Then he said, 'I might have agreed with you about that once, but things change. People change.' His voice sounded tired as he went on, 'I had to see her again to realize that the girl I loved is no more and the woman she's become wouldn't suit me any more than I would suit her. At first, after I saw her in the street that day, I told myself she'd had to change because of the circumstances you and I had thrust upon her, but I don't think that's it now. She was always a go-getter. We used to laugh about it, her and I, and she'd call me a stick-in-the-mud. But I don't think we would have continued to laugh about our differences, Olive. Not for long, anyway. I looked at her that day in her fine clothes and talking different and I told myself she was just trying to ape her betters, but the thing is she always *was* better. Better than round here, I mean. She would never have needed me like I needed her. She would have been my world but I wouldn't have been nearly enough for her.'

His world. Oh, that she could have inspired such love in him; she would gladly give the rest of her life for one day and night of him feeling like that about her. Through her misery, Olive managed to say evenly, 'Be that as it may, what I did was unforgivable.'

'No, it wasn't, because Ruby forgave you and so do I. All right? And I wasn't whiter than white, now, was I? And that night gave us Alice, don't forget that. Can you honestly say you would change it if you could and not have the bairn?'

She shook her head, her throat too full to speak.

'You're a good woman, Olive.' And when she went to protest, he held up his hand. 'You've put up with me without complaint for one thing,' he added in a lighter tone, aiming to bring a smile to her face, and when she continued to stare at him, her eyes expressing her pain and something else, something that caused him to become hot with surprise and embarrassment, he suddenly found himself out of his depth. She was fond of him. More than fond. After all he'd put her through and the way he had used her in the bedroom, worse than a man would use one of the whores down at the docks, she loved him. He didn't know what to do. Strangely, because never in a month of Sundays would he have expected to feel this way, he had the desire to comfort her. Just that, comfort her.

He stood up, moving round the table and then drawing her to her feet and into his arms, and when her thin, taut body relaxed against him and her head buried itself in his shoulder, he murmured, 'We're a team, lass, you and I an' the bairn.' He couldn't say he loved her because it wasn't true, but as he held his wife to him it dawned on him that he didn't know himself at all; perhaps no man did. Four years ago he would have sworn on oath that Ruby was the right one for him and that in losing her his life was over. And he had stubbornly held on to that belief, refusing to consider anything else, rejecting his daughter and causing this woman in his arms untold misery. But now, now he knew that if Ruby was to walk in here this minute and ask him to go away with her, he'd say no. And mean it. What did that say about him? He didn't understand it. He didn't understand anything these days, but one thing he was certain of. He cared about Olive and he wanted to make her as happy as he could, her and the bairn.

He could feel her trembling through his own body and, pity uppermost, he said softly, 'If it means that much to you I'll accept anything your sister gives with good grace, all right? I don't like it, any more than I like having to take what amounts to handouts from other folk since this strike started, truth be known. Every time I knock on someone's door asking if they've any work they want doing and see their faces, I know they're sick of us, and who can blame them? Some of the women whose menfolk are in work have had their knives and scissors almost worn away with sharpening, and they must have more tea cosies and doorstops and clippy mats than they know what to do with. I was brought up to look after me own and ask nowt of anyone and all this sticks in my craw, lass.'

'I know, I know.' Through her tears, she mumbled, 'And you do look after us.'

'Not really, and we can't win this fight. Everyone knows it but no one's saying it. The rest of the world is going along as normal – no one's interested in the coal miners any more. They're getting coal from abroad and to them coal is coal. They don't care if it comes from our old enemy the Germans or anybody else, damn them. That is, if they even bother to consider where it's from, which I doubt. The general strike came and went and folk were inconvenienced for a few days but that was all it meant to them. This struggle's been for nowt, that's what gets me the most.' He put her slightly from him, looking down into her tear-drenched face as he said, 'Come on, come and eat your dinner an' I'll eat mine but only if you add a bit more to your plate.'

'But—'

'No buts. Like you said to me, you need to keep your strength up. Alice needs you.' He paused. 'And so do I.'

In the middle of November the miners finally agreed to end the pit strike. Seeing their wives and children starve in freezing-cold houses with no heat, no hot water, no food and with everything they had in the pawnshops, accomplished what the coal owners and the government had been unable to do. Bairns weak from eating scraps that should have gone to pigs and sleeping on the floor under old newspapers because their beds and blankets were in the pawnshops had beaten the men. They had lost everything and won not one concession; it was a defeat of momentous proportions.

On the day that the colliery opened, Adam joined the other miners gathered at the gates. It was a bitterly cold day and sleet was falling, the sky leaden and dark. There was a list of names on the noticeboard on the gate beside the terms that had been up there for seven long months and which they'd fought so hard and suffered so much to change. If your name was there, it meant you had a job. If it wasn't, it meant the owners were having their final revenge on those they saw as troublemakers and agitators. Adam's name was there, along with his brothers'. His father's wasn't. The five of them stood together, staring at the board, his father's mouth working as though he was chewing something. John hadn't been the same since the night he had been so badly injured. He had barely known what day it was for some time, and when he had finally come to himself he had been subdued and distant, often not speaking for hours on end.

Now as John stared at the list he shrugged. 'Thought as much.'

'I'm sorry, Da.' Adam shook his head. 'It's not fair.'

'When did fair have anything to do with it?'

'You an' Mam'll be all right,' Walt said quietly. 'We'll all see to that.'

'You've got your own families to take care of.'

'Aye, an' you an' Mam are part of 'em. We'll all put in a bit till they take you back on, and they will sooner or later. You're one of the best hewers in the pit, everyone knows that.'

Adam had been reading the list. There were a lot of skilled men like his father who were excellent workers whose names were absent because of their political beliefs and the way they'd spoken up in the past. He swallowed hard. Those that could go back would – families were depending on them – but if they'd thought they had it bad before it was going to get a darn sight worse. The owners had them by the short and curlies, that was for sure. They wouldn't be able to wipe their noses without risking the sack.

The four brothers stood together and watched their father shuffle off down the street. Adam had never thought of his da as an old man; John was over sixty, it was true, and his life down the pit since he was a lad of thirteen had marked his body, but his zest for life and belligerence and pride of himself as the head of a family of five lads had made him seem ageless. But not any more.

As one, they walked through the colliery gates and into the yard where the deputy eyed them up and down. Most of the deputies Adam liked – they were just miners like him, he'd told himself in the past whenever one of

them had docked a lad's wage or argued the toss about
something or other – but this one, Norman Boyce, was
a nasty bit of work and a boss's man to the soul of him.

'The Gilbert crew.' The deputy smiled mockingly. 'Nice
to see you, lads.' Both the look on his face and the tone
of his voice told Adam they were in for a rough ride. And
so it proved. His father had been a thorn in this man's
side for years and now Boyce wasn't satisfied in his victory
over him; he intended to kick all the Gilberts' backsides.

Walt was as skilled a hewer as their father and all
four of them had been doing face work before the strike;
it was where the money was and every miner knew it.
Now Boyce had set the four of them doing labouring
work at seventeen shillings and fourpence a week. He
knew they couldn't refuse and what was more they had
to appear grateful for being taken back in any capacity.

It was a long day. The four of them fetched and carried,
passed stuff to the skilled men working at the face and
tidied up after them. They shovelled the pit ponies' dung,
cleaned things, and generally did the work they'd done
as green young lads fresh from the schoolyard. Each one
of them knew they were being punished for being their
father's sons, but if they were ever going to be set on at
the face again and earn real money they had to keep their
mouths shut and bide their time.

Adam's shoulders were bowed as he walked home
later that day. The earlier sleet had turned into snow and
a keen north-east wind whipped the flakes into his face,
but his physical discomfort was nothing to what he was

feeling inside. He felt like nowt, less than nowt after kowtowing to that scum Boyce all day. He didn't know how he was going to be able to stand it but he'd have to, there was no other option.

When he opened the back door and walked into the kitchen the warmth and the smell of cooking hit him at the same time. They'd had no coal that morning and no money to buy any with, and the only food in the house had been a pan of two-day old broth made with scrag ends and vegetables that had been on the turn. They'd had it cold the night before and it had tasted like something you wouldn't expect a dog to eat.

He looked at Olive who came to him and helped him take off his coat without saying a word. It wasn't until he'd sat down and unlaced his hobnailed boots that she said, 'Alice is in bed. She's worn herself out playing with your Fred's two when I popped round your mam's this afternoon. Your mam's looking after them in the day now while Bess works at the pickling factory.'

When he made no response to this, she said quietly, 'Your da was there.'

'Aye, he would be.'

'He said you and the others got taken on.'

'In a manner of speaking.' He was suddenly so tired he could barely speak. 'Boyce has got us labouring.'

'*Labouring?*'

'Aye, he's enjoying showing us who's boss. He's treated us as less than the muck under his boots and loved every minute.'

Olive stared at him, compassion and anger in equal measure in her eyes, and then she amazed Adam and surprised herself by using language a sailor would think twice about. He would have sworn on oath that his wife, his quiet, proper and somewhat prim wife, had never heard such profanities, and for a moment the indignities and ignominy of the day, the shame of which had been compounded by knowing that yet again they'd had to accept a handout from Ruby, were swept away. Olive had clapped her hand to her mouth, shock widening her eyes, and this as much as anything else brought the laughter bubbling up. He couldn't remember the last time he'd had a belly laugh but he was having one now, and when after a few moments Olive joined him, plumping down on the chair next to his, it further tickled him.

Quite when the laughter turned to something else he didn't know, but he suddenly became aware that he was crying and not quietly but with great choking sobs that were torn up from the depths of him. His head was deep on his chest and his shoulders were hunched, and even as he cried, he thought, This is the final humiliation, crying like a bairn in front of her. A man was the head of the family; his wife was supposed to look up to him, respect him, and not only couldn't he provide for her and Alice, but here he was blubbing like a baby.

He felt her arms go round him and realized she was kneeling in front of him, pressing him fiercely to her as she murmured more words he hadn't expected to hear, but these were passionate, ardent, fiery declarations of how wonderful he was, how Boyce and the rest of them weren't worthy to lick his boots, how strong he had been for her and Alice throughout the last months and how he was everything a husband and father should be.

He had lived with this woman for over four years, bitter years at first which had then mellowed and become bearable in the last months, and he had admitted to himself that he'd come to admire her, like her even, and pity her a lot once he'd understood how she felt about him because he knew he could never feel the same about her. The way she had supported him through the strike with never a word of complaint or self-pity had further impressed him, and there had been moments of late, especially when he was with Alice listening to the child's chatter and laughter and knowing how much the bairn loved him, that he could have said he was content. He didn't know about happy; happy had always been linked in his mind with Ruby and consisted of a wild joy and elation that bordered on ecstasy, but maybe Olive and the bairn made up a different sort of happiness? He hadn't examined his feelings too often because he always ended up more confused when he did, but as his respect and regard for Olive had grown, so had his determination not to use her for the relief of his body's needs. He had taken her in anger in the past, but now that anger and resentment had gone he'd felt he needed to give her peace, besides which he knew she had suffered when she had lost the babies. But in all his deliberations, even when he'd realized how she felt about him, he hadn't understood that her feelings for him were so strong.

He raised his head, wiping his face with the back of his hand as he muttered, 'What the hell must you think of me?'

'I think you know the answer to that.'

He looked into the thin plain face that of late hadn't appeared so plain to him. 'Olive—'

'No, please don't. Don't say anything. I can't help how I feel any more than you can, and it's all right. I – I don't mind you don't—' Her voice broke and as she swallowed, she lowered her head, but not before he had seen her eyes fill with tears.

Again he said her name, but now the deep tender tone brought her head lifting. This woman loved him in a way Ruby never had. The realization was part shock, part pain. She needed and wanted him and she would never have walked away from him.

Their hands were joined and she was still kneeling when she stammered, 'I – I don't expect anything from you, not – not in that way.'

Slowly and firmly he drew her up with him, and when they were both standing he lowered his head, bringing her hands to his mouth and feeling her fingers tremble as his lips touched them.

'Can the dinner wait a while?' he asked softly, and when she nodded, her eyes wide as she stared at him, he put his arm round her and led her out of the kitchen and up the stairs to their bedroom.

PART FOUR

A Woman of Substance

1928

Chapter Twenty-One

Ruby stood blinking in Foreburn's beautiful ballroom, her arm in Edward's. The glass chandeliers shone a brilliant light on the dancers in the middle of the vast room and she could see an orchestra on a raised balcony at the end of the endless space, couches and seats and small tables arranged against the walls where some women were sitting talking and looking about them and others were conversing with their menfolk standing to the side of them. A huge fire was burning in the magnificent fireplace, which took up half of one wall, and an army of maids and footmen were flitting here and there with trays of drinks and canapés. The extravaganza, the people, the sheer noise was overwhelming and she took a deep breath to steady her nerves. Edward had picked her up a little while before to bring her to Clarissa's party and although she had been expecting something grand – Clarissa never did anything by halves – she hadn't prepared herself for the dazzling vista in front of her.

But this was one invitation she couldn't have refused,

she knew that, and she hadn't wanted to. Three days ago the suffragettes' long campaign had finally come to a victorious end when the House of Commons had passed the Equal Franchise Bill giving the vote to all women aged twenty-one or over, and Clarissa was throwing the party for all her friends to celebrate, including the local branches of the suffrage movement in Newcastle and Gateshead. March had been a trying month – blizzards had swept Britain and the north in particular had suffered as temperatures had plummeted to record lows – but tonight the bitter cold and freezing winds outside the ballroom were forgotten. All was light and gaiety.

'Would you like to dance?' Edward's husky voice was deep and soft as he gazed down into the face of the woman whom he thought about constantly in his waking hours and who tormented his dreams. He didn't think she had ever looked more lovely; her long coffee-coloured dress sewn with hundreds of tiny crystals sparkling like a galaxy of stars and bringing out the deep brown of her eyes, and her hair arranged in shining blonde curls on top of her head. He was glad Ruby hadn't succumbed to the new craze of shorter and shorter hair for women; not that it wouldn't suit her – she was so beautiful nothing could detract from her loveliness – but it would be such a shame to see that silky mass cropped.

Ruby felt an inward shiver as she looked up into his face. They had never danced – he had never even held her in his arms, she had made sure of that – and she had been anticipating this moment with equal longing and apprehension. Sooner or later Edward would tire of the platonic friendship between them, she knew that. He was a man, wasn't he, and men had needs; she was amazed he hadn't forced the issue long ago, but she knew he had bowed to her demands that they remain just friends because he cared for her. How much she wasn't sure – they'd never spoken of their feelings – but whether his intention would be to ask her to become his mistress or to actually want to marry her, her answer would be the same. She could no more inhabit his world happily than he could hers, whatever hers was, these days.

'So, Miss Morgan, may I have the pleasure?' Edward said, laughter in his voice now.

The orchestra had started a waltz, and forcing herself to nod and smile she placed her left hand tentatively on his shoulder and the fingers of her right in his extended palm and they were off into the moving throng. He was a wonderful dancer, but then of course he'd had a lot of practice since he was a youth; balls and fancy occasions would be commonplace to him, she thought, her feet hardly seeming to touch the floor as they flowed as one with the music. She was vitally aware of every single thing about him as they circled the room, and for a moment she panicked.

'Play with fire,' her mam used to say, 'and you'll get burned.'

Telling herself to forget everything but the fact that she was in Edward's arms and to live in the moment, Ruby felt as though she was floating as they danced dance after dance. Clarissa came up and chatted with them at one point when they stopped for refreshments, and the chairwoman of the local suffrage group made herself known to Ruby along with several other of the members, but only one or two of Edward's acquaintances engaged him in conversation although Ruby noticed Clarissa's friends were craning their heads to observe them on more than one occasion.

At ten o'clock the orchestra stopped playing and Clarissa stood on the balcony in front of them and made a rousing speech with Godfrey at her side. Ruby had met Clarissa's husband a few times on her Sunday visits to Foreburn, although he was away more than he was at home, and had found him to be a genuinely nice man with a great sense of humour who was clearly deeply in love with his much younger wife. After giving due homage to Emmeline Pankhurst and other stalwarts of the movement, some of whom had suffered shocking maltreatment in Parliament Square on Black Friday eighteen years before and never recovered, Clarissa went on to say that it was impossible to list all the women who had died or been injured for life in the course of the suffrage agitation in England.

'But the horrors of prison, of beatings, of hunger strikes and force-feeding did not deter them from fighting for the rights of citizenship,' Clarissa said passionately.

There was a round of 'hear, hear's and some clapping before she continued, 'On the subject of laws made by men, without the assistance of women but supposedly for their protection and that of children, I'm sure many of us here today appreciate the need for continuing drastic change. Horrors like the "Children's Charter" of 1906, an Act filled with mistakes and cruelty that put the responsibility for neglect of children on the backs of their mothers who, incidentally, under the laws of England at that time had no rights as parents, meant that even if a mother living in a miserable hovel starved herself in order to feed her children, she was still in danger of being incarcerated in prison for violating the terms of the Charter, with the result that her children would be sent to the workhouse. This Act caused untold misery. Throughout history, governments have devised ways of punishing those they see as "rebellious" women, but now we see real hope of a new age being ushered in. We have two women MPs in Parliament and I believe more will join Nancy Astor and Margaret Wintringham, perhaps even among this present company. As Lady Astor herself is fond of saying, women are braver and more unorthodox than men – we've had to be to get where we are now – and we are not afraid to step out of line and flout harsh man-made rules where necessary. So, may I finish by inviting you all to raise your glasses to those women of the past, those of the present and those of the future who will take the cause ever forward, after which do feel free to make your way into the dining room across the hall where a buffet dinner will be served.'

'Well said, Clarissa,' Edward murmured as they drank the toast. 'And to think she was once a disobedient little scrap with permanently scabbed knees and torn clothes who my parents despaired of.'

'They are not here tonight, your parents?'

'Good grief, no.' Edward shook his head. 'Our dear Mama and Papa are pure establishment, my dear, and thoroughly disapprove of their only daughter's views and activities, and of course Cuthbert and Leonard do exactly as they are told.'

'But not you?'

'No, not me.' He smiled. 'In our family there are two black sheep, not one.'

In spite of his air of casualness she felt that the split in the family bothered him, and now she said quietly as people began to walk to the dining room, 'I'm sure your parents love you and Clarissa as much as your brothers.'

'Possibly.'

The tone of his voice brought her eyes to his face. 'What does that mean?'

'Ruby—' He stopped abruptly. 'Oh, it doesn't matter. Come on, let's get some food.'

'Tell me.' She resisted moving as he put his hand under her elbow to usher her towards the door.

'It's nothing – just that as you know our childhood was different to the one you experienced. Our parents had children to carry on the family name as was expected of them, but neither my father nor my mother was interested in us as people. We were given into the care of the servants from the day we were born and brought down from the nursery for a few minutes each evening, and even that was too much for them in Clarissa's case. They had expected a daughter who would be sweet and malleable and not say boo to a goose, and they got Clarissa.' He smiled.

'But they still love you, all of you.'

'Cuthbert and Leonard have fulfilled their obligations and therefore remained in favour, but I don't think my parents love them in the sense you mean any more than they love Clarissa and me. It's simply not like that, Ruby. The two of them live their lives exactly as they please – my father has his hunting and fishing and mistress, and my mother enjoys the social scene and her friends and trips to Paris and Italy.' He shrugged. 'Don't look so shocked, they're products of their class. Their parents behaved in the same way and their parents before them.'

She wanted to ask, 'And you? Is that how you see love and marriage and family life?' but instead she said, 'Is that what Cuthbert and Leonard want?'

'I have no real relationship with either of them so I have no idea of their feelings, but Cuthbert married a lady of my parents' choice some years ago and no doubt Leonard will do the same at some point. They are dutiful sons,' he added mockingly.

'It's all very cold-blooded.'

'Yes, I suppose it is.' Edward stared down into the troubled face raised to his. She had no idea of the impact she had made on his life, he thought wryly. Before he had met Ruby he had been going along in his own sweet way and had never really thought deeply about life and love. True, he had decided to break the mould and go into commerce, a vulgarity he knew his parents still hadn't forgiven him for despite his success, but his social life as a bachelor with mistresses from the top drawer who would present no complications when he decided to end the liaison had seemed natural enough. And then this changeling-like creature had burst onto his horizon, a woman who looked so fragile and ethereal on the outside but who was made of pure granite on the inside, certainly where he was concerned, that was. She had kept him at arm's length for over three years – *three years* – and he had been patient, heaven knew he had been patient, but he'd had enough. He didn't know if it was the amount of champagne he'd imbibed tonight that had brought things to a head, but he knew he couldn't carry on for much longer playing the friend, not and remain sane.

He opened his mouth to speak, intending to ask Ruby to accompany him into Godfrey's morning room where they could have some privacy for what he was about to say, but as he did so his arm was jostled, and when the woman who had bumped into them turned to apologize, he inwardly groaned. Belinda Ferne-Rice. Of all the people here tonight, it had to be one of his old mistresses and this one in particular with her airs and graces. Their affair had been over for years now but she still persisted in adopting an over-familiar attitude with him when they met socially. He had let their association go on too long at the time in spite of losing interest quite quickly, but he had found her to be a jealous and vindictive harpy of a woman once they had got together and it had seemed easier to jolly her along until she became bored with him. But she never had. And so he had taken the coward's way out and disappeared off to the States for a month or two, writing from there to end their association. It hadn't been his finest moment and even now he was ashamed of how he had behaved towards her.

'Belinda, how lovely. I don't think you've met a friend of mine? Ruby Morgan? Ruby, this is Belinda Ferne-Rice.'

'How do you do, Miss Morgan.'

As Ruby murmured a polite reply she was aware of several things at once. One, although the woman in front of her was plump to the point of fatness, she was extremely attractive. Her skin was a peachy cream colour, her eyes a deep clear green with thick curling lashes, her nose perhaps a little large but her mouth full-lipped, and although this same mouth was at present set in a fixed smile, the green eyes had darkened until they'd become almost black. She was wearing a dress that exposed the tops of her ample breasts to a point where it was almost indecent and the dress itself must have cost a fortune. The diamond combs that were holding the waves and curls of her chestnut hair in place were not costume jewellery, like Ruby's own, and the woman's fingers were so weighed down with sparkling rings it was a wonder she could move them. But it was the expression on Belinda Ferne-Rice's face as she looked at Edward that Ruby was most conscious of. It was hungry. That was the only way Ruby could describe it to herself. And then as this stranger turned her gaze on her, there was resentment and dislike in it.

'Morgan . . .' Belinda let the name trail over her lips. 'My husband's family seat is in Wales and he has a lot to do with the Welsh Morgans. Are you a relation of theirs?'

'Miss Morgan is from the north-east, Belinda,' Edward put in quickly. 'Now shall we all go through to the dining room and—'

'Really? Then you must be part of Sir Charles Morgan's family? Such a dear man. We had dinner with Sir Charles and his wife only the other day at the Savoy when they were in town.'

This woman knew she wasn't related to either of the families she had mentioned, Ruby thought, and that Edward was associating with someone from a different class. Ruby wasn't sure how she had come by the knowledge but she was sure of it. Mrs Ferne-Rice was toying with her, and the reason she was being so spiteful was because there was something between this woman and Edward. The way he had stiffened when she'd turned to face them and his almost nervous attitude now confirmed it.

'I'm sorry, Mrs Ferne-Rice, but I have no idea who Sir Charles Morgan is,' Ruby said coolly, 'or the Welsh Morgans, come to that.' She didn't add, 'Neither have I any wish to,' but let her icy tone say it for her. 'Shall we go and eat, Edward?' she added as she turned and swept away, hearing Belinda's outraged, 'Well, really!' with some satisfaction. It had been rude, but she wasn't one bit sorry.

Her cheeks burning, she didn't look round to see if

Edward was following her, but when she entered the dining room and felt his hand at her elbow a moment later, she held herself very straight. If he made excuses for that dreadful woman she would hit him.

'I'm sorry about Belinda,' he muttered in her ear. 'She might rub shoulders with the great and the good but she has the manners of an alley-cat.'

Ruby didn't trust herself to speak. Instead she concentrated on selecting a little food from the huge variety of dishes on display, and it wasn't until they were seated in a quiet alcove and Edward had fetched two glasses of wine, that she said, 'She seemed angry.'

'Belinda?'

'Yes, Belinda. Had she any reason to be?'

He might have guessed she would get straight to the point. There was never any beating about the bush with Ruby. 'Are you asking me if I have been acquainted with her in the past?'

Well, that was one way of putting it, she supposed. She said nothing and neither did she sip at her wine as he was doing; she'd had two glasses of champagne and felt a little tiddly as it was but that was probably just as well. She might not have had the courage to deal with Mrs Ferne-Rice the way she had otherwise.

Edward put down his glass of wine and then sighed. 'It was over long before I met you.'

Stupid, so, so stupid to feel so let down and jealous, but she did, which was utterly unfair as not only had he been involved with this woman before he had met her but if he was still seeing her now she would have no reason to object. Drawing on all her composure, she said quietly, 'I see.'

'Ruby, I swear she is nothing to me. She never was, not really. I was young and she was married and bored. It was one of those things.'

One of those things. How could he speak so offhandedly about something that was so important? But by his own admission, it hadn't been to him. Carrying on with someone else happened in her own class – she of all people knew that, since her world had been turned upside down because of it – but it wasn't treated lightly, far from it. It was a terrible disgrace, a sin, a crime. A man who betrayed his wife was likely to have her father and brothers and other menfolk turn up on his doorstep and knock ten bells out of him, and a woman would be hounded out of the neighbourhood and probably pelted with muck and filth into the bargain.

She and Edward were worlds apart. Millions and billions of worlds apart.

He was looking at her and she knew he was waiting for her to speak but it was beyond her. She nodded instead, a non-committal nod, and when he sighed again she felt a rage spring up that had her wanting to leap up and shout at him to stop sighing, to stop acting as though it was she who was at fault because it was him, *him*. But instead she forced herself to begin eating although she had no appetite for the delicacies on her plate.

This was all part and parcel of the reason why anything

other than friendship between them was impossible, she told herself miserably. She had been right not to let anything develop between them, although more and more as time had gone on she had wanted to. Indeed, there had been moments of late when she had wondered if she was making too much of their different stations in life, perhaps a kind of inverted snobbery? But any relationship between a man and a woman, even those of the same class, had to be built on a solid foundation or it would fail when the storms of life hit, and one with Edward would be on shifting sand. She had never seen it so clearly. But she loved him; she'd loved him for a long time.

The evening was over for her and it seemed as though Edward felt the same, because shortly after they had eaten and the dancing began again, he said quietly, 'It's nearly midnight – you must tell me when you would like to go home. I know you rise early every morning to open the shop.'

She forced a smile. 'Now would be lovely if I'm not taking you away from the dancing?'

'I've danced enough.'

He didn't smile as he spoke and Ruby felt a thrill of unease. Something had changed between them tonight and not just on her side. Once she had made her farewells to Clarissa and Godfrey and a few of the ladies from the local suffrage society, they left the hothouse warmth of Foreburn for the bitterly cold night. A frozen winter wonderland greeted them; a heavy frost had fallen on top of the fresh layer of snow during the day and now the night was crystal clear, the frost glittering like diamond dust and the stars twinkling in the moonlit sky.

Edward draped a thick fur blanket about her knees once she was sitting in the car, asking if she was comfortable and warm enough as they left, but saying little else during the journey, which was unusual for him. With every mile Ruby's heart beat faster. He was clearly vexed, and she guessed it was due to the way she had acted with Belinda Ferne-Rice and their subsequent conversation because everything had been all right before then. Was he going to tell her that this friendship, which wasn't really a friendship but something much more, was over? Had he finally accepted what she'd known all along: that they shouldn't see each other again?

The thought caused a piercing pain and panic, even as she told herself it was the best thing, the *only* thing that could work in the long run. She was a working woman, not a sophisticated socialite, and if she was truthful, that sort of women somewhat repulsed her, women like Belinda Ferne-Rice. She saw all sorts in her shop but mostly her clientele had proved to be from the middle class: wives and daughters of businessmen in the town, councillors, magistrates, solicitors and the like, women who had risen in society along with their husbands but whose basic morals matched hers.

And then Ruby shook herself mentally. Who was she to judge anyone, for goodness' sake? And who knew what went on behind closed doors anyway? Half of her clients could be dilly-dallying with other men for all she knew and it was absolutely none of her business how other folk behaved, it was just that . . . She felt a stab of the old pain surface and bit down hard on her lower lip. Just that she could never again bear to be betrayed and feel like she had done when she was eighteen; she'd never recover from it a second time. And for that reason she was looking at a single life as a businesswoman. She had never seen herself in that guise but one day at the bank one of the assistants had referred to her that way, and she'd realized that's how they regarded her.

'You're home.'

Edward's voice was soft and she came out of her thoughts with a start to find he had just drawn up outside the shop.

Before she could speak, he said, 'You're tired now, but there's something I need to say. Could I call round tomorrow before I go back to London?'

'I'm not tired.' Part of her, a big part of her, didn't want to hear what he might say but neither could she endure a sleepless night of wondering. 'What is it?'

He half-turned in his seat, settling back and surveying her through narrowed eyes. He made no attempt to touch her and they looked at each other for a few moments without speaking before he drew in a deep breath, his voice quiet and husky as he said, 'We have known each other for over three years and I have loved you that long.' As she opened her mouth, he said, 'No, let me finish before you say anything. I am thirteen years older than you but I don't see that as a problem in one way – in another, I am conscious that I have lived in a kind of limbo for some time now, and that at thirty-seven the time has come where I want a future in sight. A future that centres round you, a future where you would be my wife.'

'Edward, please—'

'You have always made it clear you wish us to remain as friends and I have respected that, while hoping that in time you would grow to feel as I do. Sometimes I feel you care about me but then at others . . .' He shook his head. 'And so I have continued to tread lightly, to give you time. I know you have had your heart broken in the past and that you carry that sadness with you – perhaps you still care about the man in question, I don't know, because we have never talked about it or anything of substance in a romantic sense.' He paused. 'Do you care about him still?'

For a fleeting second Ruby was tempted to say she did because that would be the easy way out of this, but she couldn't lie to him, he deserved better than that.

'Not in the way you mean, no. He is a different person now and so am I, and I see quite clearly we would never have been truly happy together. We were childhood sweethearts but we are children no longer and in growing up we have changed.' She swallowed hard. 'Perhaps I have changed the most because I know being a wife and having a family is not for me.'

'I don't believe that,' he said softly. 'Are you trying to let me down gently because you don't love me?'

'Edward, please—'

'That's the second time you have said that but I'm afraid tonight it won't work, Ruby. I have told you how I feel and I want an honest answer from you. Don't worry about my feelings. I'm big enough and ugly enough to take it. Do you care for me?'

'You know that you and Clarissa are my dearest friends.'

'That's not what I'm asking.'

Her voice was low as she murmured, 'Friendship is all there can be between us, Edward. You must see that?'

'No, I don't, and I ask you again, do you care for me? Do you love me, not as a friend but as a man?'

She moved her head slowly from side to side, then bit down hard on her lip. She had known this moment would come one day. 'Yes,' she whispered, 'I love you, but that makes no difference to how I see things.'

'I want you as my wife, Ruby. As the mother of my children. I want to grow old and grey with you, but before that I want us to live and love and make the most of every day together—'

'Stop.' She physically drew away so she was pressed against the side of the car as she spoke. 'Please stop. It's impossible. You must be aware of that? Things have changed a little since the war but not that much. How that woman behaved tonight – Belinda – is just a taste of how it would be. If you married me it would cause a scandal that would affect you in every area of your life, not just privately but in your business and so on. I'm sure there's been talk already, as it is.'

'Belinda is a spiteful harpy, she always has been.'

'But she merely voiced what everyone else would think and you know it. We come from the opposite ends of the social scale—'

'And you are content to bow down under such elitism, such injustice? I thought more of you.'

'Then I'm sorry to disappoint you.'

He sighed deeply and visibly took hold of himself before he said in a calmer tone, 'I'm sorry, I didn't mean that and you know it. You could never disappoint me, Ruby. I adore you, worship the ground you walk on. I've never felt like this before.'

For now. But what about when the ostracism began to occur, as it surely would? Sometimes openly, and at other times old friends would keep him at arm's length or show their contempt by snubbing her in that oh-so-upper-class way Belinda had done? It would wear him down, it would wear anyone down, and sooner or later he would tire of having to constantly fight for his wife to be accepted in society. And their children; Edward marrying so far beneath him would affect them too. Besides which – Ruby drew in a long breath – she would not allow herself to be looked down on or patronized, which would cause further problems. She knew herself well enough to realize she would be incapable of not retaliating when she was slighted by people who thought themselves above her simply because of their family background and wealth. A marriage – any marriage – would falter under such strain, and then what? Would he seek solace by taking a mistress from his own class, someone like that awful woman tonight? It was part and parcel of how he had been brought up to think, after all. Or would he simply grow bitter and resentful and come to believe she had ruined his life?

'A relationship between us is impossible,' she said very quietly. 'I'm sorry but I won't change my mind about that.'

'I'm not talking about a "relationship", damn it, but a marriage. You would be my wife.'

'That would be even more impossible.'

'No, it would not. You've admitted to loving me and I would move heaven and earth for you.'

'Love isn't enough for either of us.'

He groaned in exasperation and before she had realized what he was going to do she found herself in his arms. The kiss wasn't the gentle, warm caress she had always imagined it would be with Edward, nor did it resemble the sweet loving embraces she had once shared with Adam as a girl. This was raw passion such as she had never imagined and it called forth a response in her that was frightening in its abandonment. She was gasping for air when he finally raised his head and released her, and as he did so she fumbled with the handle on the car door and almost fell out onto the pavement.

She was fumbling with her key when he reached her, his voice desperate as he said, 'I'm sorry, I'm sorry, I never intended to do that. Don't be frightened of me, please, Ruby. I lost control but it won't happen again, I swear it. Look, let me come in a minute to talk, just talk, I promise.'

'All the talking in the world won't change how I feel.'

'But let me try. Just try.'

'It's no good, Edward.'

'But I love you.'

'And I love you but that doesn't change how I see the future.'

'Then you don't love me enough.' His face had tightened, his whole body had stiffened. There was anger in his stance now, and deep frustration. 'I mean it when I say that if I go now I won't be back, Ruby. I can't live like this any more – it's killing me.'

She closed her eyes for a moment to shut out the sight of him because it was too painful to see the hurt in his face. But she had to do this, for the sake of both of them. Marrying her would ruin him and he'd find himself a social outcast, and she wouldn't be able to live with the guilt of that or seeing their love slowly being tarnished. She gave a shiver and opened her eyes, her voice betraying none of the turmoil inside her when she said softly, 'I understand that, I really do, and – and I want you to be happy with someone else more—'

'Don't say upper-class,' he ground out grimly.

'I was going to say someone more suited to you.'

'That's the same thing as far as you are concerned, isn't it?' When she didn't answer, he went on. '*You* are the woman who is suited to me. Don't you understand that yet? No other woman I look at, no other girl, can compare to you. Everything about you is perfect for me and always will be – your face, your voice, your attitude to life, the way you speak your mind, your strength of will, except, of course, when it's opposed to what I want most in the world.' He paused. 'I adore you, every bit of you. Doesn't that count for anything?'

She felt she was going to cry and was holding on to her composure by a thread. This had to be goodbye because she couldn't go through it again. 'I'm sorry.'

'No, don't say that because you can't be or else you would agree to marry me.'

She stared at him, and as she did so a strange thought came into her mind. Edward had been born with a silver spoon in his mouth and probably had never been thwarted about a thing in his life before. He was rich and handsome and thought the world was his oyster, as indeed it was. What did he know about life, real life, the life *her* folk were forced to live just to pay the rent each week and put food on the table? He was angry and upset now, and she supposed he had every right to be, but how much of his desire for her had been prompted by the fact that she had made it clear from the start there could never be anything but friendship between them?

She didn't know if she was being grossly unfair, but nevertheless, it gave her the strength she needed to draw herself up straight. 'You are entitled to believe as you see fit.'

'And that's it? After all this time, that's it?' He turned on his heel, walking back to the car and opening the driver's door before saying grimly, 'I hope the life you have chosen brings you contentment, but I fear one day you will wake up to find yourself a little old lady all alone except for a cat or two. And don't worry about seeing Clarissa – I won't be visiting Foreburn again so there will be no danger of running into me.'

She stared at him, her eyes huge in her white face, but made no reply, and after a moment he slid into the vehicle and started the engine.

In spite of the lateness of the hour and the bitter chill, she continued to stand there for some minutes after the sound of the car's engine had died away. It was over, not that it had ever really begun, but he had gone and she knew he would not return.

A numbness had settled on her senses, and once she was inside the shop and had locked the door, she didn't immediately go through and make her way upstairs to the flat. Instead she walked to one of the full-length, gilt-framed cheval mirrors and stared at herself. The mirror was a fine piece of furniture. The shaped top, the stand with turned finials and brass side screw knobs on shaped legs with carved knees and claw-pad feet was an object of quality – but then so was every item in the room. The French carved upholstered chairs and small gilt-wood tables inset with serpentine-yellow mottled marble tops that were dotted around on the thick pile carpet screamed luxury, as did the cream-and-rose brocade wallpaper and wall mirrors decorated with acanthus-scrolled designs. The same taste and attention to detail was reflected in the adjoining fitting room with its small cloakroom and carpeted floor; all was comfortable and discreet.

Ruby turned from the beautifully dressed woman in the mirror and glanced round the quiet interior, the glow of achievement she usually felt at her surroundings absent for once.

She had opened the shop within two months of signing on the dotted line, and following Clarissa's advice, the sign above the door read 'Madame Beaucaire'.

'A French name will appeal to your clientele so much more than Ruby Morgan,' Clarissa had said apologetically. 'Trust me on this.' And Clarissa had informed all her friends and acquaintances for miles around of 'the wonderful new establishment' that had opened its doors in Newcastle, suggesting that they pay Madame Beaucaire's a visit and see for themselves. As well as that, some weeks into the refit of the premises, she had arrived on the doorstep with umpteen bags of exquisite clothes that she'd bought in London and only worn once or twice.

'For you, Ruby,' Clarissa had said carelessly. 'I thought it might help if you have a rail or two of pre-owned bits and pieces, but whatever you do, don't call them second-hand. Off-models is the term, all right? They'll boost your initial stock, won't they, and there are quite a few influential women in the town married to businessmen whose husbands are beginning to feel the pinch a little now the economy is struggling, who'll still want their fashionable evening dresses and daywear but won't want to pay as much as they once would have done. If anyone asks, as they undoubtedly will, you can truthfully say they're off-models from London shops. They will simply adore that, trust me.'

Ruby had been overwhelmed by her friend's generosity, especially as Clarissa wouldn't hear of accepting a penny for the beautiful clothes. 'Darling girl, they'd just have been disposed of by my maid,' Clarissa had said offhandedly, 'which is such a waste, after all.'

It was one of the moments when the huge divide between them had been brought home to Ruby; but the clothes were a gift from the gods, nevertheless, not only to sell but to examine in detail and take patterns from for her own pieces. Clarissa had advised her to be pricey – her intended market would expect it – but not as expensive as the shops in the capital, and with her friend's patronage business had been brisk from day one. It still was. Her clothes spoke for themselves and her order book was full, so much so that she'd been able to go ahead with the second part of her plan and convert the annexe to the building into her workroom just before Christmas. This meant her tiny flat was free of the clutter that had occupied so much of it, and could just be her home at long last. She'd had a lovely time turning what had essentially been a workplace into her first real home where she had no one to answer to but herself.

She and Edward had already painted the walls throughout the flat in a warm cream colour in the first week of owning the property, along with scrubbing the floorboards and varnishing them in the sitting room and bedroom. The kitchen and bathroom had new linoleum on the floor. Now, with the drop-leaf table that had been her workstation and had occupied the centre of the room folded away against the wall, its two hard-backed chairs standing either side, she'd found she had room for a small comfortable sofa with chintz upholstery for the sitting room, along with a small bookcase and a coffee table. A couple of brightly coloured shop-bought rugs added to the general air of cosiness, and in the winter evenings when the fire in the hearth glowed and flickered, and the thick curtains at the window shut out the darkness, Ruby was conscious of a sense of peace. Not happiness – happiness was something else and intrinsically tied up with Edward, which made it impossible to achieve.

This last reflection pierced the numbness and she hurried out of the main shop and through the fitting room into the tiny square of hall beyond. This now boasted a door to the flat. Edward had insisted the builders make this modification on the grounds of privacy and safety when they had carried out the other work, and although she wouldn't have thought of it herself, she had been pleased with the end result. It kept the shop and her home independent of each other and it was nice to have a separate key to her living quarters. She was thinking of employing an assistant in the near future – her workload was already too much for one person and she needed to delegate where she could – and although she might think about giving a key to the shop to someone in the future, her home was a different matter. As Edward had said, an Englishman's home – or Englishwoman's – was his or her castle.

Oh, Edward. *Edward.*

By the time she had climbed the stairs the anaesthetizing numbness had melted away and the full reality of what had just occurred had flooded over her. He had gone. Gone for good. She would never see him again and she only had herself to blame. She collapsed in one of the armchairs and gave vent to a paroxysm of weeping, and much later, as a quiet winter dawn broke and the street below the flat emerged slowly into life, she was still asking herself if she had done the right thing – or whether she had made the biggest mistake of her life.

Chapter Twenty-Two

Life had gone on, the days and weeks merging into a blur of hard work and such a full order book Ruby had taken on two assistants rather than one, but as the year neared its close a few days stood out from the past months. One was the death of Emmeline Pankhurst in June. The First Lady of women's suffrage was buried in an emotional ceremony attended by hundreds of her followers, many of them wearing the colours of the Women's Social and Political Union, and Ruby had attended with Clarissa and the chairwoman of their local branch. On the same day an American, Amelia Earhart, became the first woman to fly the Atlantic, battling against terrible weather to bring her seaplane down in a South Wales estuary. It seemed very appropriate that such a significant event had occurred on the same day that Mrs Pankhurst was saluted as a 'heroic leader' and a woman who had encouraged her own sex to believe they were every bit as good as men, Ruby and the others had thought.

Another less newsworthy but to Ruby even more

momentous occasion happened in August when she bought herself a little car. The thrill of holding the sulphur-yellow driving licence in her hand for the first time and knowing she was free to drive herself where she pleased was intoxicating. Her Morris Minor was the latest model from Morris Motors and she immediately christened it Alfie, although quite why she wasn't sure. 'He' just looked like an Alfie, she told a bemused Clarissa when she drove to Foreburn for Sunday lunch.

But it was in November on the first Sunday of the month that she was tested to the utmost. By unspoken mutual consent, she and Clarissa had never discussed Edward since the day of her friend's party. It was clear by Clarissa's silence about her brother that Edward must have confided something of what had occurred between them, Ruby thought, but Clarissa's friendship had not wavered and the two women had carried on as normal. But that Sunday, when she had arrived for lunch, Clarissa had taken her aside and told her that Edward had been living in America for the last few months and had been seeing a rich young heiress to whom he had just got engaged.

'I thought you ought to know.' Clarissa had stared at her with troubled eyes. 'I confess I don't think his heart is in it and I'm more than a little surprised but there it is.'

It had taken every ounce of strength for Ruby to be able to nod and say calmly, 'Pass on my congratulations to them when you have a chance. I'm sure they'll be very happy,' but she didn't linger after lunch, unlike most Sundays.

Once she got home that day she had faced the truth that had flooded over her the moment she heard the news. She regretted, with every fibre of her being, sending Edward away. She had been fighting against admitting it to herself for months, but even as he had driven away that snowy night at the beginning of April she had known it was a mistake. She should have swallowed her pride and gone to see him the next day or in the following days, but she hadn't. She hadn't. And now it was too late. A marriage between them might have been a disaster but, equally, it might not have been; now she would never know. It was a bitter pill to swallow, but swallow it she must and get on with things. The alternative was to curl up in a little ball and die, and that wasn't an option. She had felt like this once before when she had first arrived in Newcastle after Adam's betrayal, and she had got through then. She would do so again. But this was much worse. Before she could blame Olive and Adam for her suffering; this time the fault was hers and hers alone.

But now it was three weeks before Christmas and the weather was so cold no one would have been surprised if the sleety rain that had been falling for the last week or so had come down in ice cubes. She and her two seamstresses were working longer and longer hours as the festive season approached – it seemed all the well-to-do women in Newcastle and for miles around had parties and social functions they simply had to have new clothes for, but if nothing else it had convinced Ruby that she had to take the plunge and open another shop in the near future. It was simply a matter of finding the time to look for one, but then just that very morning one of her seamstresses, a sweet and rather shy young girl who reminded Ruby of Ellie, or the Ellie in the days before her friend had met Daniel Bell, had told her about a property that had come up for sale close to where she lived just a few streets away in Ridley Place at the back of Ginnett's Amphitheatre. Ridley Place was only a quarter of a mile or so from her present shop, which Ruby thought was perfect. She had already decided that a new business would be aimed at women on the large size and would stock mainly outsize clothes; it seemed among the middle class there were plenty of stout matrons who would pay the prices she asked to look as though they had been dressed by a London fashion house, at the same time as appearing pounds lighter than they were.

'It's a lovely shop, Miss Morgan,' Polly said earnestly. 'It's been a draper's ever since I can remember, an' it's in a row like this one. There's a watchmaker's next door an' a wool shop the other side if I remember right. You ought to go an' have a look.'

'I will, Polly. Thank you.' If the shop had been run as a draper's, hopefully it wouldn't need much in the way of alterations to bring it in line with what she had in mind, but she would have to see. Her first appointment that morning was with a lady coming in for a fitting and the evening dress was ready for the client to try on, so deciding there was time to quickly pop to Ridley Place before eleven o'clock, Ruby left the shop.

The premises were slightly larger than the present shop, being in a terraced row of three-storey shops with what looked like an attic room under the eaves. After she had ventured in and explained why she had come, the present owner – a dapper little man in his sixties – escorted her round the shop and the living accommodation above. The only modifications Ruby felt were needed on the ground floor were the addition of a cloakroom and indoor toilet, thereby making the privy at the end of the yard obsolete, and painting and decorating throughout. The flat, although neat and clean, had no modern conveniences, an outside tap being the only source of water for the premises. As she intended to employ a manageress to live above the shop, the cost of converting the smaller of the two bedrooms on the second floor into a bathroom and providing running water for the kitchen would have to be taken into account. The attic room was presently being used for storage and was packed so full she couldn't see much. Nevertheless, it seemed promising and she told the owner she would be in touch with the estate agent handling the sale.

True to her word, that evening she visited the agency and found out more details with a view to setting the wheels in motion, and the following morning contacted the owner of the shop to ask permission for her builder to come and view the premises so he could give her a price for the work she would want carried out.

When she had first begun considering a second establishment some weeks before, she had thought it sensible to pay a visit to the building society to enquire how they would view her buying a further property. The manager, who had been watching the success of the first shop closely, had agreed that – subject to certain guidelines – he saw no reason not to lend her the money for a second venture.

Within twenty-four hours her builder had given her a quotation and, unwilling to let the grass grow under her feet, she put in an offer for the premises, which was accepted. By the end of the week she'd been to the building society and everything was under way.

She hadn't seen Clarissa for some time while all this was going on. Godfrey had finally retired from the army and to celebrate he had whisked his wife off to Europe for a holiday, taking in the sights of Italy and Greece, and finally ending up in Paris for a week or so. And so it was with some surprise that the weekend after the purchase of the new shop was completed, Ruby answered a knock at the door to find Clarissa on the doorstep, as bubbly and effusive as ever. Over coffee, she told her friend about recent events, admitting that the speed with which her latest acquisition had happened had left her feeling shell-shocked.

'Darling, it's wonderful, just wonderful.' Clarissa kissed her on both cheeks. 'You're doing so amazingly well and so you should – your clothes are divine. My goodness, a woman of substance! Lady Russell was asking after you only the other day when we spent a few days in London after returning from Paris. She's never forgotten how you saved my life, and she thinks this new endeavour of yours is fabulous.'

Ruby smiled but didn't comment. Lady Russell had been present at Clarissa's party in the spring, and Ruby had got the distinct impression that the aristocratic noblewoman had disapproved of the friendship between herself and Edward. Women from every walk of life having the right to vote was one thing but Lady Russell, like so many of her class, believed that those walks of life should be kept clearly defined with no party stepping over into a different one when it came to marriage and family. Indeed, Ruby had often wondered what Clarissa's reaction would have been if she and Edward had told her they were in love and intended to marry. Would her friend have welcomed her with open arms, or would there have been reservations? Much as she cared for Clarissa, she rather thought it would be the latter. And she couldn't blame Clarissa if that was the case, not when she herself could list a whole host of reasons why a match with Edward could have been a disaster. Anyway, all that was incidental now. She had sent Edward away and he had lost no time in making his home abroad and falling in love with someone else, which perhaps indicated that she had been right all along.

Knowing that when she let her mind go down this particular route it resulted in bitter heartache and confusion, Ruby steered the conversation to Clarissa's recent holiday and let her friend enthuse about Paris. 'Here.' Clarissa passed over a large embossed carrier bag that had a Parisian designer's name on it. 'An early Christmas gift but I knew it would suit you. Oh, and there are some French fashion magazines too; I know you don't speak French but the illustrations will give you an idea or two, won't they. Darling, it's all little skull caps over there of silver and gold tissue designed to cover the ears as well as the hair, and skirts are set to get longer apparently but women must be pencil-thin. Godfrey wasn't at all impressed. He said this slimming craze is set to turn women into boys and he finds it repugnant, so at least I can eat my cream cakes and chocolates and other goodies with impunity.'

Ruby had delved into the bag while Clarissa had been speaking and now, as she brought out an exquisitely made dress and jacket in dove-grey raw silk, she said, 'Oh, it's beautiful, Clarissa, thank you so much.'

'My pleasure.' Clarissa leaned forward and took her hand. 'Will you come to Foreburn for Christmas Day? We would love to have you.'

Ruby had accepted this invitation for the last two years and she knew the house would be crowded with friends and family. Quietly, she said, 'Thank you but no, not this year, but it's very kind of you.'

Clarissa stared at her. 'Edward won't be coming – he's spending Christmas in America.'

With her. 'Nevertheless, I won't come.'

'About Edward.' Clarissa paused. Since her brother

had gone off across the ocean she had done some hard thinking and one thing she was sure of. He and Ruby should have been together. He had been in such a state that night of the party when he had arrived back at the house after taking Ruby home, and when he told her what had transpired, she had urged him to go straight back and bang on Ruby's door. He had almost glared at her as he said, 'You've changed your tune. The last time we talked about this you were of the opinion that there was no meeting point between her class and ours, if I remember rightly. "The class system is still alive and well." Isn't that what you said? Along with the fact that Ruby would be a fish out of water in our world the same as I would be in hers.'

'Yes, I did say all that, and I was wrong.'

'She doesn't think so. If it's any comfort, she thinks exactly like you do.'

'Did.' She had stared at Edward's tormented face as she had repeated, 'Did.'

He had waved his hand angrily. 'Did, do, it makes no difference. It's what Ruby thinks that counts.'

Remembering this now, Clarissa said softly, 'He's not happy, Ruby. I know he's not. His letters . . . Well, they don't sound like Edward.'

'Some people find it difficult to express themselves on paper.' The words were spoken so quietly as to be almost a whisper.

'Not Edward. I know he's—'

'*Clarissa.*' Now it was Ruby who paused. From barely

being able to get the words out she knew she had barked her friend's name. 'I'm sorry,' she said more calmly, 'but I don't want to discuss this. He is engaged to be married and that's the end of it. It's – it's all for the best.'

'Do you really believe that?'

'Yes.' She had to believe it, needed to, otherwise she would go mad. 'Yes, I do.'

Clarissa inclined her head. She wasn't convinced but she felt as though she had said as much as she could.

They talked a little more before Clarissa left and Ruby went downstairs to work in her sewing room. It was a Sunday morning and for once she was glad that she was so busy she had to keep her nose to the grindstone non-stop over the next few days if she was going to fulfil her commitments. It meant she couldn't think about anything else but the job in hand and that was what she needed.

Apart from stopping for a quick bite at lunchtime and again about six o'clock she worked through till midnight, and she only ceased then because she was so tired she was in danger of falling asleep sitting at her work table. But she had got through a mountain of work, which was satisfying and would also take the pressure off herself and the two girls in the coming week. She had already warned them to make it clear to customers that no further alterations could be promised before Christmas, and that any clothes must be sold strictly on that understanding until the New Year.

When she walked into the flat, her gaze was drawn to the luxurious carrier bag that held Clarissa's gift and she felt a stab of contrition. She hoped she hadn't appeared ungrateful in refusing her friend's invitation for Christmas Day, but the memories of the previous two years when she had been in Edward's company would have been too much in her present state of mind.

She had also declined the same invitation from her mother, but this time it was Olive she had been thinking about. She had seen her sister and niece several times since she and Olive had been reconciled, always at her mother's house so there was no likelihood of running into Adam, but at Christmas that wouldn't be possible. Her mother had confided months ago that things were much better between Olive and Adam, but she would have guessed this herself anyway. Olive was twenty-eight years old, but this was the first time ever that Ruby could remember seeing her sister anything other than waspish and bitter. And it was strange, but such was the power of love – and it was abundantly clear now that Olive did indeed love her husband – that there were times when her sister's face took on an attractive quality and you forgot about her plainness. How Adam felt, Ruby didn't know, but it was clear he was making Olive happy, which perhaps spoke for itself.

This thought wasn't a new one and at first Ruby had struggled with the realization that after all Olive had done, things had worked out for her sister with Adam, her old childhood sweetheart that she herself would have married. But then reason had asserted itself and she'd given herself a stern talking-to. The past was the past and she didn't love Adam any more, not in that way. Her niece was a beautiful little girl and she needed a loving family home, and whatever had happened to change how Adam treated Olive and his daughter was to be applauded. But at the same time she felt, and she didn't try to analyse the whys and wherefores, that it was better for everyone concerned if she and Adam didn't run into each other, at least for the foreseeable future. Her sister wouldn't like it, and although she didn't owe Olive anything, especially with regard to Adam, she loved her, and therefore, just in case . . .

When she fell into bed she was asleep as soon as her head touched the pillow.

It was the following morning, just before midday, that the bell on the door tinkled and Adam's youngest brother, Ronnie, walked into the shop. Ruby recognized him immediately even though she hadn't seen him since the day he had come to see her at Mrs Walton's with the message from Adam that had altered the course of her life so drastically. In those days he had been a grubbier, much younger edition of his older brother, and now he was the spitting image of how Adam had looked at thirteen or fourteen. Whether it was the memory of that other time that caused Ruby's heart to drop like a stone she didn't know, but she found herself incapable of speaking a word as they stared at each other. It was only Polly coming forward and saying, 'Aye, what is it?' in a tone that stated all too clearly this high-class shop wasn't the place for the likes of him, that enabled Ruby to turn and say, 'It's all right, Polly. I'll deal with this.'

'Mam sent me.' Ronnie, too, found his voice as he flashed an indignant glare at Polly. 'There's been a fall.'

There's been a fall. They were the words every mining family dreaded. Even before Adam had begun working at the pit she'd been afraid of those words, knowing how close he was to his father and brothers, and then when he, himself, had gone down the mine she'd never been free of the fear. 'Come upstairs. Polly, you and Sarah take over, and I'm not to be disturbed.'

Once Ronnie was standing in her sitting room twiddling his cap between his fingers, she said, 'You're frozen – come and sit by the fire and I'll get you a hot drink in a minute.'

She was putting off the moment when he would tell her, she was aware of that, and maybe he was too because he didn't move from his spot just inside the door but blurted, 'They're all down, me brothers, an' your da's bin took bad an' all. The shock, the doctor said. Mam said I had to come an' tell you 'cause her an' da are at the pit gates and Olive an' all.'

He was clearly on the verge of tears and through the horror Ruby found herself saying calmly, 'That's a good lad, you've told me – now come and sit down, all right? Just sit here and I'll get you something to warm you.' The icy rain of the last days had given way to a light dusting of snow that morning and now more flakes were drifting in the wind.

'I've got to get back.'

'I know, Ronnie, and we'll go together once you've eaten something and had a hot drink. I've got my own car so it won't take long. Have you had anything inside you this morning?'

He shook his head and rubbed at his nose. 'Me mam's bin at the gates all night, she won't leave.'

Once she had him settled in front of the fire in her sitting room she made him a cup of tea and a pile of bacon sandwiches, leaving him to thaw out while she went downstairs to explain the situation to the girls. They immediately rose to the occasion, assuring her they would be pleased to hold the fort for however long she was away.

'We'll stay late and finish all the alterations that need doing, Miss Morgan, and open up at the same time each morning. You stay as long as you're needed,' Polly said earnestly. 'Family comes first every time, that's what me mam always says and it's true. We'll keep a record of anything we sell in the book, don't worry. We know what's what by now.'

It was half an hour later by the time Ruby left, and Ronnie was looking considerably brighter for having demolished the heap of sandwiches and several cups of tea. Just before she slid into the driving seat of the car, Ruby looked up at the white sky. Why was it everything bad seemed to happen when it was snowy? she asked herself painfully, and what was she going to find when she got home? From what Ronnie had said she surmised her father's heart had been affected by the shock news, and what about Adam incarcerated underground, his brothers too. They had to be all right; anything else was unthinkable.

On the way into Sunderland, Ruby found herself regretting that she hadn't spoken to Adam since that first visit home. Not that they had parted on bad terms, not really, and she had made it clear to him that she had forgiven both him and Olive – she was glad about that – but she'd also told him that she had moved on and he must do the same. But what else could she have said? she asked herself. It was the truth, however unpalatable it had obviously been to him. And thinking about it logically, could things at home ever really settle into anything like normality with the ex-sweetheart becoming his sister-in-law and auntie to his child? It was best they didn't meet; she'd resolved that in her mind before this present fall at the pit. Maybe years hence, when they were all old and grey and the passions of youth had settled into something less fiery, she and Adam and Olive could meet in a family situation without it being a problem.

On and on her thoughts raced, interwoven with worry about her da's condition and how her mother was feeling and the terror that the fall was a bad one. Ronnie sat beside her not saying a word, and once they reached the town she drove straight to the pit to drop Ronnie off and also to find out if there was any news before she carried on to her mam's. She parked the car in Wreath Quay

Road and she and Ronnie walked quickly to the crowd standing at the pit gates. It was comprised mostly of women of all ages and a few old men, and there were two constables stopping anyone entering the yard beyond the gates. She saw Olive and Adam's mother and his brothers' wives straight away. They were standing in one of the small groups that made up the crowd and Adam's father had his arm round his wife. No one was saying anything and no one was crying; in fact, on the whole it was eerily quiet.

As Olive saw her she gave a little cry and then pushed through the crowd to fling her arms round her sister. Taken aback by the open show of affection, Ruby returned the hug and after a moment, when they drew apart, she looked into Olive's agonized face and whispered, 'Oh, lass, lass.' Olive just shook her head, unable to speak, and then slipped her arm through Ruby's and drew her over to Adam's mother and the others.

'Hello, lass.' Adam's mother's voice was dull, and as his brothers' wives nodded to her, his father said, 'They won't let me go down, damn 'em, in the rescue squads. Said they needed younger men because the air's putrid and old lungs wouldn't cope.'

Ruby didn't know what to say and as Ronnie sidled close to his father, Mr Gilbert said, 'This is why I said I don't want you going down when you leave school in the summer, all right? Nowt to do with whether you'd be a good miner or not. All the pits are in a hell of a state, your brothers have told you that. Timber's rotted, there's water gathered an' gas built up, an' the ventilation is shot – an' the owners aren't liftin' a finger to put anythin' right after the strike. Nor will they. No, nor will they. They won't spend a penny on makin' the pits safer 'cause in their eyes miners are barely human beings an' if there's falls an' explosions, so what? A few men an' lads lost is no skin off their nose 'cause they know there's more waitin' to take their places from the herd. An' that's how they look at us – animals in a herd from which they can pick an' choose whenever they like.'

'John.'

Mrs Gilbert only murmured her husband's name but it was enough to check the outburst as he glanced at her face, grey with worry. He muttered something and then lapsed into silence, his lips moving one over the other.

'There's six been brought up dead and ten others injured but alive,' Olive said quietly. 'Barney and Toby Johnson were both killed – their mam collapsed when they were brought up.'

Ruby stared at her sister, aghast. Barney and Toby were identical twins and the same age as Adam; they were their mother's pride and joy and had still been living at home. Olive reeled off the other names of the deceased, all of whom were known to Ruby, before she said, 'They were all on one side of the fall in the main road. Adam and the rest of the shift are behind it, but – but they're worried about the air.'

Suffocation. Carbon monoxide. Explosion. Death. All the words that had been with her in her early years with

Adam rushed through Ruby's mind but she found herself saying quite calmly, 'They have air pockets sometimes, you know that, and even a little clean air can be enough to keep a man alive until the rescuers reach him. Don't give up hope, Olive.'

'I don't want to live without him.' It was a whisper for her ears only. 'I know what I did was wrong and I hurt you and he suffered too, so much because he loved you so deeply, but – but we're all right now, him and me.'

'I know, I know.' She didn't want to hear this in spite of having come to terms with it.

'He's my life, Ruby. I know I can never be what you were to him but that doesn't matter. If he dies –'

'He won't, he won't. Keep believing that.'

'I'm trying to.'

Olive's teeth were chattering with the cold and now Ruby said softly, 'Where's Alice? Shouldn't you go home and see to her, lass? She needs you.'

'No, I can't leave here, not till – till I know. My neighbour's seeing to her, I couldn't take her to Mam's 'cause of Da. When he knew Adam was one of those who was down he had a sort of seizure. He thinks a lot of Adam. One in a million, he called him, the other day.'

'I'd better go and see how Da is but I'll come back if I can. Do you want me to bring you anything? A hot drink or something?'

Olive shook her head. 'All the folk round about keep bringing us mugs of tea or soup an' the like. They've been very kind.' Olive caught hold of her arm. 'What am I going to do?'

'Keep believing he's all right, that's what.'

'I can't.' Olive shivered.

'Well, I'll believe for the both of us then.' Now it was her who hugged Olive, and as her sister clung to her as though she would never let her go, Ruby thought how strange, how terrible and strange, life was. If anyone had told her a couple of years ago, before she had come back to Sunderland that first time, that she and Olive would be one in heart and mind with the past of no account, she wouldn't have believed them. By the time she turned and walked away both their faces were wet, and as Ruby slid into the car and dried her cheeks on a handkerchief, Olive was still standing where she had left her, a tall, thin figure in the falling snow.

Chapter Twenty-Three

Adam had been aware of the pain even in his sleep but now, as he surfaced from the nightmarish dream, it hit hard. Clenching his teeth to prevent himself groaning out loud, he opened his eyes. Three of the miners' lamps had survived intact – Walt and two other men had been ahead of him and the others when the roof had come down, and he thanked God again they weren't in the dark, although the rays of light were a mixed blessing. They showed the huddle of bodies of men who had been killed.

He had seen Walt swing round as a terrible, unforgettable sound like a giant grinding its teeth had told them the roof was moving, but then there had been nothing but an almighty cracking and deafening roar as the slabs of rock, choking slack and black splinters had engulfed him, Fred and Pete either side of him and the rest of the shift behind them. He didn't think he had lost consciousness at that point because he could remember the thick dust suffocating him as he tried to breathe and the feeling that a huge hand was holding him down. It wasn't until moments later when scrabbling hands had clawed at the rocks and earth and found him, and then attempted to pull him free, that the excruciating pain had sent him into blackness.

When he had come to he'd found himself cradled in Walt's arms as his brother had sat with his back resting against the wall of rock. Apparently he'd been out of it for nearly an hour and in that time Walt and the others had pulled several more men out of the mountain blocking the road, but none had been alive apart from him. Fred and Pete had gone, along with Cyril Foster whose wife was expecting their first bairn; Ray O'Leary and Archy Shelton, two old timers; and Desmond and Joe Shawe who were father and son. How many were still buried was anyone's guess; the whole shift could have bought it because the roof was monumentally unstable. In the middle of Walt and the other two trying to dig out more bodies the roof a little way down the tunnel had suddenly caved in too so they were essentially now entombed in a little pocket of the main road with a fall either end stopping rescuers reaching them.

He moved slightly, and immediately Walt said, 'You all right, man? They'll be through to us in no time, don't worry.'

Walt's breathing was laboured – there wasn't much air – and for a moment Adam almost said, 'No time might be about right,' but that would help no one. Instead he nodded, but even that slight movement of his head brought piercing pain. His whole body from his neck down to his toes felt like it was being stabbed by hot knives.

His voice a whisper, Walt said, 'You in much pain?'

He wouldn't have believed the human heart could suffer pain like this and not give up. 'A bit.'

'Aw, man. Hold on and once they get through they'll give you something.'

Walt was saying the right thing but his brother knew as well as he did that he was too smashed up to survive this, and would he want to? He'd seen other miners, one or two young men like him, who'd been involved in accidents and been left in a hell of a state, good for neither man nor beast and a burden on their loved ones. He wouldn't want that for Olive, or for his bairn to see her da as a thing to pity.

Olive . . . His head was getting increasingly muzzy – it was the lack of air. If death came like that he'd welcome it as a release from this pain because he didn't think he could stand it much longer. But Olive, Olive would miss him. Somewhere in the depth of him he felt a deep sense of regret that he had never told Olive he loved her. It wouldn't have been true, but did that matter? He liked her, cared about her after all, and she loved him with a passion that had surprised him more and more over the last months and had invoked in him a secret feeling of gratefulness because it acted like a soothing balm on the part of him that was still raw at Ruby's rejection. Olive made him feel like a king in their little house and he'd found himself actually looking forward to getting home after a shift. He'd been saving his beer and baccy money since the beginning of the year and unbeknown to her he'd bought her a ring he'd seen in the pawnshop. It had been cheap – with money so tight it had to be – but the bloke in the shop had assured him it was gold even if the three stones were blue glass rather than the real thing. But it was pretty and he knew Olive would like it. It was nothing like the small cluster of diamonds and garnets he'd given Ruby when they'd got engaged, but at least it wouldn't make Olive's finger green. He'd been planning to give it to her on Christmas morning once Alice had unwrapped the doll they'd bought her. Olive had been knitting clothes for it for weeks with any scraps of wool she could find; he'd made her laugh when he'd remarked that the doll would be a darn sight better dressed than the rest of them. He liked to make her laugh . . .

'Walt.'

'Aye, man?'

'I – I've got a ring for Olive. She never had one apart from the wedding ring with how things were back then, but – it's for Christmas.'

'That's grand.'

'It's hidden behind the wardrobe in our bedroom. Make sure she gets it and – and tell her I love her.'

'Aw, man, what are you on about? You'll tell her yourself and give her the ring an' all. Don't be daft.'

'Promise me, Walt.'

Walter adjusted his position slightly so he could look

down into his brother's face. He'd always regretted the stupid prank they'd played on Adam, which had had such disastrous consequences for so many people, but never so much as now. His voice choked, he whispered, 'Oh, lad, lad. I'd give me right arm to go back in time.'

They both knew to what he was referring. Adam wondered how something that had mattered so much was completely unimportant. He had never been able to bring himself to forgive his brothers but now, his lips hardly moving, he murmured, 'Don't take on, Walt. Olive's a good woman and the bairn's a joy, and you didn't know how it was going to pan out. Forget it. I have. Water under the bridge. But promise me you'll tell her. Promise.'

'Aye, aye, lad. Course I promise. Lie quiet now. Hear that tapping? I wasn't sure a minute ago but there it is again. They're coming. It won't be long now.'

The pain had gone and in its place was a sense of peace Adam could only wonder at. He was more tired than he had ever been in his life and a buzzing in his ears was making it difficult to think, but if this was the way God was going to take him he was thankful for it. He roused himself enough to say, 'Walt, I want to pray but I forget the words.'

'Pray? Well, aye. There's worse things we can do while we wait, eh, lad?' Walter's voice was over-hearty. 'Remember when we were bairns how Mam made us kneel every night by our beds, bless her, and say the Lord's Prayer afore she'd let us up off our knees? Didn't matter how cold we were, we still had to say it and slow, mind. No gabbling. Here goes then. "Our Father, which art in heaven. Hallowed be thy name. Thy kingdom come, thy will be done . . ."'

When Walter came to the end of the prayer he became aware that the tapping he had thought he'd heard for a while was louder, and now he could definitely hear voices too. Softly, he said, 'Adam, lad, listen. I told you, didn't I? We'll be out soon. Adam?' He looked down into his brother's face in the dim light. There was a smile about Adam's lips and his eyes were closed. For a moment Walter breathed a sigh of relief. He was sleeping. Just sleeping.

One of the other two men left alive crawled across to them and then brought his ear close to Adam's chest. He remained still for a while before raising his head and then shaking it slowly. 'I'm sorry, Walt.'

Walter stared at him and then gathered Adam's limp body fiercely against his chest with a sound an animal might make. The tears raining down his face and making white rivulets in the grime, he began to shout. He cursed the mine and the unbearable suffering it inflicted on those who robbed it. He cursed the owners who carelessly sacrificed men and boys to die in agony in filthy holes under the ground because they thought them worth less than the cattle in the fields of their country estates. He cursed the government and the whole of the middle and upper classes who sat before their roaring fires in their fine houses and toasted themselves on their victory at putting the miners back under their heels where such 'creatures' belonged. He cursed the lot of them to hell and back. And all the time, as he cried out, he held Adam against his heart as though its beat could somehow bring his brother back to life.

George Morgan lived for another hour or so after Ruby arrived home, and the doctor himself said it was only the patient's desire to see his younger daughter before he went that had kept him alive for the last twenty-four hours. Ruby and Cissy sat either side of his bed in the front room holding his hands as he slipped away, and after they had cried together, Ruby made her mother go upstairs and lie down, fearing she'd collapse.

Once Cissy was settled in bed with a stone hot-water bottle at her feet and the curtains drawn, Ruby waited until she was sure her mother was asleep before going downstairs to the kitchen. She felt odd, she admitted to herself as she brewed a pot of tea, and so full of a mixture of emotions that she couldn't have said even to herself which was foremost. Grief for her da, worry for her mother, overwhelming fear for Adam, concern for Olive. The list was endless but she had to keep calm and be strong for everyone; her mother and sister needed her to do that. But Adam would be all right, she told herself in the next breath. He had to be all right. He and Olive were happy at last and they had Alice. They belonged together, she could see that now. It hurt a little, but more because no one belonged to her than anything else. If she'd had Edward . . .

Her mam slept for a couple of hours and once Cissy

had come downstairs, Ruby asked the next-door neighbour, who was a great friend of her mother, to sit with her while she herself went back to the pit to be with Olive. She arrived just as word spread through the crowd outside the gate that the rescuers were about to break through to the men on the far side of the fall. She slipped her arm through Olive's and whispered about their da after Olive asked how he was, but she could see Olive's whole being was concentrated on Adam.

It was another hour before the survivors were brought up.

For ever and a day Ruby would remember the moment when Walter walked out of the pit gates flanked by the other two men who had been rescued alive. The sound of the gates clanking open, the falling snow, the silently waiting crowd and the hope on people's faces as they rose on tiptoe and craned their necks to look for their loved ones, and then the low moans and cries as a deputy began to make the announcement that was the worst possible news for so many.

Walter's wife had pushed through to meet him and was clinging to him as though she would never let him go as he reached his mother. He didn't have to say anything – his face spoke for itself – and as she all but fainted Olive, along with Fred and Peter's wives, helped hold her up, united in their grief and loss.

Ruby had stepped back a pace from the family group. She felt she was on the outside looking in, part of them but not part of them. She had no right to mourn as they were doing, but in this moment the loss of the Adam she had loved – the childhood friend she'd grown up with and the sweetheart he'd become – was nigh on unbearable. It was Adam's father, who when she and Adam had been together had treated her as one of his own, who put his arm round her and held her tight, the tears rolling down his wrinkled cheeks. And only then could she let her own flow.

George Morgan was buried six days later and the day after that was the service for Adam and the other miners. The morning dawned bright and cold, a white winter sun turning the fresh fall of snow during the night into a beautiful glittering winter wonderland. It was cruel that it was such a lovely day, Ruby thought, as she and Cissy made their way to Olive's house. The day before had been almost a blizzard when they had buried her father but that had seemed more fitting somehow. Today, the sunshine and the mother-of-pearl sky seemed a mockery in the circumstances.

It had been decided that Cissy would stay with her granddaughter, and Ruby would represent Adam's in-laws with Olive. The last few days had taken their toll on Cissy, and both Ruby and Olive were worried that the length of the mass funeral, coming so quickly on the heels of George's the day before, would be too much for their mother to cope with.

It seemed as though every house in every street of the town had their curtains closed as a mark of respect as the two women walked on, and when they reached Olive's back lane no bairns were playing out as would have been expected. In fact, everywhere was still and quiet with no sign of activity in the backyards and no washing hanging out even though it was a Monday. Ruby had never known anything like it and it felt eerie.

When Ruby looked back on that day in years to come, she could only picture it as a series of images in stark monochrome. The dark clothes of the townsfolk lining the funeral route under the white winter sky; the grim procession of black plumed horses pulling the hearses; the blindingly spotless snow coating the cemetery; the dark wood of endless coffins with their wreaths of white flowers, and overall the bleached pinched faces of the mourners standing like a flock of desolate crows round the graves. Black and white. All colour sucked out of the world by the scale of the tragedy that had unfolded.

When Adam's coffin was lowered into the ground side by side with Fred and Peter's, Ruby found herself holding her sister up as Olive's knees gave way. Up to this moment Olive had been quietly stoical but now she was unable to control her sobs, the sound being torn out of her like a wounded animal in a trap. All Ruby could do was to hold Olive tight, their tears mingling as their faces pressed together. And still more names were called and more coffins lowered and more wives and mothers sobbed and grieved and more fathers and sons cursed the pit.

And then, at last, it was over.

*

'But – but you don't have to do this. I mean – why would you? I can't let you . . .' Olive's voice trailed helplessly away.

It was the morning after the funeral and Olive, Ruby and Cissy were sitting at Cissy's kitchen table having a cup of tea while Alice looked at a picture book on the clippy mat in front of the range. There had been no semblance of colour in Olive's face when she had walked into the house that morning, nor any life in her voice when she had said that yes, she was all right, thank you, and yes, she would have a cup of tea, but over the last few moments her countenance had changed. Cissy, too, was staring at her younger daughter in sheer amazement.

Ruby smiled at them both. She had been awake most of the night making plans and formulating the ideas that had been at the back of her mind since Adam's death. Over the last few days her mother had suddenly become an old woman; it was as though with her husband's death the main spring that had kept her going through all the ups and downs of the last years had snapped. And Olive was like a lost soul. Most of the time she sat quietly turning the little ring that Adam had apparently bought her for Christmas round and round on her finger, her face ashen and her eyes pools of pain. Ruby didn't know if it had made her sister feel worse or better when Walter had relayed Adam's last message to her. At the time she had broken down completely and she hadn't spoken of it since.

Now Ruby said briskly, 'The way I see it, this would

be good for all of us. I need someone to manage the new shop and the couple of staff I'll employ, and the flat above the premises would mean that you, Mam, could take care of Alice while Olive's working. The flat, of course, would be rent free as part of Olive's salary and you could bring anything you like from here, both of you, to furnish it as you please.'

Olive stared at her sister. She hadn't really slept since Adam had gone; partly because of her grief but also because she had been racking her brains as to how she and Alice would survive. It had been clear that either her mother would move in with her or she and Alice with her mam because two lots of rent was impossible, but even then anything she might earn – supposing she could actually find work of some kind – wouldn't cover the rent along with food and other bills. A hundred scenarios had been played out in her head every night, and in the depths of the dark hours the spectre of the workhouse had loomed closer and closer. Even if Ruby took their mother to live with her, how would she and Alice manage? She couldn't survive on charity from her sister, she wouldn't, whether or not Ruby could afford it for a time. It would be too humiliating. But now Ruby had presented a proposition that changed everything. She would have a job, one that would provide a roof over their heads and a secure home for Alice at a time when the slump was getting worse and worse and unemployment was increasing with terrifying rapidity. There had always been a chasm between rich and poor, but now gaps were opening up between those who had work and those who did not.

Getting up from the table, she walked round it and took a chair next to Ruby, reaching for her sister's hands. 'Thank you, lass,' she whispered, the tears running down her face and dripping off her long chin. 'You didn't have to do this, I know that.'

'Olive, we're family,' said Ruby softly.

Cissy, too, was weeping, and part of her emotion was a deep thankfulness that her two girls were – as she put it to herself – kind again, the old northern term for reconciliation, because didn't Ruby doing this prove that? The new priest who had taken the place of Father McHaffie after he had succumbed to a bout of influenza two years ago was a great one for saying all things work together for good, and he was right. Father Kane also preached a lot from the New Testament about love and it was generally agreed within the congregation that Father McHaffie must be turning in his grave.

'So.' Ruby glanced at her mother. 'That's agreed then? Once the alterations are done and the flat's ready after the New Year we'll hire a vehicle and get you moved in. It'll take a while to stock the shop and get everything in order but that's all to the good. I can be showing you the ropes, Olive, and explaining what's involved.'

'Do you think I can do it?'

'With one hand tied behind your back,' Ruby grinned. 'You're a very capable lady and you can be quite scary – perfect management material.'

For the first time since Adam's death, Olive smiled. 'I'm not sure if that's a compliment or an insult.'

'The former. Definitely the former.'

'That's all right then.'

'And over the next little while you and Mam can decide between you what you want to bring, bearing in mind you're going to have to fit two households into one.'

'I'm not leaving my three-piece suite,' said Cissy immediately.

Ruby and Olive exchanged a glance. Ruby had the feeling that her sister would need to bite her tongue quite often in the coming days.

Ruby left for Newcastle the following day. Once back, she immediately visited the new premises where her builder was hard at work. Now that the attic room had been cleared of its contents, she could see the idea she'd had regarding it would work. She told the builder she wanted the space divided into one small room and a larger one, with a narrow landing outside so each room had its own door. It would be perfect for Alice and Olive, whilst her mother could occupy the bedroom on the floor below. With her sister and niece's comfort in mind, she told the builder she wanted the roof better insulated against the harsh northern winters and for his carpenter to build in wardrobes and a dressing table to make the most of the limited space under the sloping roof.

Ernest McArthur listened to 'the bit lass with ideas

above her station', as he had previously described Ruby to his wife. He knew why she had spent the last week in Sunderland, and he had offered his condolences on her return, but now, as she explained the reason for the extra work she wanted doing, he found himself re-evaluating his opinion of her. He didn't hold with all this new thinking about women being able to stand for Parliament and equal rights and the rest of it – a woman's place was in the home and that was that, and a young lass like this one setting up a business on her own with no man to keep her in check wasn't right in his opinion – but, that said, it seemed the lass's heart was in the right place. And to be fair, she'd paid him promptly for the work he'd carried out on her first property, which was more than most of the blokes he dealt with did.

Mentally knocking a few pounds off the amount he had intended to ask when she had first mentioned the conversion of the attic room, he offered a few practical suggestions of his own before they agreed a price and Ruby disappeared.

Once she had left, Ernest stood for a few minutes, puffing at his pipe as he cogitated the peculiarities of life. There was that lass, as bonny as ever he'd seen, but with no man to look after her. Nor did she seem to want one. What had happened to that fancy gent who'd been around when he'd first met her he didn't know, but as he'd said to his wife at the time, that could only end one way and to his mind the lass was lucky she hadn't been left with a bellyful. But no, she was doing all right. More than all right, and whilst he didn't begrudge her the success, where would the world be if girls, women, thought they could behave like men rather than being content looking after their own hearths? It wasn't right. Whatever way you looked at it, it wasn't right and no good would come of it. Women weren't as bright as men, never had been and never would be, everyone knew that. He nodded to the thought and then as one of his sons came in, muttering something about having dropped a hammer on his foot for the second time in as many days, George sighed. There were some blokes who weren't much cop up top an' all, mind.

The new premises were completed at the end of January and within three days Cissy, Olive and Alice had moved into their home which, as Cissy herself said, was a cut above anything she could have imagined. Mr McArthur and his sons had done a fine job in the flat; not only was it bright and modern with its own bathroom and a new gas stove and freshly painted cupboards in the kitchen, but the living room and the three bedrooms had wall-to-wall carpeting and the curtains at the windows were thick and luxurious. Once the removal men had brought the furniture that Cissy and Olive between them had decided to keep, selling the excess, the flat became home, and by the time Ruby opened the second shop just weeks later, the strained, haunted look had lifted from Olive's face.

Although Ruby had constantly assured Olive that she would be a great success as manageress she knew it had been something of a gamble on her part, but within a short while it was clear Olive had taken to the job like a duck to water. She proved to be an excellent saleswoman, and the two seamstresses that Ruby had taken on were in awe of her sister. Indeed, as Ruby remarked to Olive one day in the spring, she had been right about her sister being somewhat scary but in the best possible way, for the business at least.

Cissy enjoyed keeping the flat spick and span and seeing to Alice once the child was home from school, and at the weekends Ruby often joined the three of them for Saturday afternoon high tea when her mother would bake an elaborate spread that could have fed the whole street. Alice had settled well into her new home, and although she often spoke of her father there were fewer tears as time went on.

By the summer, when Ramsay MacDonald formed a new Labour government with a woman in the Cabinet for the first time as Minister of Labour, Ruby knew the second shop was as great a success as the first. With her bank balance steadily increasing and her order books full for months ahead, so much so that she was well on her way to paying off the first mortgage, her mother and Olive contented and fulfilled and Alice doing well at school, and her Sundays with Clarissa now and again keeping her in touch with her friend, Ruby knew she ought to be the happiest woman alive. And she was – she was happy, she told herself on those nights when she tossed and turned until the early hours. It would be terribly ungrateful to be otherwise. True, there was an Edward-shaped hole in her life that grew more painful and not less as time went on, especially when she thought of him in the arms of another woman. And yes, in spite of how close she had become to her sister and her mother over the last months, she knew there would always be a gulf between her and them now. It was she who had changed and become a different person, but that didn't make it easier to bear. And even with Clarissa she could never truly be herself. Perhaps she didn't know who she was, come to that, so how could anyone else really understand her? She didn't fit in anywhere, that was the thing. It was the price she had paid for following her dreams. And that was all right, it really was – most of the time.

Chapter Twenty-Four

Edward drove through the open gates of the Kingston estate but brought the car to an almost immediate stop. Leaving the engine running, he gazed at the huge stone house in the distance set on an incline within the six-acre parklands and gardens surrounding it. The first time he had seen it he'd thought it looked like a grand Virginian house – tall, haughty, almost isolated from the land around it. He'd later discovered that Verity's grandfather had hailed from Virginia and when he had moved to the outskirts of New York and bought the land, he'd had the house built almost to a replica of the one he had been brought up in.

There was no doubt it was one of the most magnificent houses in the area, both inside and out. The stone was a soft rosy colour and when illuminated by the setting sun, like now, seemed to be swallowed up into the sky itself. A decorative stone terrace ran the length of the property and this, along with the house, had red and green ivy climbing over it. Inside, it was surprisingly light and modern; Verity's grandfather had obviously been a forward thinker. Sunlight poured in through large Palladian windows reaching from floor to ceiling in most rooms, and from a central glass dome onto the huge winding staircase. The classical proportions and the scale of the house meant that light was carried from room to room; nowhere was there a hint of dullness or darkness. It was a residence that was meant to impress and it did, and the army of indoor servants under the jurisdiction of Josiah Kingston's butler, Hutton, kept it running like clockwork. Outside, four gardeners saw to the extensive grounds and walled kitchen garden and greenhouses, and the fine semicircular stable yard with its many horse boxes and beautiful Arabian animals was manned by two grooms and three stable hands. All those servants looking after a family of four. Edward stretched and then put his foot down on the accelerator. How had he allowed himself to be sucked into it all? He must have been mad. He *had* been mad when he'd first met Verity; mad with grief at losing Ruby and in a state that had verged on self-destructive.

As he drew up outside the massive front doors of the mansion they were opened immediately and a tall, slim woman stood in the aperture. Verity Kingston was her father's only daughter and the apple of his eye. Her older brother, Randolph, was a somewhat dour and cold-hearted individual who had none of his sister's whimsical charm and teasing ways. It had only been lately that Edward had come to realize that Verity's winsome allure concealed a nature every bit as ruthless as her brother's.

She had been denied nothing she wanted from the moment she could toddle, and she had made it clear from the outset that she wanted him. And he, fool that he was, had been flattered and gratified.

He forced a smile as he walked up the steps and onto the terrace. Verity was looking lovely; she always looked lovely and dressed in the height of fashion, choosing clothes that showed off her figure and natural poise. Her shining sleek black hair that looked like wet sealskin was cut in a chin-length bob that accentuated her large, heavily lashed blue eyes and delicate features, and her skin was pure peaches and cream. It was only her mouth that hinted at the iron will and inflexible disposition the sweet, girlish exterior concealed, being thin and on the tight side. Tonight it was set in a straight line, and she greeted him with, 'You're late.'

He could have lied and said he'd been delayed at the office but the truth was he was dreading yet another dinner with Verity and her parents and a number of their friends. Verity's mother threw dinner parties at least twice a week and keeping a high social profile was everything to the family. Her father was a highly intelligent man with a fine eye for art. He collected Holbeins, Murillos, Roman marbles and statuary, as well as antique weapons: crossbows, halberds and medieval armour. Every time he went to the house Edward felt he was expected to admire something new that had been acquired. With this in mind he had deliberately delayed his arrival until he knew cocktails would be over and dinner imminent.

Glancing at his watch, he said, 'The invitation was for dinner at eight.'

'And cocktails at seven.' Verity's eyes narrowed. Edward was in one of his difficult moods – she recognized the signs. Deciding the success of the dinner party was more important than challenging him, she slipped her arm through his, saying softly, 'But I forgive you. Come and meet everyone. The Harrisons are here and they've brought their niece from the Deep South with them. Oh, my word, such a country bumpkin and her dress must be at least ten years out of date. And Angeline and Scottie are back from honeymoon and positively glowing – it's indecent.'

She continued to prattle on as she led him into the bright lights of the house, the smell of hothouse flowers assailing his nostrils and the chatter from the guests finishing their cocktails in the huge drawing room sounding like the buzz of very well-mannered bees. Once Hutton had sounded the dinner gong and they had all trooped through to the bedecked and bejewelled dining room with its snowy linen, silver cutlery, crystal glasses and more extravagant flower displays, he found himself sitting with Verity on one side and her father on the other. Josiah Kingston was in fine form, having taken receipt of an Egyptian statue that day, which had duly been admired and applauded by those present as being one of the best in his huge collection.

At what point during the meal Edward knew he couldn't go on with the farce that was his engagement, he wasn't sure. Perhaps it was when Verity asked the Harrisons' niece, who seemed a gentle, nice girl, where, *exactly*, she had got her dress because she simply must have one the same, to the obvious amusement of a few of the other female guests. Or when one of their usual number who wasn't present that night had her reputation mauled to pieces because the lady in question was seeing an employee who worked for her father's broking firm. 'I mean, he's a runner for the firm, darling. Can you believe it? A runner.' Or yet again when someone asked Verity how the wedding plans were coming along and he knew a moment of blind, unadulterated panic that made him sweat.

He looked round the table at the life he would be expected to embrace and the people he would mix with, and he knew he couldn't do it. He had known for some time, perhaps from the morning after the night when he had drunk too much and had been manoeuvred, ever so cleverly and sweetly by Verity, into agreeing to marry her. He never had been able to remember actually proposing but one minute they had been alone in her father's study drinking champagne on an evening like this one, having escaped the throng in the drawing room for a while, and the next she had professed her love for him and he had felt obliged to return in like measure. And then she had dragged him to the drawing room and made the announcement before he could blink. Squeals of excitement and clapping and congratulations from all and sundry had followed, and he had stood there smiling gormlessly with his head swimming.

There would be hell to pay now. He glanced at Verity in her exquisite evening dress, her ears and neck and arms glittering with some of the jewels her father heaped on her, and felt a sense of relief at knowing what he was going to do. However bad it was, whatever happened, he had to tell her tonight and walk away. If he didn't, he'd be lost forever.

'Don't be ridiculous, Edward.'

The other guests had left including Randolph and his very loud American wife, and Verity's parents had retired to their separate suites on the first floor. He and Verity had been sitting having coffee in the drawing room before he drove back to the flat he rented closer to the main hub of the city, and he had just told her he couldn't marry her.

'I won't allow you to break our engagement.'

Edward blinked. He had been expecting a tantrum or tears or sheer rage, but Verity's icy cool and almost amused attitude had taken him aback.

'I'm sorry, Verity, and you are a wonderful girl for someone, just not me. I don't fit into the requirements you demand of a husband – you know that as well as I do.'

'I know nothing of the sort.' Verity took a long pull at her cigarette in its bejewelled holder, letting the smoke drift out of her small nostrils before she added, 'You are coming up to scratch very well,' and smiling as she put her hand over his. 'You've been a bachelor too long and it's natural to be a little nervous at the thought of having your wings clipped.'

Her voice had been light and teasing but her blue eyes were like chips of frosted glass, and Edward knew the signs. She was furiously angry inside but, like the consummate actress he now knew her to be, hiding it well. Again he said, 'I'm sorry but I mean it. I can't marry you and believe me, this is the right thing for both of us. I could never make you happy, Verity.'

'*Spare me the platitudes*.' For the first time her tone revealed what she was feeling, but when she went on her voice was level again. 'We are going to get married, Edward. I will not be held up as a laughing stock, I tell you that now.'

'And nor would I want you to be. You can tell everyone that you ended the engagement – you can say whatever you like and I won't disagree. Paint me as black as you like.'

'How very gracious of you.' Her voice, although controlled, was belied by the expression on her face. 'You do this to me and you will regret it, I'll make sure of it, and my father will too. He's a very powerful man, Edward, as you know. He can be a bad enemy.'

'I can't stop either of you doing your worst.'

There was a moment of deafening silence before she hissed, 'It's her, isn't it? That little shop girl in England you told me about?'

'This is nothing to do with Ruby and she is not a shop girl as you know full well but the owner of a successful business.'

'Making clothes to sell in her shop. A shop girl.'

Her face was ugly now, white lines showing round her mouth and her eyes narrowed. He shook his head, standing up as he said, 'Have it your own way but I repeat, this is nothing to do with her. There is no chance Ruby and I will get together, Verity. And I mean it when I say you deserve someone who will make you happy and I could never do that.'

Her persona changing, she said, 'You could. You do.' She jumped up and became the girl he had known in the early days, soft, warm, vulnerable, clinging. It was a front and he knew that now, had seen evidence of it time and time again when her cruelty and disdain, especially to those she considered beneath her, had made him cringe inside, but nevertheless, the little-girl act made him feel like a cad.

Telling himself he couldn't weaken, he moved her gently back from where she had pressed herself against him, the faint perfume she always wore wafting into his nostrils.

'I'm sorry,' he said for the third time.

Verity gazed at him for a moment, a combination of anger, frustration and hate showing on her white face, and then she slapped him twice across his cheeks with enough force to make his head snap back and jerk his neck painfully.

'My father said you were weak and he is right. "A typical English gentleman," he said. "All wind and little else." He warned me that if I married you I would be carrying you for the rest of our lives, but I told him I could make something of you.'

'Perhaps I never wanted something "made" of me,'

said Edward evenly, his face burning and a thin trickle of blood running down his cheek where one of her rings had caught him.

She stared at him fixedly. 'No, perhaps you never did. You're a loser at heart, after all, an under-achiever and content to be so. I thought I could take you to greatness but you're a small man, Edward Forsythe. I see that now.'

'Have you finished?'

'No wonder this other girl didn't want you, and her just a shop girl too. But she could see you for what you are, couldn't she? That is the truth and that's what brought you across the ocean to lick your wounds. She didn't want a lead weight round her neck any more than I do, so yes, I am finished. Here –' she flung her engagement ring at him – 'take this and get out. I never want to set eyes on you again.'

He made no attempt to catch the ring and neither did he retrieve it from where it had fallen at his feet. He had expected her to let fly at him and he had told himself that whatever she said or did she was entitled because he was the one at fault. What he hadn't expected was her words piercing the core of him, especially what she had said about Ruby not wanting him. And even though he knew that Verity being Verity would go for the jugular and show no mercy, the fact that she had brought his own deeply buried insecurities and fears of failure to the surface had hit him straight between the eyes.

He swung round without a word and went out of the drawing room to find Hutton standing in the vast hall holding his hat and coat. What the butler had overheard he wasn't sure, but the man was stony-faced as he thrust the clothes at him rather than helping him on with his coat as would have been normal, before marching to the front door and flinging it open. There was no 'Goodnight, sir,' or 'I trust you have had a pleasant evening,' and as Edward stepped out of the house the door swung shut so quickly it almost caught the heels of his shoes.

He stood for a moment in the balmy September air staring towards his car waiting for him in the shadowed night. There had been much in the newspapers a few days ago about America finally joining the International Court of Justice, but he didn't think he would see much fair play from Verity and her father and the rest of them over the coming weeks and months if the butler's attitude was anything to go by. But perhaps he didn't deserve it. He should never have got romantically involved with Verity in the first place, he'd known that, so why hadn't he struggled harder when she had reeled him in like a fish on the end of a line? Damn it, what an unwholesome mess.

Verity was standing quite still in the drawing room. She heard the front door close and then after some moments the sound of the car starting up. She followed it down the drive and out of the gates to where it faded to nothing once the car reached the road. Her eyes burning, she began to pace back and forth. How dared he, how *dared* he do this to her? He would pay for treating her this way, as though she was one of the countless silly little debutantes doing the rounds in New York with not a brain cell between them. She was a Kingston and she could buy and sell him a hundred times over.

After some minutes she sat down on one of the sofas after pouring herself a large glass of brandy. She was meeting some of her girlfriends at the Copley Plaza Hotel for lunch the next day and they'd planned to spend the afternoon at Long Island. She had to have her story straight by then as to the absence of her engagement ring because they would notice it was gone in the first moment.

A discreet knock at the door and her 'Yes, what is it?' brought Hutton into the room, and as she stared at the old retainer who had been with the family from the first days of her parents' marriage and whom she knew to be utterly loyal to them all, she said flatly, 'How much did you hear?'

Hutton cleared his throat. 'Enough, Miss Verity.'

'I could kill him.' She swigged back the brandy, and as Hutton coughed and said, 'Shall I get you more coffee, miss?' she said sharply, 'Oh, don't be so stuffy, Hutton. Not tonight. Sit down, I need your advice.'

Neither of them thought it strange that she was confiding in him before speaking to her parents. Hutton had always been the glue that held the establishment together, and from a little girl she had known this. As he bent and retrieved the engagement ring and then sat down, she stood up and fetched another glass, pouring a brandy and handing it to him before she resumed her seat. 'What shall I do?' she asked simply.

Art Hutton took a sip of his drink before replying. He was aware of his unique position in the household, which long ago had exceeded that of a servant. He knew everything there was to know about 'his' family as he thought of them, and he also understood Verity probably better than she understood herself. She had never treated him as she did the other staff, and he in turn was devoted to her in spite of her many failings. Quietly, he said, 'You have broken the engagement with Mr Forsythe because certain things have come to light regarding his business ethics which you are, of course, not at liberty to discuss.'

Verity stared at him, her eyes widening.

'Disappointed and sad as you are, personal happiness has to be put aside when such circumstances present themselves.' He took another sip of brandy. 'Of course, you will be brave and dignified in your distress and refuse to discuss the matter further. Insinuation, hints, nothing that could be held up in a court of law while you maintain a loyal and composed silence.'

Verity breathed out slowly. 'Hutton, you're diabolical,' she said reverently.

'A reputation is a fragile thing,' Hutton went on, 'and your father has influence in many quarters. It is often more what is not said that sows seeds of doubt. I think by the end of the year the gentleman in question might well return to England like a whipped dog with his tail between his legs. If that is what you want?' he added.

'It is.'

Hutton nodded. From the beginning he had been of

the opinion that Miss Verity had been dazzled by the young Englishman's good looks and ancestry, beguiled by the thought of a member of the British aristocracy dancing to her tune. In spite of all the Kingstons' wealth and influence and their power in America's high society, she'd regarded Edward Forsythe as a feather in her cap, which he found strange.

'Will you have a word with your father in the morning before he leaves the house and acquaint him with the facts?' he asked in his stiff way.

Verity nodded. 'Father will be furious with him.'

Hutton knew what she was saying. Where Miss Verity was concerned, Mr Kingston could well act first and think later.

'I'll make sure Mr Kingston sees the wisdom of following through on what we have discussed, and I would suggest it would be wise if your mother and brother were not told the details of what happened tonight?'

'I agree. Mother can never hold her tongue about anything and Randolph's hopeless when he's had a few drinks. We'll keep it between Father and you and me, Hutton.' Verity stretched like a sleek cat. The thought of her friends and everyone knowing she had been thrown over had been unbearable, but now she could see she'd emerge from this with her status as the most sought-after catch in society intact – which was all that mattered. And Edward *had* become a little tedious lately, like tonight with his covert disapproval when she had teased the Harrisons' niece.

Jumping up, she said, 'I'm going to bed,' and before he could rise she dropped a kiss on the top of his balding head, took the ring that he held up to her and danced out of the room.

She hadn't thanked him, and nor had Art Hutton expected her to, but the momentary show of affection was worth more to him than anything she could have said. He had denied himself a wife and children for the sake of the Kingston family, knowing that he could not have given them his all if he had distractions in his private life. His was a somewhat solitary existence, but ever since she had been a little girl Miss Verity had made it all worthwhile, like tonight. The other members of the family he served with dedication and faithfulness, but Miss Verity he loved and adored with a father's heart and he knew that in her own careless and self-centred way she loved him too.

He drained the last of his brandy and stood up, placing his glass and Verity's on the coffee tray; he didn't immediately carry it through to the kitchen but stood staring at the huge, practically life-size family portrait that hung over the ornate marble fireplace. Josiah Kingston and his wife were seated with their two children standing behind them, Randolph looking more cheerful than he ever did in real life and Verity laughing down at her father who was half-turned in his chair to look up at her.

Art stared at the portrait for a long time, and when he eventually turned away it was with a brief stab of pity for the young man who had left the house a short while ago. Edward Forsythe had no idea what he had done in spurning Miss Verity, he thought to himself as he left the room. But he would soon find out.

As it happened, a catastrophe that far exceeded the wrath of Josiah Kingston and his daughter brought Edward to his knees just a few weeks later. On a day that would become known as Black Thursday, Wall Street – the beating heart of America's financial stability – crashed.

In an unprecedented wave of fear and confusion and panic, nearly thirteen million shares changed hands on the New York Stock Exchange. Dazed brokers, wading through a sea of paper, clutched frightened investors' orders to 'sell at any price'. At the peak of the panic selling the market ceased to function and turned into a mad clamour of salesmen looking for non-existent buyers, with stocks being dumped for whatever they could bring. By midday, New York's leading bankers held an emergency meeting and police riot squads were called to try and disperse the hysterical crowds gathering in Wall Street awaiting news.

Edward stood in the throng, as stunned and disbelieving as many around him, telling himself he should have cashed in his investments months ago. The incident in June the year before, when Wall Street share prices had plunged with some leading shares falling by as much as forty points, had been a warning of things to come. That fall had been triggered by massive selling of aircraft shares and panic selling had followed, even though no particularly bad economic or financial news had been issued during the day and stock-market experts were unable to provide any explanation of what had provoked the dramatic slump. He had felt in his gut then that he should sell up and go home to Britain, but he was heart-sore about Ruby and had become involved with Verity by then. He had taken his eye off the ball. He nodded to the thought.

The bankers emerging from their hour-long discussion brought his attention back to the present, and as the mob surrounded them, desperate for some assurance, he listened to the bland statement that the situation was 'technical rather than fundamental' and that the market was essentially sound. He didn't believe a word. For whatever reasons, the spree of easy money and over-confidence was now finished and the bear market had returned with a vengeance, crushing the dreams and aspir-ations of an army of small investors, some of whom – like him – had lost everything in just a few hours. The boom was well and truly over.

It was late evening by the time he walked back to his flat and although he'd had nothing to eat all day he wasn't hungry or thirsty. He sat slumped in a chair hardly able to believe what had happened for most of the night, a hundred thoughts whirling around in his head. His father would just love this, he told himself bitterly. From the time he had put a tentative step into the business world of investments, his father had been predicting that his son's 'wheeling and dealing' would end in disaster. His brothers, like the puppets they were, had followed suit, begrudging his success more and more as the years had gone by. Only Clarissa had believed in him, and it looked now as if her belief had been misguided all along. He had failed. Spectacularly. Verity had been right. He was a loser in every sense of the word. How she would love this.

He put his head in his hands, a blackness so profound there was no end to it enveloping him. He had nothing to live for now. Someone in the crowds still milling about Wall Street when he had left had said that a dozen or more speculators had committed suicide already, and he could understand that. He had always regarded suicide as the coward's way out before this; how judgemental and arrogant was that?

He had been a fool to end fools, that was the truth of it. Even last month he had been aware that some investors had started selling shares in large numbers after a number of financial experts had warned that the American economy was slowing down, but he had let it roll over his head, more concerned with the rumours about him which he was sure were originating from the Kingstons. Stupid, stupid, stupid. The self-recrimination and bitter regrets went on and on until he started to feel he was losing his mind.

As a grey cold dawn began to break, he considered his options. A couple of days ago he had paid the rent on the flat until the end of November; after that he would have nowhere to stay. He had no prospects, virtually not a penny to his name, and since the Kingstons had been spreading their poison, no friends.

He brushed his hair back from his brow and was surprised to find he was sweating as his hand came back damp. He'd been feeling ill for a day or two and had wondered if he was going down with something; standing in the wind and drizzle of rain in Wall Street all day yesterday wouldn't have done him much good. Not that it mattered. Nothing mattered.

Standing up, he found that his head was swimming and his legs felt like lead. He stumbled into the small bedroom and threw himself down on top of the covers, too exhausted and nauseous to try and get undressed. He knew he probably ought to make himself a hot drink and have a couple of pills for the headache that was now beating a tattoo in his brain, but it was beyond him. Curling into a ball, he shut his eyes and fell into a troubled, restless doze.

Time ceased to have any meaning over the next days. He knew he was ill, more ill than he had ever been before, but the pains racking his body and the torment in his mind made rational thought impossible. Bouts of delirium made him sure at times that he was back in the apartment he had had in London before he had sold up and come to America. Sometimes Ruby was there, looking down at him with pity and sadness as she reiterated why they could never be together; once or twice Verity had stood over him, laughing as she had told him he was weak and useless and an excuse for a man and that everyone despised him. Of the two manifestations he preferred it when Verity was with him; the thought of Ruby knowing how far he had fallen made him sick to his stomach.

He had managed to stagger to the kitchen a few times and get himself a glass of water but he had eaten nothing – just the thought of food made him retch – and mostly he existed in nightmares of sweating and harrowing half-dreams, only to come briefly to himself and realize that reality was far worse than anything his subconscious could drag up. Verity had called him a dead weight and she was right; it would be better for everyone if he died, here and now, and if this influenza took him and saved him the job of killing himself then that was all to the good.

It was over a week or more when he became aware that the aches and pains that had been in every muscle and bone were now all centred in his chest. Every breath was painful like a fire burning inside him and the coughing that racked him constantly was agony. He had stopped drinking, his throat was too sore to swallow, and now he lay in damp, sweat-soaked sheets too exhausted to move.

When Clarissa first looked down at him he thought it was another of the apparitions that had come and gone since he had fallen ill. He was aware of his surroundings again now, and how could his sister be in New York? And so he had simply shut his eyes and refused to try to talk, drifting back into the semi-conscious state she had awoken him from. How much later it was when he came round to find a doctor examining him he didn't know, nor was he really aware of being transported to hospital or being stabbed with needles and having drips set up over his bed. He coughed and slept, and coughed and slept, while the doctors and nurses in the private hospital Clarissa had had him rushed to battled against the pneumonia that had filled both lungs with pus and could even now take his life.

It was four days later when he opened his eyes one evening and looked at Clarissa fast asleep in a chair by the side of his bed. He had known she was around before this but had never been able to keep his eyes open long enough to speak, just managing to smile at her before drifting off again. Now, though, his mind was clear for the first time in two weeks, and he whispered her name. 'Clarissa?'

Her eyes opened instantly and the next moment she was kneeling by the bed, tears spilling down her cheeks as she murmured, 'Edward, oh, Edward. Thank God, thank God. I must call the nurse—'

'No.' He found he was too exhausted to even raise his hand. 'First, how . . .'

She understood what he meant even though he was too tired to continue, saying, 'When we heard about the crash, Godfrey managed to secure us a cabin on the *Mauretania* and we left almost immediately. Oh, darling boy, you've been so very ill.'

He didn't know about 'had been'. He still felt at death's door. 'Lost everything,' he muttered, gasping as even the two words made him breathless.

'I know, I know, but don't think about that now. Just concentrate on getting well. Godfrey has been to see the Kingstons, by the way, and he put the fear of God in them by the end of the visit. They were trying to paint a picture of a man we didn't know and Godfrey wasn't having any of it. Your little Verity is a snake, isn't she.'

'Not – not mine.'

'No, and I'm glad you came to your senses there. Now go to sleep, my darling. I'm here and I'm staying until you are well and then taking you home. Everything is under control and blue skies will come again one day, I promise you.'

Blue skies will come again one day. He went to sleep with the words ringing in his ears but not quite able to believe them.

It was a month later, and as was the custom for the big liners, the *Mauretania* was sailing at midnight from her North River pier after a farewell party that had continued to the last minute. As the huge ship eased out of her berth festooned with paper streamers her siren, pitched two octaves below Middle A, announced her departure from American shores back to the old world. The sound carried with it a whole history of departure and arrival, longing and loss, dreams hoped for and dreams smashed, but for Edward, as he sat on deck buried under the mountain of blankets Clarissa had insisted on bundling round him, the main feeling was one of resignation.

He was still recovering from the pneumonia that had

been within a whisker of taking his life, and his doctors had told him that he would be low mentally as well as physically for some time, but he knew it was the fact that he had come to terms with his future that had gradually deadened his emotions. He had had nothing but time with his own thoughts over the last weeks, and he had realized that he would never have married Verity, or any other woman for that matter. He had allowed the American girl to bulldoze him into the engagement, but as for walking down the aisle and promising to be with her for the rest of his life – it would never have happened. Because, and here his thinking was particularly painful, his heart was so irrevocably Ruby's that he would prefer to live life alone than suffer another woman in the role of his wife. And here was where he had told Clarissa they would have to agree to disagree.

He shifted slightly in his seat, trying to get comfortable. Not that the chair itself was uncomfortable; everything on the *Mauretania* and her sister ship, the *Lusitania*, had been made with their passengers in mind. The grand staircases were on the fifteenth-century Italian model; public rooms were treated either in the Italian or French Renaissance styles and the dining rooms were panelled in straw-coloured oak in the style of Francis I, each having a dome in cream and gold. The state rooms, the first-class lounges and even the lavatories were beautiful, and the smoking room had a fire basket and firedogs that had been reproduced from originals at the Palazzo Varesi, according to Godfrey who took a keen interest in such things. Edward had travelled on her before and had great respect for the speed with which the *Mauretania* cut through the Atlantic, the roughest and hardest of seas, especially in the winter months like now. The great ship could steam hard into a head sea and lift her bow sixty feet before dipping and burying it as she cleaved through the water, thrusting it to either side, but he wasn't looking forward to what could be a choppy crossing. Though he had coped fairly well with seasickness in the past when he had been fit and well, he was neither now.

His musing brought his mind back to Ruby again, and the conversation he'd had with his sister about the girl he loved. Clarissa had told him that she knew Ruby cared for him – hadn't Ruby herself told him that, and the reasons why she felt any permanent relationship between them was impossible?

'It was all about you being so wealthy and moving in top circles and the lifestyle you had,' Clarissa had said earnestly. 'But that's changed now. In fact, she is wealthier than you. The chasm between you has gone, along with your fortune, and you can meet as equals in Ruby's eyes. It's as if the way has been cleared at last. Don't you see?'

He had stared at her as though she was mad. 'Clarissa, my sweet, you've been reading too many romantic novels,' he'd said with a smile, hoping to deflect her from further conversation. 'As you said yourself, Ruby is making a huge success of her business and what could I offer her? Any relationship between us is more impossible than it has ever been.'

'No, no, it's not, Edward.'

'It is, and with all respect to your sisterly affection, I don't wish to discuss this.'

'It's your pride, isn't it? Do you mean to tell me that you would let your pride stop you being with the one woman you love?'

He had stared at her and said, 'A remnant of pride is all I have left. I would rather be hanged, drawn and quartered than become a lead weight round Ruby's neck.' The words Verity had flung at him had cut deep. 'It's over between us, Clarissa. That is final. I mean it.'

'I can see that you do.' Clarissa had sighed and shaken her head. 'I love you, Edward, I really do, but you are a fool.'

'I love you too and you're right, I am, which is another reason Ruby is better off without me.'

'Oh, you!' She had stamped her foot and left him with a flounce. The memory of that day brought a wry smile to his lips as he watched Clarissa and Godfrey make their way towards him from where they had been standing waving to the crowds on the dock, none of whom they knew. He loved his sister, and he appreciated the devotion that had brought her and Godfrey rushing across the Atlantic to be at his side, but he wished they had arrived just a day later. According to his doctor, all his troubles in this world would have been over by then.

Chapter Twenty-Five

Edward had been installed in one of the bedroom suites at Foreburn for a week when Ruby went to see him in the middle of December. He was up and about most of the time but still frail, retiring to his private quarters most days after lunch for a nap and joining Clarissa and Godfrey again in the late afternoon for cocktails before dinner. He was irritable and frustrated by what he perceived as the slowness of his recovery, but had found he had to give in to the exhaustion and weakness for the simple reason that it brought him to the point of collapsing if he attempted to fight it.

His parents had visited when he had been back in the country for three days and it hadn't been a happy meeting. Mr and Mrs Forsythe had come in a spirit of 'I told you so' and had left within an hour after Clarissa had ordered them out of the house when Edward had become so incensed he'd been in danger of having a seizure. They had departed threatening never to return, and had been further put out when Clarissa had told them that this was a promise she would hold them to.

Now it was the third Sunday in the month and the morning was bright but bitterly cold. There had been heavy frosts for a week but no snow as yet, and as Ruby had driven to Foreburn the glinting sparkle of spiderwebs in the hedgerows and the thick white coating on bare trees carried a desolate beauty all of their own. She stopped the car at one point and wound down the window, breathing in the icy air as she gazed across frozen fields shimmering in the weak winter sun that was doing its best to melt the carpet of frost. She needed to compose herself before she saw Edward. Clarissa had called to see her the day before and invite her to lunch, but the main reason for her friend's visit, Clarissa had told her candidly, was to acquaint her with Edward's changed circumstances. Clarissa had held nothing back, emphasizing that Edward had called off his engagement some weeks before the Wall Street Crash because he was still in love with Ruby and always would be, and that on top of losing everything, he had been as near to dying as a person could be and still survive.

'But he's changed, Ruby,' Clarissa had said sadly. 'He sees himself as a failure and it's done something to him. I don't know how to reach him, I confess, and Godfrey has tried and got nowhere. He's talking about joining the RAF when he's well enough – he had some flying experience when he was younger – or failing that trying for the Civil Service. He can speak several languages and with his Eton background they'd probably snap him up. He – well, he's got this fixation about not becoming a burden to anyone.'

Ruby sighed, leaning back in the car seat for a moment and shutting her eyes. How she would eat any lunch she didn't know because her stomach had been doing cartwheels since Clarissa's visit the day before. Her mother had baked a splendid high tea as usual yesterday evening but she had only been able to nibble at a sandwich and swallow a small custard tart. While Cissy had been reading Alice her bedtime story, something she loved to do and which Alice enjoyed because her grandmother didn't mind going over the same story time and time again, unlike her mother, she had confided in Olive about Edward. She hadn't meant to, but once she had started the whole story had come out.

When she had finished, Olive had looked at her and said, 'You still love him.'

She'd nodded.

'And you would accept him now he's poor?'

'Even if he had come back rich I would have married him. I'd realized how stupid I'd been not to give it a chance after he had gone to America but it was too late then. And then he met this other girl . . .'

'So tell him that. When you see him tomorrow, tell him.'

'How can I? He'll think I'm feeling sorry for him.'

'Feeling sorry, my backside,' said Olive forcefully. 'From what his sister has said, he's not going to say anything to you, is he, not feeling as he does about himself? So it's up to you to make the first move. Look, lass, if you love him like you say you do, what have you got to lose? Better telling him and him still clearing off, than not telling him and always wondering whether it might have worked.'

She had nodded. Put like that it seemed her only option. Now, though, doubt had crept in. Clarissa had seemed so sure that Edward still loved her and that it had been that which had ended his engagement, but could she really be as sure as she claimed? He must have felt something more than affection to get betrothed to the American girl so quickly? Actually ask her to spend the rest of her life with him? Would they have got back together if the Wall Street Crash hadn't happened and then Edward had become so ill? It might have been a lovers' tiff that would have got sorted out but for the catastrophe that had followed.

She made a sound of irritation in her throat and straightened, winding up the window and starting the engine. Enough. At this rate she'd drive herself mad before she got to Foreburn. Feeling as though she was teetering on the edge of a precipice she drove on, vitally aware that the next few hours would determine the rest of her life.

'You've done *what*?'

'I've invited Ruby for lunch.' Clarissa faced her brother calmly. 'You know she often dines with us on a Sunday when we're at home.' For a moment she thought he was going to explode – certainly he had more colour in his cheeks than he'd had thus far – but then she watched him take control of himself.

'Of course,' he said stiffly. 'This is your home and you are free to do as you please, but I will take my meal upstairs if that is all right.'

'No, it's not all right. That would be positively insulting and you know it. I know things were difficult between you when you parted but surely you can be civil to her?'

Much as he loved his sister, right at this moment he could throttle her. Edward glanced at Godfrey who shook his head. 'Don't look at me, old boy. I had no idea either.'

'It's Sunday lunch, for goodness' sake.' Clarissa hid behind annoyance. 'Don't make such a drama of it, the two of you.'

Sunday lunch. Hell's bells. Here was he looking like death warmed up as his mirror had told him only too plainly that morning, and Ruby was coming. It would have been difficult enough to see her again if he had been hale and hearty and still in possession of his investments, but now? How could Clarissa do this to him? What had possessed her? He had to swallow hard before he could say, 'You didn't think to ask me if I thought this was a good idea, or at least give me the opportunity to dine elsewhere in town?'

'You're not well enough to dine elsewhere, and I knew if I asked you, you wouldn't want to see her.' Clarissa had decided it was time for plain speaking. 'Which is ridiculous. Ruby is a dear friend and you are my brother – you can't avoid each other for ever now you are back home. The first time you met was always going to be a little . . . uncomfortable for you both, so it's better to get it over and done with and everyone can relax. That's what I think.'

Again Edward glanced at Godfrey, who raised his eyebrows but didn't comment. He'd met sergeant majors who weren't a patch on his wife when she had a bee in her bonnet.

After a moment, Edward said quietly, 'I wish you hadn't done this, Clarissa.'

Clarissa had her own qualms which had been mounting all morning but she wasn't about to admit this. She smiled sweetly. 'You can meet as old friends surely? We are all perfectly civilized, after all.'

He wasn't feeling civilized, certainly not towards his sister. He was about to ask, 'What time is she coming?' when a knock at the drawing-room door and the maid announcing Ruby's name saved him the trouble.

The next moment Ruby walked in. He knew he ought to say something, to rise to the occasion, but as Clarissa jumped up and hurried forward, taking Ruby's hands as she said, 'Oh, darling, you must be frozen, it's so cold outside. Come and get warm by the fire,' he found himself unable to even stand to his feet. And then Godfrey had stood up and moved forward, giving him much needed seconds to compose himself. As he rose, he was praying his legs would hold him. She looked even lovelier than he remembered and so full of life, her cheeks pink with the cold and her beautiful hair shining like silk. Somehow he managed to smile and hold out his hand and say coolly, 'Ruby, how nice. It's been such a long time. I trust you are well?'

'Quite well, thank you, Edward.' There was a split second of screamingly awkward silence before she added, 'And you? I hear you have been ill.'

'Oh, I'm fine now, as you see.'

What she saw was a gaunt and skeletal individual who bore little resemblance to the man she had known; even his face seemed to have been hollowed out, his cheekbones showing razor sharp under the skin. Pulling herself together, she said politely, 'I'm glad. I'm sure Clarissa's been looking after you.'

'Oh, yes. Clarissa always knows what's best for us all.' It was barbed and he immediately could have kicked himself for his boorishness. Too quickly, he said, 'But enough about me. I hear your business has gone from strength to strength? You have opened another shop, Clarissa tells me.'

Clarissa had been ushering Ruby to an armchair close to the roaring fire as he had spoken, and once Ruby had sat down and they'd resumed their seats, she said quietly, 'Yes, a short distance from the original one. My sister's husband was killed in a mining accident at the same time my father passed away and so they had nothing to hold them in Sunderland. They live above the second shop. My mother takes care of my niece and my sister runs the shop. It has worked out very well.'

He was dead? The man she had been betrothed to who had let her down so badly with her sister, he was dead? And she'd taken on the sister and child, along with her mother? He became aware that he was staring and forced himself to say, 'My condolences. It must have been a difficult time.'

'Yes, it was.' This was awful, ten times worse than she had prepared herself for. He was so stiff, so cold.

Clarissa and Godfrey must have been thinking the same because over the next half an hour before lunch they fell over themselves to keep some sort of conversation going. When the gong sounded and they walked through to the dining room everyone breathed a sigh of relief, although in the event the meal was just as uncomfortable.

It was as they retired back to the drawing room where Clarissa had asked their coffee to be served, that she caught hold of Godfrey's arm, saying to Ruby and Edward, 'You two go through, we won't be a minute,' leaving them no option but to do as she said. Ruby knew she was blushing as she took the seat she'd vacated before the meal, but Edward was as cool as a cucumber to her fevered gaze.

In the event, he was inwardly cursing Clarissa. All through the interminable lunch he had been picturing the look of shock on Ruby's face when she had first set eyes on him. She had concealed it almost instantly, but not before he had seen the concern and yes, yes, the pity that had turned her brown eyes liquid. He had always known she had a soft heart. Look how she had tortured herself over her friend, Ellie, and this latest – her providing a home and employment for her sister and the child after the history between them – proved she was a sucker for the underdog. And that's what he was now, an underdog.

There were a few moments of excruciating silence after they had sat down, and then they both spoke at once, only to stop again.

'I'm sorry.' Edward smiled grimly. 'You were saying . . . ?'

'I was just going to say that – that I'm sorry your engagement didn't work out.' It was the only thing she could think of to introduce what she wanted to say.

He shrugged. 'It was just one of those things.' Looking at her was causing a physical pain in his chest – she was so beautiful, so damn perfect. 'Better to have loved and lost than never to have loved at all.'

Ruby inwardly flinched. So he *had* loved her, this American. 'I don't know if that's quite true.'

'No? Well, we always did look at things differently, you and I,' he said, his tone pleasant now. 'You were right about that. In fact, you were right about a lot of things.'

She shook her head. 'Not really.' It took all her strength to look him in the eye and say quietly, 'I missed you.'

There was an agony inside him as though he had been disembowelled. He knew he was looking at her for the last time because he couldn't go through this again. As soon as he was able he would leave Foreburn, leave the north altogether, and he wouldn't come back. Clarissa had said to him that he and Ruby could meet as equals now, but they were far from that. Her star was rising and he was glad for her, he didn't begrudge her one moment of the success she so deserved, but he was poorer than a church mouse and that had effectively finished anything that might have lingered between them. And the fact remained that she had been able to cast him off and get on with her life perfectly well; she hadn't written to him or tried to contact him all the months he had been away. There had been nothing. But now, because she saw him as a lame duck, her sympathy was aroused. But sympathy and pity and even affection weren't a basis for a relationship between a man and a woman. Steeling himself, he smiled coolly.

'Thank you. Now if you will excuse me I usually spend the afternoon resting in my room, so I will see you later if you are staying for tea?' He knew she wouldn't; her face had gone white.

'No, not today.' She rose too, offering him her hand as she said, 'I hope you are soon completely well.'

He inclined his head – speech was beyond him – and walked as steadily as he could out of the room, closing the door quietly behind him. He met Clarissa and Godfrey in the hall but he didn't speak, casting his sister one look that caused her to put her hand to her throat.

They stood and watched him as he walked up the winding staircase, and as Clarissa whispered, 'Oh, Godfrey,' her husband patted her hand but said nothing. One of the things he had always loved about his young, lovely, impetuous wife was her bravery for rushing in where angels feared to tread, but in this instance he wished she had discussed the matter with him first. Edward was broken in body and mind and the only thing he had left was a semblance of pride. Clarissa should have known that, but perhaps it was a male/female thing? Anyway, it was clear that this whole incident was an unmitigated disaster.

When they entered the drawing room they found Ruby standing looking out of the windows into the white expanse outside. She turned to face them, and before Clarissa could speak, she said, 'Thank you for a lovely lunch but I really must be going now.'

'Oh, Ruby, please don't. Please stay. Whatever has happened, whatever he's said, he doesn't mean it and—'

'*Clarissa.*' Whether it was the tone of Godfrey's voice, a tone he had never used with her before, or because the situation was beyond even her, Clarissa became quiet. He patted her hand again and then walked across to Ruby, taking her arm as he said, 'Let me walk you to the car.'

'Thank you.' Ruby managed a faint smile, and as they passed a stricken Clarissa, she stopped and gave her a swift hug before continuing. Godfrey himself fetched her hat and coat, and once they were outside in the frosty air and standing by her car, she said quietly, 'Tell Clarissa I know she meant well, won't you? But I hope she'll understand that I won't come again while Edward is with you.'

Godfrey nodded. 'I'm sorry, m'dear.'

'So am I.' This time her smile was tearful, and afraid she would break down completely in the face of his kindness and understanding, she kissed him swiftly on his cheek and slid into the car, starting the engine at once and driving away before he could see the tears streaming down her cheeks.

Once outside the confines of the estate she drove for some miles before stopping the car and letting the overwhelming sorrow have its way. It was nearly half an hour before she started the engine again and she was all cried out. She had lost him, totally and for ever, and the finality of it had caused something to die inside her. From this day forth, whatever happened and however well she did in life, she would never look at the world in the same way again. A light had gone out – that was the only way she could describe the way she felt to herself – and with its going everything would always be that little bit darker.

Chapter Twenty-Six

'Oh, you shouldn't have.' Polly gazed entranced at the silver locket in its little velvet box. 'And I haven't got you anything yet. Not that I expected a present for Christmas,' she added hastily. 'What I mean is—'

'I know what you meant and I like to give you nice things, that's all.' Daniel Bell smiled at Ruby's seamstress. Since he had been released from prison a short while ago, he'd made it his business to find out all he could about the woman who had put him in there, the upshot of this being that Polly had come across his path. Sweet, malleable Polly who had been putty in his hands from day one. He had told her that he had recently left the army after getting badly injured and losing his eye in the unrest between Arabs and Jews in Palestine in the summer, painting a picture of bravery and loyalty to king and country that had thrilled her romantic heart. He was settling back into civilian life as best he could, he'd confided, but he still found it difficult to adjust, and for that reason he would prefer to keep their relationship secret for the moment. He found it so easy to talk to her and be with her, he'd said gently, but it wasn't like that with other folk, and so if she could just be patient and give him time . . .

Polly had been flattered and smitten in equal measure, and had found – like many innocent young girls before her – Daniel's charm impossible to resist. He had been careful to remain in the role he had created at all times, asking nothing of her but a goodnight kiss, showering her with little gifts, acting to perfection the part of the damaged hero who had found love for the first time in his life. Gradually he'd established what Ruby's routine was, her comings and goings, the fact that she lived in the flat above the shop alone with no man to protect her.

Now it was the day before Christmas Eve, and he had arranged to meet Polly after work in a little cafe they'd been to once or twice. Taking her hand, he said, 'The locket is to celebrate us finding each other as much as Christmas, Polly, and I don't want you to buy me anything, all right? Just being with you is sufficient for me. I adore you, Polly, you must know that? But this Miss Morgan of yours works you too hard,' he added playfully. 'You say you'll be working right up to the last minute on Christmas Eve?'

Polly nodded. 'But it's not her fault,' she said earnestly. 'We've got a client who is getting married on Boxing Day of all days and she's been a right pain. First she was having two bridesmaids and then four, and we're making all the dresses, and now she's having a flower girl too at the last minute. Miss Morgan has got to alter the client's dress an' all because she's put on a bit the last month or two. She came in today for her last fitting and was supposed to take the dress away with her, but the buttons wouldn't do up. They go right from the neck to below her waist at the back, loads of little pearl things, they are.'

Daniel didn't give a fig about the buttons or the bride, but he nodded as though he was hanging on Polly's every word.

'Miss Morgan said it's a good job she was planning to have a quiet Christmas this year and just go to her mam's on Christmas Day for dinner, because she won't get the dress done till the last minute tomorrow. It's not fair, how some of the clients are. Just because they're well off they expect miracles. They don't think the likes of us have a life an' all.'

Daniel nodded sympathetically. So Ruby was going to be alone on Christmas Eve. Perfect. All good things come to him who waits. He looked out of the cafe window at the snow that was falling. It had started that morning and they were saying more was on the way so most folk would get their shopping done early and hunker down tomorrow, which meant the shops wouldn't stay open late. The market would, but that was a good distance from Ruby's shop. He'd have plenty of uninterrupted time to do all he intended to her. It had been the thought of that which had kept him going the last few years when Lonnie Gray and his gang had had their way with him. A huge man with arms on him like tree trunks, Lonnie, a lifer, had been the undisputed leader of the prisoners and he'd had a penchant for what he called 'pretty boys'. What he'd suffered . . .

'Daniel?'

Polly's voice was concerned and he quickly smoothed his face clear of all expression. 'Touch of stomach ache,' he said briefly. 'Just the old injuries playing up now and again.'

Polly squeezed his hand. He was so brave, so wonderful, so different to the lads of her own age who seemed gormless in comparison. She didn't know what her mam and da would say about him being a bit older when she introduced him to them once he was ready, but she wouldn't give him up. Not for anything. She would never meet someone like him again.

It was Christmas Eve afternoon, and Edward was sitting staring into the crackling flames in the drawing room's huge fireplace. Outside the house was a cold, hushed world and more snow was falling to add to the previous day's although by northern standards it still wasn't thick, being merely an inch or two, but inside there was warmth and the smell of Christmas cooking wafting from the kitchens now and again. He had a plate of mince pies to the side of him, which Clarissa's cook had sent with the maid with strict instructions he was to eat the lot or she would want to know the reason why, and a glass of – as yet untouched – sherry. Clarissa and Godfrey were out on a duty Christmas visit to the Rochdales and expected back shortly, whereupon the three of them were going to enjoy a 'nice peaceful Christmas together', as Clarissa had put it. He felt guilty that they hadn't accepted the numerous invitations that had come their way, or invited guests here to Foreburn, but Clarissa had insisted that a quiet Christmas was their choice, regardless of him. Believe that, believe anything, he thought morosely, and then chided himself on his churlishness. He was an ungrateful so-and-so and how Clarissa and Godfrey had put up with him he didn't know, but come the New Year he would send out feelers about his future with both the RAF and the Civil Service and see what transpired.

He heard a car outside, and thinking it was Clarissa and Godfrey hastily crammed a mince pie into his mouth. The whole household was on a mission to fatten him up, and although he appreciated the sentiment behind it, he found it tiresome in the extreme. Breakfast was no sooner over than he was being pressed to take elevenses, and after lunch it was the same. He would have to leave here soon or he'd be a walking barrel, although he had to admit the good food and rest over the last three weeks had begun to make him feel more like himself in the last couple of days. For three afternoons running he hadn't felt the need to take a nap.

When there was a knock at the drawing-room door and the maid put her head round it, he looked up in surprise. 'There's a Mrs Gilbert here, sir.'

Mrs Gilbert? He had no idea who that was. 'Have you told her my sister and husband are out at present?'

'It wasn't the mistress and master she wanted to see, sir. She asked for you.' The maid hesitated and then said, 'She came in a taxi, sir, and asked it to wait, so . . .'

'Yes, yes, bring her in.' Edward stood up, racking his brains. He'd heard the name before but he couldn't think where.

When Olive walked into the room and saw the man whom Ruby loved, she could instantly see what the attraction was, even before he came forward and said courteously, 'Mrs Gilbert, you must forgive me, I've been ill and my memory isn't what it was . . .'

'We haven't met, Mr Forsythe.'

'No? Well, please sit down. Can I get you coffee?'

'No, thank you, I have a cab waiting so I won't be long.' Having sat, Olive found that the words she had rehearsed for some time had completely gone. She stared into the handsome face in front of her, and after a moment, said, 'I'm Ruby's sister, Olive.'

Gilbert. Of course.

'And before I say anything more, I must tell you that Ruby has no idea I am here, Mr Forsythe. I've left the shop in the care of my assistants and—' Olive stopped abruptly. He wouldn't care about the shop, for goodness' sake.

'Mrs Gilbert—'

'No, please listen, Mr Forsythe,' she interrupted forcefully, finding her flow. 'Let me say what I need to say and then I'll leave. Ruby loves you. She always has and she never stopped, not even when you got engaged to that other girl in America. It broke her heart, that's the truth of it, and she bitterly regretted sending you away as soon as you had gone but didn't know how to put things right, and then it was too late. She'd already decided you being rich didn't matter and she had made a terrible mistake—'

'I'm not rich.'

'Not now, I'm talking about when you were. Rich or poor, it doesn't matter to her and it shouldn't to you, not if you still love her. Do you? Do you love Ruby, Mr Forsythe?'

He stared into the face of Ruby's sister and it came to him that although Olive Gilbert bore no resemblance whatsoever to the woman he loved, she certainly had Ruby's directness. 'I care for Ruby, yes,' he said stiffly, feeling as though he had been run over by a human steamroller.

'That wasn't what I asked. Do you love her?'

'I don't think that is any concern of—'

'She's desperately unhappy, Mr Forsythe. I've made her unhappy in the past, which I'm sure you know all about.' Olive swallowed hard. 'She didn't deserve what I did to her and she doesn't deserve this either. If you do still love her as much as you claimed before you left, then why are you condemning her to a mere existence as well as yourself? It makes no sense. If you do still love her?' she asked again.

Edward stood up, running his hand through his hair and moving to stand in front of the fire with his back to her and one hand resting on the mantelpiece.

'I love her with all my heart and soul, Mrs Gilbert. It sounds unchivalrous to say this but I was tricked into my engagement at a time when I think I didn't really care what happened to me one way or the other.' He paused, turning as he said, 'You know I have nothing to offer her now? Nothing at all?'

Olive's eyes were bright and her voice was eager when she said, 'You have everything to offer her – you have yourself, don't you see? Ruby has told me that she thought ultimately she would make you unhappy if she tried to fit into your world, that the pressure of society would cause you both difficulties and grief, and likewise a man of your education and upbringing would find it hard to feel accepted in our class. But after you had gone to America and she thought she had lost you for ever, she realized none of that mattered and that you would weather any storms together. The way I see it, all that could bring you closer together if you are of like mind. It might not be easy, but once the front door is closed at night and it's just the two of you that's what's important, not other people's opinions or attitudes.'

He stared at Olive, and then he surprised her utterly when he said softly, 'You'll make a great sister-in-law, Mrs Gilbert.'

'So you'll go and see her?'

He nodded.

'Today?'

He nodded again, and Olive visibly relaxed, the smile that lit her face causing Edward to warm to her still further. Whatever had gone on in the past, she clearly loved Ruby.

'Wish me luck.'

'You don't need it. I know how Ruby feels, Mr Forsythe.'

'Edward. If we're going to be related I think it's time we dropped the formalities, don't you?'

Olive stood up as she said, 'Will you come to Christmas dinner tomorrow, Edward? My mother and I would be so pleased to have you and you can meet Alice, my daughter.'

'If all goes well, I would be delighted.'

'It will, so we'll see you about one o'clock?' She hesitated, hoping Edward wouldn't think she was being pushy, before saying, 'I have a cab waiting – I could drop you off at Ruby's if you like?'

Edward thought quickly. It was nearly five o'clock and dark outside, although the snow provided plenty of illumination. Clarissa and Godfrey would be home soon; he could leave them a note explaining where he was, and asking them to send Pearson later on. 'Actually, that would work very well, if you don't mind. Give me a moment to write a note to my sister and we can be off.'

Once Edward had disappeared, Olive exhaled a long breath. She looked down at Adam's ring next to the gold wedding band. He had told Walter that he loved her when he was dying. She would never know for sure if he had meant it, or whether he was merely being kind knowing that he wasn't long for this world.

She closed her eyes for a moment. But what she did know was that he had bought the ring for *her*. He must have saved up for months to give her the engagement ring she had never had, and he had done that because he cared for her in some measure. Not as he had loved Ruby – she wasn't foolish enough to imagine that – but there were many levels of love, after all.

Ruby had always inspired love in those around her, even as a small child, and she had always been jealous of it. Bitterly jealous. And because of that she had taken something from her sister that could have destroyed their relationship for ever. *Should* have. But it hadn't. She could still hardly believe it.

She reached in her pocket for her handkerchief and wiped her eyes. Now she could atone for that awful act of betrayal, and she prayed with all her heart that Ruby and Edward would sort things out. Because she loved her sister. And not because Ruby had been so good to herself and Alice, although she had. She loved Ruby because of who her sister was, inside, where it counts. Perhaps they'd had to reach adulthood before she could do that, or maybe if things hadn't happened as they had she would have carried on hating her for ever, watching her with Adam and their babies while she remained a frustrated and angry spinster.

She blew her nose, shaking her head at herself. She was thinking too much again, and it never did her any good.

She had composed herself by the time Edward returned, dressed for outdoors in a thick greatcoat and hat and scarf. Once in the taxi, Edward kept the conversation flowing, asking her about the shop and Alice and how her mother had adapted to their new environment, and she was content to follow his lead. Both of them knew the next hour or two would be momentous, but talking about it wouldn't help.

When the taxi drew up outside the shop, Edward surprised her by putting his hand over hers for a moment. 'Thank you, Olive,' he said quietly. 'I'll never forget what you did today, however this turns out. I couldn't see the wood for the trees, that's the truth of it.'

She smiled. 'The shop will be closing in a minute or two – do you want to wait a few moments until Ruby's assistants have left?' But even as she spoke, the door opened and two young girls came out, laughing and talking, and they caught sight of Ruby in the doorway as she turned the 'Open' sign to 'Closed'.

Edward was out of the taxi in a heartbeat. Olive caught sight of her sister's face as she saw him and it told her everything she needed to know. Leaning back in the seat, her smile widening, she said to the taxi driver, 'You can go now.'

Ruby had become transfixed as she watched Edward walk towards her through the falling snowflakes. The door was slightly ajar but for the life of her she couldn't open it fully; it was as though she was frozen. It wasn't until he said her name that she was able to respond, pulling it wide as she whispered, 'Edward, Edward . . .'

Even while he had been making conversation of sorts with Ruby's sister, a different section of his mind had been planning what he would say when he saw her. Now he simply took her into his arms, kissing her as he had always dreamed of doing, long and hard and endlessly, lifting her right off her feet and kicking the door shut with one foot before he carried her over to one of the plush easy chairs and sat down with her on his lap, his lips never leaving hers for a moment.

Her head was swimming and she was gasping by the time his mouth left hers long enough for him to mutter, 'Oh, Ruby, I've been such a fool. Can you ever forgive me, my sweet? I'll spend the rest of my life making it up to you if you'll have me. Will you? Will you marry me, my love? Tell me it isn't too late, that you still love me.'

Her eyes glittering with unshed tears, she pulled his mouth to hers again, kissing him with a passion that was answer enough, even before she whispered, 'I'll love you for ever and beyond and yes, I'll marry you, but it's all my fault. I should never have—'

He cut off her words by the simple expedient of kissing her again, and it was only some minutes later when they became aware of a handful of bairns with their noses pressed up against the window and a scandalized mother attempting to marshal them away, that she said shakily, 'I think we'd better go upstairs to the flat.'

He waited while she locked the door and then extinguished the lights before pulling her in to him again, and like that, wrapped in each other's arms, they walked through to the back of the shop where Ruby opened the door leading to the flat.

The snow was falling thickly outside now but Ruby's little sitting room was as warm as toast, and by unspoken mutual consent they sat down on the small sofa in front of the fire whereupon Edward took her hands in his. 'I have to explain,' he said huskily. 'Why I was the way I was when you came to Foreburn.'

'It doesn't matter.'

'Yes, it does. You have to understand that it wasn't you, it was me. I couldn't think straight, Ruby. I've been in turmoil. But for Olive coming today—'

'Olive has been to see you?' she exclaimed, her voice high, but when she would have pulled her hands from his he held on tight to her fingers.

'And thank God she did,' he said softly. 'She's very forthright, your sister, isn't she.'

'I don't understand.'

'Then let me explain, my love.' He pulled her to him, sitting her on his lap again as he kissed her hard before beginning to talk.

Chapter Twenty-Seven

Daniel Bell stood in the small space left in the yard of the shop by the annexe, his heart thudding with excitement. The back lane had been deserted when he'd walked down it but even if it hadn't been he had made sure that with his cap pulled low over his eyes and his muffler up round his neck and mouth, no one would be able to recognize him. It was seven o'clock. He had walked down the main street first and the shop had been in darkness, but light glowed in the flat above. All was going to plan.

'Happy Christmas, Ruby,' he murmured softly, playing his finger along the blade of the hunting knife in his pocket.

The door of the annexe that led into the yard presented no problem to him. He had been breaking into buildings from the time he was in short trousers, at first under the tuition of his father who had been an accomplished burglar and then, when his father had been mortally injured in a fight with other ne'er-do-wells, on his own.

Once inside the annexe he stood looking around

Ruby's workshop in the dim light from the window. Thick rolls of expensive cloth and several beautiful outfits on wooden mannequins stood out among the paraphernalia. He walked over to one, gazing at the classic two-piece costume in a rich blue fabric edged with ermine and felt it between his fingers, running his hand over the swell of the dummy's breasts and down into its waist. Just the sort of outfit Lady Muck would wear. Perhaps she'd even made it for herself?

Once he had slashed it to ribbons he stood back, panting slightly. He'd take great pleasure in setting fire to this lot as he left, he thought, but that wouldn't be for a good few hours yet. He was going to make his fun last tonight; his Christmas present to himself. He smiled, pleased with his little joke.

Once in the small square of hall beyond the annexe he stood for a moment. The door that opened onto the stairs leading to the flat was ajar and he hadn't expected that, not that he was complaining. He looked upwards, anticipation of the night ahead making him as hard as a rock. He'd always enjoyed inflicting pain on his sexual partners – it enhanced his pleasure ten-fold – but until now he'd never contemplated the satisfaction of torturing a woman to death and he found it intoxicating. Once she was gagged and bound, he'd start on her face first. Unconsciously his hand touched the eye patch. Aye, he'd take his payment for what she'd done to him before he moved on to other things. An eye for an eye. Wasn't that what the good book said and who was he to argue?

He crept up the stairs without making a sound. The landing was in darkness but a shaft of light was showing from under the door. He paused for a moment with his hand on the door knob, thinking he heard something from inside the room, but as he waited all was quiet. Slowly, very slowly, he turned the knob and when it opened, again it was unexpected. She clearly didn't bother with locks and bolts, thought herself invincible no doubt. Foolish, very foolish, as she was about to find out. The element of surprise was always a distinct advantage.

He sidled into the room as silently as a cat, but then stopped dead at the sight that met his eyes. Ruby was wrapped in the arms of a man and they were kissing passionately, oblivious to anything but each other. They were half-sitting, half-lying on a sofa that was set at a slant to the door and meant they had their backs to him, but it would only take one of them glancing round to see him.

Daniel had been used to thinking on his feet all his life. A small bookcase stood to the left of the door against the wall and it had a pair of brass bookends in the shape of owls holding a row of books on the top of it. He grabbed one, the books falling, but in the same breath he brought the brass bookend slamming down on the top of Edward's head as he sprang to the sofa. The force of the blow was enough to send Edward slumping onto the floor, but as Ruby began to scream he thrust the knife in front of her face.

'Shut up, shut up now or I'll slit your throat and I'll do the same to him.'

She backed away from him, her hand to her mouth to prevent another scream but her horrified eyes flickering from him to Edward.

Daniel kicked at the prone figure on the floor, and as Edward made a sound in his throat, he said, 'He's not dead, not yet, but he will be if you don't do exactly as I say, you hear me? Do you hear me?'

She nodded, watching as he pulled some thick hemp twine out of his pocket, the sort that fishermen used to mend their nets.

'You're goin' to tie lover boy up real tight and no messing or I'll gut him where he lies. I was goin' to use this on you but it might be fun for him to watch if he comes round, don't you think?'

'You're mad,' she whispered.

'Aye, you're right there, mad enough to do what I say if you don't do exactly what you're told.'

He had been drinking, she could smell it, and as she stared into his face she believed him.

'I've been waiting for this for a long time, Ruby,' he said almost conversationally. 'Aye, a long time. Right from the minute we met, in fact. Remember that? With sweet little Ellie? There was I, all prepared to be nice, and you looked at me like I was scum. I knew then I'd see my day with you, but after this –' he touched the eye patch – 'it was all I lived for.'

He held out the twine. 'Tie him up.'

In the same instant that he spoke, Edward, who had been lying as though he was dead to the world, reached up and grabbed one of Daniel's ankles, jerking him off balance. As Daniel fell virtually on top of him the two began to struggle, but dazed and weak as Edward was from the vicious blow to his head, it was an unequal fight. Even as Ruby darted forwards she saw Daniel get astride Edward who was on his back and plunge the knife into his chest.

Screaming at the top of her voice Ruby snatched up the stout iron poker from the hearth as Edward feebly tried to ward off the hand holding the knife, but Daniel stabbed him again before she brought the poker swinging in a wide arc with all her weight behind it. It caught Daniel on the side of his neck just above his shoulder, and as he gave an unearthly shriek and dropped the knife, she hit him again. He rolled to one side and began to crawl towards the door as she knelt beside Edward who was covered in blood and bleeding profusely. Rushing into the kitchen she grabbed a towel and stuffed it over the two stab wounds, telling Edward to press down on it as she ran to the window and opened it, yelling and screaming for help.

The next few hours were something of a blur.

It was only later she learned that several folk from the houses opposite had come hurrying into the street, one burly individual taking it upon himself to shoulder open the door of the shop and burst in. All Ruby was aware of was the sound of people running up the stairs and attempting to help her with Edward who had lost consciousness.

The police arriving, the ambulance, the journey to the hospital, the numerous questions that continued for what seemed like hours as she sat in the waiting room waiting for news of Edward, were all part of the nightmare she couldn't wake up from. Olive arrived at some point and after she had acquainted her sister with the facts they sat in silence, holding hands tightly. Clarissa and Godfrey came a little while later, and although they talked with Olive off and on, Ruby found she couldn't say a word. She was going to lose Edward like she'd lost Ellie, she knew it. Doctors couldn't always save someone, and like Ellie, Edward had lost so much blood it didn't seem possible he could survive.

It was still dark when a constable came into the dimly lit, antiseptic-smelling waiting room and told them the body of Daniel Bell had been found some streets away from the shop. Such was Ruby's state of mind about Edward the news barely registered, but Godfrey ushered the policeman outside and returned some time later, his face grim. It appeared Bell had died of a crushed windpipe, he told the three women, and had eventually choked on his own blood. Pity he'd died so quickly, he'd added bitterly. He would have liked him to suffer more.

Dawn was creeping into the dour little room through the tiny high window when an expressionless-faced sister popped her head round the door.

'Mr Harper will see you now if you will come this way,' she said primly, although her eyes couldn't quite conceal the avid interest this case had caused among the hospital staff. A handsome rich patient, a beautiful young woman, and an attempted murder. It was like a story from the penny journals she secretly enjoyed so much when she had a minute or two to herself.

Mr Harper turned out to be a tired-looking, middle-aged man who had met Clarissa and Godfrey socially in the past, having connections in high places. He was also an excellent surgeon with a first-class reputation who had chosen to leave a prestigious London hospital for the north-east when he had married the daughter of a wealthy Durham landowner, the lady in question preferring the north to the capital. As Godfrey remarked afterwards, it had needed an Augustus Harper to bring Edward back from the brink.

The patient was still seriously ill, Augustus had told them, but miraculously the knife had missed any major organs. Unfortunately, one of the two wounds had caused significant damage to the left shoulder, which almost certainly would result in restricted use of that arm in the future. Was the patient right-handed?

Ruby didn't hear Clarissa's reply to this, having fainted clean away.

It was a full eight weeks later before Edward was allowed home to Foreburn, and four weeks after this Clarissa handed over care of the invalid to Ruby, on Ruby and Edward's wedding day.

It was the quietest of occasions, the guests comprising Ruby's mother and sister and Alice, a frail Mrs Walton and thrilled Mrs Duffy, and on Edward's side, just Clarissa and Godfrey. As far as the bride and groom were concerned, it was exactly as they wanted and they couldn't have been happier.

Ruby was a vision of loveliness in a simple white lace gown and short veil, and Alice, as bridesmaid, was as pretty as a picture in a frilly powder-blue frock and matching shoes, of which she was inordinately proud.

After the service at the small parish church, which was a stone's throw from the grand hotel where Godfrey had paid for the wedding reception as his and Clarissa's wedding present to the happy couple, they all sat down to a sumptuous five-course meal with champagne. By the time Clarissa and Godfrey took Mrs Walton back to Sunderland the elderly lady was tiddly and declaring it was the best wedding she'd ever been to. Ruby and Edward agreed with her. It had been a wonderful day. But it wasn't until the taxi cab deposited them home to the place Edward had christened 'the love nest' above the shop that Ruby felt truly married. They were alone at last, and after all the twists and turns of the last years, the sorrow and heartache, the doubts and fears, suddenly the world made sense. She was Edward's wife and he was her husband. It really was as simple as that.

Their wedding night was everything she could have hoped for and more. Edward proved himself to be a gentle but passionate lover, intent on making her first time as wonderful as it could be. And afterwards, when she lay in his arms and listened to the strong steady beat of his heart, she suddenly raised herself up and kissed him over and over again, thinking that if Daniel Bell's aim had been slightly to the left or right, everything would now be very different. Against all the odds they were together, and she knew that what had been forged in the fire would last.

They would carve themselves a good life, based on a foundation of mutual love and respect, and what better foundation could there be?

It was up to them now.

Epilogue

1935

The last few years had been busy and productive for Ruby and Edward, in more ways than one.

Eighteen months after their wedding day, twin girls had been born, and two years later a bouncing baby boy had announced his arrival into the world with a bellow that had become characteristic of him when he was demanding a feed. George Edward had weighed in at a healthy and hungry ten pounds, and his diminutive sisters, Rose Ellie and Kate Olive, had been thrilled with their new live 'dolly'. But the arrival of their children had only been part of it.

Augustus Harper had been right and Edward's arm had never fully recovered from Daniel Bell's knife wound, but twelve months into their marriage he had been elected onto the local council and had become involved in various community projects, and was currently in the process of running for government on behalf of the Labour Party. He supported Ruby in the continuing fight for women's rights in every walk of life, and the two of them ran a soup kitchen in the heart of Newcastle, which had become a lifesaver to some folk as the depression had worsened. Along with her two shops, Ruby had opened a clothing factory, employing local women who badly needed work due to family situations. They made good but cheap clothes for the less well off in the community, which were sold direct from the factory shop at the front of the premises.

When Ruby had moved a manageress into the flat above her original shop a few months after she and Edward had tied the knot, they'd purchased a small three-bedroomed house with a family-sized garden on one of the new housing estates that were springing up in Arthur's Hill and Fenham, one of Newcastle's fastest-growing suburbs. It was a modest dwelling compared to what they could have afforded, but they had decided that to be part of the local community they had to live among them and not in some grand ivory tower.

Times were still desperately hard for huge numbers of the north's working class, and although the abolition of the dreaded workhouses in 1930 meant that a significant break with the odium of pauperism had begun, Ruby and Edward knew from their welfare work that some folk would prefer to slowly starve than ask for help. Through their contacts with the soup kitchen, they'd established a link with some of these families, and had set about quietly distributing food parcels, medical supplies and clothes and shoes for the bairns on a weekly basis.

Of late, they had also been thinking about a new

venture, that of opening a small refuge for girls like Ellie who had been sucked into a life of prostitution and despair, and who needed practical help to escape it. Mrs Walton had died peacefully in her sleep some months before and, true to her word, the old lady had left everything she possessed to Ruby. It was Ruby and Edward's plan to name the refuge after Mrs Walton, something they knew would have pleased her. Ruby's businesses had also gone from strength to strength, and she could think of no better way to use the legacy and the growing wealth they'd accumulated. Edward had spoken to the local branch of the Labour Party about it and they'd been fully supportive, no doubt thinking it would increase his chances of being elected as their MP, but that wasn't why he wanted to do it. He knew Ruby grieved every day for her friend, and doing something constructive to help other girls would enable her to come to terms with Ellie's tragic death, something he knew hadn't happened yet.

He glanced at his wife as they walked arm in arm towards the park where they were taking the children for their Sunday afternoon stroll, the girls just in front of them swinging George between them who screamed with delight every time his chubby little legs flew into the air.

Ruby caught the look and smiled at him. She was heavily pregnant with their fourth child who was due in six weeks at the beginning of December. She and Edward were thrilled about this, but it had caused yet another difficult conversation with her mother. Cissy had been

scandalized when Ruby had continued working throughout her pregnancies, returning to oversee each of the two
shops and the clothing factory within weeks of the babies
being born when she would leave them in Edward's care
for a while. They worked their daily routine between
them, manipulating his council work and party work with
her business obligations, along with the soup kitchen
every other day, and the care of the children. Edward
was a complete anomaly to her mother the way he wanted
to be involved in every aspect of home life, changing
nappies and babysitting the bairns, tackling washing and
ironing and housework, and – crime of all crimes –
cooking meals. Ruby had learned the uselessness of
explaining to her mother that they shared all these tasks
between them and worked as a team, and she had given
up trying. She and Edward were supremely happy with
the way things were and that was all that mattered.

To be fair, she supposed they *were* unusual and something of a peculiarity, but she felt this was a good thing.
At one time she had felt stuck between two worlds and
that she fitted in nowhere but she and Edward had created
their own world, with their own rules. It was one where
class and wealth and social niceties had no relevance
whatsoever; they were equals in every respect. They
worked together and supported each other in a way she
could never have envisaged years ago when she had sent
him away, and they were determined to mirror their way
to their bairns. They were both aware that the future
wasn't going to be easy. Europe was beginning to beat

the drums of war and Germany's massive rearmament programme could only mean one thing. War was inevitable and that would mean everything became uncertain, but one thing *was* for sure. She and Edward would deal together with whatever came.

The sky was a heavy blue-grey and the pleasing nip in the air at the beginning of the month had already given way to several hard white frosts in the last week, the alchemy of the season turning the decaying autumn landscape into a glorious abundance of colours. As they reached the little park situated not far from the house, Edward took the children off to play on the swings and roundabout while Ruby sat down on a bench to watch them.

The baby in her womb kicked, a strong, vigorous kick as though to demand that her attention wasn't all on the rest of the family, and as she placed her hand under her coat and felt more movement she experienced a sense of deep contentment. Whatever challenges the future might bring, she was ready to face them. The road had been a long and winding one at times, but she had come to a place where she was sure of who she was and where she belonged. It was the most precious of gifts.

Dancing in the Moonlight

By Rita Bradshaw

As her mother lies dying, twelve-year-old Lucy Fallow promises to look after her younger siblings and keep house for her father and two older brothers.

Over the following years the Depression tightens its grip. Times are hard and Lucy's situation is made more difficult by the ominous presence of Tom Crawford, the eldest son of her mother's lifelong friend, who lives next door.

Lucy's growing friendship with Tom's younger brother, Jacob, only fuels Tom's obsession with her. He persuades Lucy's father and brothers to work for him on the wrong side of the law as part of his plan to force Lucy to marry him.

Tom sees Lucy and Jacob dancing together one night and a chain of heartbreaking events is set in motion. Torn apart from the boy she loves, Lucy wonders if she and Jacob will ever dance in the moonlight again . . .

Beyond the Veil of Tears

By Rita Bradshaw

Fifteen-year-old Angeline Stewart is heartbroken when her beloved parents are killed in a coaching accident, leaving her an only child in the care of her uncle.

Naive and innocent, Angeline is easy prey for the handsome and ruthless Oswald Golding. He is looking for a rich heiress to solve the money troubles his gambling and womanizing have caused.

On her wedding night, Angeline enters a nightmare from which there is no awakening. Oswald proves to be more sadistic and violent than she could ever have imagined. When she finds out she is expecting a child, Angeline makes plans to run away and decides to take her chances fending for herself and her baby. But then tragedy strikes again . . .

The Colours of Love

By Rita Bradshaw

England is at war, but nothing can dim land girl Esther Wynford's happiness at marrying the love of her life – fighter pilot Monty Grant. But months later, on the birth of her daughter Joy, Esther's world falls apart.

Esther's dying mother confesses to a dark secret that she has kept to herself for twenty years: Esther is not her natural daughter. Esther's real mother was forced to give up her baby to an orphanage – and now Joy's birth makes the reason for this clear, as Esther's true parentage is revealed.

Harshly rejected by Monty, and with the man Esther believed was her father breathing fire and damnation, she takes her precious baby and leaves everything and everyone she's ever known, determined to fend for herself and her child. But her fight is just beginning . . .

Snowflakes in the Wind

By Rita Bradshaw

It's Christmas Eve 1920 when nine-year-old Abby Kirby's family is ripped apart by a terrible tragedy. Leaving everything she's ever known, Abby takes her younger brother and runs away to the tough existence of the Border farming community.

Years pass. Abby becomes a beautiful young woman and falls in love, but her past haunts her, casting dark shadows. Furthermore, in the very place she's taken refuge is someone who wishes her harm.

With her heart broken, Abby decides to make a new life as a nurse. When the Second World War breaks out, she volunteers as a QA nurse and is sent overseas. However, life takes another unexpected and dangerous turn when she becomes a prisoner of the Japanese. It is then that Abby realizes that whatever has gone before is nothing compared to what lies ahead . . .

A Winter Love Song

By Rita Bradshaw

Bonnie Lindsay is born into a travelling fair community in the north-east of England in 1918, and when her mother dies just months later Bonnie's beloved father becomes everything to her. Then, at the tender age of ten years old, disaster strikes. Heartbroken, Bonnie's left at the mercy of her embittered grandmother and her lecherous step-grandfather.

Five years later, the events of one terrible night cause Bonnie to flee to London, where she starts to earn her living as a singer. She changes her name and cuts all links with the past.

Time passes. Bonnie falls in love, but just when she dares to hope for a rosy future, the Second World War is declared. She does her bit for the war effort, singing for the troops and travelling to Burma to boost morale, but heartache and pain are just around the corner, and she begins to ask herself if she will ever find happiness again.

Beneath a Frosty Moon

By Rita Bradshaw

It's 1940 and Britain is at war with Germany. For Cora Stubbs and her younger siblings this means being evacuated to the safety of the English countryside. But little does Cora know that Hitler's bombs are nothing compared to the danger she will face in her new home, and she is forced to grow up fast.

However, Cora is a fighter and she strives to carve out a new life for herself and her siblings. Time passes, and in the midst of grief and loss she falls in love, but what other tragedies lie around the corner?

As womanhood beckons, can Cora ever escape her troubled past and the lost love who continues to haunt her dreams and cast shadows over her days?

The People's Friend

If you enjoy quality fiction, you'll love "The People's Friend" magazine. Every weekly issue contains seven original short stories and two exclusively written serial instalments.

On sale every Wednesday, the "Friend" also includes travel, puzzles, health advice, knitting and craft projects and recipes.

It's the magazine for women who love reading!

For great subscription offers, call 0800 318846.

twitter.com/@TheFriendMag
www.facebook.com/PeoplesFriendMagazine
www.thepeoplesfriend.co.uk